UP FRO

Johnny Kovak—he ⟨...⟩ from the Flats of Cleveland. ⟨...⟩ a dream, a dream that would take a lowly warehouse hand and make a union president, a hero to millions, out of him.

Anna Melsbakas—the fiery blonde next door who played hard to get, but she too was swept up by Johnny's pride and fierce determination. She fought for him, married him, bore him a son he could not love.

Abe Belkin—orphaned at twelve, he was taken in by the Kovaks and grew up with Johnny. They loved each other like brothers, but Johnny's violent rise to power changed all that.

Babe Milano—schooled by Al Capone in the sleazy ways of the underworld, his "business deals" with Johnny turned the dream into a nightmare.

Karen Chandler—young, voluptuous, idealistic, she went to work for Johnny at F.I.S.T. by day, played with him in bed by night.

Cole Madison—the charismatic and intensely ambitious senator from Rhode Island, whose self-serving investigation of F.I.S.T.'s business practices started Johnny on the long trip down.

F.I.S.T.

A novel by

Joe Eszterhas

based on the screenplay by
Joe Eszterhas and Sylvester Stallone

A DELL BOOK

Published by
Dell Publishing Co., Inc.
1 Dag Hammarskjold Plaza
New York, New York 10017

Dell ® TM 681510, Dell Publishing Co., Inc.

ISBN: 0-440-12650-9

Printed in the United States of America

First printing—March 1978

F.I.S.T.

I.

THE FLATS

Cleveland, July, 1934. At six-thirty in the morning, Joe Kovak walked through the Flats to his blast furnace at the Baldwin and Johnson steel mill. He was fifty-two years old; a hulking, heavy-footed man whose name had been Kovacs until an immigration official misspelled it at Ellis Island.

He walked through a pit: a giant industrial valley of steel mills, smoke stacks, and time-worn docks half-sunken into the Cuyahoga River. The river snaked past refineries and coke works and was oily and blood red. At night, the pit was afire and open-hearth furnaces blazed leaping purple patterns against the sky. Joe Kovak lived and worked here. The pit was home.

His shirt was soggy. The humidity off Lake Erie choked him. Boiling, sweltering summer heat. Heat that could kill. A figure crawled in the street ahead of him. The street shimmered and Joe Kovak wiped the sweat from his eyes and walked closer.

It was the gypsy. The gypsy crawled along the red brick on his hands and knees and for a while Joe Kovak watched him. He was not astounded by the sight. The gypsy played the violin at Zigi's Tavern. Like all gypsies, he played the violin well. Like all gypsies, he was mad. The gypsy kept his nose to the ground and crawled from brick to brick.

"Did you lose something?" Joe Kovak asked in Hungarian.

The gypsy looked at him. His face was soot-stained, his eyes bloodshot. He wore a crimson vest and baggy pants, his costume each night at Zigi's.

"I have lost my job."

"Zigi kicked you out? What did you do?"

"Nothing."

Joe Kovak smiled. "My friend, did you put your hands on the waitress again?"

"Nothing," the gypsy insisted. "I played my violin."

"You are talking like a gypsy." Joe Kovak frowned. It was absurd. He was standing in the middle of the street talking to a grown man who was scuttling along in gutters.

"There is not enough money. Zigi can't pay me." The gypsy picked something out of the gutter, scrutinized it, and handed it to Joe Kovak.

"It is my gift to you," the gypsy smiled. "It is a very fine button."

"I don't want your button."

"But it is a wonderful button."

"Enough about the button," Joe Kovak said sharply. "Let us forget the button. What are you doing crawling in the street?"

The gypsy smiled beatifically. He glanced around and whispered. "I am looking for the gold."

"What gold?"

"The gold they promised. In America they said the streets are paved with gold."

Joe Kovak laughed. It was a booming, joyous laugh which echoed in the empty street.

"Fool," he said, "have you found any gold?"

"No. But I have found the button," the gypsy said. "It is a beginning."

Joe Kovak walked away from him, shaking his head and mumbling. At the corner he stopped and looked back. The gypsy was still watching him, still laughing, still on his hands and knees, holding high his button.

He walked down the narrow streets toward his mill. Bridges overhead shadowed him. Expensive, chrome-shiny cars rushed through the sky. Some days, as he walked to work, he could see smug, suit-wearing men looking down at him. Joe Kovak knew on those mornings that he was trapped; a captive of bosses who ran the mill, who ran the world. They hurled cigar and cigarette butts into the pit. Once every few years one of them drove his car over the side of a bridge. The car came crashing down. A bomb meant to remind Joe Kovak of his helplessness.

Bluffs blocked both sides of the Flats. This morning he could see the sun glinting blindingly off the glass in the Terminal Tower building. It was fifty-one stories high and Ilona said it was beautiful, the biggest building in the world. But Ilona was wrong. It was the world's tallest watchtower. It told him there was no escape. His sentence was lifelong. At night, six shafts of light flashed from the watchtower's tip.

They said they were a beacon for ships. Joe Kovak knew what they were. Searchlights.

But at least he had work. It was more than many people down here could say. He didn't have to eat fried flour, tripe, or soupbones. He didn't have to resole his shoes with the rubber strips of old tires. As he turned onto River Road, less than half a mile from the mill now, Joe Kovak smiled. Torn and faded, the billboard had big letters that said: "World's Highest Standard of Living. There's No Way like the American Way." It showed a well-dressed man, his wife, and their children riding in a new car. They were all smiling. Each morning, as he walked the two miles to his blast furnace, Joe Kovak smiled at them. Each morning, as they rode in their new car, they returned his smile.

A group of children were bouncing a rubber ball in the middle of the street. Joe Kovak stopped and watched them. A gangly boy with carrot hair took the ball. "Sally Rand has lost her fan," the boy said, in rhythm with the bouncing ball. "Give it back, you nasty man." The children giggled. Joe Kovak walked on.

Children. He wondered what Johnny would do today. At least he didn't have to worry about Abe. Abe would go down to Fleckner's and earn his wage. That was Abe. With all his speechmaking and book reading, Abe went to work each morning and earned his wage. Not Johnny. Not his own son. Johnny couldn't hold a job longer than a few months. He yelled at the foreman. Hit somebody. Caused trouble. Always trouble. Never enough trouble.

Mule-headed as a boy even. Before they came to Cleveland, Joe Kovak had worked in southern Ohio, at the Truetown mine. He didn't make very much money; the food on the table was never very good. The boy wouldn't eat it. No matter what they said to him, he wouldn't eat it. Ilona was afraid Johnny would starve; the boy had to be taught a lesson. "You sit here at this table," he told the boy one morning, "until you eat." Johnny sat there. He was four years old. He sat at that table for seventeen hours.

His son was just as mule-headed now, Joe Kovak knew. He had grown tall and handy with his fists, but he hadn't changed. Nothing ever really changed in the Flats. Ilona said it was his fault and maybe she was right. He even looks like you, Ilona said. Yes, but there was more to it. Johnny had his size, his thick black hair, his cheekbones. But his eyes were different. It was the anger. There was burning coal in his son's eyes.

When Joe Kovak got to the Baldwin and Johnson gate and showed the guard his card, he was overcome once again, as he was each morning, by his hatred for the mill. The heavy lifting strained his back. The hours were so long that some nights he was too tired even to eat. The roar of the booming big machines was deafening. But what he thought about each morning when he woke up was the mill heat. His face was his work record: his eyes bore a permanent squint;

his skin was the texture of baked leather. But he had made peace with the way his face had changed. His face was worth sixty-eight cents an hour; the pension he would get at sixty-five.

It was his difficulty breathing that frightened him. Sometimes, in the past few years, he had felt momentarily weak. He had had to ask the foreman's permission to go outside for a breath of fresh air. Kraus was an okay guy; he had never given him a hard time about it. So Joe Kovak never said anything to anybody about his breathing problems. He knew that Ilona would become alarmed. And a doctor might find something that would cost him his job.

As he walked into the mill this morning, Kraus waved him over with a smile. He knew what was coming.

"Did you hear the one about the horse, goes into the bar, asks for a bottle of dago red and some horseradish?" Kraus said.

"Bullshit," Joe Kovak told Kraus. "Always more bullshit."

"Listen to it," Kraus laughed.

"Okay, I listen."

"This horse walks into a bar and asks for some dago red with some horseradish," Kraus said.

"I listen that already."

"The bartender hands the red over and then he gives the horse the horseradish. The horse the horseradish, get it?"

"I get it, yah yah," Joe Kovak said.

"The horse drinks the red and knocks off the horseradish and he says—'You probably think it's pretty funny. Me comin' in here askin' for dago red and horseradish.'"

"Real funny, yah yah," Joe Kovak said.

"'Hell no,' the bartender says. 'I like my red that way myself.'"

Kraus roared and slapped him on the back.

"Bullshit," Joe Kovak said, smiling. "Always fulla bullshit."

Kraus stopped laughing. Joe Kovak waited. He knew it was coming.

"Listen, Joe," Kraus said. "I'm sorry I gotta do it to you, but I got nobody else right now. I need you up above, to clean out the carbon."

It was the job in the mill which he hated the most. Kraus rarely gave it to him: he respected his difficulty with the scorching heat.

He grinned. "You think I'm gonna tell you I'm not gonna do it?"

"You're a helluva man," Kraus said, smiling. "I always said that."

"I'm a helluva man, what the hell I'm doin' in this goddamn place?" Joe Kovak said and walked away toward the coke works. He could feel the awful intensity of the heat already.

He climbed up a narrow ladder which led to a six-inch planking built around the mouth of an open oven. He stood on the planking, looked into the oven, and swore. He'd have to keep the flues of the oven free of carbon.

He wrapped his hands in burlap and picked up the

iron bar which he'd have to jam into the flue. When his hands touched the bar, the burlap went up in flames. He swore again, got some more burlap, wrapped it around his hands, and tried it again. He could feel the heat of the bar but this time the burlap didn't catch. He jammed the bar into the flue and tried to duck the smoke and gas which billowed toward him. The heat of the oven blew directly into his face. He turned away and tried to breathe but now he couldn't see what he was doing with the bar.

After forty-five minutes, he felt weak and slightly dizzy. He put the bar down, climbed down the ladder, and asked Kraus if he could go outside for a few minutes.

"Sure," Kraus said, "another ten minutes, I'll get somebody else in."

He walked toward the door, feeling off-balance again. He noticed that a button was missing from his shirt. He thought about the gypsy crawling around in the street. He smiled. I should have taken his damn button, Joe Kovak thought.

Heading for the door in the dim mill light, he felt the dizziness rush him again. He staggered, then fell. Steam rose on all sides of him.

His mother and Abe beside him, Johnny sat in the front pew, a few feet from the casket, watching the priest's mouth. The priest's mouth was moving, but he couldn't hear the words. Pretty words, though; he was sure of that. The priest had a whole bookful of pretty

16

words for every poor sap who got himself killed down here.

Looking at the casket, he caught Abe's eye. It was the cheapest one they could find; a plain wooden box he was sure the old man would have approved of. It didn't cost too many of "The Dollar." That's the way the old man always said it: "The Dollar." "The Dollar" he busted his ass for all his life. "The Dollar" they doled out to him for working in that hellhole.

Work, Johnny, the old man had said. Work puts the food on the table. Work puts the clothes on your back.

Work put you into the ground, pa.

He looked around the church, glancing occasionally at the priest to make sure the pretty words still flowed from his mouth. He had been an altar boy here. Anybody who went to school at St. Stephen's, the only Hungarian parish in the Flats, had to be an altar boy. It was one of their rules. They had a lot of rules. And every time he had broken one of their rules, the nun spread his hands out on the desk and cracked them with the sharp edge of a ruler until they bled. His hands had bled a lot, but their rulers hadn't stopped him from breaking their rules.

When he was in the eighth grade, a nun took him into an empty classroom and told him to kneel.

"Where did you get this dirty picture?" she asked. It was a picture of a naked girl which she had found in his catechism book.

He didn't answer her.

17

She slapped him.

"Where did you get this filth?" Her hands were shaking.

"I found it in the catechism book."

"Liar!" she yelled. She slapped him again.

He grinned. "It's only a venial sin, sister. It doesn't matter."

She slapped him hard, twice. Her face was purple.

"Cry," she said, "you're going to cry."

"I don't cry, sister."

She hit him in the mouth with her fist. Blood dripped down his chin.

"Cry!" She hissed it.

"Hit me again," he said, "and you're gonna be sorry."

She raised her arm. He caught it, jumped to his feet, picked her up, and slammed her hard against the blackboard wall. She sunk to the floor, whimpering and dazed. He wiped the blood off his chin, looked down at her, and smiled.

"Don't cry, sister," he said.

When the old man came home that night, his mother told him what had happened. The old man took him down to the basement and looked like he was really going to give it to him. He had the catechism book in one hand and the picture of the naked girl in the other. He gazed at the picture a while before saying anything.

"Johnny, why you keep the picture in the holy book?" Joe Kovak said.

"I don't know, pa. I figured they wouldn't find it in there. It's a big book."

The old man nodded and shifted his attention back to the picture of the girl. The girl was bent over and the picture was taken from behind her. Her bare ass stuck high into the air.

"How come you got this picture?" the old man said.

"Whatsamatter with it, pa?"

The old man hesitated. "Ain't too pretty, this girl," he said. "You got a picture like this, it oughta be a pretty girl."

The old man gave him the book and the picture and they went upstairs. On the top step he stopped and turned to him.

"Johnny," he said. "Don't tell your ma what I says to you."

He sat now in the front pew of the church, looking at his father's casket. He was angry. He could feel tears welling in his eyes.

Why, pa? Why'd you let 'em kill you? Why'd you let 'em push you around? How many times did you come home bruised up? Cut? Burned by the oven? Why, pa? Why?

The priest's singsong was his only answer.

Yet he knew that his father hadn't been a weak man. When he was ten years old, the old man took him up to Public Square to buy him a new jacket. They walked into a little shop off Superior Avenue. It was a cruel, cold day. An icy wind lashed off the lake. The old man took his cap off and told the clerk in his broken accent that he wanted to buy a jacket for the boy.

"I don't have any jackets," the clerk said curtly.

The old man pointed to a long row of jackets in the back. "Many jacket. What you mean?"

"I don't have any you can afford," the clerk said.

"How much the price?"

"How much can you afford?"

"Two dollar."

"We don't have anything under three."

"Okay. Three dollar."

"We don't have anything under four," the clerk said.

"You say three."

"Four. Four dollars. I said four," the clerk yelled. "Now get the hell outa here or I'll call the police."

"Police!" Joe Kovak shouted. "Yah! Police! You call police!" He grabbed the clerk by the lapels and pulled him close to him. He clutched the clerk's throat and squeezed it.

"Please," the clerk said, pale. "Please. Lemme go."

The old man kept squeezing his throat. "Two dollar?"

"Two dollars," the clerk said. "Fine. Please. Two dollars."

It was a beautiful jacket, too, Johnny remembered, the best jacket he'd ever had.

The priest finished his sermon now and walked back to the altar. His mother and Abe knelt down; Johnny knelt with them. It was a meaningless gesture, a reflex from his childhood.

He kept thinking about his father. How, at the same time, the old man kept telling him not to get into fights.

"You got a head, Johnny, so you don't gotta use your fists."

"I know, pa, I know."

"You got a head or don't you?"

"I got it, pa. It's right here."

"Then you use it."

"I got fists, too, what am I supposed to do with them?"

"Stick 'em in your pockets."

You stuck 'em in your pockets at the mill, pa. Look where it got you.

The priest turned now and gave them his blessing. They got up and surrounded the casket. He looked at his mother: a slight, brittle woman who wore a black dress and a black babushka. She was crying.

"You okay, ma?"

She nodded but didn't say anything.

"You wanna ride in the funeral car?"

"I walk."

"You sure, ma?" Abe said. "Maybe it'd be better if you rode in the car."

The priest came out of the sacristy with the two altar boys, Johnny and Abe and some of the men who were Joe Kovak's friends—Mishka Biro, Anton Jugovich, Zigi Zagon—picked the casket up and walked it out of the church into the blazing sun. They carried it down the steps and placed it gently into the flatbed of the funeral-home hearse.

With the hearse leading the way, they walked through the Flats toward the cemetery halfway up the hillside. It was the same route, Johnny knew, which Joe Kovak had taken to the mill each day.

Al Dorsett stood in the soup line and watched the hearse. His guts were on fire. His feet felt like they had a thousand jagged splinters in them. The hearse creaked its way down the bumpy, potholed street. At least that guy's got a ride, Al Dorsett thought. Come my turn, they'll pick me off the cement, toss me into a trunk, and shovel me into a field.

He had been out on the street since six o'clock this morning. He had gone from fence to fence, from plant to plant. This morning, when he kissed Julie good-bye, he had found a smile in himself somewhere, and said, "Maybe this is our lucky day." Julie had smiled back. "Maybe it is." And now Al Dorsett stood in the soup line on his lucky day, waiting for his lunch; a cipher in a line of ciphers waiting for warm greasy water.

The soup line stretched to the end of the block. Still more men joined it and it spilled into the street. In a few minutes, Al Dorsett knew, the street would be blocked. The cops would come. He hoped he'd have his soup by then. When the street got blocked, the cops got angry and shut the soup truck down.

"What have we got for dessert today?" someone shouted behind him. No one laughed.

Ahead of him, a man was talking to a friend. "What we all oughta do, we all oughta go down to a grocery store. We all oughta walk into the place and take whatever we want. All of us." The man waved his hands excitedly as he spoke.

A mirthless laugh. "You dumb shit," his friend said, "they'd shoot you dead."

"Naw. Naw, they wouldn't. Not if we all goes down there in a big-ass group. They ain't gonna shoot all of us. Hell, they wouldn't even call the cops. I'm tellin' you they wouldn't."

"Hell they wouldn't," his friend said. "You're dreamin' now. The hell they wouldn't."

"I'm tellin' you. They'd be afraid to, see? They wouldn't want it to get out what we done. If it got out what we done, that we all gone down there and took whatever we wanted, hell, everybody'd do it. They'd have to close up all the stores, they'd have to." A pause. "It'd start a revolution."

"A revolution my ass," his friend growled.

"We would. We'd start a revolution."

"All I want's some soup," his friend said.

If I don't find work soon, Al Dorsett thought, listening to them, the landlord will throw us out. If I don't find work soon, I'm going to have to take Julie and the kids and move into the Hooverville by the lake and fight off the rats. The rats were getting fatter each day. It was always like that. When people went hungry, the rats got fat. The sweat poured off his forehead into Al Dorsett's eyes and for a moment everything blurred in front of him.

"I wanna go to California," he heard a young man say. "I got me a pal that went out there. He's in the gravy now. You can live for about nothin' out there offa the ocean. All you gotta do is, you gotta go out each day and catch the fish. Besides of which, they got palm trees. And it's warm all the time."

"Palm trees," somebody said. "Can you eat one of them palm trees?"

"Warm," somebody else said. "He wants it warm. It ain't warm enough for him right here."

"Sure you can eat 'em," somebody said. "Ain't you ever heard of palm tree stew?"

Al Dorsett laughed. He had begun this day at the West Side Market: "shopping" at the market dump. There was already a crowd when he got there. When the trucks dumped their loads of garbage, men, women, and children attacked the new mounds, poking around in it with their hands. Maybe it was the smell this morning, or the heat. Maybe he was losing his grip. But all he could do today was watch them. He couldn't force himself to dig in. He felt as if he were outside of himself; watching himself standing there; paralyzed. They dug into the rotted piles and picked out tomatoes, lettuce, squash, bits of meat. They were excited and joyful and Al Dorsett cursed the God that had put him on this earth.

Then he had gone to Arnold's Bakery on West Twenty-eighth Street and had stood in line for the two-day-old bread. He stood in line for two and a half hours. When there were only four people in front of him, the fat woman closed her window and said, "We got plenty inside, nice and hot, just out of the oven."

24

Now here he was, in a soup line again, shuffling toward the back of the truck. He took his shirt off and toweled his face with it. He rolled the shirt up and stuck it into his pants, which were a size too big for him.

"Fuckin' Jesus!" somebody said. "Look at that thing!"

A big black car came down the street toward them. Al Dorsett loved cars and looked at this one closely. A 1932 Packard, the new ports on its hood, its interior gleaming black leather. Three men in it. The two in the front were young, wise-looking guys who smirked out at them. An older man sat in the back reading a newspaper with gold spectacles. All three wore suits and ties; the man with the gold spectacles wore a straw hat. On the side of the car were the words "Baldwin and Johnson Steel Co." The letters were painted in gold.

Al Dorsett watched the Packard and thought how good it would feel to drive a car like that. To grasp that steering wheel, his head high, and coast down a country road. To press himself, on a day as hot as this, against that cool black leather.

He watched the car go to the end of the block and then stop. The soup line had snaked completely across the street now and the car couldn't get through. He heard the car horn, heard one of the men in the line yell, "Eat shit, you rich bastards!" Some of the other men picked it up and laughed. The horn honked again. The men didn't move.

It's too late, Al Dorsett thought, I'll never have a car like that.

He was forty-four years old: a good husband, a good father. He had never done anything in his life to cause harm to another man. He had fought bravely for his country in the Argonne Forest, where he'd been wounded, and now here he was. Waiting for a cup of greasy water. Worrying about the rats getting fatter each day.

"The hell with 'em!" Al Dorsett heard himself shout to the men blocking the car. "Don't move!" The men in the line picked it up. "Don't move! Don't move! Don't move!" It was a full-throated roar.

The hell with them! With all of them! With all of the rich, stinking bastards who had big bellies and owned big houses and read newspapers with gold spectacles and blocked the sun with straw hats. With Presidents and bosses who made big speeches and bigger promises filled with bullshit and hot air. With the men who had sent him to war and still wouldn't pay him the money they owed him.

"The hell with 'em!" Al Dorsett shouted to the men in the street. "Don't move!"

It was just as hot then, he remembered, a day just like this one. Four years ago. He had gone to Washington to demand what they owed him: a $500 cash bonus for the war. The whole town was filled with veterans; jobless and hungry men who set tents up for themselves in that hell-hot sun; so hot the cherry blossom trees were burned completely bare. They had called themselves the Bonus Expeditionary Force.

Then, one afternoon, the bastards came down on them. Cavalry, with their shiny sabers. Machine guns. The Thirty-fourth Infantry. Six tanks, their trucks eating up the concrete. That tinhorn leading them all, General Douglas MacArthur, high on his white horse as a goddamn Hun. They set their machine guns up and came marching into the camp, destroying the homes they had fashioned out of fruit crates, chicken coops, gunny sacks, beached old cars. "Where were you in the Air-Gone, buddy?" he had yelled. And then he had screamed, until there was nothing left in his lungs, "Yella! Yella! Yella!" They kept on coming, burning everything down. A kid had a rabbit he kept in a tent. The tent on fire, the kid tried to go back in for it. A tinhorn saw the kid. He stuck his bayonet through the kid's leg. Next morning, the garbage trucks came around. Bodies all over them.

Down the street, the Packard honked its horn again.

"Let's get 'em!" Al Dorsett yelled.

He ran for the car along with a dozen other men. They surrounded it. Their fists banged on its hood. The two wise guys in the front looked scared. The one with the gold spectacles in the back looked up from his paper and said something to them. The car moved into reverse and backed away. The men cheered. They had won.

The car stood a few hundred feet from them in the middle of the street, its engine idling. More and more men crowded into the street, laughing, shaking their fists.

Then, suddenly, the car came roaring at them. The driver had his eyes and his mouth wide open. The one next to him was laughing. The one with the gold spectacles wasn't even watching. He was reading the newspaper again.

The car was coming straight at him, Al Dorsett saw, its engine screaming, a hurtling black cannonball aimed right at his guts.

He threw himself desperately to the concrete.

The Packard exploded by him.

He lay on the pavement, bleeding from his elbow but otherwise unhurt, and then he got up and went back to the line to wait for his soup.

Behind them, in the cramped little living room, the women were asking the priest to say the Rosary.

"Pray pray pray," Mishka Biro said to Johnny and Abe. "If Joe was here, he say enough pray already, we go down the basement and get the wine." He was a barrel-chested little man with silver hair and a snow-white moustache. "What the hell," he said. "Joe was a good man or no. He go to hell or no. Make no difference now."

"Quiet!" one of the women hissed. "We will say the Rosary."

"Say it," Mishka said loudly. "You gonna say it, say it. Me, I'm not gonna say it. I'm gonna go home."

Johnny and Abe laughed. Mishka waved and walked out.

The priest was halfway through the Our Father when the three men walked into the living room. The priest stopped praying; the women watched them. The men were wearing new suits and brightly shined shoes. They looked like they didn't belong there. The room was quiet.

"Excuse me," one of them said, smiling. "I'm looking for Mrs. Kovak." He had a straw hat in his hands and a pair of gold spectacles on his nose. He had very white teeth. "We didn't mean to interrupt," he said.

There was a pause and then Johnny stepped to him. "I'm Johnny Kovak."

The man smiled again. "I'm Charles Holden." He stuck his hand out. "I'm the personnel manager at Baldwin Johnson."

Johnny nodded and looked at his outstretched hand. The man pulled it back.

"I'm sorry about your father. He was a fine man, one of our best workers. I always liked him." He smiled again.

Johnny said, "Did you?"

The two younger men stepped closer to Holden.

"I'll get ma," Abe said.

"Good," Holden said, "thank you."

"Wait a minute," Johnny said. He looked at Holden challengingly. "What do you wanna talk to her about?"

"It's a business matter?"

"What kinda business matter?"

"Really," Holden said, "can't we talk somewhere else? We're interrupting the ceremony." He looked at the priest apologetically.

"She's in the kitchen," Abe said.

Holden turned to the priest and the women in the living room and smiled. "I'm sorry, father."

Abe led them into the kitchen. The priest continued saying the Rosary.

Ilona Kovak stood at the stove making coffee. There was a battered table in the room, four chairs, along with the white stove and a nearly empty larder. Joe Kovak's ancient cap hung on a peg on the wall not far from a portrait of the Blessed Virgin Mary.

Holden introduced himself to her. "I'm so very sorry about your husband," he said, and held her hand consolingly. Johnny leaned against the wall, not saying anything. Holden's men eyed him.

"Sit, please," Ilona Kovak said. "You like coffee?"

"I'd love some," Holden smiled. He sat down at the little table.

"My English no good," Ilona Kovak said. "My boys, they translate."

"Of course," Holden said.

She turned to the two men with Holden. "You? Coffee?"

"No thanks, ma'am," one of them said.

"It's good coffee," Johnny said. "Go on, have some." He leaned against the wall and grinned at them. They watched him suspiciously.

She served the coffee and sat down at the table across from Holden. Abe sat at the head of the table. Johnny slouched against the wall. The two men stood by the door.

Holden sipped his coffee. "It really is excellent."

"See what I mean?" Johnny said, grinning at the two men again. "You guys shoulda had some."

There was a pause. "Well," Holden said, "As I was telling your boy, Mrs. Kovak. Your husband was one of our best workers. He was a fine man. I always liked John."

Johnny laughed. "You musta known him pretty good."

Holden ignored it and continued. "I am here to express the company's condolences."

"Con-do-lenz," Ilona Kovak said to Abe. "What is that?"

"Big word, ma," Johnny grinned.

Abe translated it for her.

Holden said, "We are a generous company, Mrs. Kovak. We always try to take good care of our workers and their families. Especially in these times. These are such difficult times for everyone."

She nodded slowly.

"Your husband worked for us a long time, Mrs. Kovak. Baldwin and Johnson wants to demonstrate its appreciation. I've bought you this check as an expression of our sympathy."

"Get the fuck outa here," Johnny said sharply, his voice very low.

Abe turned on him. "Hey," he said. "Come on. Ma's here."

Holden held the check up in the air. Ilona Kovak looked at it, then reached for it slowly.

"You understand, Mrs. Kovak," Holden said. "We

F.I.S.T.

don't have to do this. Your husband died of natural causes. We are in no way responsible."

Johnny laughed bitterly. "Did you hear that, ma?"

Holden pressed it. "Do you understand that, Mrs. Kovak?"

"Yes," she said, her face blank. "I understand."

"Good." Holden smiled. "We understand each other then." He pushed his chair back.

"How much, ma?" Johnny said.

"We'd better be going," Holden said.

Ilona Kovak nodded.

"Ma, how much?"

"One hundred dollar," she said. She didn't look at him.

"A hundred dollars," Johnny said quietly. He stepped to Holden. "A hundred lousy dollars!" he shouted. He turned to his mother. "They killed him, ma. You know that."

"Hold on, bub," one of Holden's men said.

"Give it back to him, ma." He stood over her, staring at her. She avoided his gaze and kept her eyes on the check.

"Ma, give it back to him!"

She stared at the check and didn't say anything.

"Good-bye, madam," Holden said. "Good luck to you." One of his men looked at Johnny and smiled. "Thanks for the coffee," he said. They walked out of the room.

"Good-bye," Ilona Kovak said. Her voice was a hollow whisper. She kept staring at the check.

"Jesus Christ, ma!" Johnny turned sharply away

from her. In the momentary silence, he could hear the cadence of the Rosary coming from the living room.

"Johnny," Ilona Kovak said softly, "we gotta eat."

"I'll get a job, ma. I'll get some money."

She nodded and didn't say anything.

"Ma, I promise you."

They looked at each other a moment.

"Johnny, Johnny," she said. She got up and walked out into the living room.

Johnny went to the window and watched the big black Packard with the gold letters on its side. Holden was reading a newspaper. The two men in the front seat were laughing.

He turned from the window in fury.

"He didn't even know his fuckin' name!"

Abe stared at the table's scarred surface. "Let it alone, Johnny."

"Sure," Johnny said. "Let it alone. He wasn't your old man."

When Abe Belkin was twelve years old, a slight, fair-haired boy who liked to stand by the river and watch the ore boats go by, his father died. Ivan Belkin had raised the boy alone from the age of four and when he was crushed to death by a motor at the Olson Tool Company, the boy locked himself in the house for five days and lay on his bed staring at the peeling-plaster ceiling.

On the evening of the fifth day, there was a knock at the door; the knock turned to louder and louder banging, and the next thing the boy knew the door came crashing down and Joe Kovak, who had been Ivan Belkin's best friend, stood there swearing at him.

Joe Kovak took him home. Ilona Kovak fed him hot bean soup with kolbasz in it and put him to bed. The next morning, Joe Kovak woke him at six o'clock and told him to get his skinny, lazy ass out of bed. No son of Ivan Belkin's was going to sleep the day away. Joe Kovak fed him, paid for the clothes on his back, hugged him before he fell asleep each night. And almost before he knew it, Abe Belkin had the family he'd only read about in his books.

He barely remembered his mother, knew her only from the things Ivan Belkin had told him. His mother, Ivan Belkin said, had the gentlest heart in the world. She liked books, fine music, and walks in the spring rain. And he had had no business, Ivan Belkin said, bringing her to America. She was not built to endure the hardships of an immigrant's life. She was afraid of this raucous and often hostile country and cowered from it inside her books and music. And until the day he died, Ivan Belkin blamed himself for his wife's death. She died of appendicitis. The doctor who spoke Slovak and Hungarian was away for the weekend and Rose Belkin didn't want an American doctor to see her naked. So she hid her pain and waited for the old-country doctor and by the time he got back, she was dead.

Ivan Belkin had always been a man of wildly shifting moods, but after her death he sank into an overwhelming depression. He reached for his bottle more often, spoke little to his son, who reminded him of his dead wife, and spent most of his time at the plant or at Zigi's Tavern.

Abe was a shy boy who didn't like arguments, yet he was stubborn and unyielding when he felt he was right, but always in a rational, soft-spoken way. He didn't like fights and he didn't do well in them. Not only because he was small, but also because he never seemed to be able to get his heart into a fight. Fighting proved nothing. He preferred his brains to his fists. Joe Kovak understood these things, encouraged his reading, bragged to his friends about Abe's grades in school, and used him as an example whenever Johnny came home with a bloody nose.

In the beginning, in the first few years after Abe moved in with the Kovaks, Johnny would pick at him. He'd challenge him, call him names, make fun of his reading. But as the years went by, as they spent more time with each other, as Ilona Kovak kept telling them to "help your brother," they made an unstated pact with each other. Abe was two years younger than Johnny, yet he had a skill with numbers and words that far surpassed his age. Johnny had the same precocious skill with his fists and with the harsh, crude word that could hack someone off. So they took care of each other, in their differing ways, almost becoming brothers even though they remained almost total opposites. Johnny was big; Abe was small. Johnny always had a girl; Abe always had a book. Johnny was trigger-tempered; Abe was always patient. Johnny couldn't hold a job; and Abe, like Joe Kovak and Ivan Belkin, was a "good worker."

Not that he cared for his job at the Fleckner Brothers warehouse. He was abused and underpaid and each day he had to face the foreman he despised. But the job supported him and two years ago, when he was eighteen, he had moved out of Joe Kovak's house and taken out a single room on Front Street. To prove to himself that he was a man. That he could support himself.

And while he hated his job, his reading taught him that workers were abused and underpaid everywhere. Fleckner Brothers was just a symptom of a worldwide disease called Capitalism. Capitalism robbed the worker of his dignity and self-respect. And since it was the same everywhere, in every warehouse and mill, it did no good to lash out at individual places and bosses—the way Johnny always did. They would just fire you and you'd be out on the street again begging for another job where the same thing would happen.

But while he knew that the game was rigged, that the system itself was at fault, Abe didn't know what to do about it. He liked much of what Communist Party organizers said, but he couldn't bring himself to approve of their solutions. Revolutions meant bloodshed and violence. And while he believed that the injustices had to be wiped out, Abe Belkin didn't believe in bloodshed and violence. It was a position which paralyzed him.

So he continued his reading, seeking illumination and insight, and went to work in the dingy Fleckner

Brothers warehouse each day, being a "good worker," earning his wage.

He tried to talk to Johnny about these things sometimes and got nowhere.

"I don't give a shit about all that stuff," Johnny would say. "All I care about's me."

"It's all tied in, don't you see? I am talking about you."

"What's a buncha big words gotta do with me? I just don't like gettin' fucked over, that's all. All I know's they can't fuck me over."

"They can kick your ass out, can't they?"

"Not before I get a coupla punches in," Johnny would grin.

That had always been Johnny's solution to everything. When he was fourteen and Johnny sixteen, he and Johnny were walking around Public Square late one winter afternoon. Snow was piled high on the ground and it was so cold Abe could feel his hair frozen in clumps. It was just before Christmas; the Swearingen Company had its mammoth tree lighted up on the square. They were standing in front of it, staring at it.

"Look at the flatheads," somebody said.

There were six of them. They were in their late teens. They wore fur coats and fur caps and gloves, scarves that dangled all the way down to their shiny, expensive boots.

"What are you lookin' at, flathead?" one of them said to Johnny. He looked about eighteen. He was bigger than Johnny and he had a bright red scarf.

"Haven't you ever seen a Christmas tree before? Don't they have them where you come from?" The others laughed.

It was getting dark and they were badly outnumbered. Abe glanced around the square. He desperately wanted to see someone who would break this up. No luck. Their side of the square was empty.

"Don't you have a mouth?" the red scarf said to Johnny. "Can't you—*spikka the linguige?*" The others laughed again.

"I got a mouth," Johnny said. "But you—you're gonna need a new one."

"Ooh-hoo-hoo," one of them laughed. "Listen to the flathead."

"I know you've got one," the red scarf said, his eyes locked on Johnny's. "You use it to go to the toilet every day."

Johnny swung.

"Look out!" Abe screamed.

The iceball exploded against Johnny's right eye and in a second all six of them converged on the two of them, flailing and kicking. They hit the ground. Three of them were on top of Johnny, Abe saw, smashing away at his nose and mouth, and then Abe felt a boot go deep into the back of his skull and the Christmas tree lights swirled . . . tilted upside down . . . turned black.

"Get up!" Johnny was screaming at him. "Get up!"

Johnny was bleeding from his nose and mouth, holding his right eye. Abe got up, dazed and numb, and saw the six of them running down Euclid Avenue, hooting and laughing.

Johnny was running after them, still holding his eye. Abe ran behind him, trying to stay on his feet. They were splitting up now. Three of them ran toward Prospect Avenue and at Fourth Street two of the others headed for Superior. The red scarf kept running down Euclid. He was a block ahead of them.

"Come on!" Johnny yelled back to Abe.

"We can't get him."

"The *fuck* we can't!"

They ran past Ninth Street, dodging heavy traffic. Past the policeman standing inside his booth directing cars. Past Playhouse Square. Through a ticket line in front of the Palace Theater box office. Past a woman in the line who said, "Oh my God, oh my God!" when Johnny ran by her.

A block past Playhouse Square, they stopped to catch their breaths. A block ahead of them, the one with the red scarf had stopped, too, and was spread-eagled against a doorway, gasping. Johnny's right eye was a purple grapefruit. Much of his face was dark brown. The freezing cold had clotted the blood there.

They started running again down Euclid Avenue, gaining on the red scarf now, in the section known as Millionaire's Row, where the houses had gables and white pillars, where the driveways seemed a mile long.

The red scarf tripped and got up again and just as he turned into a driveway, Johnny caught him. "Help me!" the red scarf screamed. Johnny knocked him to the ground. He was beating at the kid's eyes, landing one punch after another, always to his eyes. The kid was sobbing.

Abe heard a woman scream inside the house and then the front door of the big white house opened and a man was running toward them down the long driveway.

"He's got a gun, Johnny!"

Johnny jumped up and they ran into the street. Behind them they heard a shot and then another. In an alley between Euclid and Chester, they threw themselves down behind a row of garbage cans. They lay there panting, not saying anything. They heard sirens; a police car came down the alley with a spotlight and passed them. They crouched in the alley for several hours, half frozen now, and then ducked down a network of back alleys which led them down to the Flats.

When Ilona Kovak saw them, she made the sign of the cross and ran into the bedroom to wake her husband up. When Joe Kovak saw the purple grapefruit that was Johnny's eye, he yelled, "Jesus Christ! What happen? What the hell happen?" He couldn't stop yelling it. "What the hell happen?"

Johnny told him and he yelled, "You stupid, you coulda got killed."

"It wasn't that bad, pa," Johnny said.

"Shut your mouth!" Joe Kovak yelled. "You, Abe? Where's your big brains?"

"I'm sorry, pa."

"Yah," Joe Kovak said. "You sorry. You both gonna be sorry. Down the basement."

They got down to the basement and Joe Kovak lined them up under the bare bulb in the middle of the room.

"Now I tell you. No, Johnny? No more trouble!"

"What the hell was I supposed to do?" Johnny said. "Let him go?"

"You do what I tell you," Joe Kovak said. "No more trouble!"

"Okay, pa," Abe said.

"Johnny," Joe Kovak said, "you hear me?"

Johnny looked away from him. "I hear you," he mumbled.

Joe Kovak nodded, looked at them, and walked away to his cabinet. He reached up, pulled down a bottle of wine he had made, a bottle of his best, and said, "Drink. Drink all. Warm you up."

The day after Joe Kovak's burial, Abe Belkin walked toward the Fleckner Brothers warehouse and remembered that bottle of wine. It was the best bottle of wine that he had ever had.

Lines Lines Lines. The whole goddamn country was one big line. Guys waiting around till their legs gave. And for what? Greasy water. Old bread. Blank faces. Empty words.

Johnny had sworn to himself that he would never stand in a line again. Yet here he was, the day after the old man's funeral. Hundreds of saps in front of him, hundreds of saps in back. Waiting around the City of Cleveland's Free Employment Bureau. Not even for a job. Just for the chance of getting one.

It was nuts. What the hell was he doing here? What chance? With this long line of guys waiting for the same thing? Why was he kidding himself? Still . . . the old man was dead. He was the man of the house. Who would pay the rent? Who would put the food on the table? Abe? Sure, Abe would do it. Maybe that's why he was here. If he didn't do it, Abe would. Good old Abe. He always did what he had to do.

The line moved ahead of him and Johnny could see the men who'd been in the Employment Bureau Office upstairs being herded out. There were four shifts each day. You waited two hours downstairs. Then they let you upstairs for an hour. You stood around for the hour and hoped some job would come in over the phone. Some job they thought you could do.

Big deal, he told himself. What if you do get something? What the hell is that gonna prove? You've washed dishes. You're swept floors. You've worked three different kinds of assembly lines. It always ends up the same way and you know it. They push you around. They pay you peanuts for working yourself stiff. Then somebody says something to you. You don't like his tone. You tell him off. They can you.

He offered his own defense: maybe it'll turn out different. At least I haven't sold any apples yet. He grinned to himself.

Maybe that's next. Listen, get the hell outa here.

Go see Vince Doyle. Wouldn't that feel great? To walk away from here, go over to Vince's place, knock down a few beers, shoot the shit with Jocko? Vince'll find you something.

He almost heard himself say: I don't wanna do that stuff no more.

You want to stand here in line with these guys, Johnny? Is that what you want to do? Look at 'em. Look how their shoulders sag. The way they keep their eyes down on the ground. You're not like them. You don't belong here. You don't crawl.

He remembered his promise to his mother.

So what? You've promised her a lot of things.

It was different now.

How? You need some money. Go see Vince. He's got his own club. Everything's aboveboard.

It was bullshit. He could get into trouble. His mother needed him.

Forget it then, Johnny. Crawl.

The men in front of him moved. He followed them up the stairs to a large, cavernous hall. A thick rope was stretched from post to post at the front of the room. Behind it sat three clerks with telephones in front of them. Off to the side, a bored-looking man in a rumpled suit stood behind a microphone. Johnny knew the routine. The man in the rumpled suit was the "auctioneer."

A telephone rang. The men in the room froze. A clerk picked the phone up, wrote something down on a card, and hung up. He got up and handed the card to the auctioneer.

43

The auctioneer leaned into the microphone. "No-wicki Meats. Two men. Clean-up. Five hours' work. Twenty-five cents an hour. Clerk number three."

Johnny muscled toward the clerk's desk. It was too late. The clerk already had four men picked out, twice the number needed. The boss had to be given a good choice. The four men ran from the room with the cards in their hands. A man who hadn't been picked said, "Please, they're gonna shut off my gas."

The room quieted again. The men stared at the telephones. One of them rang; somebody cheered. "Shut up, goddammit!" a man yelled, "he can't hear." The clerk wrote something down again and handed the card to the auctioneer.

"The Manor Hotel. Twelve men. Fifteen cents an hour. Day's work. Garbage detail. Clerk number one."

More men pushed toward the clerk's desk. The rope stretched taut and looked like it was going to snap.

"You break the rope," the auctioneer said, "you're gettin' outa here! Alla yousel"

Johnny watched them. A hundred men trying to knock each other down for a job collecting garbage. A hundred men yelling, "I got three kids, mister" and "I'll do a good job, mister." He moved out of the way and let them squeeze in front of him.

I'm not collecting garbage, he told himself. I need the money. It's fifteen cents an hour, but I'm not collecting anyone's garbage.

Thirty minutes and three calls later, he had battled his way up to the front of the room. He looked at the clock. He knew that if he didn't find something in the next ten minutes, it would be too late. They would clear him out with these men and bring the next group in.

The telephone rang. The auctioneer got his card.

"Fleckner Brothers warehouse. Two men. Strong. Loading. Seventy cents an hour. Full time. Clerk number two."

It was the big one. A full-time job. The jackpot. What all of the men prayed for.

The clerk was right in front of him. He felt the mass of men squeeze into his back, pushing him against the rope. The clerk stood up and looked at them. He was young, his hair was combed to the side. He wore a clean white shirt.

Pick me, Johnny thought. Pick me, you little cocksucker. I'm right here.

"Hey, right here!" he yelled. The clerk looked through him. On Johnny's right, somebody was trying to squeeze up to the rope. He put his elbow out, jammed it back, felt soft flesh, and heard a groan. The clerk looked off to his right and picked another man. He looked behind him into the crowd and picked two others. Then the clerk raised his hand toward somebody behind him.

"Mister," Johnny said, "please."

The clerk look at him and hesitated for what seemed hours. "Okay," he finally said, "you."

He took his card, ran out the side door, down the stairs, and into the street. He ran through the Flats in the heat, the sweat pouring off of him. One of the other men who had been picked was half a block ahead of him. He speeded up. His sides hurt and his lungs felt like they were going to explode. He was thirsty. He hadn't eaten yet today. He tripped on a chunk of cement and almost lost his footing.

Fleckner Brothers, he thought. That was funny. He and Abe working in the same place. Ma wouldn't believe it. The two of them working side by side. Maybe it would work this time. Abe would be there. Maybe it wouldn't be so bad.

When he got to the Fleckner Brothers gate, he could hardly breathe. There were a dozen men there already. They had come from other employment bureaus. He had forgotten about that. That there were other employment bureaus for other men to come from.

An hour later, he was still standing at the gate with the others. Waiting again.

"Here comes Gant," one of the men said.

He was a fat, beet-faced man with a cigar stuck in his mouth. He walked toward them from the warehouse, a shotgun-toting guard beside him.

He stopped on the other side of the gate. "Well, what have we got here today?" He smiled.

The guard opened the gate and Gant walked out. He looked them over. The guard stayed close to him.

"Another fine lot," Gant said. He walked among them, his face close to theirs, smiling.

"I need two men," he said. "Food on the table for two of you."

He stopped next to a middle-aged man with a pale

face. Johnny watched him. "What's your name?" Gant said.

"Dorsett. Al Dorsett."

Gant puffed on his cigar. "Dorsett, huh?"

"Yes, sir."

"Sir, he says. I like a man calls me sir."

Dorsett smiled.

"Course, maybe you're tryin' to fool me," Gant said. "Maybe you're one of these Red troublemakers. You tryin' to fool me?"

Dorsett said, "No, sir."

"Are you a responsible man, Dorsett? Are you married?"

"Yes sir." Dorsett smiled.

"She pretty?"

Dorsett hesitated. He was wary. "Yes, sir. She's kinda pretty."

The guard laughed. Johnny watched them.

"She is?" Gant puffed. He laughed. "Why would a pretty gal marry a man like you?"

"Lucky, I guess," Dorsett said.

"A lucky man." Gant laughed. "Did you hear that? Dorsett here is a lucky man." The guard laughed. Everyone else was silent. There was a long pause.

"Tell me something, Dorsett," Gant said. "Man to man." He lowered his voice conspiratorially. "You put it into her at night?"

The guard laughed. Dorsett flushed and looked away from him. Johnny felt his skin crawl.

"Do you?" Gant said.

Dorsett looked at him and didn't say anything.

47

"I asked you a question."

Very quietly, Dorsett said, "Sometimes." He was trying to grin. It came out as a grimace.

"She like it?"

The guard laughed again. Dorsett stared at the ground. His face was taut. He clenched his fists.

"You want me to hire a man doesn't answer my questions?" Gant said. "Okay, let's see who else here wants a job." He moved away from Dorsett.

"I guess she does," Dorsett said. He whispered the words.

"What'd you say?" Gant said, smiling.

"I guess she does."

"She does what?"

"She likes it," Dorsett said, louder now, forcing the words.

Gant smiled, pleased with himself. "She does, huh? Well, what the hell do I care? What are you tellin' me for?" He laughed. Dorsett looked away.

"Get in there," Gant said to him. "You earned yourself a job. The rest of you bums, get the hell outa here."

"What about me?" one of the men said.

"You?" Gant said. "You can kiss my ass."

"You said two. Two men. That's what you said."

"You're not a man."

Gant strolled across the yard, puffing on his cigar. Johnny pressed his face against the gate and grabbed it with his hands.

Sap, he told himself. What did you expect?

* * *

Day after day, he kept trying. After two weeks, he was still jobless, but he recognized the faces in the lines now, knew many of them by their first names. They knew him, too. He wondered if that meant that he was one of them.

He got home each night and his mother said, "How it go today, Johnny?" He shrugged and grinned. "Still tryin', ma." She made him something to eat which he didn't feel like eating. He fell into bed exhausted, got up early the next morning, hit the lines, got home that night, and his mother said, "How it go today, Johnny?" He shrugged and grinned . . . and wondered if this was how the old man had felt going to the mill each day.

Discouraged and worn out, he went over to the West Side Market one day to see Mishka. Mishka was like an uncle to him. Even as a kid, whenever he had a problem, it was Mishka he had gone running to. Mishka always understood. He stuck up for him, even against his parents. When his mother insisted that Johnny speak Hungarian at home, it was Mis who had convinced her. "You gonna send him back the old country, Ilona?" It was Mishka who had taken him down to League Park every Sunday to see the Indians play.

The market was nearly empty this morning and up ahead he could see Mishka in his undershirt, the leather apron hanging over his belly. He was arguing with a well-dressed young woman who reeked of money.

"You want orange," Mishka was saying to her, "I

pick orange. My orange. Your orange when you pay. You no pay me yet. You no pay, I pick the orange."

"I don't want them then," the woman said haughtily. "You can keep your oranges."

"I keep," Mishka said. "Good. Fine orange. Good-bye." He bowed elaborately. The woman walked away in a huff.

"Hey, Mish," Johnny said. He laughed. They hugged.

"You! Good for nothin'!" Mishka said. "What the hell you do here?"

"How's it goin', Mish?"

"Wonderful. Couldn't be no goddamn better. Big business. Big money. I'm gettin' rich, Johnny. See?"

He opened his strongbox. It was empty.

Johnny laughed.

"Gonna buy me a big mansion in the Shaker Heights, Johnny," Mishka laughed. "Where the hell's Abe? I don't see him no more."

"He's workin'."

"Workin'? All the time he's workin'? He don't got time to see me? Bullshit, Johnny." He laughed. "He still livin' above that goddamn butcher?"

"Yeah."

"A thief, the goddamn butcher. Horsemeat in the sausage. A day, the bacon is green."

"What are you talkin' about?" Johnny laughed. "He makes pretty good sausage."

"Croat, Johnny. Don't ever trust no Croat. Horse-meat in the sausage. They rob you."

"They all rob you," Johnny said.

50

"Smart guy," Mishka laughed. "Always smart guy. So—what you doin', smart guy? You work or you gettin' in the trouble again?"

Johnny looked away and fingered the oranges.

"I been lookin', Mish. I can't find nothin'."

"What the hell you mean you can't find nothin', Johnny? Everybody gettin' rich. Everybody gonna be —millionaire. You, me, every-goddamn-body."

"Yeah, that's for sure," Johnny said. He paused and cleared his throat. "Listen, Mish." He stopped again. "You don't need no help—loadin'—packin' stuff. Do you, Mish?"

Mishka looked at him. "Shit, Johnny. If I can— shit, Johnny. I can't pay nothin'." He opened his empty strongbox again. "What the hell I'm gonna pay you with? Them?" He pointed to the oranges. Johnny laughed.

"I hear somethin' about down at the Fleckner Brothers," Mishka said. "You go down there?"

"Yeah. I been there."

"They didn't hire you to run the goddamn place?"

Johnny grinned. "Shit for the birds, Mish. Shit for the birds."

He made the rounds again that day, but it was a day like the others. He got nowhere. Late in the afternoon, as he walked home, he saw a group of people in the square in the Flats. He heard loud voices he couldn't make out and he walked over. It was only Bela Szabo, standing on top of his soapbox again.

Bela Szabo weighed over three hundred pounds and had the largest head Johnny had ever seen. He was completely bald. He bellowed all the time and wore the same mud-brown suit each day. He was the Communist Party organizer among the workers in the Flats. He was a man who started bellowing the moment he saw more than five people standing around.

Johnny stood there, watching him, and remembered the day Bela Szabo had come to his house to try to convince the old man to join the Communist Party. The old man listened to it and listened to it and he finally said, "Enough. We will have some wine." Bela Szabo said he didn't want any wine and the old man told him he'd either drink the wine or get out. So Bela Szabo drank the wine and three hours later he was still bellowing and finally Joe Kovak said "No more!" and led him by his brown suit to the door.

Johnny stood on the square and listened to Bela Szabo bellowing his big words. He noticed Abe in the crowd, glued to Szabo like he didn't want to miss a single word.

He went over to Abe and said, "Let's get the hell outa here."

"I want to hear him, Johnny."

"Aw, come on. I know it by heart. You wanna hear it? I'll give the speech."

Abe kept his eyes on Szabo. "I want to hear him," he said.

Some people booed and catcalled. Szabo bellowed over the noise. "Listen to me! You know I don't lie. You know me!"

Johnny looked at them booing Szabo and laughed. "They want to hear him too," he said to Abe. He glanced back at the crowd and that's when he saw her.

She was standing a few hundred feet away from him, at the far edge of the crowd. She looked to be about twenty. She had blond hair down to the middle of her back and the whitest skin he had ever seen.

"Holy shit!" he said to Abe. "Look at that."

She had cheekbones that hung way out, a nose that perked up at the tip, and big, emerald-green eyes. She was tall and had the best legs he had ever seen. From what he could see, there was an awful lot more inside her simple dress.

"I'm tryin' to listen to Szabo," Abe said.

Johnny kept his eyes on the girl. Szabo, he heard dimly, was trying to overcome the rising jeers of the crowd.

"Who the hell is she?" Johnny said.

"Will you cut it out?" Abe said.

"Look at her, will ya? Just look at her."

"Who?"

He grabbed Abe's neck and twisted it. "There. You dummy. There."

Abe looked at her. "I've never seen her," he said. He turned back to Szabo.

Szabo kept bellowing. "I live down here in the Flats with you! And how do we live? Look at you!"

Johnny kept looking at the girl.

"Knock the Bolsheviki down!" someone said.

And suddenly the girl yelled, "It's a free country! Let him talk!"

"Tell him, Anna!" a woman near her yelled.

Johnny laughed. What the hell. He couldn't resist. She was the prettiest girl he had ever seen.

"Yeah," he yelled, "let him talk like Anna says."

Abe turned to him. "What are you pullin', Johnny?"

Johnny kept his eyes on the girl and grinned. She looked at him, saw him grinning at her, and looked angrily away.

Abe watched them. "Jesus Christ, Johnny," he said.

"And when they let us get jobs," Szabo bellowed, his three hundred pounds jiggling and shaking, "what do they pay? Nothing! Serf wages!"

"Serf wages!" Johnny yelled. He kept looking at her. "Serf wages!"

"We don't want no Reds here!" a man near the girl yelled at Szabo.

"You got no right to stop him," the girl said.

"It's a free country, ain't it, Anna?" Johnny yelled. He kept grinning at her.

"Shut up, sister!" the man said to her. "You don't know what you're—" He pushed her.

The girl pushed him back. "Don't you push me!" she said angrily.

Johnny dove through the crowd. He stood between them. "Don't you push Anna," he said to the man. He still had the grin on his face.

The girl turned to him. Her green eyes flashed. "Stay outa this, you!" she said to Johnny. She tried to push him away.

"What are you pushin' me, for?" Johnny said, laughing now. The girl had a pretty mouth. He wanted to kiss her. "I'm tryin' to help you."

"I didn't ask you to help me," she said, and at that moment the man she was arguing with slapped him in the face. Johnny swung at him, missed, and hit someone else. He was laughing. He couldn't control himself. A dozen people were suddenly swinging at each other aimlessly. Johnny stood there, swinging away, watching the girl, laughing.

Abe heard the sirens, raced into the middle of the fray, dodging blows, and grabbed him. "The cops, Johnny. Come on. We gotta get outa here."

"I thought you wanted to stay," Johnny grinned.

Abe pulled him away toward an alley. He went reluctantly and looked back. The girl was still yelling at someone.

"Hey, Anna," he shouted, laughing. "I wanna talk politics with you, Anna!"

The sirens were closer now and they ran down the alleys until they found themselves on the riverbank, behind a shipping terminal. Johnny was still laughing.

"Did you see her, Abe? Wouldn't you love to—"

Abe looked at him angrily. "You caused the whole thing. Szabo's probably gonna go to jail for inciting a riot."

Johnny laughed. "What the hell you so upset about? He's been there before."

Abe shook his head and finally grinned. "Asshole," he said.

Johnny walked down to the river.

55

"Look at this shit," he said, "it really is dirty." He paused. "Remember when we were kids. The old man made us those carts. We came down here and raced 'em all the time."

Abe smiled. "You got pissed off the only time I beat you."

Johnny laughed. "What are you talkin' about?"

"You did. You got all pissed off."

"You never beat me."

"I did too. I beat you fair and square. You wanted to deck me."

"Bullshit," Johnny laughed. "You never beat me. Come on, I'll deck you right now. Come on." He faked a couple of punches at Abe's face, then grabbed Abe in a hammerlock and, laughing, swung him around.

"Who's the asshole?" Johnny said.

They laughed and he released his hold.

Abe walked down to the water and after a pause he said, "You find anything yet?"

Johnny looked away from him.

"Huh? Did you?"

"Naw," Johnny said. "Nothin'. I been out every day."

Abe nodded. "I talked to Gant," he said, down at the warehouse."

"That bastard. I saw him take this guy. Asked him about his wife. Busted him into little pieces."

"If you want it," Abe said, "I can get you on."

Johnny stared at him. "How you gonna do that?"

Abe walked a few steps away from him. "Listen," he said. He hesitated. "Just—just get a bottle of the best whiskey you can. I'll give it to Gant."

Johnny looked at him dumbfounded. "Just like that," he said. He shook his head. "As easy as that."

"As easy as that."

Johnny grinned. "Anything else?" he said. His voice was getting louder. "I gotta mow his lawn Saturdays? Shine his goddamn shoes? Huh, Abe? Anything else?"

"Nothin' else," Abe said. "I gotta go, Johnny." He looked at him. "I'm tryin' to help you, Johnny. That's all."

"Kiss his ass, maybe?" Johnny said.

"Play it smart, Johnny. Let me know," Abe said, and walked away.

In mid-afternoon, Vince Doyle sat at the polished mahogany bar of his nightclub and sipped Johnnie Walker. It was raining outside. If it kept up, it would boost tonight's take. Rain always brought them in.

"Red," he said to the bartender, "give me another one of these."

The club was empty and he swiveled around on the bar and looked it over. It had only been open three months, but it was already known as the liveliest place in town. They came all the way from Bratenahl, Lakewood, even Shaker Heights to drink at "Vinnie's." They drove big cars and carried big wads and they came because they knew it was a class joint. They knew Vince Doyle didn't cater to riffraff. The bar brass shined; the floor gleamed; the mirrors sparkled; the fans overhead were painted gold. Red even wore a gold velvet vest.

There was nothing cut-rate about this place, Vince

Doyle said to himself. Not too bad for a mick from the Flats.

He smiled, turned back to the bar, and glanced at himself in the mirror. He was thirty years old and he felt like a million bucks. His suit cost $150; his shirt was silk; his shoes genuine alligator. He had a penthouse apartment in the Lakeshore Hotel. He drove a new Stutz Continental Coupe. His auburn, brilliantined hair was swept back from a ruled part. He had a small head; a mouth wary and dubious of everything and everybody. His eyes were indifferent, feline. He was a little pale and maybe he'd put on some weight, but that couldn't be helped. Horizontal exercise was the only kind he liked and horizontal exercise didn't do much for pallor.

A newspaper boy dashed in with the *Cleveland News.*

"Here's your paper, Mr. Doyle," the boy smiled.

Vince Doyle took the paper, gave the boy his five cents, and glanced at it. The same old malarkey. The Communists were marching on City Hall. The city was issuing scrip to its employees. The Kennel Club Dog Show was judged the best in the city's history. Vince Doyle laughed. The fucking Kennel Club Dog Show!

"Hey, Red," he said, "listen to this." He read from the paper. "The City Council announced plans yesterday for a massive Great Lakes Exposition which will cost several million dollars. The highlight of the exposition will be—get this!—Billy Rose's Aquacade with Johnny Weissmuller. Several new buildings will

be erected, including an Automotive Building and a
—listen to this, Red!—a Hall of Progress." Vince
Doyle roared.

"A Hall of Progress, did you hear that? Now listen
to this—the City Council said that Cleveland for
several years has been depressed by . . . Adverse Circumstances . . . isn't that good? . . . Adverse Circumstances . . . and that a forward-looking enterprise is
needed to revive civic pride."

He put the paper down. "Jesus Christ," he said,
laughing.

"That's pretty funny all right," Red said.

"Adverse circumstances. You get half the city out
on the streets goin' hungry. What do they do? They
give 'em a fuckin' Aquacade. A fuckin' Hall of Progress."

Vince Doyle laughed again and when he had finished laughing, he thought What the hell do I care?
It's no skin off my ass. I don't live down there anymore. I got smart and got out. I've got a fresh carna-
tion on my lapel each day.

He had grown up in the Flats. When he dropped
out of high school, he went to work alongside his
father at the lumber company. Making five and six
dollars a day. His mother worked as a scrubwoman on
a Great Lakes passenger ship. He gave them half of
what he made each week, but even with all three of
them working, it had never been enough. His parents
didn't seem to care, though. They were decent, law-
abiding people who went to Mass and Holy Com-
munion at St. Malachi's each Sunday. Decent, law-

abiding people who wore secondhand clothes. Lived in a secondhand house. Lived secondhand lives.

Finally Vince Doyle couldn't stand it anymore. He stopped working, moved out of the house, and started hanging around the pool halls. It didn't take long. He was a smart, street-wise kid with suddenly big ambitions. They spotted him.

First he ran numbers for them. Then he got in with some of the Huron Road gang and he started lining broads up for them. Then they asked him to run one of their speakeasies. He realized one day that he had enough money stashed away to go into business for himself. He opened a speak of his own on the near West Side. He soon had a reputation for handling the best booze in the city. He didn't fool around with bathtub gin and near beer. He went to Detroit and made a deal with a man named Babe Milano. The liquor came from Canada. It was delivered once a month by boat to a pier near Avon Lake. Babe Milano got a big slice, but even so Vince Doyle sometimes made as much as $5,000 a week.

Word of his success spread and he branched out. Babe Milano gave him advice on how to do it. He gathered his own crew of guys from the Flats and, using them as his muscle, Vince Doyle formed a Neighborhood Protection Association on the near West Side. As far as he was concerned, he was simply capitalizing on the merchants' own greed.

For example: he went to a theater owner on Lorain Avenue with two of his boys and told the man that unless he joined the Neighborhood Protection Association, Certain People might vandalize his theater. All Vince Doyle wanted to do was protect the owner against these Certain People. He wanted to help the man. For a cut of his box-office profits.

The theater owner said he didn't need any help like that and threatened to call the cops. The next night, Certain People dropped stink bombs on the theater's floor. They dropped more stink bombs the next week. The theater owner called Vince Doyle and told him he had changed his mind. Would he help him?

Vince Doyle helped him and a month later he asked the theater owner a hypothetical question. There were two other movie houses in the same district on Lorain Avenue. What would happen if both of the other houses went out of business? How much would that improve the theater owner's profits? How much would he like to see that happen? Enough to raise the cut Vince Doyle was getting each week? The theater owner didn't have to think about it. He was happy to raise his cut. A month after Vince Doyle had asked him the hypothetical question, both of his competitors were out of business.

Sometimes it worked in other ways. He went to a grocery store owner and told him that if he joined the association, he guaranteed that his competitors would go out of business. The owner was happy to join. Then he went to the competitors and told them that unless they joined, he would have to shut them down. The competitors were also happy to join. Then he went back to the first store owner and said he'd need a bigger cut to shut his competitors down. He got his bigger cut. Then he went back to the competitors and said he'd need a bigger cut to keep them open. He got his bigger cut. Everybody wanted to make money. Everybody, Vince Doyle learned, was willing to pay money to make more of it.

"Boss," Red said, interrupting his thoughts. "You want another?" Vince Doyle nodded and Red poured him another shot.

The front door opened and Jocko walked in. He was in his mid-twenties. He wore his hat brim low. His collar was high and shiny. His suit was patterned, his pants tight, his shoes pointed. He was dripping wet.

"Hiya, boss," he said. He showed a snazzy mouthful of gold teeth. "Wet out there." He took his suit coat off and exposed a shoulder holster and a Colt .38 automatic.

"What are you doin', modeling that thing?" Vince Doyle said.

"Sorry, boss." He smiled again self-consciously, hesitated, then put the wet coat back on. "Hey, Red," he said, "how's about a pop?"

Vince Doyle glared at him. "Did you talk to that singer I told you to call?"

"Right away, boss," Jocko said, looking forlornly at the drink the bartender had poured him, and walked away.

Vince Doyle lighted a thick Cuban cigar and watched the smoke drift to his gold fans. I was smart to get out of the Flats, he thought. I was lucky, too. The cops didn't nail me. No problem now. The cops are under control. A couple bucks, a free meal. They call me Mr. Doyle. Everybody, Vince Doyle grinned to himself. Everybody calls me Mr. Doyle.

Behind him, Jocko said, "She won't do it for less than thirty a week, boss."

"She'll do it," Vince Doyle said, "I'll talk to her."

He walked to the telephone in the back of the room and he was right in the middle of telling the uppity bitch how much good he could do her when he saw the kid walk in the front door.

He hadn't seen the kid in a year. The kid was wearing an old leather jacket and he looked tired, but other than that he still looked the same. That cockiness was still in his walk. The fire in his eyes.

He had found him at Andras' Pool Hall, a grimy dump of a place where the cockroaches usually outnumbered the customers. The kid hung around there every day. He was sullen and unfriendly and the only reason Vince Doyle approached him was that he had heard how good the kid was with his fists. Nobody fucked with Johnny Kovak, Vince Doyle had heard, and that was the only qualification necessary for the job he had in mind. Which was to have somebody no one would fuck with ride in the truck with Jocko as he brought the booze back from the dock in Avon Lake. Somebody who could handle the small-time ginzos who every now and then would try to knock off a truck filled with prime Canadian whiskey and peddle it themselves. Jocko always had his gun, yeah, and was always willing, too goddamn willing, to use it, but that was exactly what Vince Doyle wanted to avoid. He didn't like leaving corpses around. Cold bodies brought a lot of heat.

The kid agreed to take the job, did as he was told, even if he did it without any apparent enthusiasm, and one dawn, when a carful of punks from Toledo forced the truck over, the kid and Jocko took them all on and left the punks crawling around, battered up, and alive, at the side of the road. That was the last time any amateurs ever tried to muscle in on Vince Doyle's action.

There was something always distant about the kid, though. He took his pay and did his job but Vince Doyle got the feeling that the kid didn't really want to do what he was doing—that he was just doing it to make his buck and that he resented all of it somehow.

Then, about a year ago, he had quit. They were setting up the Neighborhood Association on Bridge Avenue then and there was a tailor named Mogyordy who wouldn't give in. A shriveled-up acorn of a little man who looked like he could be blown over by an Indian summer wind. It figured. It was always this kind of man who wouldn't give. So one night Vince Doyle walked into his shop with Jocko, Johnny, and another kid from the Flats and Jocko slapped the tailor around a little bit. Nothing serious, no marks, no bruises, but the tailor decided that he would join the association and the next day Johnny told Vince Doyle that he was through.

"Whatsamatter?" Vince Doyle had said, "ain't I payin' you enough?"

"That guy last night," the kid had said.

"What guy?"

"The tailor."

"The tailor?" Vince Doyle had laughed. "You got a soft spot for tailors?"

"He was Hungarian," the kid had said.

"So what," Vince Doyle had roared. "I don't give a fuck if he was from County Cork. If he kissed the fuckin' blarney stone when he was a kid. What are you talkin' about, the fuckin' tailor?"

The kid had looked at him, unsmiling, the fire in his eyes. "See you, Vince," the kid said, and that was it. He was the best kid who had ever worked for him.

The kid and Jocko were bear-hugging each other at the bar and Vince Doyle finally told the uppity bitch to go fuck herself with a broom handle, hung up, and walked up to them.

"Long time, Johnny," he said. He punched the kid playfully in the stomach. "Look at him, Jocko, he's still growin'." They laughed.

Johnny looked around. "I wanted to see how the big shots live," he said.

"In style," Vince Doyle grinned. "That's how."

He threw an arm around Johnny. "It's great to see you, kid. Come on, let's take the load off."

Johnny kept looking the place over. "Not bad," he grinned. "Not bad."

Vince Doyle slapped him on the back. "You're fuckin'-A right it's not bad."

They sat at a back booth. Jocko brought them a bottle and walked away.

"I heard about your old man," Vince Doyle said. "I always liked the guy." He poured Johnny a drink.

Johnny grinned. "He loved you too, Vince."

"Yeah, I'm sure."

Johnny laughed and they downed their drinks.

"So. What brings you back after all this time?" Vince Doyle said. "You need work? You got it."

"Come on, Vince," Johnny said. "That stuff."

"What stuff?" Vince Doyle said. "What are you talkin' about?" He smiled. "We're businessmen. Look at Jocko. Look at that fancy suit he's got over his ape body."

Johnny laughed.

"Hey, Jocko," Vince Doyle yelled across the room. "How's the teeth?"

Jocko turned from the bar, gave them a dazzling gold smile, and made a circle with his fingers.

"Aces, boss," he said.

Johnny laughed. "Good old Jocko."

"What's the matter, Johnny?" Vince Doyle said. "We got a good business. We take care of the club. We're nice and legit. We all got shiny suits." He rubbed the sleeve of his suit coat.

"Yeah?" Johnny grinned. "What's that Jocko's got under his arm?"

Vince Doyle laughed. "Insurance, kid. Everybody's got insurance nowadays."

"You know what I been wonderin', Vince," Johnny said, teasing him now, a rueful smile on his face. "I been wonderin' how the Protection Association's doin'?"

"It's doin' real good," Vince Doyle said.

"I was just wonderin', that's all," Johnny smiled.

"Listen, kid," Vince Doyle said, the color rising to his face. "Don't get so fuckin' high and mighty with me. How the hell you think it is in this country? It's a war. The big business guy fucks over the little business guy. Except he makes it sound high and mighty. He joins the fuckin' Rotary and he talks about building Halls of Progress and shit."

Johnny laughed. "Halls of Progress? You're really somethin', Vince."

"Yeah! He builds churches and sends his kids to fuckin' college so he can be a holdup guy just like him. Now what do we do? Do we fuck over the little guys? We fuck the merchants over. Nice and legitimate businessmen, guys that have been robbin' the little guy blind a hundred years. What the hell's wrong with that?"

Johnny laughed. "Nothin'. You put it like that."

"Okay," Vince Doyle smiled. "So how about it? I could use you."

"You shoulda been a salesman," Johnny grinned.

"I am a fuckin' salesman," Vince Doyle said. "Besides all kindsa other things."

There was a pause. Red turned the fans on overhead. They made a grating, rhythmic noise. Johnny watched them.

"I been lookin' for a job, Vince," he said quietly.

"I just gave you a job."

"Naw, a regular job."

Vince Doyle looked at him. "What the hell's a regular job?"

"You know what I mean."

"A regular job," Vince Doyle said, shaking his head. "Sure. Find a regular job. Work your balls off. Bring home a coupla bucks nice and regular each week. I don't give a fuck."

Johnny looked away from him and didn't say anything. The fans whirled and chewed at his nerves.

"So what do you want, Johnny?" Vince Doyle said.

Red turned the fans off. The clicking noise got louder for a moment, then stopped.

"I need a—a bottle of whiskey, Vince."

"A bottle of whiskey?" Vince Doyle said. "You shittin' me?"

"I don't have the dough."

"Jesus Christ, Johnny," Vince Doyle said. He stared at him, his eyes disbelieving and thin. He dug into his pocket and threw a hundred-dollar bill on the table.

Johnny avoided his eyes. "I don't want it."

"Jesus Christ, Johnny," Vince Doyle said, his voice husky and low. "You could have been somebody."

The next morning, with Abe at his side, Johnny walked across the gravel of the yard toward the rectangular Fleckner warehouse. I did it, ma, he thought to himself. I promised you. Here I am. I did what you wanted. I got a job. I crawled.

"It looks like a fuckin' casket," he said to Abe.

Abe grinned. "It's bigger. Come on, we'll go in the back."

Last night, home from Vince Doyle's, Johnny had put the hundred-dollar bill on the kitchen table. His mother was sitting there writing her weekly letter to the old country. She glanced at the money, didn't say anything, and finished the letter. She stamped the envelope, sealed it firmly, put the letter on the table next to the money, and looked up at him.

"Where you get, Johnny?" Her voice was soft; her eyes accusing.

"I stuck up a bank, ma, what do you think? But this bank wasn't doin' too good. It only had a hundred bucks in it." He smiled.

She was unyielding; her tone rock hard. "Where you get?"

"What are you lookin' at me like that for?" He turned away from her. "What difference does it make?"

"Where you get?"

His face felt hot. He pressed it to the wall for a moment, then turned back to her. "All right, ma, you wanna know? I'll tell you. I'm not gonna . . . lie to you. I never . . . lie to you." He said it bitterly, paused looked at her. She wasn't giving an inch. Her eyes were nailing him to the wall.

"I was down by the river," he said, "and there was this big black car stuck in a ditch down there. And this guy inside. This *gentleman*. That nice Mr. Holden. The one you took the money from after pa died. Remember him, ma?"

69

"I remember, Johnny." Her face was a mask.

"He was in a big hurry to get to some important meeting, some *conference,* ma. And cause he was so nice to us, givin' us all that money, I helped him with his car."

"You lie, Johnny," she said quietly. "Always lie."

He ignored it, fought not to let the hurt show on his face. "And after we got the car out," he said, "he just handed me a hundred bucks. That's how nice a guy he is, ma."

"Why you lie?" she said.

"Cause you make me, that's why." His voice was thick with anger and pain.

"Johnny, Johnny." She shook her head and looked away from him. She picked the envelope up and drummed it against the table. "Your big-shot friend," she said, "the gangster, Doyle, how is he?"

"Aw, ma," he had said, turning away from her. "What do you want from me, ma?"

On the truck dock outside the warehouse now, a group of men were unloading crates. Abe stopped and waved one of them over. He was breathing heavily; there were purple pouches under his eyes.

"Hey, Al," Abe said. "I want you to meet a friend of mine. Al Dorsett, Johnny Kovak."

"How you doin'?" Johnny said. He remembered him: the man with the pretty wife who had let Gant humiliate him at the front gate.

"New man, huh?" Al Dorsett grinned. "Did you take him over to see fat-ass yet?"

"Not yet," Abe smiled. "What kinda mood's he in today?"

"He's on a real tear. Good luck, you're gonna need it." Dorsett looked at Johnny. "I've seen you someplace."

"I was down at the gate," Johnny said, "the day you was hired."

"Oh yeah," Dorsett said. He looked at him a long moment, then looked away, his eyes hooded. "Well," he said. "I better get goin'. I'll see you around."

They walked into the warehouse, a cavernous, dimly lighted hall filled with fruit and vegetable crates. At its center was a raised platform four feet off the ground with steps leading to it. Behind a lectern on the platform stood the foreman, Gant, checking invoices.

"Mr. Gant," Abe said.

Gant ignored them. Abe looked at Johnny and winked.

"Excuse me, Mr. Gant."

Gant kept his eyes on his invoices. "Why the hell aren't you out there unloading the celery?" he said.

"Mr. Gant, this is Johnny Kovak."

"So?"

"He's the one we—the one we—talked about."

Gant looked up from his papers and looked down on them from the platform.

"Ain't you got work to do?" he said to Abe. "You wanna hold hands with your boyfriend here all day?"

"No sir," Abe said, and walked away.

Gant turned back to his papers. Johnny stood in front of the platform. An hour later, he was still standing there.

"Kovak," Gant finally said, grinning at him. "What kinda bohunk's that?"

"Hungarian."

"Hungarian, huh?" Gant's grin widened. "Now let me tell you somethin', Kovak. I don't like hunkies. I don't like any of you goddamn flatheads. The boats shoulda sunk that brought you over here. You screw around with me just once, Kovak, you're out. There's a hundred other bohunks out there every day beggin' to take your place. You hear me?"

Johnny nodded and didn't say anything. I've been hearing you all my life, he thought. I hear you twenty-four hours a day. I hear you when I see the look in ma's eyes. I hear you in my dreams.

"You get here at seven o'clock sharp every day," Gant said. "You stay as long as I want you to. If the delivery don't get here till ten at night, you stay till ten. You get paid eight hours, period. You get sick, tough shit. You don't like the deal, get outa here right now." He paused. "One more thing. You drop some of the stuff, you damage the merchandise, it's outa your pay. You hear me?"

"I hear you," Johnny said.

Gant pushed a button on his platform; a buzzer echoed loudly through the hall.

"Polack," Gant yelled, "put this hunkie to work."

A towering black man walked toward him. His

head was completely shaved. Tied across his sweating forehead was a red bandanna.

"Come on," the black man said, and led him toward the dock outside. "All we need here's another hunkie."

Johnny stared at him.

"What are you gawkin' at?" the black man said. Ain't you never seen a . . . Polish person before?"

Johnny grinned. "You're—Polish?"

"The name's Lincoln Dombrowsky."

Johnny laughed. "*Lincoln* Dombrowsky? Jesus."

"You Jesus?" Dombrowsky said.

Johnny laughed. "Kovak. Johnny Kovak."

They shook hands, grinning at each other.

"For reasons of my own," Dombrowsky said, "I like people to call me Link."

"How come? Ain't you proud of being Polish?"

Dombrowsky laughed and looked at him. "Yeah," he said, "we're gonna get along just fine."

The buzzer startled them.

"I said get him to work!" Gant yelled.

They hurried to the truck dock.

"*Idz Do Piekla!*" Dombrowsky grumbled.

"What the hell does that mean?"

"It's an old Polish saying."

"Okay," Johnny said, "it's an old Polish saying. What the hell does it mean?"

Dombrowsky handed him two crates from a tall stack of celery.

"It means yes suh, Mr. Gant. Yes suh."

"It sure didn't sound like that to me."

Dombrowsky smiled. "We better get these on in there."

"How come I got two and you're only takin' one?"

Dombrowsky looked at him with a mischievous grin. "Cause all us polacks is lazy," he said. "Don't you hunkies know that?"

The next day Johnny went to work at seven in the morning and at ten o'clock at night he was still there, waiting for a delivery. He sat on the dock with the others. Some of the men were smoking; others were asleep. Dorsett and Abe were kidding with Dombrowsky. Johnny watched them restlessly.

"Lincoln comes from my mama," the black man said, "Dombrowsky's my dad. One plus, one minus."

Abe grinned. "Which one's the plus, Link?"

"Depends on who it is that's looking at me," Dombrowsky said. They laughed.

"Christ," Johnny said, "it's eleven o'clock."

Dorsett looked at the clock. "That's what it is all right."

"Did the same thing with my boys," Dombrowsky said. "One of 'em I named Tadeusz. The other, he's Roosevelt. Balances out." They laughed again.

Johnny got up. "How can you guys just sit around? We been here sixteen goddamn hours already."

"Yeah, but we ain't been paid yet for the eight," Dombrowsky said.

Abe said, "What are we waitin' on, anyway?"

"Tomatoes," Dorsett said.

Dombrowsky smiled. "Never did like the taste of tomatoes."

"Don't you worry, Link," Dorsett said. "Gant's not gonna offer you none." They laughed.

Johnny kept pacing. "We just gonna sit here till dawn?"

They looked at him. None of them said anything. The buzzer went off. Johnny jumped and turned toward the platform.

"You wanna go home, Kovak," Gant yelled. "Go on."

Johnny stared at him, then sat down slowly. The men watched him.

"He pushes that fuckin' thing one more time," Johnny said, "I'm gonna—"

Dombrowsky smiled. "What are you gonna do then, Johnny?"

As the days went by, he did nothing.

He went to work each day.

He collected his paycheck each week.

He was too tired at night to do anything but eat and sleep.

He felt caged.

He thought often of the old man and how he had trudged through the Flats to his mill each day. And he thought about what Vince Doyle had said to him: "Johnny, you could have been somebody."

Six months later, in the freezing cold, he was still there, still lugging his crates. He had never held a job this long. He wore the old man's cap to work each day.

* * *

The buzzer whipsawed his nerves. Kovak, get up here! Stack these crates up straight! Straight, I said! You deaf and dumb, hunkie? Get off your ass, Kovak!

Sometimes, when he got home at night, he could hear the buzzer for hours afterward. It went off deep inside him, at the center of his being. He held his ears and blinked his eyes. It stopped and then, minutes later, it would go off again. Once it woke him in the middle of the night. The house was cold but the sheets were wet from his sweat. He sat up in bed, shaking, and waited. The buzzer went off again and he buried his head in the pillow.

"Eat, Johnny," his mother kept saying. It was her solution to everything. He was losing weight. The walk to the warehouse seemed longer each day. The crates he lifted were loaded down with lead. His battered leather jacket didn't seem to protect him from the cold. He couldn't ever seem to get warm.

A few weeks before Christmas, Gant summoned them to the platform. There was another man up there with him Johnny had never seen before. He wore a woolen overcoat, a fur hat, and spit-shined black leather boots. He was jowly, balding, and in his sixties. The men whispered among themselves. It was the owner, Dietrich Fleckner.

"Keep it down, you guys," Gant smiled. "Mr. Fleckner's got somethin' to say to you." Gant's tone was different, Johnny noticed, almost kind.

"What's goin' on?" Johnny said to Abe.

Abe grinned. "Santa Claus."

"You men, you vork hard alla da year, alla you men," Dietrich Fleckner said with a thick Bavarian accent. "I know zis. You don't gotta tell me zis. I vant to say Merry Christmas. We give alla you twenty dollars bonus."

The men cheered. Fleckner called their names off: Abruzzi, the prune-faced little *paisan;* Sweeney, whose brogue was so thick sometimes Johnny couldn't understand him; Faflik, who chewed tobacco and went around hawking all the time; Knowles, who was always showing his kids' pictures around; Baker, who handed out cigarettes last week because his wife had a baby; Dorsett, whose name had to be called twice because occasionally he was hard of hearing; Dombrowsky, who Amos 'n' Andied up to the lectern and got a big laugh. A dozen other names were called and then Belkin and then, finally, Kovak.

Johnny climbed the steps to the platform. Fleckner pumped his hand, smiled, and handed him the envelope with the two crisp ten dollar bills in it.

"Kovacs?" Fleckner said. He pronounced it the old-country way: Kovach.

"Yeah," Johnny said, "that's what it used to be."

"Magyar." He said the word with feeling, respect.

"Yeah." Johnny smiled.

"*Jo munkas a Magyar,*" Fleckner said with his German accent. He turned to Gant and translated it. "Good vorker, zee Hungarian."

"Yes, sir, you bet," Gant said. His eyes were laughing.

"*Koszonom,*" Johnny said. Thank you.

"*Boldog Karacsonyt,*" Fleckner smiled. Merry Christmas.

Johnny went back to his crates, grinning, the twenty dollars securely pocketed. The guy's all right, he thought. He even spoke Hungarian. Maybe the company wasn't the problem. Maybe it was Gant. Fleckner never came around. He probably didn't even know how Gant treated them.

On the truck dock, he talked to Abe about it. Abe laughed at him.

"What the hell's so funny?"

"There ain't no Santa Claus, Johnny. Don't you know that?"

"I got the twenty bucks right in my pocket."

"Don't go spendin' it too fast," Abe said. He gave him a strange smile.

Late that afternoon, after Fleckner had left, Gant hit his buzzer and called them up to the lectern one by one. Johnny saw that money was being exchanged.

"What does he want?" he asked Abe.

"His Christmas presents." Abe laughed. "You'll see. I don't wanna ruin it for you. It's a surprise."

Johnny heard his name and walked up to the platform.

"Let's have it," Gant said.

"Huh?"

"If you don't hand it over right now, Kovak, you're back out on the street."

"Hand what over?"

Gant looked at him. "My Christmas present."

"Your what?"

Gant snapped his fingers. "The ten bucks."

It hit Johnny then. His body felt rigid. He couldn't move.

"I'm not gonna tell you again, Kovak."

He dug into his pocket, took the envelope out, and handed Gant a ten.

"Nice of you, Kovak," Gant smiled. "Thanks."

Walking home that night, Abe said, "It's like that every year. Fleckner hands the bonuses out. We hand half of it back to Gant. That way Fleckner gives Gant a nice big bonus every Christmas." He laughed.

"How come somebody don't tell Fleckner about it?" Johnny said.

Abe stopped. "Listen, don't you think it's real convenient we get *two* bills every year?"

"That don't mean Fleckner knows."

"Hey, Johnny," Abe laughed. "No shit. There really ain't no Santa Claus."

Three days before Christmas, Gant buzzed them to his platform again.

"I got good news for two of you guys," he said. "We're cuttin' down. Two of you guys can get home early for Christmas." He smiled. "You know I like all you guys. So who's it gonna be? Why don't you make it easy for me? How about some volunteers?"

Gant laughed. The men shuffled their feet nervously.

"Come on," he said, "I wanna see some hands."

Nobody moved.

"How about you, Dorsett? You wanna go home to that pretty wife of yours?"

"No, sir," Dorsett mumbled.

"Polack, how about you? Can't you get a job shinin' shoes?"

Dombrowsky didn't say anything.

"I got an idea," Gant said. "Kovak. How about you? You ain't got any kids. Do these guys a favor. Get your hand up."

Johnny felt the men looking at him. His face flushed. Gant laughed at him.

"All right," Gant said, "you and you! Get your vouchers!" Johnny looked at them: Knowles and Baker. The two men were watching him, their eyes pleading. Johnny looked away.

He went back to his crates. Through an ice-crusted window, he could see Knowles and Baker trudging across the snow in the yard to the gate.

The bastard was right, Johnny thought. I should have put my hand up. I should have quit. I was scared. He picked up a crate and hurled it furiously into place.

"You damage the merchandise, Kovak," Gant yelled, "it's outa your pay!"

Dorsett brought a crate over to his stack. "He was just raggin' you, Johnny," Dorsett said. "He already had Knowles and Baker picked out."

Dombrowsky said later, "It ain't your fault, Johnny. You need the money like everybody else."

But he blamed himself anyway and brooded. It couldn't go on like this. They had to do something. He had to do something. He thought about going down to Fleckner's office downtown. He even looked the address up: the forty-sixth floor of the Terminal Tower building. He would tell Fleckner about the Christmas bonuses, about the sixteen hours' work for eight hours' pay. He dismissed the thought. What if Abe was right? What if Fleckner was in on it? Even if he wasn't, though, if he went up there to see him, Fleckner would think he was some sort of trouble-maker, some sort of Bolshevik. That wouldn't work. But what if some of the men went up there with him? Better yet, what if all of the men got together? What if they pulled something at the warehouse to show Fleckner they really meant business?

At Christmas dinner with Abe, Johnny could hardly wait to tell him about it.

Ma put a steaming pot on the table. "Stuffed cab-bage and dumplings," she said. "Make you strong."

"Looks great, ma," Abe smiled.

"Yeah, we gotta be strong to work, don't we, ma?" Johnny said.

"They pay the money," she said.

"We're gonna buy mansions up in the Heights. Right, Abe?"

Abe looked at him. "What's raggin' you?"

"That goddamn Gant," Johnny said. "What the hell you think's raggin' me?"

"It's not him," Abe said, "it's the company."

"That damn buzzer of his, I'd like to—"

"It's all the companies, Johnny. They all got buzzers."

"Listen," Johnny said slowly. "I been thinkin'. What if we talked to some of the guys?"

Abe laughed. "About what?"

"Naw, I mean it," Johnny said. "What if we—"

"No more stuffed cabbage and dumplings," Abe grinned. "That's what."

"What if we all got together?"

"And did what?"

"I don't know," Johnny said. "Stopped workin' maybe."

Abe roared. He stopped eating. "Stopped workin'?" he said loudly. "You hear that, ma? It ain't me. He's tryin' to start a revolution."

"What if we got old man Fleckner down there," Johnny said, "and told him—we don't work till you get ridda Gant."

Abe shook his head, still laughing. "And the buzzer, right?"

"Sure. The goddamn buzzer, too."

Abe looked at him seriously. "They'd kick us outa there in five minutes, Johnny. That's what."

"Not if we did it late at night. Not if we was packin' somethin' that'd freeze if we left it out all night. Abe, don't you see?"

Abe chewed his food, paused. "I'll tell you what I see, Johnny. Guys like Dorsett and Link, what's gonna happen to 'em if they lose their jobs? Did you think about that?"

"They're not gonna lose their jobs," Johnny said.

"What if they do? Are you gonna risk that? You got a right to risk that?"

"I'm tellin' you they're not gonna lose their jobs," Johnny said.

"You don't know that."

"I do know it."

"Bullshit," Abe said heatedly. "You're just pissed off at Gant. You're just thinkin' about yourself, Johnny. You gotta think about them."

"I am thinkin' about them."

"No you're not."

"The hell with you," Johnny said angrily. "I'll talk to the guys myself. We'll see how they feel."

"Yeah," Abe said, "you do that, Johnny."

They ate their food in silence.

"Don't start trouble, Johnny," Ilona Kovak said. "Always trouble. Your pa never complained."

Johnny pushed the plate away from him. "That's right, ma," he said bitterly. "Pa never complained."

At the warehouse the next week, as they waited for a delivery at midnight, he tried to talk Dorsett and Dombrowsky into it. They laughed at him.

"Too much of that Tokay for Christmas," Dombrowsky said.

"Let's just try it," Johnny insisted.

"Try it?" Dorsett grinned. "You think we'll get a second chance?"

"Look at the hours we gotta work. It ain't fair."

Dombrowsky smiled. "One thing I learned growin'

83

up Polish," the black man said. "Ain't everything that's fair."

Dorsett laughed. "Ain't nothin' that's fair."

"That sonofabitch," Johnny said angrily. "We just gonna let him kick us around?"

"Hell, Johnny," the black man said. "I been kicked around and I been kicked around. That man, I ain't even worried about him kickin'."

"I ain't either," Dorsett laughed.

Johnny flared at them. "Don't you guys got any guts?"

"Guts," Dorsett smiled. "Listen to him."

"I know I got 'em, Johnny," Dombrowsky said. "They's always hungry."

Gant's buzzer shattered the silence.

Dombrowsky said, "Yes suh, boss, yes suh. I hears you callin' me," and ran exaggeratedly toward the truck dock.

"Take my word for it, kid," Dorsett said sadly, "you can't beat 'em. You're young. You'll see."

Abe stood by and watched as Johnny kept after the men. He wasn't surprised. Johnny was like that. When he got something into his head, come hell or high water . . . It was like he wanted to prove that he could do it. That he could convince them. That Abe was wrong. That the men had more guts than Abe did.

He cornered all the guys and gave them his pitch. "How can you guys take that shit?" Johnny said. "Why should we beat our brains out like fuckin' slaves? He took the dough we got for Christmas. We gotta do somethin' about it! We gotta!"

They said, "What, Johnny?"

Johnny told them.

That ended it.

"Things are bad, yeah," Dorsett said. "Not that bad. Not to pull somethin' like that."

"You know where I was before I got this job," Abruzzi said. "Down by the lake. There's a big sandpile down there. You ever been down there, Johnny? You walk down in the summer, you can see the stovepipes stickin' outa the ground. People are livin' in that sandpile. I was livin' in it. I don't wanna live there no more."

"I got me a brother I'm takin' care of, Johnny," Faflik said. "Six months ago, he was drivin' a delivery truck in Detroit. He had a house and a car. He was happy. The kinda guy that's always tellin' you a joke. A good joke, too. Then he got laid off. He tried to get somethin' every day after that. He couldn't. You look in his eyes now, there's nothin' there. They're dead. Big blue dead eyes. They say he's had a mind breakdown. Somebody's gotta pay the doctor."

They all had their reasons, Abe saw. Good reasons, too. He was glad he wasn't helping Johnny. It was Johnny's crazy bullheadedness, his hatred for Gant, his pride, that was driving him. It was a personal battle between Johnny and Gant and Abe wondered whether he was just using the men to get rid of Gant. To win the fight.

Johnny kept at it with the men. He badgered them

over and over again. With his eyes; the sarcastic look on his face. You don't have any guts, Johnny was saying. The men listened to it and, Abe saw, some of them were getting upset. It was a shit job. All of them knew it. They didn't need to get their faces rubbed into the shit.

Some of them started grumbling about Johnny behind his back. Dorsett cooled them down. "He's all right," Dorsett said. "He's a young, fiery kid. When I was his age, I was just like him. He reminds me of me."

"Can't you talk to him, Abe?" Dombrowsky said. "Somebody's gotta talk to him."

Abe tried. He stopped him on the sidewalk one night after work. "You wanna go down to Zigi's for a beer?"

Johnny shook his head.

"You wanna come up to my room?"

"What for?"

"What do you mean what for, Johnny? I gotta give you a reason? I wanna talk to you."

"Yeah, well," Johnny said, "I got nothin' to say."

"Lay offa this, goddamnit. You're makin' a lotta enemies outa guys that like you."

"You're a real big help to me, Abe," Johnny said. "You know that? Thanks a lot."

"Don't you understand, Johnny? Jesus Christ. It wouldn't do any good. It's crazy. They'd just can all of us."

"Not if we got Fleckner down here," Johnny said.

"The hell with Fleckner. Fleckner *is* Gant. Don't you see that? He's worse than Gant."

"How the hell's he worse than Gant?" Johnny said. "You tell me that."

"Cause at least Gant's straight. We know how he feels about us. He don't hide nothin'. Fleckner feels the same way, I'm tellin' you. He just goes through a show."

"You don't really know that, do you, Abe?"

"Johnny. Every goddamn company in this goddamn country is the same goddamn way. Open your eyes."

"You're the one that can't see straight. You're up to your fuckin' eyeballs in that garbage Szabo says all the time. You don't wanna help me, Abe, don't help me. I don't need you to help me. Why don't you go home and get out one of your fancy books? Why don't you get the fuckin' Communist Party Manifesto, Abe? And why don't you stick your dick into it and jack off?"

The next day at the warehouse, Ned Sweeney got canned and Abe was almost ready to help Johnny then. Ned had come in twenty minutes late. Gant hit the buzzer as soon as he saw him. The men watched.

Gant said, "All right, Sweeney, you're through."

"Mr. Gant," Sweeney said, "I'm sorry I'm a little late. Mr. Gant, my boy's sick."

Sweeney kept talking but they couldn't hear him because Gant kept hitting his buzzer. He hit it four times. It was the signal for the guard, who came in and led Ned Sweeney away.

At lunch that day, the men were silent and subdued. Johnny sat there looking at them. He didn't say a word but Abe knew the man heard what he was saying. Johnny was saying it so loud that it hurt. Then he got up and looked at them. "Well, that's it for Sweeney," Johnny said. "Who's it gonna be next week? You, Abruzzi? How about you, Link?" He grinned and walked away. "Maybe he's right," Abruzzi said. "No, he ain't," Link said.

When Abe got to work a few mornings later, he knew it would be a bad day. Only seven o'clock and the booze was already coming off of Gant. It looked like it would be Dombrowsky's turn that day. Gant kept after him. Hitting his buzzer. Calling him "polack" as if he were saying "nigger." As Link was eating lunch, Gant hit the buzzer again. "Polack! Get up here! Stack those crates! Proper! Right now!" Gant kept getting off the platform all day to go to the john. By mid-afternoon, there was a cloud of whiskey around him.

At four o'clock in the afternoon, they got a delivery of peaches in a boxcar. They started lugging them inside. Gant came out to the loading dock and started screaming at Link.

"You think I can't see you, you lazy bastard?"

"I didn't do nothin', Mr. Gant."

"Take three more of these crates."

Gant picked the crates up and piled them onto Link's arms. "Now get in there!"

All the men were watching them. Link had six crates in his arms, too heavy a load for one man. His body strained. He was off balance as he walked inside. Then Gant shoved him and the crates fell. Peaches splattered and rolled all over the warehouse floor.

"That's three crates of peaches, polack," Gant said. "Company says—"

"You put 'em on there, Mr. Gant," Link said, "I didn't."

"You break 'em, you pay for 'em."

Link shook his head. He kept his eyes on the ground.

"You hear me, polack?"

"I heard you."

"Then get down there and pick 'em up!"

Gant walked away toward the platform. Link stood there a moment, then hunkered down and crawled on the ground after the peaches. The men stood there staring at him, too stunned to move.

Suddenly Johnny was down there on the ground with Link, helping him pick up the peaches.

"You guys just gonna stand there?" Johnny said.

The men got down on the floor to help them.

Gant saw them and hit the buzzer.

"What are you doin'? Get back to work!"

The men stayed there and pretended they didn't hear him.

Gant hit the buzzer. He hit it again and again.

"Get to work all of you," he screamed.

The men ignored him.

Then, suddenly, Gant was on top of them, off his platform, standing right above them, screaming.

"Didn't you hear me?"

The men backed away slowly until only Dombrow-sky and Dorsett were left on the floor.

"Dorsett," Gant said, "you're fired."

"What?"

"You're through."

"I didn't hear you, Mr. Gant," Dorsett said. "I got hurt in the war."

Gant walked away toward his platform again.

"It's true," Dorsett said. "I can't hear good."

The men stood there looking at him. Link was still on the ground, motionless, staring at the cement.

Dorsett walked slowly after Gant and stood in front of his platform.

"It's true," he said. "Please. I didn't hear you."

Gant laughed. "Go get a hearing aid," he said.

Then, suddenly, as the men watched in shock and disbelief, Dorsett was up on the platform. He had Gant by the throat. There was a funny sound coming from him, a scream and a moan. Gant's finger was on the buzzer. The guard came rushing in, the billy in his hand. He swung it at Dorsett's head. The men heard the thunk. They heard it again and again. The guard kept clubbing him. Blood was gushing from Dorsett's ear. Dorsett fell off the platform onto the cement.

The men stood there, ashamed that none of them had helped him.

In the dank and airless corridor outside the hospital emergency room, Abe sat on the floor with the men, his head in his hands. Come on, Dorsett, he said to himself. You can make it. You can. You've got to. And then he thought, we just stood there. All of us. We didn't help him. We let the guard hit him. Why? Why? Are we men? Am I?

After what seemed like a very long time, a doctor was walking out of the emergency room toward them.

"He has a concussion," the doctor said flatly. "Not too bad. He should be all right."

Abruzzi laughed. "God bless you."

"Can we go see him?" Link asked.

"See him," the doctor said, "absolutely not."

"How come?" Johnny said.

"The police are moving him now."

"Police?" Link said.

Johnny looked at the doctor. "Moving him where?"

"The prison ward. He's been arrested for assault."

"Assault," Johnny said. He laughed. The laugh was bitter and choked.

"You'll have to move from here," the doctor said, looking at him. "We always keep this corridor open."

They looked at each other, got up from the floor, and walked down the corridor to the door. There was a police car outside.

Dombrowsky looked at it. "Fuck it," he said. "Fuck it. I don't care."

At eight o'clock at night, the twenty-second day of February, 1935, the temperature in Cleveland was 19 degrees. A howling thirty-mile-an-hour wind whipped the snow, which had been falling for two days, into three-foot drifts. Most Clevelanders were inside, trying to stay warm, listening to Eddie Cantor's "Camel Caravan" or the "Voice of Firestone" or "Phil Spitalny's All-Girl Orchestra." Radio station WTAM interrupted its programming to say that three more inches of snow were expected that night. "Leapin' lizards, it's cold out there," the announcer laughed.

On West Twenty-fifth Street, on the near West Side of the city, Mike Monahan sat at the wheel of his half-ton Chevrolet truck and felt every one of his fifty-four years. He was freezing. His heater didn't work. For three weeks now, he had been after his supervisor at the Consolidated Terminal to fix it. The supervisor still hadn't done it. He probably wouldn't do it until the spring and Mike Monahan knew well the reason why.

They wanted him to quit. They didn't have any cause to fire him except for the fact that he headed up Local 302. But they didn't want to fire him for that. They knew the other drivers liked him. They knew, too, that times were changing. FDR was a friend to the workingman; as much of a friend as it was ever possible for a politician to be. The yellow dog, the contract which forbade a man to join a union, couldn't be enforced anymore. So they wouldn't fire him. But they wouldn't fix his heater, either. And, knowing that his heater didn't work, they sent him, on a day as raw as this, for a load of tomatoes thirty miles away. A load which he had to haul back to the city that night in the hellish cold.

Mike Monahan knew the road by heart. Billboards were his signposts. Buy Iodent Toothpaste . . . Camel

92

Cigarettes are the highest quality regardless of price
. . . and, there she was now, good old Kate, Kate
Smith Says Buy Borax. Tonight Kate Smith was the
best friend a man could possibly have, even if she did
weigh more than Mike Monahan's truck. Kate Smith
meant that in another fifteen or twenty minutes, he
would be at the Fleckner warehouse and this long and
brutal day would be over. And he could go home once
again to his empty house. And he could soak his ach-
ing joints in a hot bath. Swirling snow blew across
the road ahead of him. The big truck shuddered in the
wind.

Inside the Fleckner warehouse, as Mike Monahan
drove toward them, the men were huddled in groups
against the wall. Gant sat on his platform, a newspaper in front of him.

"Gehrig," Abruzzi said, glancing at Gant. "It's
Gehrig that makes 'em work. Ruth, he's a show-off.
For my money, I'll take Gehrig any day."

"What money?" somebody laughed.

"Baloney," Faflik said. "He's a line-drive hitter. A
line-drive hitter, that's all. He don't win the games."

"How long?" Dombrowsky said nervously.

"Any time," Abe said. "He oughta be here any
minute now."

"I wish he'd hurry," Dombrowsky said.

The others looked at him.

Abruzzi said, "What do you mean he don't win the
games? He gets on base, don't he? You gotta get on
base to get the runs."

"I don't know," Johnny said. "You can't beat the

long ball. How can you beat a guy, he points to the fence, and there the sonofabitch goes. Huh? The size of that guy's balls."

"Luck," Abruzzi said, "that's all."

Faflik said, "I'll take that kinda luck any day."

Dombrowsky looked at Gant. He got up and started to pace. "Ain't he gonna get a surprise," he said.

"Link," Johnny said. "Sit down. Relax."

"Yeah, Link," Abe grinned. "Tell us what you think."

"I think I'm scared," Dombrowsky said.

"About Gehrig and Ruth," Johnny grinned. He looked at Abe. "That's what the subject of this here get-together is, ain't it?"

Dombrowsky shook his head, sat down, and didn't say anything.

"What's the matter, Link?" Abe smiled. "Don't you like baseball?"

"Did you hear the one about the pigeons in the park?" somebody said. "Things are so bad, it ain't the people feedin' the pigeons no more. It's pigeons feedin' the people."

It wasn't very funny, but they roared. Gant glanced at them. They heard the truck honk at the gate and they stopped laughing.

At the gate, the guard came out of his shack.

"Consolidated," Monahan said. "Tomatoes."

"What took you so long?" the guard grinned. "Did you knock off a piece on the way up?"

"Just get the damn gate, will you?" Monahan said. "You didn't have to drive five hours in this shit."

When Mike Monahan got out of his truck at the loading dock, Gant was already standing there.

"You wanna check 'em?" Monahan said.

"Goddamn right I'll check 'em."

"I didn't eat any of 'em," Monahan said. "If that's what you're worried about."

"We inspect the merchandise," Gant said. "You know the rules."

The men stood on the loading dock in their coats and jackets, shivering, looking at each other.

Gant opened two crates of tomatoes, felt them with his hands. "All right," he said. "Get 'em in there before they freeze." He walked back into the warehouse.

Mike Monahan watched them as they started unloading the crates. Something's wrong, he thought. He couldn't put his finger on it. They were moving slowly. They kept looking at each other. They finally started taking the crates out of the truck, but what in the Sam Hill? They were stacking them up on the loading dock.

"Jesus Christ," Monahan said. "You gotta get 'em inside. Inside! They're gonna freeze out here."

"That so?" Lincoln Dombrowsky said.

They kept piling the crates up on the dock.

"What the hell's wrong with you guys?" Mike Monahan said.

Johnny looked at him. "Keep your nose out, Jack," he said.

Mike Monahan had had a long day. He didn't need this. "It ain't Jack, Jack," he said angrily.

Johnny looked at him calmly. "It's jackshit to me, pal." He walked into the warehouse carrying a crate of tomatoes. The men followed him inside, some with crates in their hands. Monahan trailed them.

Johnny stopped in front of Gant's platform. The men stood behind him.

Gant saw them line up. "What the hell you doin'? Get those crates in here!" He pushed his buzzer.

Johnny handed his crate to Abe and walked up the steps to Gant's platform. Gant stared at him wide-eyed. He looked scared. Except for Dorsett, none of the men had ever been up here. Johnny grinned.

"Excuse me, Mr. Gant," he said. He reached around Gant and yanked the buzzer and its wiring out of the stand.

Mike Monahan couldn't believe what he was seeing. "Holy shit!" he whispered to Dombrowsky.

"You're fired!" Gant sputtered. "You bastard! I knew you were trouble! You hear me? You're fired."

Johnny laughed at him. "Kiss my ass, Mr. Gant."

The men cheered.

Johnny walked off the platform.

"Has he gone nuts?" Monahan whispered to Dombrowsky.

"We all gone nuts," Dombrowsky said. "You want a tomato?"

Mike Monahan looked at him. "What?"

"A tomato." Dombrowsky was handing him one.

Monahan stared at him bug-eyed. "No, thanks."

"I don't like them neither," Dombrowsky said.

Mike Monahan shook his head and walked away from him. The day had gone on too long. These guys were nuts. The whole crew of them.

"Guard! Guard!" Gant screamed. He was jumping up and down on his platform. His face was crimson. He moved his hand toward the buzzer, stopped, and realized it was no longer there.

"Here," Johnny said. He threw the buzzer up on the platform. The men laughed.

The guard came through the door, his club in hand, and headed for the platform. Dombrowsky tripped him and kicked the club out of his hand. The guard stayed on the ground and looked around, stunned. Dombrowsky picked the club up and tapped it against his palm. The black man smiled down at the guard, still tapping his club. The guard made no move to get up.

Gant looked at the guard, at the men in front of him.

"Get Fleckner down here," Johnny said. "I wanna talk to him."

"Mr. Fleckner?" Gant said. "Mr. Fleckner? You don't talk to Mr. Fleckner. Who the hell do you think you are?" He looked away from Johnny to the other men. "Get those tomatoes in here!" he screamed.

"You want a tomato, Mr. Gant?" Dombrowsky said. He tossed a tomato up on the platform. Gant watched as it rolled across the platform and fell to the floor.

"You're fired! Alla you!" he yelled. "You're out in the gutter, alla you!"

Johnny smiled and turned to Abe. "Gimme some of

97

those tomatoes." Abe handed him a crate. Johnny smiled at Gant, raised the crate high above his head, and slammed it to the cement floor.

"You're destroying my merchandise!" Gant yelled. "You can't—you can't—" The words stuck in his throat.

"Gimme another one," Johnny said. He raised another crate high, still smiling, and slammed it to the floor. Another and another. Gant looked pale.

"I'm gonna keep takin' these," Johnny said, "and I'm gonna keep smashin' 'em till you get Fleckner down here."

Gant stood on the platform, breathing loudly, dazed. Johnny smashed another crate to the cement.

"Maybe he wants to get down on the ground and pick 'em up," Dombrowsky smiled.

Gant looked down at the black man, fear in his eyes. He rushed down the steps and across the warehouse floor to a telephone. The guard jumped off the floor and tried to catch up with him.

"Hurry it up," Dombrowsky shouted after him, "we ain't got all night."

The men laughed uneasily.

Mike Monahan smiled. Yes, they were all nuts. Yes, it had been a long day. But goddamnit, he hadn't enjoyed anything as much in years.

An hour and a half later, Johnny, Abe, and Dombrowsky, representing the other men, sat in a brightly lighted office on the warehouse's top floor. Across from them sat a middle-aged, impeccably dressed man trying, unsuccessfully, to light his pipe: Peter Andrews, the business manager of Fleckner Foods.

"I don't know who the hell you are," Johnny said, looking at him coldly. "It's Fleckner we want."

"I told you who I am, Mr. Kovak," Andrews said. His manner was friendly and understanding. "Now look, it's late and it's rather silly to beat around the bush, no? Mr. Fleckner is in Florida, vacationing. I told you that. I'm sorry he can't be here to talk to you but we didn't exactly have advance notice of your plans." He smiled. "Now did we?"

Johnny didn't say anything.

Abe grinned. "Well, I guess that part of it is true."

"All right," Andrews said. "Thank you, Mr. Belkin. Now let's get down to business, shall we? I don't want those tomatoes out on the dock to freeze and you don't, either."

"Why not?" Johnny said.

"Because those tomatoes are your trump card," Andrews smiled. "Am I not right? Once they freeze, you've lost your leverage. And it's very, very cold out there." Andrews finally lighted his pipe. "Now what is it, exactly, that's upset you so much?"

Uncomfortable in this brightly lighted room, they told him, hesitantly, about the things that they felt were unfair. Andrews listened to them solemnly, nodded, and puffed his pipe. When they were finished speaking, he put the pipe down and said, almost gravely, "I want to be fair about this."

Dombrowsky laughed. "Here's somethin' new."

"I'm happy you told me these things," Andrews said. "The version I heard of the incident with Mr. Dorsett was completely different. And I certainly had no idea of the situation with the Christmas bonuses. The amount of time spent to earn the eight hours' pay is, I must say, a company decision, a decision of the board of directors. I was aware of that. Let me say this to you. It certainly sounds like you have some legitimate complaints and perhaps one lesson is that we should set up some program whereby either Mr. Fleckner or I can talk to you men more often."

Dombrowsky laughed. A drink after work maybe," he said.

"Look," Andrews continued. His tone tolerated no levity. "Let's agree on this. We'll drop the charges against Mr. Dorsett and we'll permit him to come back to work. As far as Mr. Gant is concerned, I will see to it personally that he returns the money he took from all of you. And from now on, Mr. Gant can't fire anyone without my approval. Mr. Fleckner is a busy man. I don't want to bother him with it, but I'll attend to it. No firings without my approval. How's that?"

"Sounds okay," Johnny said warily.

"And from now on, when there is an accident and the goods are damaged, you won't be docked from your pay."

Dombrowsky laughed again. "That's a little late for this polack," he said.

"No, no," Andrews said. "We will, of course, return your money for the peaches. How's that?"

They looked at each other.

Abe said, "What about bein' paid for regular hours waitin' on deliveries?"

Andrews paused. "As I said, I want to be honest

with you. It would be very easy for me to lie and give you everything you want just so you bring the tomatoes inside. But I'm not going to do that. As you'll see, I don't operate that way. I can't tell you that we'll change that policy, Mr. Belkin. It's not up to me. It's up to our board of directors. I will take it up with them, though. I give you my word of honor. I will raise the issue. But I honestly can't do better than that. The decision will be theirs."

Johnny and Abe looked at each other. Neither of them said anything.

"Now, to be fair," Andrews said, "will you move those tomatoes inside right away?"

There was silence in the room.

Dombrowsky broke it. "How do we know you ain't lyin'?"

"Well," Andrews said. "I suppose you don't. But I haven't made any grand promises to you, have I? I haven't agreed to everything you want. And I've been honest with you about that. If I were lying, wouldn't it make sense for me to promise you anything you want just to convince you to bring the tomatoes in here?"

"Maybe," Johnny said.

Andrews smiled. "Now look, Mr. Kovak. I can see you're a sensible man. Those tomatoes, left out there much longer, will freeze. You don't want them to freeze, do you? It would mean a significant loss to this company. And wouldn't that be a shame? For all of us? Haven't we made some progress in this room? In terms of our relations in the future?"

No one said anything.

"How do we know you're really gonna talk to 'em about the extra pay?" Abe said.

Andrews shrugged his shoulders. "You have my word."

"Is that any good?" Johnny said.

"Yes, it is," Andrews said coldly. "As you'll see."

He knocked the ash from his pipe and pulled a black leather pouch from his pocket.

"Now," he said slowly, "do we agree?"

Johnny looked at Abe and Dombrowsky. He learned nothing from their expressions.

"We wanna go out and talk," he said.

"Fine," Andrews said. "But please don't take too long. Remember those tomatoes and how cold it is out there."

Out on the truck dock, next to the stack of tomatoes, Johnny talked to the men and told them what took place in the brightly lighted office. Mike Monahan stood among them, listening.

"But all we got's his word," Dombrowsky said.

Abe said, "That's more'n we had before."

"How do you know he ain't lyin'?" Dombrowsky asked.

Johnny dragged on a borrowed cigarette. "I don't," he answered.

"That guy must sleep in his suit," Dombrowsky said, "how can you trust anybody sleeps in his suit?"

The men laughed.

Abruzzi said, "What do you think, Johnny?"

"I'm freezin' my ass," Faflik said.

"Abe," Johnny said finally, "what do you think?"

"It ain't good," Abe said. "Maybe not as bad as before."

"Link?"

"I think this polack's gonna get lynched," the black man said, "that's what I think."

The men laughed uneasily, their eyes on Johnny.

"Come on, Johnny, it's cold out here," Faflik said.

Johnny looked at them, tossed the cigarette away, and took a deep breath.

"What the hell," he said.

In the brightly lighted room, Andrews shook Johnny's hand. "Excellent, Mr. Kovak," he said. "You'll find it will be a good agreement. Now please, those tomatoes."

Johnny grinned. "Don't worry. We'll get 'em right away."

"Good. What I'll do right away is have a talk with Mr. Gant." He raised his voice. "Guard! Get Gant in here."

Gant walked into the room. The big man seemed to have shrunk. He avoided their eyes. He was hunched over and looked unsteady on his feet. Johnny grinned at him.

Andrews said, "And by the way, I want to thank you personally, Mr. Kovak, for bringing all this to my attention." Gant stood there listening to Andrews, his head bowed.

As Johnny walked out the door, he heard Gant say, "You wanted to see me, sir?" And he heard Andrews. "Some things, Mr. Gant, we'd better get straight."

Johnny laughed in the corridor. "Did you hear that, Abe?" he said. He grabbed Abe and lifted him into the air, laughing. "We won! Jesus fuckin' Christ! Wait till we tell Dorsett! Wait till I tell ma! We won!"

Mike Monahan watched him as he hugged Abe and stalked triumphantly down the stairs. Monahan smiled. This hellish day. This freezing cold. The pain in his bones. It had been worth it. All of it.

The plate-glass windows of Zigi's Tavern were dusty and frosted, but from their table the world outside was a shimmering and unspoiled place. Peaceful. Immaculate. Inviting.

They sat in the corner around a little table with a torn, red-checked tablecloth—Johnny, Abe, Dombrowsky, Abruzzi, and Faflik. Celebrating. Recounting the details of their triumphant night. Telling each other that, honest to God, it had really happened. They had really, really won.

They babbled.

Abruzzi: "Did you see the look on Gant's face when Johnny got up on that goddamn platform?"

Dombrowsky: "I can't believe Gant's finally gonna get his."

Faflik: "That fuckin' guard down on the floor. I thought Link was gonna squash him."

A waitress brought them mugs of foamy pilsner. She was young, redheaded, and curvy, and when she walked, everything jiggled. And when she bent over them with the mugs, she stuck right into their faces.

"I'd like to squash those," Johnny said to Faflik.

"Come on," Abe said, "she's gonna hear you."

At the long bar, Anton Jugovich, a beefy, broad-shouldered steelworker who had once been a prize-fighter, challenged anyone to arm-wrestle. None of the half dozen tired men standing there were eager to accept, not even for the penny stakes. The bar was old and worn. On top of it were this week's Hungarian, Serbian, and German newspapers. Above it were five framed photographs of Vilma Banky, the pouty Buda-pest movie queen who was the girl of Zigi Zagon's most feverish dreams. Greasy wooden doors led from the bar to the kitchen, where the cook, even at this hour, prepared goulash and chicken paprikash for the men who came in from the late shifts at the mills.

They sat in the corner, boisterous and happy, the pilsner and their adrenalin fueling them, and raised their mugs, clinking them together, spilling some of the beer on themselves.

"Here's to Johnny!" Abruzzi yelled.

"Abe," Johnny said, "here's to Abe."

"Here's to Lincoln!" Abe laughed.

"Abe Lincoln!" Johnny roared.

Faflik, slurring his words, said, "Franklin Delano Roosevelt."

Link said, "Don't forget Roosevelt Dombrowsky!"

They laughed and downed their mugs. The waitress edged over to them, leery of their raucousness.

"You want another?" she said.

"Another?" Johnny laughed. "We want the whole damn barrel."

She turned and he reached out and grabbed her

around her thin waist, laughing, and pulled her against him, pressing her breasts against his shoulders.

"Don't touch the merchandise, buster!" she snapped. She pushed herself away from him.

"You break it, you pay for it," Faflik slurred, imitating Gant, and they roared again.

The girl stood there angrily, resenting their laughter. "Why can't you be a gentleman?" she asked Johnny. She looked at Abe. "Like your friend here."

"A gentleman?" Johnny boomed. "A gentleman? Did you hear that, Abe?" Red-faced, slightly tipsy, he pounded Abe's back. The girl looked at him reproachfully and huffed angrily away.

"Pig, Johnny!" someone shouted from the bar in a deep voice. It was Zigi Zagon, the owner. "What you do to the girl?"

He went to their table. He wore black boots, black pants, a rumpled white shirt, and a black leather vest which strained over his beer belly. He had a curled and waxed moustache. He was fifty-seven years old, an irascible, crotchety man who was father protector to his customers. Zigi helped them with their naturalization papers and legal problems. He collected the money for their fraternal life-insurance policies. He made sure they paid their Holy Name Society dues. He made out the money orders when they wanted to send three or four dollars back to the old country. Zigi let them run bar tabs (short ones). He let them roll the dice for drinks (quietly). He sold them bottles after the liquor stores were closed (for a nickel extra). He was the kind of man who kept his first twenty-dollar bill framed above the bar. And he was the kind of man who told no one that out of that first twenty dollars, he had to hand back $19.90 change. His tavern had but one rule: all the fighting had to be done inside. Any man who fought in the street outside could never come back in again. Zigi was a good American citizen, a man who paid his taxes and helped the ward boss put all the votes into the Democratic column. Permanent banishment was the price of tarnishing his spotless civic reputation.

"You're a pig," Zigi Zagon said to Johnny. "You attack her."

"I didn't do nothin'," Johnny laughed. "She fell right into my arms. She attacked me."

"Ya, ya, sure," Zigi said. "Abe, you witness. You good boy. He grab her bazoom."

"Bazoom?" Johnny roared. "Her bazoom? Jesus Christ, Zigi."

They laughed. Zigi laughed with them and sat down. Johnny introduced him to Faflik, Abruzzi, and Dombrowsky.

"Ya, ya," Zigi said. "Dombrowsky. Very funny."

"It's his name," Abe said.

"Ya. Ya. His name. And I black."

They told him about their victory at the warehouse tonight and Zigi, as expected, said, "Ah, you fulla the crap, Johnny," shook his head, and bought them a round of bourbon to go with their pilsners.

"Hey, Zig," Johnny laughed. "Where's that gypsy of yours, anyway? How come he ain't here with his fiddle? I wanna show this polack some good music."

"In Deet-a-roit," Zigi said. "Rich man."

"The gypsy's a rich man?" Johnny laughed. "How'd he get so rich?"

"His woman," Zigi said. "Gypsy woman. She tell the fortune from the bump in the head. She got a little place up offa Columbus Avenue. She tell the future in there. The people go see her, most of 'em women. Women got money, come down in the car, see the gypsy woman. They wanna know if the husband attack somebody. Grab the bazoom."

They laughed.

"Gypsy woman look at bump on the head, freckle on the nose, say—ya ya. Husband attack. Grab the bazoom. Ya ya. See offa the bump."

"The bump," Johnny laughed. "That's great."

"One woman, go up to the gypsy woman. Go alla time. Good customer. So she go one time, say she no feel good. Pain in the belly. Gypsy woman look at the bump, she say—Oh, oh, big trouble you got. Big trouble. You got the cancer. Woman cry. Big cry, big cancer. Gypsy woman say—you come back, we fix up the cancer. Big trouble but you come back. All fix."

"That bump's gotta be a helluva bump," Johnny laughed.

"Woman go back. Gypsy woman look at bump. She say—money the trouble. Money you got is devil money. Devil on the dollars you got, we gotta fix the dollars up. We fix up dollars, you got no more cancer. Woman very happy. Very happy. No more the cancer. No more the pain in the belly. Woman say—how we fix up the dollars? Gypsy woman say—we clean 'em.

Woman say—how we clean 'em? Gypsy woman say—
ya ya. You bring all the dollar you got. Big bill.
You bring 'em in the big bill."

They laughed. Abe said, "Didn't fool around with
nickels and dimes, huh?"

"The truth," Zigi said. "Woman go back next week,
she got ten thousand dollars. Hundred-dollar bills.
Every penny she got, she took 'em to gypsy woman
she can fix the cancer. Gypsy took money, put in a
little bag. Sew up the bag good with the needle. Magic
words. Dominus vobiscum. Requiescat in pacem.
Money clean. No more devil. Gypsy take bag with
money, sew bag in woman's dress, put bag over heart.
Gypsy woman say—you keep dress on, two week. You
go bed with dress. No take off. No bath. No nothin'.
Two week, no cancer."

Johnny laughed. "Shit, Zigi."

"Truth. All truth. Woman sleep with dress. No bath.
No nothin'. Stink like hell. Two week go by. Still the
pain in her belly. She take dress off. Smart woman,
she take bag, open up. Paper inside. No money. She
cry. Big cry. Still got the cancer and got no money.
Big, big cry. She go to police. Police come to me. No
gypsy. Gypsy go away with woman. He say—Deet-a-
roit. Rich gypsy. Ten thousand dollars."

They laughed.

"Gypsy say allatime," Zigi said. "Street in America
fulla gold."

They laughed again.

"Gypsy no kidding," Zigi said. "He find."

Zigi laughed, ordered them another round of bourbon, told Johnny to keep his hands off the waitress's bazoom, and went back to the bar.

"That gypsy's gotta be like all hunkies," Dombrowsky said. "I heard alla you was thieves."

Johnny laughed. "He's a helluva guy, Zigi. Anything gets outa hand, he gets this seltzer bottle, nails you to the back of the head with it. Anybody that's a customer here dies, he buys 'em a big wreath, shows up at the funeral. He comes back here and everybody gets free drinks for an hour. He tells 'em—it ain't on me, it's on that poor sonofabitch that can't buy drinks no more."

Johnny looked away from them. "My old man loved him."

"You know what?" Faflik said. "I think I'm gettin' stiff. That stuff about the bump, what the hell was that about?"

They laughed. At the bar, Anton Jugovich had run out of challengers.

"Johnny," he yelled. "You come on. We rassle."

"I don't wanna wrestle," Johnny laughed.

"Go on, Johnny. Bust his damn arm," one of the men at the bar yelled.

Johnny was still laughing. "Go on, Link. You can take him."

Dombrowsky looked at him pop-eyed. "I aint rasslin' nobody in a bar fulla hunkies."

Zigi flipped a penny to their table. "Get up here already."

Johnny stood up and as the men hooted and laughed, he took his jacket off with a flourish and walked up to the bar. Jugovich, who had his elbow up on the bar already, flexed his hammock hands.

"Now wait a minute, Jugs," Johnny grinned. "We gotta get a couple things straight." He winked at Zigi. The men laughed.

"Lotta gab," Anton Jugovich said, "let's go."

"First." Johnny paused and looked at the men in the tavern theatrically. "You beat me, you ain't gonna jump up on the bar again and start doin' your dance. Okay?"

The men laughed.

"Come on," Jugovich said, his hand in the air.

"Second. I beat you, you're not gonna spill no booze on the bar and light the place up again. Okay?"

"He do that," Zigi said, "I'm gonna break his head."

"Okay, okay," Jugovich said.

Johnny put his arm down on the bar and with all the men standing around them they locked their hands. Zigi lighted a match, dropped it, and when it fell to the bar, they strained at each other's arms.

Three minutes later, they were still at it. Back and forth and back and forth until Jugovich's arm sunk slowly to the bar. The men cheered. Johnny flexed his muscles.

"Now remember what I told you, Jugs," he said.

Zigi poured him another shot of bourbon and Johnny downed it in one gulp.

"Who's next?" he laughed. "Come on up here and lose."

Abe took his jacket off and as the men cheered, walked up to the bar.

"You really wanna do this, huh?" Johnny grinned.

"I can take you, Johnny," Abe smiled.

"Never."

Zigi dropped the match again and, as Johnny strained, he could see the waitress. She had moved closer and was watching them. Johnny pushed his arm back and then, suddenly, he slammed Abe's arm roughly to the bar. He winked at the girl. She looked disdainfully away from him.

"Two out of three?" Abe said. He was holding his sore arm. It got a big laugh and another free drink for both of them.

When they walked out into the snow, all of them were off-balance, shuffling against each other.

"Jesus Christ, it's cold," Faflik said.

Johnny laughed. He felt on top of the world. He had won. It was one of the best days of his whole life. "It ain't cold," he said, "it's a hundred degrees."

They staggered happily down the frigid, windblown street.

When he got home, his lurching and fumbling woke his mother up. She looked at him and saw that he had been drinking.

"Hey, ma," he said, holding her. "We won! We won, ma! We won."

"What you win, Johnny?" she said. "You drunk."

She went back to bed, peeved, and left him in the kitchen. He smiled to himself and dug it out of his pocket.

I brought it home for you, pa, he thought.

He stumbled up the stairs and fell into bed, secure

112

in the knowledge that it was down there in pieces on the old man's kitchen table. That he would never have to hear Gant's buzzer again. That, finally, for the first time in his life, he had really won.

When he opened his eyes, his head felt like it weighed more than six crates of grapefruits. He turned it gingerly toward the window. Foot-long icicles hung from the roof, but the snow had stopped.

The house was quiet. He remembered that it was Friday. First Friday. His mother had already left for the six-thirty mass at St. Stephen's. She never missed one. She wanted to have all the bonuses when she died. His mother was probably already worth a couple centuries of sanctifying grace. She was rich.

He smiled, lifted his head again, grimaced from the pain, and rested it back on the pillow. He had a couple more minutes. He couldn't fall asleep again, though. Wouldn't that be funny? He could just see it? After last night. Oversleeping today. Of all days. They would can him for sure.

He tried to remember his dream. It was about that girl again. The one he got into the brawl over down on the square that time Szabo was giving his speech. The girl they called Anna. The tall, willowy blond with the sensational legs. With the white skin. It was a funny dream. He had the girl in a car. It was his car; a car as flashy as Vince's Stutz. He was putting the make on her. The girl wouldn't go. Go, hell. She wouldn't even kiss him. He had his hand on that gossamer hair. He was looking right into those green eyes. "Please," he said. But the girl wouldn't kiss him. "I don't know you well enough," she said.

Johnny brought his head up suddenly from the pillow and, bolting straight up in bed, shook it. His head felt like it was going to explode. He shook it again. Christ! Zigi's goddamn whiskey. It was probably made out of tree leaves in the kitchen.

What an asshole dream, Johnny thought. Saying please. He had never said please. He had never had to say please. But then he had never had a girl like that one, either.

He smiled and got out of bed. One of these days, he'd see her again. He'd ask her out. He wouldn't have to say please. She'd get to know him well enough all right. She'd go. Sooner or later, they all went.

He chose one of the old man's flannel shirts, pulled the blue sweater his mother had knitted for his birthday over it, and went downstairs. He made himself a cup of coffee, walked over to the kitchen table, and sat down. Gant's buzzer was still there. He wondered what his mother had thought this morning when she had seen it there. She probably thought that he had stolen it. Ma always thought the best of him.

He took the slab of *szalona* off the wall, cut himself a few slices of it, found a stale loaf of rye, and washed it down with what was left of his coffee. He felt like another cup but there wasn't enough time, so he drank three glasses of water. He stuck the old man's cap on his head, put his battered jacket on, and walked out. The cold numbed him and he started to shiver as he walked down the street, his hands in his pockets. His head boomed with each step. His bloodshot eyes burned. He started to tremble, cursed Zigi's whiskey again, then realized it was something other than the whiskey and the cold. It was fear.

There's nothing to be afraid of, he said to himself. Andrews promised us. We made a deal. He had to be straight with us; he didn't give us everything we wanted. He even thanked me for talking to him.

Then why was he scared?

He walked through the Flats, avoiding the snowdrifts. The snow trucks were out already, trying to shovel it away. On the bridges overhead, cars honked. Traffic was snarled.

Johnny looked around. It didn't look too bad when it snowed. It was in the summer that everything felt right on top of him, weighing him down. It was in the summer that he felt he couldn't breathe. When the Terminal Tower looked like a hard-edged stone ruler; ready to bloody him when he broke some of their rules. Maybe that was why he hated the summer so much.

A block from the warehouse, he saw cars around the gate, a mob of men. What were all those guys doing there? What were those things off to the side? They looked like . . . armored cars! He raced down the icy, snow-covered street. His head throbbed. His body trembled. He felt nauseous.

It can't be, he said to himself. It can't! It can't!

Closer now, he saw the scene clearly. The dazzling whiteness opened up in front of him like a black, ugly hole. Behind the gate stood a dozen uniformed guards.

All of them were holding shotguns. Gant stood next to them, a bullhorn in his hands. Two armored cars blocked the truck dock. Near the front door of the warehouse he saw Andrews and, with him, in his fur coat, stood . . . Fleckner!

Fleckner, who had come from the old country just like him. Fleckner, who could even speak some of the Magyar. Fleckner, who had called him a good worker. Fleckner, who was supposed to be thousands of miles away, vacationing. Fleckner, who had put all those words into Andrews' lying, cocksucking mouth. Fleckner, who had his office high up in the Terminal Tower.

Suddenly Abe was standing in front of him. He was yelling something into his face, but his words were all jumbled up somehow. They wouldn't sink into Johnny's brain. Everything was moving too fast.

"Lock us out," Abe was saying. "Everybody's canned . . . Christ, Johnny . . . Didn't I tell you? Didn't I? Didn't I?"

He stumbled away from Abe, dazed, the acrid taste of the bacon and coffee in his throat. He fought it down, lost now in the middle of the mob of shouting men. A hundred, a hundred and fifty men, shoving toward the gate. Wild-eyed, hungry, excited men. Men who would take their jobs.

Up ahead, cut off from him by the new men, Dombrowsky held the gate with both hands. He was pulling at it with all his might. He was trying to bring it down. He was screaming. Empty, futile, blasphemous words exploded from his mouth. A guard moved toward him. "Get off the gate!" the guard said.

Link kept screaming. The guard used his gun butt. Link's hands were bloody. He wouldn't let go of the gate. The guard used his gun butt again. Link kept screaming, holding on. Abruzzi grabbed him around the neck and wrestled him away. Link's hands were a clump of blood. Bone stuck out of the clumps. Link turned, still screaming, Abruzzi hanging onto his neck. He shook Abruzzi off roughly and threw himself into the snow. He dug his bloody hands deep into it. The snow turned pink. Then, slowly, a bright red.

Johnny kept watching Link. He felt someone's eyes off to the side. He turned to Faflik. Faflik didn't say anything. He kept his eyes on him. Johnny could hear his eyes. Faflik's eyes were deafening him.

He was dizzy. He could hear Link's screams. He could hear Gant's buzzer. He could hear the thunk of the billy club on Dorsett's head. He could hear the tired whine of the hearse as it drove his father's casket to the cemetery.

"Johnny," Abe said. "Johnny, you okay?"

He stepped away, bent over, and his vomit gushed onto the snow. Black and brown and green vomit. He forced himself to watch. He felt his whole body shake. The vomit wouldn't stop.

He cleared his head and shook off Abe's arm. He could see Fleckner now. Fleckner, who had been watching him vomit. Who was smiling. Andrews stood next to him, puffing his pipe.

Gant held his bullhorn. "We need twenty-six men today. The company is changing personnel."

Johnny staggered toward the mob of men crowding the gate. He stopped. Ned Sweeney stood a few feet ahead of him. What was he doing here? He used to be one of them. He had been fired because he'd been a few minutes late. Was he here because he wanted to take . . . one of their jobs?

"Sweeney," Johnny mumbled.

Sweeney looked away from him.

"Sweeney, listen."

"I'm sorry, Johnny," Sweeney said. "I got my kids. I gotta get a job. Maybe he'll take me back."

"But Sweeney," Johnny said, "when you got canned. All the guys. We—Sweeney, Jesus Christ. What are you doin' here?"

Sweeney stepped away from him and raised his hand into the air. "Right here, Mr. Gant," Sweeney said. "I'm a good worker. I'm not gonna be late again."

Johnny watched Sweeney begging, then hurled himself against the gate, at Gant. He felt the cold steel snap against his body. Gant was inches away from him, protected by the gate. A guard moved toward him and swung his gun butt at the gate. Johnny ducked. The butt just missed his face.

"Lemme in there!" he screamed. "I wanna see Fleckner!"

Gant smiled. The guards were his audience. "Mr. Kovak wants to see Mr. Fleckner," he said, "I'm sorry, Mr. Kovak. Mr. Fleckner is in Florida on vacation."

Gant and the guards laughed. In the background, Johnny could see the smile on Fleckner's face.

"Come on," he yelled. "We're goin' in!"

He pushed at the gate as the guards swung their shotgun butts at it. He could feel bodies behind him trying to push him out of the way. Then someone tried to pull him back from the gate. He turned and saw that it was one of the new men waiting for a job. He shoved the man away. He felt a punch to his kidney and doubled over. He could see Abe swinging at someone now; Abruzzi; some of the other men who were with him last night. Men who had lost their jobs battling men who would get their jobs. Gant and Andrews and Fleckner were smiling.

Johnny felt something loosen inside him.

It didn't matter anymore.

He didn't care.

He felt his fist hitting flesh. Hitting again. He felt a punch above his eye. A punch snapped his nose. Blood dripped down his face. Then he was down on the ground in the snow, men on top of him. A kick to the back of the head. He heard sirens. The men around him scattered.

He looked up from the ground. He couldn't see clearly. A blurred figure stood above him. He blinked his eyes. A policeman was holding a billyclub, his mouth was a snarl. The club rose into the air. It was coming down. Lower now. Lower . . . He threw his hands in front of his face. His head exploded. The snow turned coal black.

Inside the blackness, there were three of them in the police wagon. The old man held him in his lap. His mother was crying. The wagon thudded through the streets of Truetown. They had come in the middle of the night for them. They had wakened them from their beds, pushed them into the wagon. They were taking them to jail for the night. Because they were greenhorns. Because their papers had to be checked. Because, maybe, they'd be deported. It was by order of the attorney general, a man named Palmer. The wagon thudded. The old man held him in his lap. His mother was crying.

Johnny opened his eyes. The blackness became dim light. The police wagon thudded through the chuckholed streets of the Flats.

Abe said, "Johnny, you okay?"

He nodded. There were a dozen men around him on the floor. Men who could thank him for losing their jobs. Faflik held his head in his hands. Abruzzi's eyes were closed; there was a deep gash across his forehead. Dombrowsky sat across from him, his blood-crusted hands lifeless in his lap. The other men stared at him. Johnny glanced at them, then looked shamefully away.

Abe said to them, "It's not Johnny's fault."

No one said anything.

Johnny felt their eyes. He had to say something to them. But what could he possibly say?

"Listen," he said. He stopped, cleared his throat. His mouth was dry. His lips wouldn't form the words. "I didn't know they'd . . . " He stopped again. He looked at Dombrowsky. "Link, you were there, You heard—"

"Ain't nothin' new." Dombrowsky said, his eyes on the floor of the police wagon.

Abe said, "He told us, Link. He even said you'd get paid back for the peaches."

"Nothin' new," Dombrowsky whispered. "Johnny, don't you know? We're all of us . . . polacks." The black man held his broken hands out to him and smiled.

He stood in the line in front of the desk sergeant's desk at Central Police Station. The desk sergeant had a veinous nose which squatted over his face. He spoke in a droning monotone and never looked up at the men in front of him.

"Last-name-first-name-middle-initial."

"Kovak, John J."

"Address."

"122 Bentson. The Flats."

"Previous arrests?"

Johnny shook his head.

The desk sergeant didn't look at him.

"Previous arrests?" he said again.

"Nothin'."

"Age."

"Twenty-two."

"Place of birth."

"Ellis Island, New York."

"I didn't ask you where you come in," the desk sergeant said. "I ask you where you was born."

"I was born there."

The desk sergeant looked up at him for the first time and smiled. He had dirty yellow teeth. "Wise guy, huh?" he said. "Nobody's born there."

Johnny didn't say anything. The desk sergeant wrote it down.

"Louie," he said to another policeman. "Let's put this joker in the tank with the boes. Let's see how wise he is in there."

The policeman led Johnny to a small cell filled with ragged, unwashed men. Their sour stink overpowered him as he stepped into the cell and for a moment Johnny thought he was going to vomit again. He gagged. The men watched him and laughed.

"Sit down, boy," a tattooed man said to him. "Make yourself at home."

"What the hell'd you do?" said another, looking at Johnny's bruised face, "take on the whole mother-humping police department?"

The tattooed man said, "He looks worse than you smell, Harry, that's why they put him in here."

"They put him in here," Harry laughed, "cause they figured he ain't got enough of a nose left to smell us with."

They sat there slapping their knees and laughing. Johnny looked them over and tried to smile. The one called Harry was in his sixties. He had bright, perceptive eyes which peered out from under tufted eyebrows. Most of them had flat chests, skinny arms, and sagging bellies. Their shoes were flattened or had adhesive tape wrapped around their arches. The skin was stretched so tightly across their faces that they almost looked like dead men. A few lay on folded newspapers which were their pillows.

"Give him a cigarette," the one called Harry said.

Johnny took the cigarette, lighted it, sucked on it, and gagged again. He realized he couldn't draw much air through his nose.

"It's gonna kill him," the tattooed man said.

"There's worse ways to die," Harry smiled.

After a few hours, he got used to the smell. They asked him about his face and he told them that he had gotten into a fight he should have known he couldn't win. They thought that was funny. In a way, it wasn't even a lie. He was happy to be away from Abe and Dombrowsky and the others. Happy to be away from their eyes, their bloody faces, their scars. Happy to be away from Link's busted hands. To the men here, he was just another down-on-his-luck stiff. They didn't know what he had done.

He liked them. They were a kind of family of hoboes from down by the riverbank. Harry, the eldest among them, was their leader. They had lived contentedly in their tar-paper shacks until the snowstorm blew in off Lake Erie. Their shacks were blown to the ground; they couldn't even keep their bonfires going. They went down to the Salvation Army and asked for shelter. They told the truth: they were freezing to death. The Sallies wouldn't take them in. So they trooped down to the Relief and the same thing happened.

They realized they only had one chance to stay

alive: jail. They went down to Central Police Station, confessed petty thefts, and surrendered themselves. Nine hoboes who wanted to come in from the cold. The cops wouldn't accept their crimes and threw them back outside. Then Harry came up with his idea. They went back down to the police station, this time with bricks in their hands. They hurled the bricks through the police station's glass front doors. They were arrested for malicious destruction of property. They got a two-week sentence.

"Here we are," Harry told Johnny, "out of the cold. With our own lovely cell. Alive."

"For another two weeks," the tattooed man said.

Late at night, when the others were asleep, Johnny huddled against the wall and thought about this day, the longest day of his life. Last night at about this time he had been at Zigi's, grab-assing that waitress, getting drunk. He thought he had won. Now here he was in jail for the first time in his life. With a cellful of hoboes. Jobless again.

And worse: all those guys were jobless because of him. Guys with families, children, doctors' bills. What would happen to the brother Faflik was taking care of? Would Abruzzi have to go back to his sandpile? And Link? What kind of job would Link get with those hands?

He knew that they didn't want to do it. He had talked them into it. But did he really think they'd have it better if they went up against Gant? Or was Abe right about what he had said at Christmas? Did he put them all up to it just because he couldn't stand

Gant? Because he knew he couldn't beat Gant alone? Had he just been using all those guys? Playing games with their lives? Their kids' lives? Just to beat Gant?

And what would he do now? Go back out on the street and start looking for another job? Forget what had happened? Forget how they had kicked the shit out of him? Or could he get even with the bastards somehow? But how? How could anybody ever get even with them? How could it ever end any other way except the way it had ended today?

But what about Dorsett then? Why did Dorsett go after Gant on that platform? After the way Dorsett had let Gant humiliate him at the gate. After what he had told him: "You can't beat 'em, kid. You're young. You'll see." Then why did Dorsett do it? If you couldn't beat them, then why did Dorsett do it? And look where it got him? Into the prison ward, facing six months for assault.

In the morning, a policeman woke him. "Okay, Kovak. You got friends. Get your ass outa here."

Harry and the other hoboes looked at him. "Glad it ain't us that's gettin' out," Harry said.

He didn't know what to say to them. Finally he said, "Thanks. For the cigarette and stuff."

"Stay warm, kid," Harry said.

"Go get a new face," the tattooed one laughed.

He walked out of the cellblock into the hall. Jocko stood there flashing his teeth.

"Who'd you run into?" Jocko said. "Joe Louis?"

It hit him then. "You got friends," the policeman had said. They shouldn't be releasing him for another day. Abe and the other guys were still in their cells. And he was getting out because of Vince. The guy who had caused it all and he was going free. Was that fair? "Ain't nothin' that's fair." That's what Dorsett had said.

"The boss heard about it," Jocko said. "He's outside waitin' for you, Johnny."

He hesitated and thought about telling the desk sergeant he wanted to go back inside. Then he thought about that smell hitting him again and changed his mind. He walked out after Jocko, breathing deeply of the fresh air. Vince's Stutz was at the curb. He got into the back seat next to him. Jocko started the car up and drove it away from the jail.

Vince Doyle looked at Johnny and grinned. "How's the jailbird?" he said.

"Who asked you, Vince?"

"You gotta go out and save the whole fuckin' world, don't you, Johnny?" Vince Doyle said.

He didn't know what to say. Finally he said, "That sonofabitch at Fleckner's. He shook my hand."

Vince Doyle laughed. "Yeah, I know. I know you were down at Zigi's celebratin'."

"Lay offa me, Vince," Johnny said. "I didn't ask you to get me out."

"Christ, Johnny. You don't go screwin' with people like that. You got no push."

"He shook my hand," Johnny said. "He said we had a deal."

Vince Doyle laughed. "He shook your hand? What

the hell is that? Some kinda blood oath? This ain't the
old country, Johnny."

"I'm gonna get the fuckers," Johnny said, spitting
the words. "They're gonna pay."

"Yeah, sure," Vince Doyle grinned. "Sure. You come
back with me, Johnny. They'll pay." He laughed.
"We'll both get rich."

Johnny shook his head. "Money," he said angrily.
"That's all you care about, isn't it."

"That's all there is," Vince Doyle said. "There's
nothin' else."

They dropped him in the Flats, a block from his
home, but he thought about what his mother would
say. About the way she'd look at him when she saw
his swollen face. He turned around and walked away
from the house.

He passed a soup line and realized suddenly how
hungry he was. He had never stood in a soup line
before. He had never sunk that low. But the soup
didn't smell bad and there weren't very many men in
the line and he thought—what difference is this soup
line gonna make? He had caused more than twenty
men to lose their jobs. He had just spent the night
with a cellful of hoboes.

He waited in line a few minutes, then stepped up
into the back of the truck. A man ladled some soup
into a paper container and handed it to him. Johnny
looked at it. He saw that it was nothing but greasy
water. He stumbled out of the truck, drank the grease,
and walked on.

He walked aimlessly. He didn't want to go home.

He didn't want to see Vince again. Abe was still in jail. He kept walking. He didn't know where to go. He didn't know what to do.

Then he remembered Dorsett. That was it. Dorsett. He'd go to see Dorsett again. He'd ask Dorsett why he did it. Why he had gone after Gant. He had to know why. It would help him to know why.

He walked up the long hill out of the Flats, through Public Square, and an hour later he stood in front of a policeman in Metropolitan General Hospital's prison ward.

The policeman sat at a desk talking to someone on a telephone. He looked up at Johnny, the phone still in his hand.

"I'm here to see Al Dorsett," Johnny said.

The policeman looked at him and didn't say anything.

"He's a friend of mine."

"He isn't here," the policeman said.

"Where is he?"

"He's down at the morgue."

Johnny could feel himself starting to tremble again.

"He hung himself," the policeman said, and started talking into the telephone again.

Johnny stood there a moment and then he heard himself say, "Why?" It came thin and mushy out of his mouth.

The policeman hung the telephone up and looked at him annoyed.

"What?"

"Why?"

"How the hell should I know?" the policeman said.

The jalopy sputtered and then stalled. Mike Mona-han cursed, turned it over, and tried it again. It figured. The hunk of shit belonged to the union. It wasn't much of a union. So why should it be much of a car?

Yesterday, on his way back through the Flats to the Consolidated Terminal, it was some sort of wild reflex that had stopped him. He hadn't even thought about it. He just punched the horn and hit the brake and swung the cab door open and the kid stood in the street gawking at him and at the big truck.

"Hey, Johnny," he had yelled, "get in."

The kid stood there and didn't move.

"I'm Mike Monahan."

The kid eyed him suspiciously.

"Jackshit to you," Monahan grinned. "Remember? Down at Fleckner's."

"Yeah, so what," the kid said.

"Get in, that's what. It beats walkin'."

The kid hestiated, climbed into the cab, and looked it over. Monahan drove through the Flats.

"I heard what happened to you guys," Monahan said. "Can't say I was surprised."

"I sure as hell was," the kid said.

Monahan looked at him, at the bruises and blue-black colors of his face.

"Yeah, I guess you were," he said. It was another

block before Monahan tried to break the ice again.
"Ever ride one of these things?"

"My old man, he loved 'em."

"Did he drive?"

"Naw. He didn't talk the language good enough. He used to move stuff. With a horse and wagon. Back in the old country. He always wanted to try one of these."

The kid seemed self-conscious about what he had said and looked out the window.

"So what are you doin' with yourself?" Monahan asked.

The kid looked at him sharply. "What do you care?"

Monahan laughed. "Well, I thought maybe you were lookin' for a job."

"Could be," the kid said.

"Well, could be I can offer you one."

"Doin' what?"

"Oh, doin' somethin' where maybe you can get even for what they done to you."

The kid grinned. "You want me to blow up the fuckin' place? Sure. How much?"

Monahan laughed. "Just do a lotta hard honest work, that's all."

The kid didn't say anything, then he suddenly said, "Drop me here."

Monahan stopped the truck and the kid opened the window.

"Well, how about it?" Monahan said.

"How about what?"

"How about if I drop by tomorrow and we talk about it?"

"What the hell," the kid had said, "I'll be home."

Then, at home last night, Mike Monahan had thought about it. He didn't even really know anything about the kid and here he was going to offer him the job. All he knew was what he had seen at Fleckner's. But that was enough, wasn't it? There was something about this big, tousle-headed kid. Those guys at the warehouse had trusted him. And he had led them. He was younger than most of them but he had led them. It wasn't the kid's fault that the whole thing had blown up in his face. He had tried. At least he had tried. And as far as Mike Monahan was concerned, he'd settle any day for a big, tough guy who'd really try.

Every time that he picked up the paper these days, it seemed like working stiffs somewhere were fighting for what was rightfully theirs. Longshoremen in California. Auto-Lite workers in Toledo. Textile workers on the East Coast. And, right here in Cleveland, the newspaper boys were talking about a strike. Newspaper boys! Kids barely out of their diapers! A strike yet!

Every union in the country, it seemed to him, was fighting for its men. Every union in the country, except his own.

He'd been a member of the Federation of Interstate Truckers since 1906, the year it was formed nationally. He'd been president of the local here, 302, for the past seven years. President, vice-president, secretary, treasurer, chief cook and bottle washer, number one (and only) organizer. And in all those years, as far as he could see, they hadn't made any progress.

A lot of it, no doubt, was Matt Rafferty's fault. Yeah, sure, he knew that, but there wasn't much he could do about it. Matt was an old, road-driving buddy of his. Matt had been the national president since that very first year the union was formed and it seemed to Mike Monahan that all Matt ever did was endorse Democrats and send out bee-in-the-bonnet newsletters about John L. Lewis being a rabble-rouser and a threat to the country. And then Matt came through Cleveland once a year, on his way back to the national headquarters in Flint, and gave his speech about paying dues on time. Matt hobnobbed with all the political wheels and big cheeses and when he came to town he had his whiskey straight and his fluff every which way and each time Mike Monahan saw him, Matt Rafferty seemed more eager to do what he had always done. Not a helluva lot.

Matt had a whole vocabulary full of bromides which he used all the time in his newsletter. He talked about "moral duty" and "capital being the worker's best friend" and how "every manjack in the union had to work hard to prevent the next Depression." It was all balloon juice and banana oil, Mike Monahan knew. The *next* Depression? Well, what about this one? And "moral duty"? What kind of mothering Christer babble was that? And capital as the worker's best friend? Since when? Was that why the supervisor wouldn't

132

put a heater into Mike Monahan's truck? The whole trouble was, Mike Monahan sometimes thought, that Matt started wearing suits when he stopped driving a truck. And now Matt's suits had vests inside them and the vests always had a gold watch and a gold chain hanging off of them.

Mike Monahan knew that if there was ever a time for working stiffs to get a better deal in this country, that time was now. Now that FDR was in the White House and the medicine-ball-headed Great Engineer was hiding out someplace. Now that the Blue Eagle was flying its battle colors all over the place. Now that working stiffs didn't have to join company unions anymore. Now that the scurvy yellow dog was howling in pain and looked ready to die. Now that, thanks to Section 7A of the NIRA, working stiffs everywhere had the right to organize themselves. To bargain with their two-faced, fat-assed bosses. Through men they themselves picked to represent them. Men who wouldn't sell them out for an extra buck a week in their paychecks.

Meanwhile, with all this going on, with workers reaching for picket signs everywhere, Mike Monahan's own union was all talk and no cider. Unity, hell! They didn't even have much communication with each other. There were some locals which didn't even bother to tell Matt Rafferty what they were doing. Which meant that no local could ever really back another one up. Not that there had ever been any need for that, anyway. As far as Mike Monahan knew, no federation local had ever gone out on strike. A few

guys walked out now and then and if there were
enough guys involved, then Matt Rafferty would show
up and take over. He would temporize and pattycake
and asskiss the bosses and get the guys their jobs
back. Their jobs and nothing else.

What the hell kind of union was that? Mike Monahan often thought. Was it any wonder that guys
weren't beating on his door to sign up? To sign up
for what? If somebody who belonged to Local 302 had
a problem and Mike Monahan went in to talk to the
supervisor for him, he barely got the time of day.
Jesus Christ, he was the president of the goddamn
local and he couldn't even get a heater for himself.
And whenever he did go in for somebody, he had to
go in on his belly. If they said no, or if they laughed at
him, what could he do about it? Call a strike? With
the number of men he had signed up? The goddamn
newspaper boys were probably better organized.

Mike Monahan knew, too, that some of it was probably his own fault. He was no leader. He was just an
ordinary truck driver. He knew the road. He'd been
driving since the time a highway meant a gravel path;
back in the days when trucks could only carry candy-
ass payloads; when they were equipped with solid
rubber tires and couldn't be pushed much over thirty
miles an hour. He was a motor man. He knew how to
get a truck from one place to another as fast as possible. But he didn't have the same talent with men.
From what he had seen that night at Fleckner's,
though, this Kovak kid did. The kid had a more

powerful drive than any truck Mike Monahan had ever seen.

He parked the jalopy now in front of the kid's door. There was a light on inside. Mike Monahan knocked. "Come on in," the kid said.

Mike Monahan walked inside the small living room. There was another kid there, even younger, whom Monahan remembered from Fleckner's.

"Good to see you, Johnny," Monahan said.

The kid shook his hand but didn't smile. "I figured you wouldn't mind if Abe was here," he said. "Abe Belkin, Mike Monahan."

Monahan shook hands with Abe Belkin and looked at his bruised face. "Both of you guys look real pretty," Monahan said.

Johnny said, "Listen, you got somethin' to say, say it."

Monahan smiled, sat down, and lighted a cigarette. There it was again. The fire. What he liked so much about this kid.

"Sure, Johnny," Monahan said. "I don't want to take up your time. You're a busy man."

The kid caught it and grinned at him for the first time. "Yeah," he said, "we're real busy all right."

"Well, listen, Johnny," Monahan said, "I'm the president of the Federation of Interstate truckers here and—"

"The president," Johnny interrupted, smiling. "Did you hear that, Abe?"

Monahan grinned. The score was tied. The kid

didn't miss a trick. "You heard of it, Johnny?" Monahan said.

"A union," Abe Belkin said.

"Not much of one. I figure we got maybe a hundred guys signed up here right now. I don't know how you feel about unions, Johnny, but I saw you at the warehouse. You got a way with men."

The kid looked away from him, his face pained. "Yeah, I really did a lot for 'em."

"You know how to talk to 'em," Monahan said gently. "They listened to you."

"They sure as hell did that," the kid said.

"I need a guy like that to sign men up," Monahan said.

The kid smiled. "I don't even know nothin' about unions, trucks."

"It ain't a pretty way to make a livin', Johnny," Monahan said. "I'll tell you that."

The kid laughed. He said. "You know any pretty ways, Abe?"

"I'll tell you," Monahan said. "You got no insurance. You get into a wreck, we pay for the damage. No overtime pay—we just get paid for the haul. You know what that means, Johnny? That means you run your ass into the ground gettin' as many hauls as you can. That means a lotta guys—when they hit forty or forty-five, they gotta piss every three minutes 'cause their kidneys been beaten into pus from too many bumps in the road and too little rest."

Monahan stopped and looked at them. Johnny was expressionless. Abe shook his head.

Monahan glanced at his hand and saw that the cigarette had burned down between his fingers. He raised his hand up and let them see that the lighted butt was stuck to his skin. He took the butt out with his other hand and let them see how scabbed the hand was. They watched him.

Monahan grinned. "Can't hardly feel a thing. It's my alarm clock."

"What do you mean?" Johnny said.

"We get paid for what we haul," Monahan said. "Like I told you. So you ain't got much time for sleepin'. You feel yourself dozin' on the road, you pull it over to the side and take a little snooze. You light up a cigarette and hold it. You set your alarm clock."

He lighted another cigarette. "When she runs down and tickles you," he said, "it's time to get back on the road again."

"Christ," Abe Belkin said.

Johnny's eyes were hooded and emotionless. "Maybe you oughta get yourself a new alarm clock," he said.

Monahan grinned. "Maybe you're right, Johnny."

He put the cigarette into his other hand. The fingers on this one were just as scabbed. He saw Johnny watching his hands.

"The companies we work for, Johnny," Monahan said, "they're fulla guys like your Fleckner and your Andrews. They smile and stick it into you. They give you nothin' for killin' yourself." He dragged on his cigarette.

"So," Johnny said, "what's it gotta do with me? What do you want me to do about it?"

137

Monahan grinned. "Work for us, Johnny. You can go out there, sign every trucker up you can. Tell 'em that unless they join up, unless they all join the federation, we're never gonna beat 'em."

Johnny smiled. "Beat 'em, huh?"

"That's what I said. Beat 'em."

"Tell me somethin'," the kid said. "What the hell am I gonna live on while I go around preachin'?"

"We'll pay you, don't you worry about that," Monahan smiled.

"How much?" Johnny said.

"Not much. But every guy you sign up, you get a commission."

"A commission," Johnny said.

"You get an office," Monahan said, "you get a car."

The kid grinned. "You guys got a car?"

"Well, she ain't much," Monahan said. "But she runs—most of the time."

Johnny laughed.

"Listen to me. What's more important, Johnny," Monahan said, "you get a chance to get even."

"What if there ain't no way to get even?" Johnny said.

"You don't believe that yourself," Monahan said. "To get even with every smilin' flabby company bastard you ever saw."

Johnny looked at him, got up, and paced around the room. He didn't say anything for a long time.

"I don't know," he said finally. "I don't know. I don't hardly know nothin' about trucks even."

"I'll teach you, Johnny," Monahan said. "You ride with me and I'll teach you."

He kept pacing around the room. "Shit," he said. "I don't know. A union. I don't know. I never thought about no union before."

"Sure you did," Monahan smiled. "What do you think that was down at Fleckner's?"

Johnny looked at him and didn't say anything.

"Look at it this way, Johnny," Monahan said. "You got any better offers?" He grinned.

Johnny nodded. "What do you think, Abe?"

"Where do I sign up?" Abe said.

Johnny laughed. "Abe's your guy. Abe's a ball of fire."

Monahan laughed and got up. "Well, think it over," he told Johnny. "I gotta go."

At the door, Monahan turned back. He had been saving it. He wanted this big kid to take the job. Maybe this would do it.

"Jesus, Johnny," he said, leading him into it, "you took that bastard's buzzer."

"Yeah," the kid smiled. "At least I got that."

Monahan measured him and threw the punch. "I was back there yesterday," he said. "He's got a brand-new one."

The kid stopped smiling and stood there like he'd been coldcocked.

Between the eyes, Monahan thought, I got him between the eyes. "See you, Johnny," he said, and walked out of the house.

* * *

Johnny stood at the living room window watching Monahan trying to start his jalopy.

"Look at that clunker," he said. "He calls that thing a car?"

Abe sat on the couch, lost in his thoughts. "That was something about Gant's buzzer," he said.

Johnny turned away from the window and looked at him.

"You gotta do it, Johnny," Abe said softly. "It's more'n a job. It's somethin' to believe in."

Johnny turned away from him. "That's the trouble with you. All your life you've been lookin' for somethin' to believe in. What if there's nothin' to believe in?"

"I know what you're doin'," Abe said. "You're blamin' yourself for what happened. You don't know what you're gonna do. So you just wanna smash out at somethin'. Like you always do." He smiled. "Isn't that right?"

"Maybe," Johnny smiled. "I don't know."

"Johnny, listen to me," Abe said. "Listen to me. This thing this guy's talkin' about. It makes a lotta sense. I don't know a helluva lot about unions, but I do know they're the only chance the workin' guy's got. Nobody can do nothin' alone. They'll just stamp down on you and leave you crawlin' in the dirt. They're too big. They don't give a shit. Look what happened to us."

"And we weren't alone," Johnny said. "Were we?"

"Sure we were. We had—what? Twenty-three

140

guys?" Abe laughed sarcastically. "That's alone all right. They've got the cops. They've got the judges. They've got all this respectability they wear all the time. What can twenty-three guys do against a big, powerful machine like that? But think about it, Johnny. What if we woulda had a union of guys? What if we woulda had a hundred guys in it? A thousand guys? Ten thousand guys?"

"You're dreamin'," Johnny said. "They woulda come down on us anyway."

"No, they wouldn't have. Not if the rest of our ten thousand guys woulda been workin' every other warehouse in the city. Not if all those other guys woulda stopped workin' when we did. Not if all the warehouses in Cleveland woulda had to worry about their tomatoes freezin'. I'll tell you what woulda happened. They woulda canned Gant. We woulda really won. And listen, don't tell me I'm dreamin'. You're the one who had all the faith in Fleckner just cause he told you what a hotshot hunkie you are."

Johnny grinned. "You're right about that."

"See," Abe smiled. "I'm right about somethin'." He paused, got up, and paced the room. "Johnny, don't you see? What this guy Monahan's askin' you to do. You can do somethin' about all the things that are wrong in this country."

"I'm gonna save the world," Johnny said. "Vince was right. They're gonna put that on my tombstone. Johnny Kovak saved the world. People are gonna come by and kneel down and kiss my stone."

141

Abe looked at him. "You think you're gonna be able to afford a tombstone, huh?"

Johnny laughed.

"Look at somebody like Dorsett, Johnny," Abe said. "Look at his life. He goes off into the army. He gets wounded. He comes back, gets married, has kids, has his whole life in front of him. Then it all comes crashing down. The big money boys step on him. They won't even give him his veterans' bonus and he's gotta go out on the street beggin' food. Then he gets a job and he gets canned from that cause he's hard of hearing on account of being wounded in the war. So when he hears he's been canned he goes after the fuckin' guy. They beat his head in. And they tell him he's gonna go to jail. Jesus Christ, Johnny, can you blame the guy for hangin' himself up on the ceiling? At least if he's dead his wife can go on relief. There must be hundreds of Dorsetts out there ready to hang off the ceiling. Can you blame 'em? But if guys like that had a union behind 'em, had people fightin' for 'em, maybe it'd be different. Maybe they'd have a better chance."

"You really believe that?" Johnny said.

"You're goddamn right I believe it," Abe said.

"And I can change all that, huh?" Johnny said.

"Sure," Abe smiled. "No sweat. We're greenhorns, Johnny. We're flatheads. All our lives they've been screwin' us. But you know somethin'? This is our country much more'n it's theirs. We make this fuckin' country work. They don't. We're on the assembly lines

142

makin' cars. We're in the mills stokin' the furnace. We're in the refineries. We're on the ore boats. They own everything and give us the orders. But we make the whole thing work. So help this guy Monahan because of that. Because he's right. Because it's a way of gettin' even with the Rockefellers and the Holdens and the Andrewses and the Gants and all the other gutter bastards like your friend Fleckner."

Johnny walked away from him. "But I don't know nothin' about unions," he said. "You know that."

"You don't have to know nothin'," Abe said. "You'll learn what you gotta know. All you gotta do is keep that goddamn anger that's always been inside you goin'."

Johnny stared out the window speechlessly. Abe sat down on the couch, drained.

"You think we could really do it?" Johnny finally said.

"We?" Abe said, "What do you mean we?"

"You really think it'd turn out different this time?"

"Johnny," Abe said, "I'm tellin' you."

Johnny turned to him. "I'll do it if you come in with me," he said.

"The guy wants you, Johnny. Not me."

"I can't do it without you, Abe." His voice was low.

"You're the one the men listen to," Abe said. "I saw that at Fleckner's."

"We can do it together, Abe," Johnny said. "Like that time we got that kid with the red scarf when we were kids."

Abe smiled. "You beat that kid up yourself," he said. "All I did was watch."

Johnny put his hand out. "Shake on it, Abe."

"You don't need me, Johnny. You can do it yourself."

"Shake on it," Johnny said, "you're my brother, ain't you?"

Two days later, Mike Monahan led them up a long and rickety stairway toward a little room which would be their office.

"It's gonna be a great office for you guys," Mike Monahan grinned.

They glanced at the unpainted walls of the stairway, the peeling plaster of the ceiling, the broken stairs, the thick dust which was everywhere.

"Once you get it fixed up a little bit," Mike Monahan said.

"Fixed up?" Johnny grinned. "You didn't say anything about fixing anything up."

"Hasn't been used a while, Johnny," Mike Monahan said humorlessly.

He stopped at the top of the stairs in front of a locked door. He tried a key but it didn't work. Mike Monahan looked at them sheepishly, then savagely kicked the door down. Johnny and Abe stood in the doorway, looking at their incredibly cluttered and dusty new one-room office.

Abe whistled. "Holy shit!" he said. Johnny laughed.

Monahan led them into the room and went to its single window, which was caked with dirt. He cleaned a spot with his shirtsleeves and peered through it.

"It's got a great view," he said.

Johnny and Abe stepped to the window and looked down on a truck terminal, its vast yard filled with trucks and men. Behind a long fence stood a fortresslike, multistory red brick building. Fronting it was a sign that said "Talbot's Consolidated Trucking Company."

"Your neighbors," Mike Monahan smiled. "The biggest in the city."

Johnny stared at the huge complex below.

"Come on, Johnny," Abe said, looking at the clutter of the room. "We've got work to do."

"One day," Johnny said slowly, "they're gonna walk up here and knock on the door and ask for *Mr.* Kovak and *Mr.* Belkin."

Abe looked at the dust-covered room.

"We're sure gonna have to get our hands dirty before that," Abe said.

The jalopy which he and Abe shared sputtered worse than ever, but Monahan was right. It ran. Johnny had never had a car before and, driving down the street toward his own office, on a day as sunkissed and beautiful as this one, he could even pretend that it was a Stutz.

The streets of the Flats were teeming this morning with cars and people. There was a boisterousness in the air, an early-spring light-headedness caused by the sudden mildness of the weather and by the realization that while many people here were still jobless and hungry, at least they didn't have to face the cruelties of snow and freezing temperature anymore.

Johnny shared this mood on this pretty day, cutting in and out of traffic, honking his horn for no reason except to hear the sound of it. He turned the corner on River Road, a long line of cars ahead of him, and idly watched the people on the sidewalk.

When, suddenly, he saw her.

She was wearing a plain blue dress, walking down the street with her head high in the air, her back straight, her eyes looking nowhere but ahead. Her blond hair was up in a bun on the top of her head and he could see her thin, swanlike neck. He had been thinking about her all these months and he couldn't believe now that she was only a few feet away from him. But he was hemmed in by traffic and all he could do was watch her. He honked the horn at her. Once, twice, three times. The driver in the car in front of him turned back and waved his fist, but the girl didn't even look back. She marched resolutely down the street, taking long, loping steps which showed off her legs and figure.

Traffic had come to a complete stop ahead of him now and as the girl got farther and farther away with each step, he suddenly swerved the jalopy wildly to the curb, blocking a driveway, jumped out, and left it there. He ran down the street after her. She didn't even glance back when she heard his pounding foot-steps behind her, didn't even look at him when he was right next to her, his heart pounding and out of breath.

"Hey, Anna," he said, "remember me?"

She glanced at him and kept walking. "So?"

"So?" He laughed. "So can't you slow down a little? You runnin' a race?"

She looked at him angrily and took even faster steps.

He grinned. "Listen, you got me into a fight."

She kept marching ahead and didn't say anything. "I didn't ask you to stick your nose in," she finally said.

He smiled. "I was just tryin' to help you, Anna." He said it as innocently as he could.

"Yourself, you mean," she said.

"Myself?" He laughed.

"I heard you," she said curtly. "Whistle."

"Can't a guy whistle?" he laughed.

"Go ahead and whistle," she said. "I don't care." She kept walking ahead.

"My name is Johnny Kovak."

She didn't say anything.

"What's your name?"

"You know what my name is," she said.

"Your *last* name."

She stopped and looked at him. "Why?"

He laughed. "What do you mean why? You got a last name, don't you?"

She started walking again without answering him. He caught up with her.

"Well, don't you?" he said.

"Melsbakas."

"Melsbakas, huh? What's that? Some kinda polack?"

"Its *Lithuanian*," she said, proud, offended.

"Last polack I met was colored," he grinned.

147

She stopped and turned to him angrily.

"I am *not* a polack," she said. "I'm Lithuanian. And there are no colored Polish people, either."

"That's what you think," he laughed.

She started walking faster, trying to get away from him.

"Leave me alone," she said.

"Jesus. I didn't mean nothin'. It's true. His name's Dombrowsky. He's a helluva guy. I swear to God."

She walked briskly and didn't say anything.

"Hey, Anna," he said, trying again after a pause. "Can't we go have a beer or somethin'?"

"I don't drink beer," she said.

"Well, then let's just go someplace." He smiled.

She looked at him angrily, her face crimson. "I said leave me alone," she said, her voice loud. "I'll call a policeman."

"Hey," he said. "I didn't mean nothin' like that. Hey, really, I just want—we could talk. You know, talk. That's all."

"What do you wanna talk about?" she said.

"Hell. I don't care. Anything. I'll talk about anything you wanna talk about." He grinned. "Anything. Baseball. Joe Louis. The Depression. The price of nickel apples." He thought that was funny and smiled.

She didn't smile. "Maybe I don't wanna talk about nothin'," she said.

"Jesus, you gotta wanna talk about somethin'."
"Why?"

"Why? I don't know. So you can get some air in your mouth." He laughed. "I don't know. Jesus."

She looked at him. "Do you always swear?"

"Jesus, Anna," he said, shaking his head.

She looked at him reproachfully and kept walking.

"Where you goin'?" he asked.

"Why?"

"Is that all you can say—why?" He laughed. "I got a car. I can give you a ride."

"I don't go for rides," she said.

"Well, where you goin' anyway?" he said, exasperated now.

"Here," she said. "I work here," and she turned into the doorway of a dime store, leaving him on the sidewalk with his mouth hanging open.

"Damnit," he said, "can't you even say good-bye?"

"Good-bye." She walked into the store and didn't even look back at him when she said it.

He spent his days learning to be what Monahan grinningly called him. A union man. But almost everything he learned about his local discouraged him. They only had ninety-two men. They didn't even have a place to meet. They held their meetings infrequently, in a variety of places. A bowling alley off of Public Square. The backroom of a saloon in Little Italy. A funeral parlor near the West Side Market.

"A funeral parlor!" Johnny said to Abe. "Can you believe that? That's the first thing we're gonna change around here. We're not gonna hold no meeting with no dead bodies around." The priest at St. Stephen's in the Flats agreed to let Johnny use the church hall for meetings as long as he promised the men wouldn't disturb the nuns next door with their noise. Johnny promised the priest the meetings would be quiet and then he told Abe, "One day we're gonna make so much noise in there they'll hear us on the top floor of the Terminal Tower."

Monahan wanted to call a meeting immediately to introduce the two of them to the membership but Johnny dissuaded him. "I've got nothin' to say to 'em now, Mike," he said. "I wanna find out some stuff first. I wanna try to sign up some guys before I go makin' any speeches."

He soon discovered that many men were afraid to join the union. And even many of those who had joined were afraid to go to the meetings. "It works like this," Deke Mossi told him over a beer in Monahan's kitchen. He was a lanky, scar-faced man who'd been driving for more than a decade. "If they know you've joined up, they won't do nothin' open against you. But they'll do sneaky things. They'll give you bad trips, or they'll send you out on the road knowin' somethin's wrong with the truck, knowin' you're gonna break down. You lose time that way and you lose money. Or they'll overload you. That's probably the worst. You can't handle the rig when you're overloaded and it's easy to get into an accident. And even if you don't get hurt, you're gonna have to pay the piper on the damage."

Other men wouldn't join the union, Johnny found, because they couldn't afford the dues. "I don't blame 'em," said Bucky Bankston, a freckle-faced hillbilly who drove for Endicott. "It's three bucks a month.

You know all the stuff you can buy nowadays for three bucks a month? It's a goddamn fortune. Even if Monahan here looks the other way for a coupla months, still you're gonna have to pay up sooner or later. Three dollars a month buys a lot of baby clothes."

"Who says it's gotta be three bucks a month?" Johnny asked.

"Matt Rafferty," Monahan said. "It's been three bucks for years."

"What happens if somebody don't pay?"

"If they don't pay for three months," Monahan said, "they're outa the union."

Bankston laughed. "Listen, Johnny. If Monahan wouldn't always be fidgin' what he sends in, if he wouldn't be months late with his report sometimes, there wouldn't be no Local 302."

Of the four major trucking companies in the city, Johnny learned, of Endicott, Westin, Collett, and Talbot's Consolidated—Consolidated was the most powerful. "Sometimes I think old man Talbot and his kid run all of 'em," Monahan told him. "The Talbots set the wages, the others just follow. If old man Talbot agrees to somethin' on Friday, I know sure as hell the others are gonna agree Monday morning."

"What kinda guy is this Talbot?" Johnny asked.

"The old man?" Monahan laughed. "He's okay, I guess. For one of those big-money boys. I don't see him, hardly, though. None of us drivers see him and when I gotta talk to 'em about somethin', they have me talk to their lawyer, a guy named St. Clair."

"What's he like?" Johnny said.

"He's a prick. An eighteen-karat, thousand-percent prick. You'll find out."

Johnny liked the plain-spoken, hard-nosed union men that he met. He read the newspapers carefully now each day for the first time in his life and read about union men in other places fighting their battles. And while he certainly didn't feel like a union man himself yet, just reading about these things excited him. He had been an outsider all his life and these union men, they were outsiders just like him, fighting to stay alive.

It was a battle, the newspapers told him, which was sweeping the country. In Georgia, they were setting up a concentration camp for pickets. In Pennsylvania, a district attorney said, "Give me twenty tough armed men and I'll clean the sonsabitches off the picket line." In Pittsburgh, a company kept loaded machine guns aimed at its workers.

And sometimes, Johnny saw, they were perfectly willing to use those guns. In a company town in Wisconsin, two pickets were killed and thirty-four wounded. Fifteen striking textile workers were killed in New England. Over in Toledo, twenty-seven strikers were shot, many of them in the back.

Johnny read about men named Green and Dubinsky and Hillman. Men who, like him, had made it their business to build unions. But the man he kept hearing and reading about the most, the man who fascinated him, was John L. Lewis. Big John. Who sent sound trucks into the coalfields saying that anybody who wouldn't join his union was unpatriotic. Who punched out a man on a speaker's platform, in full view of thousands of people, because the man had called him a bastard. Who took seventy thousand men out on strike in Pennsylvania and West Virginia.

"Seventy thousand guys!" Johnny said to Abe. "That's a whole city."

Abe laughed. "All I said was ten thousand, Johnny, and you thought I was nuts."

A few days later, Abe read him something from the paper. It was part of a speech John L. Lewis had given.

"The aim of our movement is to organize the workers in order that they may obtain a large participation in the benefits of modern industry." Abe read the words slowly and carefully. "Now listen to this, Johnny," he said. "I am not blind to the fact that such a movement has other consequences. Its by-product is political, in the sense that through their organization the workers of America will acquire greater participation in the government of this country. What we want to create is an industrial democracy."

Abe put the newspaper down and looked at him. "An industrial democracy, Johnny. I told you. I told you we could do it. We can change the whole country. Make it ours. It starts right here. With guys like us. Signin' men up into the union."

Johnny thought about it and nodded. "Yeah," he said bitterly. "But you notice it wasn't Matt Rafferty sayin' all that."

He was bitter because the more he learned about

other unions, the less respect he had for his own. Truckers. Big, tough guys. And they had never been out on a strike. They had a national president, he discovered as he talked to the men of the local, who was thought of as a blowhard and a drunk. A national president who sent his men a mimeographed letter twice a month, a letter with his picture on top of it and the words, "Matt Rafferty Sez to You."

Letters which said, in the middle of the greatest poverty in the country's history:

"I've been around this world of ours for a while and do you know what? I've found that the best thing you can do is to start the day with a big smile. A big smile at breakfast helps you start the day. A big smile at work shortens your day. A big smile will always make you good friends. . . . "

Letters which said, with unions all over the country going out on strike:

"It's impossible to win a labor dispute with fists. You can only win them with understanding and patience. Mutual understanding is much more effective than a hot temper. Mutual understanding gets lasting results. . . ."

And letters which said, over and over again, in a hundred different ways:

"If you're a good union man, you'll pay your dues in advance. You won't wait until the last moment to pay them. It's a poor union man who only pays when he has to. . . .

"Make a promise to yourself today. From now on, you'll pay your dues on time. From now on, you'll make sure that your buddy pays his dues on time. That's what solidarity is."

Every letter was addressed "Dear Brother" and was signed "Fraternally yours." One letter was filled with telegrams congratulating Matt Rafferty on a speech. In another letter, Matt Rafferty urged his "brothers" to be "proud of your union by wearing cuff links and watch-fob buttons with the union insignia on it." The cuff links and watch-fob buttons could be ordered from the national headquarters at 246 Summit Road in Flint, Michigan, by mail. Three dollars for the cuff links. Two-fifty for the watch-fob buttons.

"Cuff links!" Johnny exploded, waving the letter at Monahan. "What is this, a fuckin' country club? Who the hell's got shirts that need cuff links in 'em? Who the hell can put any money out for watch-fob buttons?"

Monahan laughed.

"I'm not kiddin', Mike," Johnny said angrily. "What the fuck is this?"

"I know you're not," Monahan said. He paused. "I guess maybe Matt's just gettin' old."

One night Monahan let him get behind the wheel of his big truck. Monahan watched him as he battled with the gears and careened around the curves of a woodsy two-lane blacktop.

"So what do you think, Johnny?" Monahan said.

Johnny laughed. "It feels like if I reach out, I can touch the goddamn trees."

"Yeah, and if you push her anymore," Monahan said, "we'll be touchin' the goddamn cement."

They laughed. A truck barreled toward them and as it roared by, the driver waved. Johnny grinned, waved back, and shifted gears. The big truck bucked, lurched, then speeded up.

"They're gonna make me pay for a whole new rig when you're done," Monahan laughed.

"Honest to God, Mike, it feels like it's alive," Johnny said. "The goddamn power."

"I know what you mean, Johnny. Slow her down, though. Myrtle's is right around the bend."

Johnny eased the big truck in front of a small white clapboard shack a few hundred feet from the road. A glaring red neon sign announced, "Myrtle's Eats." Two other trucks were parked in front.

Monahan bustled into the place. Johnny tagged behind him.

"Myrts!" Monahan boomed, his arms outspread. "How I've missed you, Myrts!"

She was a tired blonde in her mid-forties, shapeless and sweating.

"Don't you dolly me, Monahan," she said. "It's still gonna cost you five cents."

Monahan laughed and leered at her kiddingly. "I'd pay a hundred dollars for it, Myrts. You know that."

"You wouldn't pay a hundred dollars for Mae West," she said.

They sat down at the counter and Myrtle automatically handed them steaming cups of black coffee.

"Here," Monahan said, resting his hand on hers. "I want you to meet Johnny. Johnny Kovak. He's our new organizer."

Myrtle smiled at him. "You must be hard up, kid," she said. "How about some raisin pie?"

He shook his head. "I'm not that hungry."

Monahan elbowed him lightly in the ribs. "Make your pecker stand up," he whispered.

"Okay," Johnny laughed, "that case, I'll have a piece."

Myrtle brought them two pieces of pie.

"I didn't ask for one, did I?" Monahan said.

"I figured you need it worse than him," Myrtle said.

They laughed.

Two truckers walked up to the counter from a back booth, plunked their change down, and started toward the door.

"Jenkins, O'Brien," Monahan said to them. "Come on over here. Meet Johnny Kovak. He's our new organizer."

One of the men glanced back. "Gotta run, Mike. You know how it is."

Monahan watched them leave. "Sure, go on," he said. Bitterness iced his voice.

"Chasin' my business away again, huh, Mike?" Myrtle said when the men had left from the other end of the counter.

"Aww," Monahan grumbled. "How much you wanna bet those guys still wet the bed at night?"

Myrtle kept washing her dishes. Her back was to them. "You know better than that, Mike," she said softly. "They got families. They can't afford no trouble."

"Yeah, sure," Monahan said. He ate his pie. He was sullen and silent.

"You hear anything, Myrts?" Monahan said after a while.

"Same old pot of beans," she said. "Joe Harper's real sick. Kidneys. You heard about that, I guess."

Monahan nodded and sipped his coffee. He got up suddenly. "Thanks, Myrts," he said. "Take care of Johnny if he needs it, huh?"

Myrtle smiled at Johnny. "He can take care of it himself when he needs it."

Monahan bustled out the door. Johnny hurried to catch up with him.

"What's the big rush?" Johnny said. "I wasn't finished with my pie."

Monahan didn't say anything.

"What's the matter?" Johnny said.

"Hell. Joe Harper and me," Monahan said. "We used to drive five-ton electric ice trucks together. One of the first guys I ever signed up."

Monahan started climbing in the passenger side of the big truck. He suddenly changed his mind.

"I'll take her," he said gruffly.

He got behind the wheel and gunned the big truck out of the parking lot.

The motor screamed.

* * *

The jalopy stopped at the Consolidated gate. A guard came out of the booth and looked at Johnny and Abe.

"We're from the Federation of Interstate Truckers," Johnny said. "We wanna talk to the men."

The guard grinned. "Just a minute." He walked into the booth and picked up the telephone. Johnny and Abe watched him closely from the car. The guard hung up and walked back to them slowly, still grinning.

"You gotta leave the car here," he said.

"Is it still gonna be here when we get back?" Abe grinned.

"Sure," the guard smiled. "I'll keep an eye on it for you."

"Thanks," Johnny said. "That's real nice of you."

As they walked into the lot, they noticed they were being followed by two men. They approached the truck dock and saw the truckers watching them nervously.

"I'm Johnny Kovak," he said to one of them. "I'm with the Federation of Interstate Truckers and I wanna talk to you about—"

"Not interested," the trucker said, looking away from him.

"Listen," Johnny said, "I just wanna talk to you a coupla minutes."

"Didn't you hear me?" the trucker said, his voice loud now. "I said I ain't interested."

Johnny turned from him to another man.

"I'm Johnny Kovak. This is Abe Belkin. We're with the Federation of—"

"Give me a break, will you?" the trucker said. He was trembling. He kept looking around.

"I thought we'd talk about the pay you're gettin'," Johnny said.

"I'm a member," the trucker said, whispering. He kept glancing at the two men who were following Johnny and Abe. "I pay my dues. Just leave me alone, will you?"

Johnny looked back at the two men following them.

"Monahan's a friend of mine," the trucker said. "Come on. I don't need no trouble."

Johnny hesitated.

"Please," the trucker said.

Johnny and Abe looked at each other, then turned disgustedly from the truck dock and walked back across the lot to the gate. The two men were still following them. When they got to the gate, the guard opened it for them.

He slammed the gate shut behind them and it was then that they saw that one of the jalopy's tires was flat. Johnny wheeled in fury on the guard. "You bastards!" he cried.

"Somethin' wrong with the car?" the guard said. He was grinning.

"Come on, Johnny," Abe said, "let's get the hell outa here."

Johnny looked at the jalopy. At the guard smiling at them. At the drivers watching them from the dock.

"We gotta fix the tire, Abe," he said.

He got down on the ground and when he was finished, he was dirty from head to toe. His old man's blue suit was ruined.

He yelled to the men in the truck dock, "See you guys!"

A few of them waved at him good-naturedly.

Inside the jalopy, he laughed.

"I'm glad somethin's funny," Abe said.

"Abe, old buddy," Johnny said, "I got a big idea."

A few days later, they pulled the jalopy up behind the truck, which was parked at the side of the road.

""I don't know," Abe said. "This better work better'n goin' to the docks."

"Well, we ain't gonna get any flat tires," Johnny said, "that's for sure."

They got out of the jalopy and Johnny walked to the driver's side of the truck jauntily, Abe a few steps behind him.

"Anybody home?" Johnny grinned. He put his hand on the door. A lead pipe smashed down on the door and missed his hand by inches. Both of them jumped back.

"Jesus Christ!" Johnny said.

"Get the hell away from my rig!" a voice inside the cab said. They saw him now. He was in his mid-forties, red-faced and sleepy, a cap pulled low over his eyes.

"Listen, we're with the union," Johnny said.

"Bullshit you are."

"We're signin' up members," Abe said.

"Last time somebody knocked on my door," the man said, "they took my whole load."

"We got cards," Abe said.

He held up a card. The man snatched the card suspiciously out of the air, the lead pipe still in his hand.

He laughed. "Okay, you're from the union," he said. "Now get the hell outa here."

Abe said, "Don't you wanna do somethin' about what the companies are doin' to the drivers?"

The man laughed again. "What'd you say your name was?"

"Abe. Abe Belkin."

"Abie," he said. "I shoulda known. Now listen here, Abie. Monahan's been tryin' to get me signed up for years and he ain't got no place. You can't do me no good. Your union can't do no good. And that rummy president of yours, Matt Rafferty, I know sure as shit he can't do me no good. So get the fuck outa here and let me get some sleep."

"If you sign up for the union," Johnny said, "they can't fuck you that bad."

"Upside down they can fuck you," the man said. "And start all over again."

"If everybody signs up," Johnny said, "they can't fuck you at all."

"Yeah?" the man said. "I'll sign up when everybody's signed up. How's that?" He grinned.

"But we can give you more clout with the company," Johnny said.

The man laughed. "You two jokers?"

"The union."

The man looked at him knowingly. "You sure you and Abie here just don't wanna collect dues?"

"The dues aren't much," Abe said, "considerin' how we could help you."

The man laughed again. "Will you get outa here?" he said. "You're worse than a travelin' salesman."

"You don't have to pay no dues," Johnny said. Abe looked at him quizzically.

"What was that again?" the man said.

"I don't give a shit when you pay 'em," Johnny said. "How about this—you don't have to pay no dues till we do somethin' for you."

The man considered it a moment, then said, "Bullshit. I still gotta pay 'em sometime." He smiled. "I bet you thought you had me there, smart guy."

"What the hell do you want, for Christ's sake?" Johnny said loudly.

"I told you what the hell I want," the man shouted back at him. "I want you to get outa here."

"All right, fuck you," Johnny said angrily. "You wanna end up like Joe Harper, go on. Let's go, Abe."

They turned and started walking away.

"Wait a minute," the man called after them.

They walked back to him.

"I ain't gotta pay no dues?" the man said.

"I told you," Johnny said.

"I ain't gotta sign nothin'?"

"Nothin'. We got a meeting Friday. Eight o'clock, St. Stephen's basement. Just show up."

"What the hell's your name, anyway?" the man said.

"Johnny Kovak," he said, grinning. "What the hell's yours?"

"Higgins. Tom Higgins. Hell, everybody knows me." He paused. "But I ain't signin' nothin'."

"See you Friday, Tom," Johnny grinned.

Inside the jalopy, Abe said, "Who's Joe Harper?"

Johnny smiled. "Joe Harper's the best friend we got."

The St. Stephen's basement was a cramped, boxlike place with a low ceiling, few windows, and walls badly in need of repainting. Behind a table at the front of the claustrophobic room sat Monahan and Abe, both wearing old suits. On the table were a gavel, a pitcher filled with water, and water glasses. Draped over it was a banner that said, "Federation of Interstate Truckers, Local 302."

A hundred and fifty men sat stiffly in front of the table on folding wooden chairs. They smoked and fidgeted and called out to each other.

"We gonna sit here all night?" Higgins blustered impatiently from the front row.

"Where's Johnny?" Monahan whispered to Abe.

"I don't know. He said he hadda talk to somebody."

"He picked a terrific time," Monahan said. "He's twenty minutes late."

"I ain't been in a church twenty years," Higgins said loudly. "This is worse than goin' to mass." Some of the men laughed.

Monahan shook his head, swore, got up, and banged his gavel.

"You guys know I'm no speaker," Monahan faltered.

"Yeah, we know that all right," Higgins yelled. The men laughed.

"We called you together here tonight," Monahan said, "so alla you could hear Johnny Kovak, our new organizer. He oughta be here any minute now."

"And I oughta go home any minute now," Higgins shouted. The men laughed again.

"But I guess I might as well say a few words," Monahan said distastefully.

"Get 'em out already!" Higgins cried.

Monahan smiled lamely. "I'm tryin', Tom." The men laughed again.

"You guys know the federation's been around a while," Monahan said. "I don't have to tell you that. But I wanna tell you that it's never been needed as much as now. Cause the companies are puttin' it to us like they never did before. And the only thing we got to hold 'em off is by gettin' together. So that when they pick on one of us they're pickin' on alla us. That's what a union's all about. That's what our national president, Matt Rafferty—"

"Come on, Mike," Higgins blustered. "For the love for Christ."

"That's what Matt's been tryin' to get across all these years," Monahan said.

"He's been drunk for most of 'em," Higgins shouted. The men laughed.

"I wouldn't say that, Tom," Monahan said over

their laughter. "Every man likes a few now and then." The men laughed harder.

At the back of the hall, the door opened loudly. The men turned. Wearing his battered leather jacket, Johnny was supporting a weak and shriveled man who walked with great pain. The men quieted down as Johnny walked the sick man to the front table. The men smiled at the emaciated man but kept staring at his condition.

"Well, now that Johnny's here," Monahan said with great relief, "he'll just go on for me."

Johnny took his jacket off, rolled up the sleeves of his faded workshirt, and looked at the men. The room was quiet.

"I'm not gonna give you guys any goddamn sermons," Johnny said. "I'm not gonna bullshit you. You guys know your problems a helluva lot better than me. You wanna sign up for the union, okay. I'm not gonna twist your arm."

He paused nervously. He didn't know how to continue. The men watched him closely, assessingly.

"You guys know Joe Harper," Johnny said. He looked at Harper. Harper kept his eyes to the floor.

"Well, Joe Harper was one of the first guys in this union. He's been comin' to meetings more than twenty years. Mike and Joe used to drive together."

Monahan put his arm around Harper at the speaker's table. The men watched them.

"Joe's sick," Johnny said, "cause all his life he busted his ass runnin' from one place to another to feed his family. The only shit the company ever gave about

166

Joe was to bust his ass more and more. Till Joe busted up his kidneys. Then the company stopped givin' any shit at all. Joe's through. As far as the company goes, Joe's a dead man."

Johnny paused. No one in the room said anything. No one moved.

"But I wanna tell you guys," Johnny said, louder now, his eyes flashing. "As far as this union's concerned, Joe's no dead man. We're payin' Joe's doctor bills. We're takin' care of his family. Cause Joe Harper's been a union man all these years and goddamnit— *goddamnit!*—we're gonna take care of him and the people he loves."

Harper nodded. His eyes were glazed. Monahan kept his arm around him.

"And I wanna tell you somethin' else," Johnny said. "If you guys sign up and join this union and if other guys like you sign up for the union, then we can make the companies give a shit about your kidneys. We can get you money for the doctors and overtime and you won't have to kill yourself makin' a buck." He paused, then in a softer voice, he said, "Like my old man did."

"You sign up," he said, "and you make this union tough and we'll make you tough." His voice was hard and steel-edged. "I promise you that! No goddamn company bastard livin' up in the Heights is gonna fuck over your life! I promise you that!"

He stopped abruptly, looked at the men defiantly, then turned suddenly away. "Come on, Joe," he said, "let's go home."

He put his jacket back on, helped Harper up, and

walked him across the hall to the door. The men watched them quietly as they left.

Then Higgins got up sheepishly and walked up to Mike Monahan.

"Count me in, Mike," Higgins said. His voice was a whisper.

The other men started lining up behind him.

Two weeks later, more than three hundred men had signed up to be members of Local 302. Johnny and Abe were out on the road sixteen hours a day.

Johnny sat in his office one night, exhausted, his shoeless feet on his desk, when the door opened. The man was expertly tailored, tall and silver-haired, in his early fifties. He smiled. It was a thin smile.

"Mr. Kovak?"

Johnny nodded, kept his feet on the desk, and didn't move.

"I'm Arthur St. Clair, Mr. Kovak," the man said. "I'm the general counsel for Talbot's Consolidated."

"I know who you are," Johnny said. His voice was flat.

St. Clair smiled. "May I sit down?"

Johnny shrugged. "You climbed the stairs, pal."

"So I did," St. Clair said. He sat down across the desk, and looked at Johnny. He was sizing him up.

"It occurs to me, Mr. Kovak," he said, smiling, "that we have some concerns in common."

Johnny grinned. "Yeah?"

"In different ways," St. Clair said, "we are both

concerned about truckers. You for the union"—he paused—"and your commission, of course."

"Course. Course," Johnny smiled.

"And I—I'm concerned for the company and our profits—of course."

"Your profits," Johnny smiled. "Sure. That makes sense."

St. Clair returned his smile. "Now it's been brought to my attention, Mr. Kovak, that you have a special talent for—uh, communication—with drivers. I'd like to put that talent to work."

"How you plan on doin' that?" Johnny said.

"By hiring you to work for us," St. Clair said.

Johnny laughed.

"Think seriously about it, Mr. Kovak," St. Clair said. "Think of the good you can do inside the company helping our drivers."

"You think I could really help 'em?" Johnny smiled.

"I'm sure you could," St. Clair said. "A man with your talents."

"What about the union, though?" Johnny said. "What's gonna happen to that?"

St. Clair smiled. "Well, your associate, what's his name? Mr. Belkin, he could carry on for you, couldn't he?"

"Sure, Abe," Johnny grinned. "Why didn't I think of that?"

"Salary, of course, is no problem," St. Clair said. "We'd be happy to double whatever you're making."

"Not bad," Johnny said, "not bad."

St. Clair said, "It's very fair, I think."

Johnny got up, walked to the window of his little office, and looked down at the fleet of Consolidated trucks.

"You know somethin', St. Clair?" he said. "The first day I moved in here, I knew then that if I did my job, the day'd come when you'd climb the stairs."

St. Clair smiled wryly.

"I knew then what I'd say to you when you got up here."

St. Clair looked at him curiously. Johnny smiled, leaned very close to his face, and almost whispered.

"Get the fuck outa my office!"

St. Clair blinked with the words, stared at him silently a moment, then smiled.

"As you get older, Kovak," St. Clair said, "you'll find civility can be learned." He paused. "Sometimes even taught." He got up and went to the door. "When you change your mind," St. Clair said, "give me a call."

Johnny watched her from a distance. Sheriff's deputies were piling an old woman's furniture onto the tenement sidewalk. The old woman, who wore a black dress and a black babushka, was sobbing. Anna was trying to comfort her in a language he couldn't understand.

When one of the deputies passed her, Anna stopped him. "You're real proud of yourself, ain't you?" she said.

"It's my job, lady," the deputy said.

"Putting her into the street," Anna said. "She's eighty-six years old. She can't even speak English."

"It's a court order, lady," the deputy said. "She didn't pay the rent. Here, the judge signed it, see? It's the law."

"The landlord's law," Anna said.

Johnny walked up to her. "Hey, Anna."

"What do *you* want?" she said. Her eyes were brimming with tears.

"You're cryin'."

"I am not," she said.

"You are so."

"Well," she said, "don't you ever cry?"

Johnny smiled. "Naw, I just get into fights."

She looked at him.

"It's better than cryin'," he said.

She wiped the tears from her eyes.

"Hey, Anna," he said gently. "let me buy you a—"

"I don't drink beer. I told you."

"Naw. Coffee. A cup of coffee."

She was hesitant.

"At the Penny Pantry," he said, "round the corner. Where all the rich people eat."

The deputies were driving away. The old woman was being led down the street by someone. Her furniture was piled high on the sidewalk. Anna watched the old woman walk slowly away.

"Those bastards!" she said.

She looked like she was going to cry again. Johnny didn't know what to say.

"Let me ask you a personal question," he said formally. She looked at him, surprised at his tone.

"Do you always swear?" he said.

For the first time, she smiled at him.

"Come on," Johnny said, "one cup of coffee."

She nodded slowly. He grinned and took her arm. She quickly and forcefully yanked the arm away and stepped away from him. He laughed.

"Okay, okay," he said. He stuck his hands into his pockets dramatically. "No hands. See?"

At the Penny Pantry, they sat across from each other over a little table, drinking coffee. She volunteered nothing, eyed him suspiciously, but answered his questions. She was nineteen years old. She lived in another part of the Flats, in a Lithuanian neighborhood, with her mother, who was a seamstress. Her father died when she was four years old, on the ship that brought them over from the old country. She asked him nothing about himself except where he worked. Johnny told her about Monahan and the union. He kept ordering cups of coffee. He didn't want this conversation to end. He wanted to keep looking into those big green eyes.

"That's what we're tryin' to do with the godda—with the union," he said. "To make sure that guys can't be—you know—can't be screwed over by those—those bastards—anymore."

"It must feel good doin' your work," Anna said.

"Yeah. Course, I'm just learnin' about it yet." He paused. She looked at the clock on the wall.

"Listen," he said, his words hurried. "How about if we go to a show sometime?"

She smiled. "At the dime store," she said, "we had two girls that tried a union there. They threw 'em out."

"They got Ginger Rogers in that show on Detroit Avenue," he said.

"The girls couldn't get jobs anymore after that," she said.

He looked at her. "But, see," he said, "you get everybody together. Hundreds of guys. Thousands of guys. They can't do that no more."

She glanced at the clock again.

"You look a little like Ginger Rogers," he said, "you know that?"

"I do not," she said. "Nobody ever told me that before."

He grinned. "How about Saturday night? I'll pick you up."

"I've got plans," she said loftily.

"Sunday night."

"I've got plans."

He laughed. "You sure got a lotta plans."

"You always push people?" she said.

He grinned. "When I really want somethin'."

"It's not polite."

"Next Saturday," he said.

She shook her head.

"Okay," he grinned. "The Saturday after that."

She smiled.

173

"Come on, Anna."

She lowered her eyes to the table, then lifted them. She was thinking about it. She looked at him seriously.

"No hands?" she said.

"A statue," he said.

"I'll bet."

He leaned closer to her over the little table, laughing.

"You know you got pretty eyes, Anna?"

She moved back from him. "I'll bring 'em," she said.

Johnny was walking out of Myrtle's one night when a trucker he had never seen before said, "Hey, Kovak. The guy in the rig over there. He wants to sign you up."

Johnny walked over to the truck, which was parked at the far edge of the lot.

"Hey, you wanna sign up?" he said.

"You Kovak?" a man in the cab said.

"That's me," Johnny smiled.

Then a voice behind him said, "Yeah, we all wanna sign up."

There were three of them. All of them had tire irons in their hands.

"Well, come on," one of them said to him, "aren't you gonna sign us up?" He laughed in a high, thin falsetto which was almost a giggle. He was a hawk-faced, pale man with blond hair and a jagged scar running down the right side of his face.

They moved toward him. Johnny stepped back from them to the cab door, but the door was suddenly slammed into his back. Knocked forward, he went down on the gravel. The man with the scar kicked him in the chest. He reeled back and was kicked again. One of them stood over him with a tire iron and swung it at the back of his head. It was a glancing blow which knocked him semiconscious. They lifted him up into the back of the truck and threw him over the seat. They took turns hitting him with their fists.

"We want you to remember this, Kovak," the one with the scar said.

Three of them held him down and the one with the scar lifted his knee into his groin. And then he did it again and again. He could hear the man's thin laughter until the moment he passed out.

When he got out of bed three days later, his right eye was black and the lower part of his body was riddled with pain.

"Telephone, Johnny," his mother said.

He walked painfully to his new telephone, which Mike Monahan was paying for.

"Arthur St. Clair, Kovak," the voice said. "I thought perhaps you had changed your mind."

He hurled the phone furiously against the kitchen wall. His mother stood there in shock. Johnny walked to the wall, bent down, the pain almost unbearable now, picked the pieces of the telephone up, and put them on the kitchen table. His mother watched him openmouthed.

He looked at her and slowly smiled.

"We need a new phone, ma," he said.

Matt Rafferty sat behind the speaker's table in the crowded church hall, a snowy-haired, cherubic, florid-faced man in his sixties wearing an expensive three-piece suit with a gold chain dangling across its vest. He listened amusedly as this new kid organizer with the black eye spoke to his men.

"It's no goddamn mystery who did it," Johnny said. "I'll tell you guys. If they pound the shit outa me and get away with it—then they can pound the shit outa you, Higgins, or Mike or anybody in here."

"Not me, Johnny," Higgins said. "I got my iron."

The men laughed nervously, then became somber.

"So maybe we oughta think real hard about that," Johnny said.

"Strike the bastards!" one of the men yelled.

There was a sudden, overwhelming silence.

"Strike my ass," Higgins mumbled.

Matt Rafferty smiled. No one said anything.

"I guess I got nothin' else to say," Johnny said.

He sat down next to Abe behind the speaker's table and Monahan got up.

"Well," Monahan said. "We got here today from Flint, Michigan, a man all of you know or heard about, a man who's a real livin' legend in the union movement—"

Higgins couldn't restrain himself. "It's Henry Ford!" he shouted.

The men laughed. Matt Rafferty laughed with them.

"Aw, the hell with this," Monahan said. "Matt Rafferty, the national president of the federation."

Matt Rafferty stood up and waved broadly as the men cheered him.

"Let 'er rip, Matt!" Higgins yelled.

The men kept cheering.

"All right, all right," Matt Rafferty laughed over the noise, "you're gonna turn your hands into sausage already."

The men laughed and Matt Rafferty reached for the gavel and pounded it several times.

"Thank you, Mike," Rafferty said. "I'm happy to be back here in Cleveland. It's always a pleasure to see old and good friends. Even if they are the biggest noisemakers God ever created."

The men laughed again.

"What I want to talk to you men about here today," Matt Rafferty said, "is something that I've been seeing everyplace I go—"

"Skirts!" Higgins yelled.

Rafferty looked at him and paused.

"If any of you real smart guys want to crack wise," Matt Rafferty said, "get the hell outa here and do it outside. This is a union meeting. I don't want to think the companies sent some of you in here to disrupt it."

The men quieted down. Rafferty savored the silence, then continued.

"That's better," he said. "What I want to talk to you about today is this business of Red Bolsheviki agitation. I've seen them in Pittsburgh, in Detroit, you've got them right here in Cleveland, trying to stir up good union men against the system of government all of us love."

"Let 'er rip, Matt!" Higgins yelled again.

Rafferty glanced at Higgins, at some of the men who were laughing at Higgins's defiance, then ignored him and continued.

"Now I know we've got problems with some of the companies now and then. But that's why we're here. That's why the federation's here. To iron those things out with your bosses. To get more into your pay. And, sure, to make sure the companies can still cut a profit. Because—we all know—the company stops makin' a profit, we stop makin' a profit."

Johnny nudged Abe. "I thought he was on our side."

"I'll tell you men something," Rafferty continued. "The one thing we always want to avoid is the strike. Everybody loses in a strike. The company loses. You lose. And you don't want to let any rabble-rouser on the come for his own self stir you into that. Now these Reds. They don't care about the company. And that means they don't care about you men, either. They just want to go into the street and hold marches. Give big speeches. Stir you up into losing your jobs."

Abe leaned closer to Johnny. "I know I ain't on his side."

"Now the other thing I have to talk to you men about," Matt Rafferty said, "is paying your dues on time."

The men moaned.

"Here we go," Johnny said.

"All right, all right," Rafferty said, "I know you don't like to hear it, but without your dues, this union can't exist."

"And with 'em, we can't exist!" Higgins shouted.

The men laughed.

"So it's very important that you don't—procrastinate," Rafferty said. "That when you get your pay you come right down here—"

"To the fuckin' church?" Higgins shouted.

The men laughed again.

"You know what I mean," Rafferty said. "To the federation office, pay your dues and get it out of the way and—"

The men catcalled and laughed. Johnny laughed with them. Rafferty noticed it and glanced at him sharply.

Zigi's Tavern was full and noisy. Rafferty sat at a table drinking straight bourbon, the shot glasses lined up around him. Johnny, Abe, and Mike Monahan sat with him.

"We by God've come a long way since then, Mike, haven't we?" Rafferty said, downing a shot. "The holes in the road back then, the dust, the ice. Yes, sir, those were the good old days. Yes, sir, they were."

"I'll be right back," Johnny said.

He walked across the crowded tavern and saw Mishka and some of his friends drinking at a table.

"Get over here, you!" Mishka roared. "Don't you come see your friends?"

Johnny was watching the sexy, red-headed waitress. "I wanna buy Mis a drink," he told her.

"Big shot," Mishka laughed. "Won't even drink with us." He shouted after him. "I seen you when you got diapers on, Johnny."

Rafferty kept watching Johnny from his table.

"Every bohunk in here know him?" Rafferty said.

"Johnny?" Abe laughed. "Everybody likes Johnny."

Rafferty looked at Abe, glowered, and didn't say anything.

On the other side of the tavern, Johnny caught up with the waitress.

"Hey, Molly," he said.

"How'd you know my name?" she said.

"Never mind," he grinned. "He wants to go out with you."

"Who?"

Johnny grinned. "The *gentleman* you like. His name's Abe."

She walked haughtily away. Johnny laughed, went back to his table, and sat down.

"Christ," Rafferty was saying to Monahan, "One time, outside of where-the-hell-was-it, Mike? Fort Wayne?"

"Her name's Molly," Johnny whispered to Abe. "She wants to go out with you."

"She don't even know my name," Abe said shyly.

"She does so, she told me."

Abe looked at her across the tavern.

"If you don't," Johnny laughed, "then I will."

Abe laughed.

"Couldn't fix the damn truck," Rafferty was saying to Monahan. "Near froze to death."

He glanced at Johnny and Abe and saw them whispering to each other.

"You're not a driver, are you, Kovak?" Rafferty said.

Johnny turned to him. "Huh?"

"I said—you're not a driver, are you?"

"Yeah," Johnny said. "I drove some with Mike."

Monahan laughed. "You shoulda seen Johnny out there, Matt. Hammerin' down on her like—"

"I bet you did," Rafferty said harshly, his eye on Johnny. "Joy-drivin' around. Never worked at it, did you?"

"Not at drivin'," Johnny said evenly. "Not at that."

"Didn't think so," Rafferty said. "Talk a pretty hotheaded game, though, don't you?" He laughed at him. "You never even drove. You don't even know what you're talkin' about, do you?"

Johnny glared at him.

"Matt," Monahan said pleadingly. "Get offa this. Since Johnny come in, we've grown, Matt. We've tripled the men. We've—"

"You get a black eye," Rafferty said to Johnny, "you start talkin' strike right away. You want these poor sonsabitches to lose their jobs?"

"What the fuck do you wanna do?" Johnny said angrily. "You wanna go in and crawl. Beg 'em to listen to you?"

"You don't fool me," Rafferty said. "I've seen a

dozen ambitious guys like you. Stirrin' the men up. Grandstanding. Gettin' 'em signed up. Puttin' money in your mattress."

"Goddamnit!" Johnny said. His face was flushed.

"Pretty soon the company comes along," Rafferty said, "and offers you somethin'. You take. All you punks take. More money in your goddamn mattress."

Johnny leaped up and grabbed Rafferty by his lapels. He pulled him over the table. The bar hushed. Johnny held onto Rafferty and pushed his face next to his.

"I don't take nothin'!" he said.

He released the red-faced old man suddenly, turned, grabbed his jacket, and walked out of the tavern without saying anything. Rafferty reached for a shot glass.

Abe got up from the table. "I gotta go, Mike." We'll have another beer."

Abe walked away from the table and on his way to the door bumped into the waitress.

"Gees, I'm sorry," he said. He paused. "Molly."

She smiled. "It didn't hurt . . . Abe."

He laughed, looked at her, and hesitated.

"I was thinkin'," he said haltingly. "Maybe sometime—"

"I'm off Saturday," she smiled.

In the executive conference room on the eighth floor of the Talbot building overlooking Public Square, Winthrop Talbot carefully lighted his cigar and blew the white smoke to the ceiling. He was sixty-three years old, a lean, ramrod-straight man with chiseled features who wore a checked heavy tweed suit.

The room mirrored his rugged masculinity. Leather chairs, a massive oak table, framed photographs on the wall showing Winthrop Talbot hunting, Winthrop Talbot playing polo, Winthrop Talbot in uniform, his arm around Teddy Roosevelt's shoulders.

Around the table sat his son, Phillip, thirty-two years old, the vice-president of Talbot's Consolidated Trucking Company, who shared his father's penchant for tweed as well as his leanness; Arthur St. Clair, the company counsel; and Russell Fitzpatrick, the company treasurer, an owlish, deaconlike man.

Winthrop Talbot puffed on his cigar and grinned.

"I should do what John D. did," he said. "Walk about the universe handing out dimes. Eh, Phillip? Then we wouldn't have these problems."

"I don't think so, dad," Phillip Talbot laughed.

"Seriously now, Arthur," Winthrop Talbot turned to St. Clair. "What exactly is all this union business leading up to?"

"I'm not sure, Win," St. Clair said. "But I don't much like the signs. They've signed up—rough guess —about sixty percent of our drivers. That's after years of no real activity. Is that about right, Russ?"

"Correct," Fitzpatrick said. "To the best of my calculations. In my discussions with some of the other companies, they seem to be having the same rate of success in those places."

"They filled up some church basement the last meeting they had," Phillip Talbot said.

"But are they actually doing anything?" Winthrop Talbot asked. "Besides collecting dues, Arthur?" He smiled at the men around the table. "Getting rich?"

"This Kovak is giving us the most trouble," St. Clair said. "The drivers seem to like him."

"Why can't we hire him then?" Winthrop Talbot said.

St. Clair had a wry smile on his face. "I've tried," he said. "But he won't listen."

Winthrop Talbot seemed incredulous. "Is he one of these anarchists?"

"No," St. Clair said, "not as far as we've been able to tell. He's held a succession of small jobs. He's been unsuccessful at all of them. His father died recently."

"Did he?" Winthrop Talbot said. "Well, I'm sure his family needs money then. Offer him more money."

"He refuses to listen," St. Clair said. "We even tried to convince him."

"Oh?" Winthrop Talbot smiled. "And?"

"And he still refuses to listen."

"Perhaps," Winthrop Talbot said, "you weren't persuasive enough."

"At their last meeting," Fitzpatrick said, "the word 'strike' was used."

"Strike?" Winthrop Talbot said. He got up from the table and walked to the window, his back to the men.

"Well," he said. "We certainly don't want any damned strike occurring here."

He walked back to the table and puffed on his cigar.

"You can convince him, Art," he said. He smiled. "I know these foreigners down in the Flats. They're good, simple people. They love to laugh and have a fine time. Marvelous musicians, you know. I like many of them. No real fiber, though. Sooner or later, this fellow will listen to us."

A radio in the living room crackled "I Can't Give You Anything but Love, Baby," and Johnny stood in front of the cracked bathroom mirror humming along with it, preening. His hair was slicked with grease. He wore a new, secondhand suit he had bought yesterday at the Volunteers, along with his new, secondhand ten-cent tie. He adjusted the tie, ran the comb through his usually unruly hair—saw that a single strand was still out of place, and smoothed it. He looked himself in the eye, turned to profile, and tried to peer his eyes around to see himself. He laughed.

The phone rang in the kitchen. "Johnny," his mother said, "Abe."

He took the phone, saw his mother glance at him, and noticed that she was staying in the room, trying to overhear his conversation.

"The car, Abe?" he said, watching his mother, grinning. "Tonight? I can't do that, Abe. I got a date. Never the hell mind with who." He noticed his mother's rising interest. "Yeah?" he said. "I told you she wanted to go out with you. I was startin' to worry about you, Abe, you know that?"

He glanced at his mother. "Thought you'd hurt it

somehow, Abe, you know what I mean? Pullin' on it all the time." Ilona Kovak blushed and, flustered, left the room hurriedly. Johnny laughed and hung up.

He reached into a cupboard, pulled down an old bottle of wine, tilted it to his lips, and took a big slug.

His mother walked back into the room, saw the wine bottle in his hand, looked at him, and said, "Valentino!"

He grinned. "Gotta go, ma."

"You no eat?"

"I'll eat later, ma."

"You should eat, Johnny. No drink."

He laughed, grabbed his suit coat, which was draped over a chair, and started walking away.

His mother said, "A nice Hungarian girl, Johnny?"

He looked at her and smiled. "She's colored, ma. *Fekete, Korom fekete.*"

She shook her head and looked away impatiently and he suddenly rushed to her, laughing, twirling her around, and kissed her in a flurry.

"You oughta see her, ma," he laughed. "Prettiest colored girl you ever saw."

"Ah, you!" she said.

He laughed, reached for the wine bottle again, and finished what was in it.

He drove the jalopy down the narrow residential street, craning over, looking for her address. It was warm, an early evening in spring, and the street teemed with activity. Children played hopscotch. Women gossiped on their stoops. Men puffed corncob pipes on their porches.

Johnny was uncomfortable in his new suit. The tie choked him. His hair felt like warm glop on top of his head. He found Anna's house finally but couldn't park the jalopy in front of it. Two doors down he found a spot, thought about putting his suit coat on, then said the hell with it and left it in the car.

When he got out of the jalopy, he felt the whole street watching him. A fat, drooping-moustached man in an undershirt was playing an accordion on a second-story porch. But he stopped playing when he saw Johnny getting out of the car and waved excitedly to his wife, who came running out to the porch.

Conscious of all these eyes, of all these amused smiles, Johnny walked to the house. Out of the corner of his eye, he saw that the accordionist and his wife were leaning over their porch watching him.

Johnny knocked on the door. There was no answer. He knocked louder. Still no answer.

He could hear the accordionist laughing.

He could feel the sweat soaking through his shirt.

He was ready to pound his fist on it when Anna opened the door.

"Jesus Christ, Anna," he said. "We've got a date. I've been waitin'."

She looked at him, her green eyes darkening.

"We don't have no date!" she said.

She slammed the door in his face.

He stood there dumbfounded. He didn't know what to do. He could hear the accordionist's horselaugh. It seemed like the whole street was laughing at him.

He stomped angrily back to the car and slammed the door.

The accordionist started playing again.

The jalopy roared off.

Abe walked down the street with Molly, laughing with her, kidding her. It was dark now and the streets of the Flats were filled with people out for a Saturday night walk. Molly was just telling him how she always had to be ready for anything in a tavern filled with hard-drinking men when Abe saw the jalopy stop suddenly in the middle of the street.

Johnny jumped out of the car. His shirt was sweated through. His tie was unbuttoned. His suit coat was wrinkled and thrown over his shoulder. Johnny ran over to them. The jalopy was still in the middle of the street, its motor running.

Molly and Abe were flabbergasted. "Johnny," Abe finally said, "what are you doin'—"

"Take the damn car!" Johnny yelled.

The people on the street stopped and stared at them.

"What's the matter with you?" Abe said. "Where's your date?"

Johnny stalked away from him and shouted, "Just take the damn car, will you, Abe?"

They stared after him, stunned, as he disappeared

down the street, then looked at the jalopy in the middle of the street, its motor running.

"Jesus!" Abe laughed.

They got into the car and after a while Molly said, "Is he always like that?"

"That's just his way," Abe said.

"Is he your best friend?"

Abe laughed. "Johnny? He's my brother."

Molly didn't say anything for a moment.

"There's something about him," she said haltingly. "He looks at me like—"

"Aw, you're pretty, that's all," Abe said.

Molly didn't say anything.

"Hell, you're beautiful."

She smiled.

"You're gorgeous," Abe said.

"You're worse than him," Molly laughed.

They went to see *Young Man of Manhattan* and when Ginger Rogers said, "Cigarette me, big boy" and everyone in the theater laughed, Abe hesitantly put his arm around her. She noticed his hesitancy, grabbed his hand, pulled the arm completely around her, snuggled closer to him, and smiled.

He kissed her good-night outside her tenement apartment, looked at her seriously, and said, wary and shy, "Tomorrow night?"

She didn't say anything, watched him, amused.

"Tomorrow afternoon, maybe," he said, "we could go for a ride."

Molly laughed.

"Cigarette me, big boy," she said coyly.

They laughed and Abe kissed her again and then Molly said, "Tomorrow afternoon." She waved a last time at him and walked in the tenement door.

Abe skipped happily down the street toward the jalopy. It was late now and there were few people in the street and as he approached the car door he saw a man leaning against a car parked behind his. He was a hawk-faced, pale man with blond hair and jagged scar running down the right side of his face.

"Nice night, huh, Abe?" the man said. He laughed. The laugh sounded more like a high-pitched giggle.

Abe looked around and saw two other men behind him now.

"We'll give you a ride," the scar-faced man said. He laughed again.

The two men behind him grabbed Abe's arms and the man with the scar opened the back door of the car for him.

"After you, Abe," he said.

The man with the scar drove. Abe was hemmed in by the two in the back. The windows were shut tight. It was hot and they were all sweating. They stopped the car by the riverbed in the Flats and for a moment nothing happened and nothing was said. Then the one with the scar backhanded Abe viciously across the mouth and the two in the back hit him with their fists. The door was opened and he was dumped out onto the ground. He was kicked in the stomach and then they just stood there, laughing at him.

The one with the scar went back to the car, opened the trunk, took something out, and walked back. Abe watched him as he came closer. He saw what he was holding now. It was a three-foot long rubber hose. The scarface swung it and giggled again.

Dr. Rosen was a thin little man with a long and bushy black beard and as he hovered over Abe, who was lying on Johnny's bed, bandaged and semiconscious, Johnny and Mike Monahan watched him from the doorway.

The doctor came out of the room, shaking his head and angry, and Monahan said, "How bad is it, doc?"

"A rib, cracked maybe," the doctor said with a Yiddish accent. "His left leg, I don't know, maybe broke."

Johnny's mother, who had come in from the kitchen, heard this and crossed herself. "*Jezus, Maria,*" she said.

"Inside damage," the doctor said. "Maybe he will be lucky."

"Lucky?" Johnny smiled.

"He should be in the hospital," the doctor said.

"They'd call the cops, doc."

"So?" the doctor said. "The *polizei.*"

"The cops don't like us."

Dr. Rosen shook his head again and went to the door.

"How much, doc?"

"I come by, look tonight," the doctor said.

"Thanks, doc."

When the doctor had left the room, Ilona Kovak said, "I tell you. Don't make no trouble, Johnny."

"Ma, please."

"You see what happen," Ilona Kovak said. "Always trouble."

"Ma," he said, "please don't."

His mother left the room and Johnny slumped down in the living room across from Monahan. He said nothing a moment, then he dug a greeting card out of his pocket and handed it to Monahan.

The card said, "Best wishes for a speedy recovery." It was signed by Arthur St. Clair.

Monahan looked at the card and said, "Those bastards. Those filthy cocksucking bastards!"

"That ain't enough, Mike," Johnny said quietly.

Monahan looked at him questioningly.

"What are we gonna *do* about it, Mike?"

"We can't call the cops, Johnny."

"Cops? Who's talkin' about cops?"

Monahan said, "I don't understand."

"What are *we* gonna do about it?"

"What can *we* do, Johnny?" Monahan said. "We got no pull. They got the cops. They got the judges, they got—"

"No more kid games, Mike," Johnny said.

He picked the card up and looked at it.

"That sonofabitch," he said, his voice violent and low. "He's gonna eat this."

He looked at Monahan and crumpled the card in his fist.

There were so many men at the meeting that they were sitting on the floor and standing against the walls. Their voices were loud and angry.

"We can't just go runnin' out and strike," Higgins said. "Just like that. I mean, what Rafferty said—everybody gets the screw then. What the hell, Johnny? I didn't sign up here to lose my job." Higgins looked at the men. "Huh, did we?"

A few cheered him; others catcalled.

"Siddown, Higgins!" someone yelled.

"You company suck, Higgins!"

Higgins spun around in anger.

"You talkin' to me?" he said.

Johnny got up angrily. "Hold it now, goddamnit!" he yelled. "I said—hold it!".

The men quieted down and listened to him.

"Nobody calls nobody else a suck in here," Johnny said. "I told you guys when you signed up. You make the goddamn decisions. That's what we're doin'. Nobody start calling each other all kindsa names."

The men were very quiet now.

"Listen, Tom," Johnny said to Higgins. "Yeah. You're right. You didn't sign up to get the can. But you signed up so we can help you. So everybody who signed up can help the other guy, right?"

"Well, yeah," Higgins said. "That's right, I guess."

"Okay," Johnny said. "But all we been doin' so far is talkin'. And all you been doin' is comin' in here and lookin' at each other's faces. And all they been doin' is beatin' the shit outa us. Ain't that right?"

Higgins didn't say anything.

"Well, come on, Tom, how about it?"

"Yeah," Higgins said, "but that don't mean we oughta strike."

"No it don't," Johnny said. "But tell me somethin', Tom. We made anything better for you yet? They payin' your doctor's bills? Your kids' bills? They payin' you overtime? They payin' you any more'n when you signed up here? Huh?"

Higgins didn't say anything.

"Fuck no, they're not. And they ain't gonna, neither. Long as we sit around here on our ass."

"That's right, Johnny!" one of the men yelled.

"They ain't gonna," Johnny said, his voice hard and intense now, "less we push 'em."

A few of the men cheered.

"I don't want a strike no more'n you do, Tom," Johnny said. "But I don't wanna just keep talkin', either, while they keep bustin' us up. So what Mike and me are gonna do—we're gonna go in and talk to 'em. We're gonna go see Talbot. And if that don't work, I don't know. Then we'll see. How's that?"

The men cheered in approval.

"All right with you, Mike?" Johnny said.

"Fine with me, Johnny," Monahan said.

"You wanna take a vote?"

"All those in favor of Johnny and me goin' in," Monahan said, "get 'em up."

The men put their arms up into the air.

"All right," Monahan said, "that's it."

He banged his gavel and the men started to leave.

"Hey, Johnny," Higgins yelled challengingly.

The men looked at him. The room quieted. Higgins smiled.

"Don't take no shit from 'em, neither," he said.

* * *

Johnny waited for her one morning in the doorway of the dime store. He watched her walking down the street toward him. She was wearing a green dress the color of her eyes. Her long blond hair was blowing in the wind. When she saw him, she put her head down and tried to get by him into the dime store without even looking up. He blocked her way and grabbed her arm.

"Let go of me!" Anna said loudly.

"What'd you do it for?" he said.

"Lemme go." She tried to pull her arm away.

"Goddamn it!" he said, angry now, "just tell me why."

They had attracted a small group of interested and smiling onlookers.

"You were drunk," she said loudly.

"I was—what?"

"I smelled it on you."

"I wasn't drunk."

"Now you're lying," she said.

"Look, I wasn't drunk. I had some of my old man's wine. He made it."

"I don't go out with drunks," she said.

"I just had a little bit, Anna. It's for—special occasions. It was a goddamn special occasion, wasn't it?"

She looked at him and softened a bit. "The *gentlemen* who take me out—"

"Aw, shit!" he said.

"The *gentlemen* who take me out park the car and wear suit coats. Then they—"

195

"I had my goddamn suit coat," he said.

"You did not."

"It was in the car."

"Well," she said. "They don't leave 'em in the car."

"It was hot, Anna."

"They wear their suit coats and they knock on the door and they talk to my mother and—"

He laughed. "Your mother?" he said. "Your mother? What the hell can I talk to your mother about?"

She seemed stumped for a moment. Then she blurted, "The weather."

"The weather?" he cried.

"The weather."

"Jesus Christ, Anna," he said.

"And they wait for me in the living room. Then they walk me out to the car—"

Johnny looked at her, amazed.

"And open the door for me. Sometimes they even bring me flowers."

He stared at her in utter disbelief.

"Flowers?" he said.

"Flowers!"

She turned from him suddenly and went in the dime-store door.

He looked after her a moment and then he shouted, "You're nuts! You know that, Anna? Raving goddamn nuts!"

The chair at the head of the massive oak conference table on the eighth floor of the Talbot Building was empty. On one side of it sat Phillip Talbot, Arthur St. Clair, and Russell Fitzpatrick. Two empty chairs faced them on the other side of the table.

When Johnny and Mike Monahan walked into the room, Phillip Talbot got up and said, "My father should be here in a moment, gentlemen. I'm sorry for the delay. Please sit down."

He motioned them to the two empty chairs and Mike Monahan said, "That's all right, Mr. Talbot. We got the time. What the hell." He smiled nervously.

The three men returned the smile condescendingly and Johnny and Mike Monahan sat down in the empty chairs.

"What are we sittin' here for, Mike?" Johnny whispered to Monahan.

"What—what do you mean, Johnny?" Monahan said.

"If he's gonna sit over here, Mike," Johnny whispered, "at the head—then you oughta sit over there. At the other head."

"This is okay right here," Monahan said.

Johnny glared at him. "No, it ain't," he said.

He got up and took his chair and Monahan's to the other end of the table and placed Monahan at its head. The three men watched them in disbelief. Johnny sat down next to Monahan and grinned at them, a distance removed from them now across the table.

Winthrop Talbot walked into the room and said, "I'm sorry I'm late, gentlemen, these meetings—"

He looked at the table arrangement, saw Monahan and Johnny at the other end, and said, "Why don't you move down here? Perhaps we can hear each other better."

"Naw, this is fine," Johnny grinned. "Less you guys wanna come down here."

Winthrop Talbot smiled at him.

"Of course," he said. "Go ahead, Phillip, Russ."

Winthrop Talbot and the three men moved down to the other end of the table, leaving Monahan at its head. Johnny and Winthrop Talbot smiled at each other.

St. Clair said, "You know Mr. Monahan, Win, and this is Mr. Kovak."

"Chief organizer," Johnny said quickly.

"The chief organizer," St. Clair smiled.

"Well, Mr. Kovak," Winthrop Talbot smiled. "What is it that we can do for you?"

"Mike's the president," Johnny said. "He's gonna lay it out for you."

Winthrop Talbot smiled at Johnny and said, "Certainly. Mr. Monahan?"

"The thing of it is," Mike Monahan said fumblingly, "the men in our local are upset about some things— well, we wanted to talk 'em over with you."

"I'm always happy to discuss the men's problems," Winthrop Talbot said. "I like our men. I want them to be happy."

"There's the matter of insurance," Mike Monahan said. "Doctor's bills. The way the men see it, the company oughta be payin' the docs when any of the

198

guys gets hurt and maybe set up some kinda insurance plan for the wife and kids."

Winthrop Talbot looked at St. Clair. "How do we stand on that, Arthur?"

"Our policy is the same as that of the other companies," St. Clair said. "While we don't have our own insurance program, as you know, we have on occasion lent some of our men money—at the standard rates—for medical emergencies."

Fitzpatrick said, "Some of our men have personally expressed their appreciation to me."

Winthrop Talbot nodded approvingly.

Mike Monahan said, "I was thinkin', Mr. Talbot, not of you lendin' money but of payin' the bills."

"Well," Winthrop Talbot said. "Our policy, as Arthur said—"

Johnny interrupted him. He had a tight smile on his face. His voice was calm and low. He kept his eyes on Talbot's.

"We're gonna cut your balls off, pal, you know that, don't you?" Johnny said.

The room was suddenly very quiet.

"What did he say?" Talbot said to St. Clair.

St. Clair said, "I told you, Win."

"I said we're gonna cut your balls off," Johnny said again, louder now.

Winthrop Talbot looked at Johnny and said, slowly, "And what exactly do you mean by that—that crudity —Mr. Kovak?"

Johnny grinned. "I mean we're gonna shut your fuckin' company down."

Winthrop Talbot stared at him a moment and then said, "I see." He turned to Monahan. "What other—uh, areas, do you wish to discuss, Mr. Monahan?"

"Overtime. Pay raises," Johnny said.

"Is he speaking for you, Mr. Monahan?" Talbot said.

Monahan looked at Johnny nervously, then at Talbot, and said, "Johnny's our organizer, Mr. Talbot. He—"

"I see," Talbot said again.

He turned to Johnny.

"The answer is no, Mr. Kovak," he said, accentuating each word. "No insurance. No overtime. No pay raises."

Monahan seemed taken aback. Johnny grinned and got up from the table.

"Okay, Mike," he said, "let's go."

"Maybe we oughta talk some more, Johnny."

"We got his answer," Johnny said.

"There's no need to be hasty about anything," Phillip Talbot said.

Johnny looked at Winthrop Talbot and grinned. "It's your balls," Johnny said.

Winthrop Talbot looked at him, his blue eyes chunks of ice.

"We'll see whose—balls—it will be," Winthrop Talbot said.

"Yeah," Johnny said. "You're fuckin'-A right. We're gonna see."

*   *   *

This is my company, Winthrop Talbot considered, alone now in the half-light of dusk in his conference room. No one had ever told him how to conduct his business. He had worked long and hard and his father and grandfather had worked long and hard and he would permit no man, no horde of men, to undermine generations of ceaseless and single-minded effort.

It was understood from the beginning, naturally, that Winthrop Talbot would one day assume command of the family business and he had been groomed for it from an early age. He was exposed while young to those things which his station in life would demand knowledge of: the theater, the symphony, the dance—and, of course, to horses. Serious and somewhat withdrawn as a child, he applied himself to his assigned duties. He developed into a superb horseman and took long rides with his mother through their Clarion Hills estate.

Exposed early to tailored clothes and blooded stock and people, Winthrop Talbot took these things as a natural part of his life, as natural as it was to apply himself to the study of business and finance. He attended private schools, graduated with honors from Western Reserve University, spent a year working as the general manager of the Talbot Wagon and Carriage Company to learn the rudiments of the family business, then announced that he was seeking a commission in the horse cavalry and was commissioned a second lieutenant at the age of twenty-four.

Upon his return to Cleveland from the Spanish-

American War, where he took part in the Kettle Hill assault with Lieutenant Colonel Theodore Roosevelt, he was hailed as a hero. His father immediately named him vice-president of all Talbot enterprises. He had built up an increasingly complex web of companies, trusts, and interlocking partnerships and Winthrop Talbot devoted himself to long hours of financial study. An excellent staff man, he studied reports and statements and learned all aspects of the business.

He got married, had two children, built himself a separate house on the Clarion Hills estate, supervised construction of the Talbot Building on Public Square, and helped guide his father's business. And in 1918, when his father, having turned the Talbot Carriage Works into the Talbot Automotive Corporation, died of a stroke, Winthrop Talbot took over the business and followed his father's lifelong advice: "Move boldly." He announced that the Talbot Automotive Corporation would become the Talbot Trucking Company.

He had been influenced in his decision by a combination of elements. The first was an act of Congress: in 1916, a measure called the Federal Aid to Roads Act had been passed in Washington. It called for the expenditure of $75 million in state aid to build and improve roads throughout the country. The second element was an act of war. In 1917, France had ordered thousands of American-made trucks for the European war theater. Normally the trucks would have been loaded on flatbed railroad cars and transported east. Instead, the head of Woodrow Wilson's

Highway and Transportation Committee ordered that the trucks be driven to eastern seaports—filled with rifles, uniforms, and other war matériel.

Those big trucks, bumping and pitching eastward along rutted rural roads, told Winthrop Talbot that the railroads were dead.

His basic plan was simple. He undercut both rail freight rates and the rates of his trucking competitors. At the same time, he took pride in guaranteeing faster deliveries than anyone in the transportation business.

He proved to be a genius at scheduling and logistics. He spent long hours studying lines of colored ink on road maps, weighing the merits of primary roads with steep gradients against secondary roads which were flat. He studied city traffic patterns, night versus day hauling, and kept intricate records of all operations.

When General Tire introduced pneumatic tires, he was among the first to adopt them. He switched truck manufacturers with equal ease if he felt an advantage was to be derived: from Republics, one of the earliest trucks built for heavy hauling, to Diamond Ts, Whites, Macks, Fords, and Internationals. He was the first in line to buy new trucks with hydraulic cylinders which could lift the front end of the truck bed to dump a load of gravel or dirt in seconds. Winthrop Talbot was peering far down the road and he had made a decision to link his fortune with that of the future of American mobility.

Sensing correctly that there would be an explosion of road building for decades to come, he organized his business so he could take advantage not only of the new and better roads but also of the road building itself. His trucks hauled gravel, cinders, slag, and bricks. They carried away or brought in dirt, as the need demanded. They participated in the building of private roads and they worked under state and county contracts.

Once the roads were built, they were immediately used by Talbot trucks hauling food, groceries, steel, tires, lumber, finished goods, and raw materials. From a single terminal in Cleveland, Winthrop Talbot expanded the line outward in rays reaching to Akron, Canton, Youngstown, and Alliance. He made deals with other hauling and transfer companies, then gobbled them up. He built terminals, shaved turn-around times, bought fleets of small trucks to haul small shipments to and from his warehouse staging areas.

By 1927, Talbot trucks hauled more tonage than any other trucking firm in the Midwest. Talbot six-wheelers ran Route 8 from Cleveland to Akron; the Akron-bound trucks, loaded with oxygen tanks and cylinders or steel and iron products, passed Cleveland-bound trucks loaded with rubber goods. And while the state of Ohio load limit for trucks was twenty thousand pounds, rare was the driver who hurtled down the road with less than twenty-two. The same was true on the Detroit-Toledo-Cleveland run along Route 102 and U.S. 20, where Talbot trucks loaded with automobile bodies and parts tore up the macadam with unrestrained disregard.

With the advent of the Depression, Win Talbot's decision to change the nature of the family business from automotive bodies to truck transport seemed all the more prescient. By 1932, automobile sales had slid to 1.3 million from the 1929 figure of 5.3 million. Many old and solid automotive names had tumbled into bankruptcy or receivership: Locomobile, Moon, Kissel, Gardner, Jordan, Stearns. Even the Peerless Motor Company of Cleveland couldn't survive. It sold its assets and converted its facilities for the production of what it hoped would be a more salable and profitable commodity. Ale.

Winthrop Talbot knew that he would survive this Great Depression in prosperity and style, but as he talked to his friends at the Union Club, he grew to fear what they all spoke of in quiet but intense terms. The hordes of unemployed workers ready to be seduced by the agents of communism. Hordes which could mean the death of the free-enterprise system itself.

Goddamn Roosevelt, Winthrop Talbot thought, alone now in the encroaching darkness of his conference room. It was all Roosevelt's fault. Revolutions always began with multisyllabic, high-toned, and idealistic words. Then, sooner or later, someone walked into your office, smiled, and said he was going to cut your balls off.

The accordionist saw the jalopy turning into the street and immediately started laughing and calling for his wife. His wife ran out to the porch, saw the jalopy, laughed, and yelled something in Slavic over to the second-story porch next door.

By the time Johnny parked the car and got out, they were all out on their stoops and porches, tittering at him, waiting for the show to begin.

It was a warm, early summer night, the kind of night when the humidity in Cleveland is suffocating, but when Johnny got out of the car, he reached back inside and got his suit coat and put it on over his dripping wet shirt. He glanced up at the accordionist and saw the fat, moustached man panting at him in great merriment. Johnny reached back into the car then and clumsily, self-consciously, pulled out a bouquet of roses. The accordionist clapped.

Johnny held the bouquet gingerly, as if it were a bomb, and walked to Anna's porch. He looked around at the people in the street watching him, shifted the flowers nervously from hand to hand, and knocked. There was no answer. The accordionist started playing a slow and lugubrious melody. The people in the street laughed.

He knocked again. The door opened and a pleasant, middle-aged woman with glasses and a round face stood there looking at him.

He blinked, startled. "Hi, I'm Johnny Kovak. I'm lookin' for Anna's mother. I mean, I'm lookin' for Anna. I got a date with Anna."

She smiled. "I'm Mrs. Melsbakas," she said. "Come in."

He walked into the living room, holding the flowers clumsily.

"What beautiful roses," she said.

"Yeah, I got 'em for Anna." He held the bouquet out to her and said, "Here."

"Why don't you give them to Anna when she comes down?" she said.

He pulled the bouquet back suddenly. "Oh yeah. Sure."

He kept shifting the flowers from one hand to the other and she noticed his discomfort and, smiling, said, "Maybe we should put them in a vase."

"That'd be great," he said quickly. He almost flung the flowers into her arms.

She walked into another room with the flowers and yelled, "Anna, your friend is here."

"I'll be right down, mama," Anna said.

He sat on the couch in the living room. Sweating. Waiting. He started to unbutton his tie, then stopped and tightened it, making sure that it was on right.

Anna's mother came back with the flowers in a vase, saw him squirming on the couch and wiping his brow, and said, "Can I get you a lemonade?"

"A lemonade?" he said. "Uh—sure."

"Something stronger?" she smiled. "A glass of wine maybe, a cold beer?"

He hesitated, then said, trying not to grimace, "Naw. The lemonade's fine. Thanks."

She brought him the lemonade and sat down across

from him. He took the glass and gulped half of it. His hands shook slightly. He put the glass down and he and Anna's mother looked at each other.

"Gee," he said, eyeing her. "This heat's really somethin', huh?"

She smiled slightly. "The humidity from the lake, I think."

"Yeah. I like it when it gets cold. You can feel yourself breathe."

"This is one of the hottest spells we've had in years," she said.

He wiped his brow. "No shi—." He almost choked on it. Oh my God, he said to himself. Oh my God. He coughed and corrected himself. "No lie," he said.

Anna came bounding down the stairs wearing a thin summer dress which accentuated her figure.

"What have you two been talking about behind my back?" she said brightly. She saw the flowers. "Oh, what beautiful roses. Johnny, you shouldn't have."

"The weather," he said. "We been talkin' about the weather."

"The weather?" She smiled at him. Their eyes met.

"I love it when it's so nice and warm," Anna said. "Don't you, Johnny?"

He got up from the couch and said, "Yeah, it's great. You ready?"

"Johnny was just saying how much he likes the cold," her mother said, smiling.

"Uh, I like it both ways," he said. "When it's hot and cold."

They started walking out. He was almost pushing Anna out the door.

"Have fun," her mother said.

"I'll try, mama," she said, smiling.

He caught the crack and looked at her, then at her mother. "Thanks for the—lemonade and all," he said.

Her mother smiled. "It was nice meeting you."

"Yeah. Well, Bye."

On the porch, he stiffly offered Anna his arm. She took it and he walked her down to the car. The accordionist and his wife and the neighbors were all staring at them. Johnny opened the door for Anna, closed it, glanced up, and saw the accordionist laughing in his face.

He got into the car, turned to her, and said, "Okay?"

She smiled. "You can take your suit coat off, you know."

"Naw," he grinned. "I never go no place without it. I'm a *gentleman*, Anna."

He laughed, started the motor, put his left arm out the window, and saluted the accordionist as he pulled away.

With the upraised middle finger of his left hand.

Riding the Roller coaster at Luna Park, she screamed. He put his arm around her; she left it there. When they got off, laughing, dizzy, they stumbled into each other. He put his arm around her again, supporting her, but she brushed it off. He stopped, looked at her, then put his hand out and grinned. She smiled at him and took his hand.

At a gaudy penny arcade inside the amusement park, they watched a group of people around a machine. The machine was a toy boxing ring with two toy figures of boxers operated by levers. Johnny and Anna watched for a while and then Johnny turned to her and said, "You wanna fight?"

He grabbed a lever excitedly. She hesitated, looking around ladylike.

"Sissy," he said.

She grabbed the other lever. He plunked a penny into the machine and they manipulated their fighters. Johnny's lever didn't work. His fighter stood in one place. Anna's fighter threw a punch at him and knocked him out. A sign went up on the machine that said, "KO!"

"Who's the sissy?" she laughed.

He laughed and pulled her away toward another machine in the corner. Inside a glass case was a crane which stood over a large pile of penny treasures— miniature pocketknives, cars, cigarette lighters, "diamond" engagement rings. A sign atop it said, "Mountain of Gold." Johnny dropped a penny into the machine.

"The knife," he said, excitedly. "Get the knife."

The crane stuck to something and popped it into the slot. He reached in, grabbed it, and held it up. It was a "diamond" engagement ring.

"What the hell am I gonna do with this?" he said.

He looked at her and grinned.

"Oh, no!"

"You can give it to your mother or somethin'," he said.

He held the ring in midair. Their faces were close together, looking at it.

"Hey, Johnny," someone said.

They turned, still close together, the ring between them. Vince Doyle stood there with Jocko and two cheap-looking, heavily rouged women.

"You gettin' married, Johnny?" Vince Doyle grinned. He eyed the ring.

"It came outa the machine," Johnny said.

Vince Doyle looked at Anna appreciatively and said, "She come outa the machine, too?"

Anna flinched and looked away from him. Doyle laughed.

"Hear you're becomin' a regular labor leader, Johnny."

"We're up over three hundred men, Vince."

Doyle smiled. "They're gonna cream you, Johnny." The smile was still on his face. "You'll never know what hit you. Nobody says they're gonna slice that old man's nuts off. Not in this town."

"We got a lotta guys, Vince," he said, "tough guys—"

"Pigeons," Vince Doyle said, his tone harsh. "Beer hangin' off their bellies. That's what you got, Johnny."

Johnny stared at him and said nothing.

"I gotta go, kid," Vince Doyle said. He winked at Anna. "Bye, doll."

Vince Doyle and his friends walked away from

them and Johnny stood there in the penny arcade, his mood shattered. He realized that the ring was still in his hand.

He turned to Anna. "You want this?"

"Who are those people?" she said.

"You want it or don't you?"

"Are all your friends like—*that*?" she asked.

He turned on her harshly. "Yeah. All of 'em. So what."

She looked at him. He saw the fear in her eyes.

"Aw, come on," he said disgustedly, his voice broken. "I'll take you home."

In the sweltering hot church basement, the men were subdued and grim.

Johnny spoke to them, but without force, quietly. "I don't see what the hell else we can do. No insurance. No overtime. No pay raises." He paused. "What the hell we supposed to say? We back off now, we're never gonna get any of it." He paused again. "We're gonna be a bluff," he said, his voice almost a whisper.

He looked at the men a moment, then sat down. They were absolutely quiet; none of them cheered.

Monahan got up, looked at the men, and cleared his throat. He waited, not knowing what to say.

"We go out against Talbot," he said, "I know the way it's gonna be. I know the kinda clout they got." He paused. "But it's like bein' out on the road, passin', and a guy's comin' at you full bore, and what are you gonna do? You either hit the guy you're passin' or smash full into the guy comin' at you. It ain't any bet-ter'n that." He paused. "I know it." He stopped, looked down and cleared his throat again. "Now we got no place to go. Either we do this or we get licked. And maybe we're gonna get licked anyway."

Some of the men grinned.

"I'm gonna pass these papers back to you," Mona-han said. "Put down yes or no, whether you wanna strike or not." He looked at the men reflectively. "Me, I'm gonna vote yes. I been drivin' a lotta years. You get tired eatin' shit."

The men got their pieces of paper and marked them; they passed them back to Monahan and Johnny. They waited impatiently. The room billowed with clouds of smoke.

Johnny got up and looked at them.

"We're gonna strike," he said quietly.

For a moment there was stunned silence. Then a loud, thunderous cheer. Then, just as suddenly, the cheer died and the men stood there, looking at each other.

When Johnny got home that night, Abe was waiting for him in the living room. He was on crutches, hob-bling around.

"What happened?" Abe said urgently.

"What are you doin' up?" Johnny said.

"Come on, Johnny, what *happened?*"

"We're goin' out on strike," Johnny said quietly.

"We're goin' out?" Abe said, loud, excited. "Oh, Jesus, Johnny! We did it! We're gonna beat 'em! We did it, Johnny! We're gonna get the bastards! Jee-zus!"

He hobbled toward Johnny on his crutches and fell to the floor.

"You dumb shit," Johnny said, "what the hell's wrong with you? The doctor—"

Abe ignored him. He got up from the floor and continued. "We'll show 'em! They can't push the little guy around! Johnny, you're somethin'—boy! *You* did it, Johnny!"

Johnny turned away from him. "Yeah."

Abe looked at him. "What's the matter with you?"

"I don't know," Johnny said. He shook his head. "You think we're doin' the right thing?"

"What? *Hell, yeah!* We got somethin' good. Somethin' that can help guys that have never been helped before. It's worth it, Johnny."

Johnny looked at him. "I wonder what they'll pull."

"Listen," Abe said, "we'll take our lumps. What's new? We've been takin' 'em since we've been kids."

"That's for sure."

"With guys like me out there," Abe said, "we can't lose."

'We can't, huh?"

"You know how good I'm gettin' takin' a punch?"

"Primo Carnera," Johnny grinned. "Ain't you, Abe?"

"I'm the champ," Abe said. "I can take a punch better'n any guy you know."

Johnny faked a punch at him and laughed.

Early the next morning, a small dirt truck pulled up to the Talbot's Consolidated gate. Johnny, Monahan, Higgins, and some twenty of the men jumped down, signs in their hands. They milled about on the sidewalk. Uniformed guards with shotguns stood facing them on the other side of the gate. Johnny stuck a sign on the fence that said "F.I.S.T. Local 302 ON STRIKE."

A burly guard walked to the fence as Johnny put the sign up. He held his shotgun so it was only a few feet from Johnny's face. Johnny looked at the guard and grinned.

"I want Slim here," Johnny said, "to hear this so he'll know the rules. We're on strike! That means no trucks come in here, no trucks go out. This is the boundary!"

He smashed the fence with his fist. The guard, startled, stepped back. Johnny grinned at him.

"We don't go in there," Johnny said, "Slim and his girlfriends don't come out here. One more thing. Nobody does nothin' on his own. Nothin'. You got that?"

The men nodded, milling about.

"Hey, Johnny," Higgins said, "can I go take a leak?"

The men laughed.

Winthrop Talbot and St. Clair watched them picketing from the third floor of the Consolidated terminal.

"Are the police ready?" Winthrop Talbot said.

"They'll be arrested the minute they destroy any property," St. Clair said.

Talbot nodded and watched the picket line.

"What this country needs," he said slowly, "is Douglas MacArthur."

A truck came down the street heading for the Consolidated gate. Johnny and the men ran toward it. The guards flung the gate open and pointed their shotguns at the picketers. The driver stopped the truck in front of the gate.

"Get it in here, damn you!" one the guards yelled.

"It's Bailey," Monahan said.

"Bailey!?" Johnny said. "Bailey's signed up."

The men surrounded the truck, yelling. Johnny pulled himself up one side of the cab, Monahan the other. The driver, a ferret-faced little man, looked scared.

"What are you doin'?" Johnny said. "We took a vote!"

"I—I voted no, Johnny."

"You voted no? What do you mean you voted no? Jesus Christ, we voted to strike."

"Please," Bailey said to Monahan, "I gotta go in there. My wife—"

"Your wife!" Johnny yelled.

"The hell you do," Monahan said angrily. "Nobody goes in there."

He jumped down from the cab and stood in front of the truck, blocking it.

"You gotta go in there?" Monahan yelled. "Well, come on!"

Bailey hesitated, then put the truck into reverse and pulled away. The men cheered.

Behind the fence, the guards grouped together and withdrew inside the building. Johnny watched them.

"I wonder what they're doin'," he said to Monahan.

At the other end of the line, Higgins yelled out in pain and held his face. Johnny and Monahan ran to him and suddenly rocks and bolts started falling around them. Some of the other men were hit.

"The roof!" Monahan yelled.

A half dozen men stood on the Consolidated roof throwing rocks and bolts at them. The picketers picked the rocks up and hurled them back at the building. Windows broke.

"Stop it!" Johnny screamed. "It's a trap!"

Police cars and a police wagon swooped down on them as Johnny tried to calm them. The policemen leaped out, billyclubs in their hands, and headed for the picketers.

"Hold it, for Christ's sake!" Johnny yelled.

The men looked at the policemen and hesitated. Some of them had rocks in their hands. The policemen eyed them warily.

"Put 'em down!" Johnny yelled.

The men hesitated, the rocks still in their hands.

"That's what they want!"

The men threw their rocks to the ground slowly and waited for the policemen.

"We're gonna go for a ride," Johnny said, "that's all."

The policemen led them toward the wagon. One of them opened the back up and started herding them inside.

Monahan looked at the wagon and said, "All of us goin' in there?" A policeman pushed him inside.

Johnny waited at the end of the line. A boy stood there, watching them.

"Go up to the office, kid," Johnny said, "get Abe Belkin. Tell him to bring the bail."

The boy watched them being herded into the wagon and said, "How much?"

"Huh?"

"How much you gonna pay me?"

Johnny grinned. "A quarter."

"I want a dollar," the boy said.

"A dollar? You're robbin' us."

A policeman pushed Johnny inside.

"Okay," he yelled from the wagon, laughing, "I'll give you a dollar."

Inside the wagon, he was pushed against Higgins, whose face was badly bleeding. They were so close together that they couldn't turn their bodies. The wagon slid through the streets of the Flats.

"They musta had it planned," Monahan said.

Johnny grinned at Higgin's face. "You're gonna look awful pretty, Tom."

Higgins tried to grin back at him.

"They musta been waitin' for us." Monahan said.

No one said anything as the wagon thudded through the streets of the Flats.

"Hey," Johnny said quietly, "none of you guys fart."

The next morning, they were back. Johnny stood on top of the jalopy with a megaphone in his hands.

Abe stood next to the line on crutches. The men walked the picket line. Across the street, a large group of people from the Flats watched them.

"We're here!" Johnny shouted. "We're back! And we're gonna stay here!" He looked up at the Consolidated terminal. "You hear me up there? You beat me up. You beat Abe up. You threw rocks at us. You sent us off to your goddamn jail. And we're still here! And we're gonna stay here till we win!"

The men cheered.

When a Consolidated truck pulled up to the gate, the men surrounded it.

"Jenkins and O'Brien!" Monahan said.

"Goddamn scabs!" Higgins yelled.

The two men had tire irons in their hands.

"We ain't scabs, Mike," one of them said. "We didn't sign up. You know that."

The guards behind the fence watched them but there were so many men on all sides of the truck that they couldn't see what was going on.

"We got our jobs to do," one of the men in the truck said.

The men yelled at the two men in the truck. Johnny nodded to Higgins. Higgins crouched down and slashed two of the truck's tires.

"You wanna go in, Jenkins," Johnny smiled, "go ahead." The truck drove in with its slashed tires. The men cheered.

A police car arrived and two policemen walked up to Johnny.

"You're under arrest, Kovak."

"Again?"

"Disturbing the peace. Malicious destruction of property."

"Let him alone!" Higgins yelled.

"You guys aren't cops," Abe said, angrily, "you're scabs in uniform."

Johnny grinned. "What are you gettin' so excited about, Abe?"

The policemen led him across the street to their car. As they opened the back door for him, the group of people from the Flats yelled at them. Johnny spotted Anna in the crowd and smiled.

"He didn't do nothin'!" Anna yelled angrily. "Let him go!"

One of the policemen looked at her.

"You bastards!" she yelled.

Johnny grinned. "You gonna let her call you that?" he said to the cop.

"You're disturbin' the peace, lady," the policeman said to her.

"Arrest her," Johnny said.

The cop looked at him. Anna stood there stunned.

"She's disturbin' the peace," Johnny said, "arrest her."

She smiled. The policeman put him into the car and drove away.

At Central Police Station, the desk captain said, Name?"

Johnny grinned. "You remember me, don't you, cap?"

"Name."

"Johnny Kovak. I was here yesterday."

"Charge?"

"Disturbing the peace," another policeman said, "malicious destruction of property. Consolidated."

The desk captain looked up.

"Take him over to the lieutenant's office," he said.

"Great seein' you again, cap," Johnny grinned.

He was taken to an office where two plainclothes policemen smiled as he walked in. One of them had a blackjack in his hand.

"Mr. Kovak." One of them said, smiling.

Johnny shook his head. "Fifteen rounds, no gloves, right?"

"Wise guy," one of them said.

"We gotta go up on the third floor," the other said, grinning. "The lieutenant's up there."

They took him to a narrow stairway. Johnny stood at the bottom of the stairs. There was no one else there.

"Lieutenant's downstairs," one of them smiled. "Run."

He ran downstairs and one of the detectives said, "Lieutenant's back upstairs."

Panting, out of breath, he looked at them.

"How long we gonna run?"

"Till we find the lieutenant."

"That's what I was afraid of," he grinned.

The detectives ran him up and down the stairs until he collapsed. They picked him up and dumped him into a cell.

* * *

It was a brutally hot day and more than a hundred men paced the picket line. Water pails and dippers had been placed on the sidewalk for them. Many were bare-chested and suffering in the heat.

"Fuckin' oven," Johnny said, looking at the sun.

"They're tired, Johnny," Abe said. "Thirsty. Hungry."

"We're probably gonna have to stay out here—"

"You know what'd be great," Abe said.

"Till that old man croaks—huh?"

"If we had a place. Guys could rest. Some bread. Water. Get away from the heat."

Johnny grinned. "You wanna put 'em in the church basement, Abe? Up in the office?"

"Some place close."

"Maybe Talbot'll give us a room."

"There," Abe said, pointing.

"Where?"

"There."

Johnny looked where Abe pointed—to a weed-grown field catty-corner to Consolidated.

"There ain't nothin' there."

"The field," Abe said.

"What's the matter with you? You got sunstroke?"

"It's empty, Johnny."

Johnny looked at him half-seriously, grinning.

"We could put up a tent, set up cots—"

"You're a fuckin' genius," Johnny said, "you know that, Abe?"

When Monahan got there, they dragged him over to the field. Monahan stood there dumbfounded.

"We could put up a tent," Abe said.

"A tent?" Monahan said. "What the hell—"

"We'll get a buncha gunnysacks, put 'em together," Johnny said.

"Get some rail ties down at the yards," Abe said.

"Get the guys outta the heat," Johnny said.

"Put some cots in," Abe said, "sleep in shifts."

"Give 'em some food," Johnny said, "I bet ma'd even help—"

"Myrtle," Abe said.

"Sure, Myrtle."

Monahan stood there in a daze, looking from one to the other.

"The whole neighborhood," Abe said.

"Wait a goddamn minute!" Monahan said.

"Bring in big barrels of water," Abe said.

"Ice," Johnny said. "Some beer maybe."

"Beer?" Monahan said. "What are you talkin' about, for Christ's sake?"

"Guys are tired, Mike," Abe said.

"But this," Monahan said, "it don't belong to us."

Johnny looked at him, smiled. "We're gonna buy it, Mike."

"Buy it?" Monahan said, astounded. "You gotta be kiddin'—"

"You are, Mike," Johnny said. "You're gonna buy it for us outa the treasury."

"Buncha weeds," Abe grinned. "Shouldn't cost that much."

"It's gonna be our own field, Mike," Johnny said. "Think about it."

"Our own field?" Monahan said. "Holy Jesus. What are you talkin' about?"

Beams had been hammered into the ground in the empty field. A group of the men with poles in their hands were trying to balance a large hand-sewn burlap tent over them.

Anna and Molly, together with Johnny and Abe, who was on his crutches, were watching them.

"You like the five and dime?" Molly asked Anna.

"It's all right. Sometimes it gets so hot you feel like takin' everything off."

"You oughta," Molly laughed.

"Yeah, Anna, you oughta," Johnny said.

"That's all you ever think about, isn't it?" Anna said.

They laughed and Abe said, "It's gonna be great, Johnny. We'll bring the mats in, the food—"

The tent fell to the ground.

"We gotta put the damn thing up first," Johnny said. Abe laughed.

"But how'd you get this field?" Molly said.

"We didn't even have to buy it," Abe said. "It belongs to the church. We leased it. Johnny talked the priest into it."

"How?" Molly said.

"By payin' him five bucks," Johnny said, "that's how."

Near the tent site, a group of women were making lemonade and sandwiches. Johnny saw his mother among them and took Anna over to her.

"This is Anna, ma," he grinned, "the colored girl I told you about."

Anna smiled. "I'm Lithuanian, Mrs. Kovak."

She looked at her. "You—good friend of Johnny's?"

She laughed. "He tried to get me arrested last week."

He laughed. "She got me a punch in the nose, ma."

"Good," his mother said. "A smart girl."

The tent fell again and Higgins yelled, "Will you get your ass over here, Johnny?"

He ran to help them.

"For Christ's sake," Abe shouted, watching them, "you buncha clowns."

He hobbled toward them on his crutches. Disgusted, he threw the crutches down to the ground and hurried to help them. Molly ran after him.

"What are you doin', Abe?"

"I'm gonna help 'em," he said angrily, "they can't even put a goddamn tent up."

"Abe," she said, "the doctor said—"

"Fuck the doctor."

She ran after him as he grabbed the tent. "Don't you talk to me like that, Abe!"

They balanced the burlap over the beams, Molly and Anna helping them.

"This time we're gonna get it," Abe said, "come on, Higgins, watch it!"

"I'm tryin'! I'm tryin'!"

They balanced it carefully over the beams and Johnny watched Anna's figure as she stood there. She held a pole in both hands and her body was rigid, extended with effort. The big burlap finally fell over the last row of beams to the ground.

In the sudden darkness inside the tent, the men cheered. Johnny grabbed Anna suddenly, roughly, and pulled her close and kissed her. She tried to break free, then let him kiss her.

One of the men lifted the flap up. Light flooded into the tent. Johnny let Anna go. He stepped back and looked at her. She smiled.

"Aren't you gonna hit me?" he grinned.

She slapped him.

In the executive conference room on the eighth floor of the Talbot Building, Winthrop Talbot said, "It's gone on long enough. The mayor said they will give us all the support we need. But we must act."

"Any possibility of state help?" St. Clair said.

"I spoke to the governor yesterday," Winthrop Talbot said. "He is, as you know, running for re-election this year. And after that shooting last year at the Auto-Lite plant in Toledo, he is not anxious to get the National Guard involved.

"It's up to us, then, isn't it?" St. Clair said.

"Yes. Specifically, Arthur, it's up to you. You make the necessary arrangements. I don't wish to know the details, but I want this mockery ended. Move boldly, Arthur. At whatever cost."

St. Clair smiled. "I'll start working on it this afternoon."

"But maybe if we talk to them again," Philip Talbot said, "discuss some sort of insurance program—"

His father interrupted angrily. "No. They don't listen to reason. They will not break any more of our windows. They will not vandalize any more of our trucks. I will not permit them to interfere with this company any further."

"But they broke the windows only after—"

"Enough," Winthrop Talbot said. "Enough, Phillip. That bohunk is not going to put a circus tent on our doorstep."

A huge federation of Interstate Truckers banner was stretched across a makeshift stage in the church courtyard. A violin and accordion band played the czardas and the polka. The courtyard was jammed with people, many of them in native costume. Mishka was there, and Jugovich, the arm wrestler, and Zigi Zagon, and Monahan, who was trying to learn the czardas. Sausages were being grilled on open fires. Johnny, Abe, Anna, and Molly sat at a small table eating sausages and drinking red wine. Johnny's mother sat with them, not far from a sign that said, "Help the Strike."

"Bloody nose all the time," Johnny's mother said, looking at him. "First I look—see how bad, then I slap to face." She pretended to slap him.

Johnny held his face in mock pain. "That hurt, ma."

"Did he learn his lesson?" Anna asked.

"Never do no good. Next day. Bloody nose again."

"Mule-headed," Anna said, smiling at him.

"Mule-brains," his mother said.

They laughed and Monahan came over to them.

"Hey, Mike, sit down."

"I gotta go back out to the line, Johnny. If it's okay with you, though, I'd like a dance with this pretty lady here."

He extended his arm to Anna, who got up, smiling.

"He stole my girl!" Johnny said to the others. "Come on, Molly."

She looked at Abe.

"Hell, he can't dance," Johnny said.

Abe grinned and waved them away and, laughing, they headed for the dance floor.

Jocko came up to them. "Vince wants to see you, Johnny."

"We got a union dance," Johnny said, peeved. "What's he want?"

"He wants to talk to you."

Johnny looked at Molly and grinned. "Tell Abe he's a lucky man."

He walked behind Jocko into the street, where Vince Doyle's Stutz was parked. Jocko opened the door for him and he got in the back.

Johnny grinned. "We gonna hold hands, Vince?"

Doyle smiled and looked away from him. "They're gonna hit you tomorrow, Johnny."

"Aw, Jesus, Vince, what are you talkin' about? I got Anna in there—"

"All right, you don't wanna hear, I'm tryin' to do you a favor."

Johnny looked at him. "Okay, so do me a favor."

"They got guards. They got all sorts goons—"

"We got our guys, Vince—"

228

"They went down to the yards, hirin' hoboes. They're gettin' armored cars—"

Johnny shook his head.

"They're gonna beat you into the ground, Johnny." "Is that it?" Johnny said. "How about planes? They got planes, Vince? Gas, maybe?"

"That's it," Doyle said.

Johnny yanked the car door open angrily. He started out.

"Don't say I didn't warn you," Doyle said.

Johnny turned on him. "What the fuck you care, Vince—"

"You wanna whistle past the graveyard," Doyle said, louder now, "go ahead, Johnny."

"What's it to you?"

"Come on, Jocko," Doyle said, "let's go."

Johnny got out of the car. He looked back inside.

"What's in it for you, Vince?" Johnny said bitterly. "You give such a big shit?"

Doyle looked at him angrily and the car sped off.

Johnny walked back to the courtyard where the band was still playing. The music was loud. He saw Anna standing with Monahan. He went up to her and grabbed her hand roughly.

"Let's dance," he said.

"What's the matter?" she said softly.

He led her to the dance area and he didn't answer her. They danced the czardas. Johnny put his anger into it. He twirled her around more and more forcefully.

"Johnny," she said, "stop it."

He turned her around roughly.

Early the next morning, four armored trucks revved their engines at the end of the street by the Consolidated fence. Wire screening covered their windshields and radiators. Dozens of shotgunned guards stood around behind them. St. Clair talked to them, then got into a car and was driven away.

Johnny stood in the picket line with his men, watching, as the four trucks pulled up and stopped, one alongside the other, at the end of the street.

"What are they gonna do with those?" Monahan said.

"They look like tanks," Abe said.

"I wish we had more guys," Higgins said. "Maybe I oughta go down to the church and see if I can get more guys."

Johnny looked at him and grinned. "You're stayin' right here, Tom."

The armored trucks advanced toward them loudly as a phalanx of the uniformed guards, spread side by side across the street, moved up behind the trucks.

"We got a picket line here!" Johnny said to the men as the trucks and guards headed toward them. "We're gonna stay right here."

He leaned close to Abe and whispered, "Get the hell outa here."

"Like hell—"

"You wanna get your leg busted up again?"

"I'm stayin' right here!"

Johnny grinned at him. "You're a stupid shit, Abe. What a dumb shit you are."

The men grouped behind Johnny as the trucks and guards headed toward them.

Around the corner, two big Consolidated trucks pulled up at the tent. Goons carrying baseball bats and sticks leaped from the trucks. They attacked the strikers by the tent. The men resisted but they were outnumbered and unarmed.

On the picket line, Johnny saw what was happening at the tent and ran with the other picketers to help the men at the tent.

As they ran for the tent, the armored trucks speeded up and some of the guards fired their shotguns into the air.

At the tent, Johnny kicked a goon in the groin. He took his baseball bat away from him and started swinging. Monahan also grabbed a bat from one of the guards and knocked two of them down with it.

Abe was struck across the legs and yelled in pain. Johnny ran over and knocked the goon down with his bat. Abe and Johnny fought side by side, and as the battle wore on they were more and more outnumbered.

A group of the goons spilled gasoline over the tent. One of them threw a match onto it and the tent burst into flames.

Two of the armored trucks were parked on either side of the Consolidated gate, which was wide open. Shotgunned guards defended it.

Johnny and Abe, fighting off goons, worked their way down the street.

A group of goons took turns hitting Higgins with their fists. Higgins, bloody, dazed, got up and was knocked down again.

Monahan's bat was knocked from his hand. He was struck across the face with a stick and, bleeding, he ran down an alley to the jalopy. Bleeding and exhausted, he started the car up and pulled it to the end of the ally, facing the street.

He saw the tent burning.

Smoke was everywhere.

Injured strikers lay on the ground.

Police wagons arrived and policemen started handcuffing the injured men.

Then, as Monahan sat there in the jalopy, he saw a whole convoy of scab Consolidated trucks heading for the open gate.

He realized that the strike had been broken.

He gunned the car suddenly into the street and aimed it for the gate in a desperate attempt to block it.

Policemen, guards, and goons leaped out of the jalopy's way.

A guard aimed a shotgun at the jalopy and fired.

Monahan's windshield shattered.

Monahan screamed.

His car crashed into one of the armored trucks.

The undertaker stood next to Monahan's body, a pencil and piece of paper in his hand.

"What about the next of kin, Johnny?" the undertaker said.

"I don't know."

"I gotta put somebody down. On the paper, Johnny. It's the rule."

"He didn't have no family."

"I gotta put somebody down. How about if I put you down, and Abe?"

He nodded, said nothing.

"What kind of casket—"

"I don't know."

There was a pause.

"We buried your father in a—"

"Sure. That's good."

Johnny and Abe stood at the end of the alley, watching the Consolidated lot. Floodlights shone on it. It was filled with scabs and trucks. The armored trucks stood on either side of the gate. Guards stood inside the fence. The trucks were being loaded; Consolidated was back in business.

"Where'd they get their scabs?" Johnny said slowly.

"They musta got 'em from outa town. Got some guys from the other companies."

Johnny watched a truck being loaded and mumbled, "You're jackshit to me, pal."

"What?"

"That's the first thing I ever said to Mike."

Abe looked at him, but said nothing.

"Jesus, Abe."

"He believed in it, Johnny."

"And they killed him." He paused. "Just like they killed the old man."

"Don't you see, Johnny?" Abe said quietly. "He hadda go after 'em."

Johnny didn't say anything.

"What are we gonna do?" Abe said.

"I don't know."

"We can't just—walk away. What about the guys? What's gonna happen to the union?"

He looked at Abe, but he didn't answer him.

Cots had been placed on the church pews. Injured strikers lay there being cared for by Dr. Rosen. Anna and Molly helped him tend to the bleeding men.

"We got everybody here, doc?" Abe said.

"A few are still at the *polizei.*"

"You need anything, doc?" Johnny said.

He shook his head. "We do okay."

A reporter walked up to Johnny. "I'm Kane from the *News*, Mr. Kovak. What are you going to do now?"

Johnny ignored him. He saw Higgins on a cot and walked over to him.

"How ya doin', Tom?"

"Terrific. Don't you worry about me, Johnny."

Johnny looked at his battered, bloody face. "You big lug," he smiled.

The reporter leaned close to Higgins. "Is it true you've got Communists backing you?"

Johnny suddenly swung at the reporter. He hit him, then swung at him again. Abe and Anna pulled him away.

"Johnny, Johnny," Anna said, holding him.

* * *

They sat in front of her house in Dr. Rosen's car, staring straight ahead into the darkness, saying nothing. Johnny put his head down on the steering wheel. Anna reached over and held his head. He started to cry softly.

"Johnny—"

He lifted his head and smashed the steering wheel violently with his fist.

His voice was choked. "Goddamn 'em! Goddamn 'em, Anna."

She was crying now, too. She pulled his face close to hers and kissed him tenderly.

The church was filled. The priest finished his requiem. Johnny, Abe, Higgins, and some of the other men lifted Monahan's casket up and carried it outside. The casket was covered with a F.I.S.T. banner.

There was a throng of people outside. The men put the casket down.

"We're gonna stop at Consolidated on the way to the cemetery!" Johnny shouted. "Nobody get outa line!"

They formed a procession, standing abreast across the street their arms linked. Johnny, Abe, Anna, and Molly were in the front row. Monahan's casket led the march.

As they walked, the people of the Flats joined them. Mishka was there, Jugovich, Zigi Zagon, Szabo, carrying a red flag. More and more people joined the march at every corner. Rowdy teen-agers straggled at the sides. People in tenement windows tossed flowers to them.

A few hundred feet from Consolidated, Johnny saw a long line of policemen blocking the street. The armored cars were behind them. A police captain stood in the middle of the street with a megaphone.

"Stop were you are!" the captain said. "This is an illegal march! I'm ordering you to disperse!"

The marchers kept moving toward the police line.

"Stay calm!" Johnny shouted. "Everybody stay calm!"

"This is the last time you will be warned!" the police captain said. "I am ordering you to disperse."

A hundred feet from the police line, Johnny stopped the marchers. The marchers broke ranks and milled chaotically over the street. Many of them were yelling.

"Stay in line!" Johnny shouted. "Everybody stay in line!"

Rocks were thrown from the ranks of the marchers toward the policemen. Johnny and Abe saw some of the policemen duck.

"Stop it!" Johnny shouted. "Don't throw nothin'!"

He and Abe headed through the crowd for the rock throwers. They saw a group of teen-agers throwing the rocks. They pushed through the crowd for the kids.

"I am ordering you to disperse!" the police captain said. "You will be arrested!"

There was a gunshot.

Johnny and Abe stopped and looked toward the policemen.

They saw the gunman. He stood among the marchers, a cap pulled low over his eyes, a pistol in his hand. They recognized him: he was the hawk-faced pale man with the scar running down the right side of his face; the man who beat both of them up.

"No!" Johnny screamed. "No!"

The gunman fired once more, then ran down an alley.

There was chaos in the street, screams and panic.

The policemen fired at the crowd. Several people went down. The marchers turned in desperation to flee.

Johnny and Abe raced down the alley after the gunman. He was a block ahead of them.

The police charged the mourners, who were trying to flee. Anna stood in the street in shock, not moving, looking at the body of a woman who had been shot.

Johnny and Abe chased the gunman through the Flats. He ran toward the railyard.

Anna remained on the street, unable to move. A policeman hit her with a billyclub and she went down. The cops turned past her. Anna got up and went to the woman's body. She kneeled over it and sobbed.

Johnny and Abe chased the gunman to a row of boxcars. They knew he was in one of them and they went from car to car. Johnny jumped in an open boxcar. The gunman came out of the shadows, holding the gun. He fired it point blank at Johnny's head and laughed. Johnny stopped, stunned, but he was unhurt. He hurled himself at the gunman. He knocked the gun from his hand, then knocked him to the floor. He punched his face, then slammed his head into the floor of the boxcar.

"You're gonna kill him!" Abe shouted.

Johnny kept slamming the gunman's head to the floor. Abe jumped at him, trying to knock him off the man. Johnny hit Abe, knocking him against the side of the car. Again and again, he slammed the gunman's head against the floor. Abe got up and tackled Johnny.

In the street, the police were piling the wounded into a wagon. Anna was brought to the wagon. Her skirt was bloody and she tried to wipe the blood away.

In the railyard, Johnny gasped for air outside the boxcar and staggered back inside.

Abe crouched over the gunman. "He's dead, Johnny."

Johnny picked up the gun. He opened it and looked inside.

He hurled the gun against the side of the boxcar. "Blanks!"

Vinnie's was dark and empty. He sat in the back, a bottle of whiskey in front of him, his funeral suit rumpled, his tie undone. His face was pained; his eyes empty and brooding. Vince Doyle walked up to his table and looked at him. Johnny didn't look up.

"I'm sorry, kid."

"Whistlin' past the graveyard, Vince. That's what you said."

Doyle sat down and poured him another drink.

"Leave it alone, Johnny. For Christ's sake, will you

leave it alone? What's gotta happen to convince you?"

He drank the bourbon. "I can't, Vince."

"Walk away, Johnny."

He shook his head. "You know how many men I got'd lose their jobs."

"*You* got? They your family?"

"They'd have it worse'n they ever did."

"What's it got to do with me, Johnny?"

He grinned, paused. "What's *in* it for you, huh, Vince?"

"Yeah," Doyle said, his voice harsh. "What's in it for me? Sure. And let me tell you something—what the hell's in it for you?" He glared at him, then looked away, his voice lower. "Get off it, Johnny."

"I need push, Vince."

"You need a goddamn army."

He slammed his fist to the table. "I ain't gonna bury nobody else! Help us knock 'em off, Vince. This one time."

"I'm a businessman, Johnny."

"Those people we buried were *ours*, Vince."

Doyle grinned. "My people's anybody that can pay me."

"*Our* people, Vince." He paused. "This one time. That's all I'm askin' you."

Doyle didn't say anything.

"This one time," Johnny said. "I give you my word."

"Come on, Johnny."

"My word, Vince."

There was a long pause.

"You know what it'd cost to get enough guys to—"

"We got a fund," Johnny said.

Doyle looked at him and smiled.

Abe sat in the living room, listening to the radio. Johnny walked in, a bit unsteady, though he was not drunk.

Abe turned the radio up.

"Police, meanwhile, said they are still seeking the striker who fired a handgun at a cordon of policemen standing near the Consolidated terminal. 'When they were fired on,' a police spokesman said, 'they returned the fire.' "

Johnny grinned. "Hell, yeah, they did."

"Four persons were killed, a score injured, in the incident which United Mine Workers president John L. Lewis called 'The Funeral Day Massacre' at a press conference in Pittsburgh today. Federation of Interstate Truckers president Matthew J. Rafferty blamed "Red agitators" for the shootings and said in Flint, Michigan, he was coming to Cleveland to take over negotiations. Local union organizer Johnny Kovak was unavailable for comment."

Johnny laughed.

"But Consolidated president Winthrop Talbot said he welcomed Rafferty's announcement. 'Rafferty is a professional who has the best interests of his men at heart,' Talbot said."

Johnny abruptly shut the radio off. "And we don't, Abe? Hear that?"

He paced around the room. "Over my dead body

Rafferty is gonna talk to 'em, that's what my comment is."

"Where you been?" Abe said.

He hesitated. "Aw, I went over, saw Vince Doyle."

"Vince Doyle? How come you saw him?"

Johnny avoided his eyes. "I asked him to help us."

"Vince?" Abe said. "Those hoods of his, Johnny? The punks he's got?"

Johnny turned to him. "Abe, listen to me. He's got push."

"Jesus, Johnny."

"You wanna keep buryin' people, Abe? Is that what we do?"

"They're gonna fuck it up," Abe said.

He got up, faced Johnny. "You hiring Vince and those guys, Johnny, I'm tellin' you. They're gonna fuck up this union."

"I ain't bringin' 'em in to be lifetime members."

"Vince comes in, Johnny, he'll never get out."

Johnny turned on him angrily. "Jesus, will you listen to me? What are you talkin' about? We need the push. Without the push, we ain't got a union." He paused. "You fight fists with fists."

Abe thought about it, then shook his head.

"Then how we gonna know, Johnny?"

"Know what?"

"The difference."

"What difference? What are you talkin' about?"

"Between them and us, Johnny."

Johnny glared at him.

* * *

The church hall was packed with men standing around in groups, talking. Johnny walked in with Vince Doyle and Jocko, both of whom wore fedoras and snazzy suits.

Higgins looked at Vince Doyle and said to Abe, "Who's he think he is, Al Capone?"

Abe grinned and walked over to Johnny. He ignored Doyle and Jocko.

"Rafferty's here," Abe said.

"Where?"

Abe motioned. In the back of the room, Johnny saw Matt Rafferty surrounded by a large group of men.

"You guys said hello?" he said to Doyle and Abe.

Vince Doyle put his hand out and smiled. "Long time, Abe."

Abe forced a smile and shook his hand. "How ya doin' Vince."

"Hiya, Abe," Jocko smiled, his hand out. Abe ignored him.

"Come on," Johnny said.

He led them toward Rafferty. As he neared him, he heard some of the men around Rafferty say, "What about our jobs? What are you gonna do about it?"

Rafferty saw Johnny and the others. Johnny smiled.

"What are you gonna tell the men now, Kovak?" Rafferty said belligerently.

"I'm glad you come down, Matt," Johnny said quietly.

"Talbot's agreed to have a meeting with me tomorrow," Rafferty said, his words loud for the benefit of the men around him.

242

"That's good news, Matt," Johnny said quietly.

"Anytime anyone in this union needs my help," Rafferty boomed, "I'm here."

Johnny turned him away from the others and whispered, "Let's go someplace we can talk a minute."

Rafferty looked at him suspiciously.

"I need your help on somethin'," Johnny said.

"I'll see you men in a couple minutes," Rafferty said to the others.

Johnny turned. Rafferty followed him with Abe. Johnny motioned for Jocko to follow them. They went out a side door and up a stairway.

"You should have asked me for help when you started all this," Rafferty said. "Getting all these people killed." He looked around the stairway. "We going to church?"

Johnny grinned and opened a door. They followed him into the church sacristy.

"Get the door, Jocko," Johnny said, his tone suddenly hard. "We don't wanna be disturbed."

Jocko left the room and closed the door. Johnny and Rafferty stood around in the middle of the sacristy, surrounded by vestments and crucifixes, facing each other. Abe watched them from the side.

"What is this?" Rafferty said.

"You're goin' in to see Talbot, huh?"

"You're damn right I am!" Rafferty said angrily.

"You're gonna sell us out, Matt. Have us go back for nothin'."

"I'll discuss this with the men," Rafferty said. He started for the door.

Johnny blocked his way. "Train leaves in an hour, Matt." He smiled.

Rafferty looked at him.

Johnny kept smiling. "You're goin' back to Flint. Nobody sells me out."

"Like hell I am!" Rafferty said.

Johnny slapped him viciously across the face. Still smiling, he grabbed Rafferty by his lapels and pulled him very close to him.

"Christ, Johnny," Abe said.

"Aren't you, Matt?" Johnny said.

"You sonofabitch," Rafferty said.

Johnny slapped him again. Abe winced.

"Aren't you?" Johnny said.

"This is a church, Johnny," Abe said.

"Let go of me, you bastard," Rafferty said, his voice choked.

"Come on, Johnny," Abe said, "let him go."

Johnny pushed Rafferty away to the wall. He started out of the room, then turned back and went to Rafferty, who cringed from him.

"Jocko'll ride you to the station," Johnny said. He smiled. "One more thing, Matt. Next time you come to Cleveland—"

He raised his hand toward Rafferty again. As Rafferty flinched, he patted him softly on the cheek.

"Call me," Johnny said. "Let me know you're comin'."

He started out of the sacristy. Rafferty and Abe looked at each other. Abe hesitated, then followed Johnny out of the room.

When they got back into the church hall, there were so many men they could hardly move.

Abe went to the table and banged the gavel. "If you guys that got seats'd sit down we could get goin'."

As Abe kept banging the gavel, Higgins introduced Johnny to two men—Petey Marr of the dockworkers and Ed Noonan of the steelworkers, local labor leaders who had simply walked into the meeting and told Tom Higgins that they were here to help Johnny Kovak, here to help F.I.S.T. Because they were all brothers. Because, as Petey Marr said, they weren't going to stand around with their fingers up their you-know-whats and let their brothers get shot down on the hard, cruel, boss-run city streets. Johnny shook hands with the two men warmly and, when the room was quiet, he stood behind the table and smiled at his men.

"All right," he said. "Before we get to anything else—I've got to tell you that Matt Rafferty got called back to Flint sudden on account of a sickness in the family. He wanted me to tell all of you that he's with us two hundred percent and he'll help us whatever way he can."

The men cheered. Johnny smiled. Abe looked at him.

"We got a coupla guys here," Johnny said, "that wanna say somethin'. First, Ed Noonan from the steelworkers."

Noonan, a little man with a thin voice, got up and said, "I got a Western Union from John L. Lewis I'd like to read."

245

The men cheered Lewis's name.

"It says—'To our brothers of Local 302 of the Federation of Interstate Truckers. We stand behind you with our hearts and bodies in the great and noble struggle you must continue.'"

The men cheered.

"Together, the American labor movement will never be van-kished. Yours in solidarity. Signed, John L. Lewis."

The men cheered wildly.

"Thanks, Ed," Johnny said. "We also got Petey Marr here of the dockworkers."

Marr got up. He was a burly moustached man in his early forties. "Whatever you guys need, Johnny," he said in a gruff voice, "you let us know. I talked to the men yesterday and we voted to give you guys whatever you need out of our emergency fund to tide you over."

Marr sat down. Then, as the men cheered, he got up again and shouted, "Till you get what you got rightfully comin' to you!"

Johnny grinned and waited until there was complete silence in the room.

"Thanks, Petey. Thanks a lot for that cause we're gonna need it." He paused. "All I got to say to you guys is that Monahan was right."

"That's right, Johnny!" one of the men yelled.

"You tell it, Johnny!" Higgins shouted.

When he continued, his voice was intense and rock hard.

"We go back out there, they're not gonna beat us no

more! They're not gonna burn us down! They're not gonna start shootin'! Cause if they do we're gonna do what Mike did! We're gonna go after 'em with whatever we got!"

He paused as they cheered him, then continued, his voice an angry cry.

"I'm sayin' to Talbot right now I don't give a shit! We gotta do anymore shovelin' in the cemetery, they're gonna shovel some too! We're through takin' punches! You don't win fights takin' punches!"

He paused in the overwhelming silence and picked up a sign that said, "Local 302 F.I.S.T. on Strike." He held the sign up and pointed to the union initials.

"What does this say?" he bellowed. "It don't say Federation of Interstate Truckers! It ain't a buncha letters like any other union! It says fist!"

He held his fist high in the air.

"One fist! Every guy in here! That's what we are! A fist!"

He paused, then lowered his voice. "Any of you guys don't believe that, get outa here right now! I mean it."

He waited and looked at the men. No one moved.

"We're gonna take a week, get organized. Then we're gonna go out and shut Consolidated down. We're gonna get what's comin' to us! We're on strike!"

The men cheered. He watched them. He raised his fist, then grinned.

"I want you to meet Vince Doyle. Vince, get up."

Doyle stood up and smiled.

"Vince is a friend of ours. He's gonna be our . . .

business agent for a while. He's gonna help us get organized."

Doyle sat down. Some of the men grinned.

"Meantime," Johnny said, "everybody can keep pickin' up your strike benefits at the office. We'll have somebody there all the time. Okay, that's it."

"We're with you, Johnny!" Higgins yelled.

Afterwards, Vince Doyle walked up to him.

"Business agent, huh?"

"Sounds good," Johnny grinned.

Abe watched them.

The window in the tiny union office was open. They were hot and sweating. Doyle was the only one who wore a tie. Higgins and Petey Marr of the dockworkers were in their undershirts. Johnny and Abe had their shirts unbuttoned. There was a map of the city on the wall. They talked fast, excitedly, sometimes at the same time.

Doyle: "But what's gonna convince 'em this time?"

Johnny: "We'll have more guys."

Doyle: "So what? They can still bring scabs in from the other companies."

Johnny: "Not if we hit all of 'em."

Higgins: "All the truckin' companies in the city?"

Johnny: "Fuck, yeah. Set up a line at all of 'em."

Doyle: "I like it. Shut everything down. Putsa lotta push on Talbot."

Johnny: "Petey, what do you think?"

Marr: "What about trucks comin' in from outa town?"

248

Johnny: "Stop 'em before they get in?"
Doyle: "Right."
Abe: "How you gonna do that?"
Johnny: "Send some guys out."
Doyle: "Bust their ass out on the road."
Abe: "And do what with 'em?"
Doyle: "What the fuck you think?"
Marr: "Take the scabs out."
Doyle: "Play tiddlywinks."
Marr: "Give 'em some exercise."
Johnny: "We cut their tires."
Doyle: "Leave the heaps block up the road."
Marr: "Have the cops get ridda the rigs."
Higgins: "Beautiful. Give 'em somethin' to do."
Abe: "How you gonna know where to send the guys?"
Johnny: "Shit. You're right. We can't have a hundred guys all over the road."
Doyle: "Send some kids."
Abe: "Kids?"
Doyle: "Kids hangin' around the pool halls. Tell 'em to get their bikes. Take a ride out on the highway."
Higgins: "Two from Toledo, route six from Erie."
Marr: "Seventy-one down south."
Doyle: "Give 'em a lollipop or somethin'."
Johnny: "Have 'em call in."
Higgins: "A pack of rubbers."
Doyle: "Sure. Now you're thinkin'. They see a truck, they call. We send the guys out."
Abe: "Call in where? Here?"
Johnny: "We're gonna need a place."

Doyle: "Get that old warehouse—what is it? A block from Consolidated."

Johnny: "We're gonna have trouble gettin' anything, if old man Talbot can help it."

Marr: "We'll rent it for you. They'll give it to us."

Johnny: "That's great, Petey."

Marr: "I'll set it up tomorrow."

Doyle: "Have the kids call into the warehouse. Set up a buncha phones."

Higgins: "Beautiful. The headquarters."

Marr: "Can you get enough kids?"

Doyle: "You get enough rubbers, I'll get enough kids."

Higgins: "I'll get the rubbers."

Doyle: "Concentrate on Talbot, though. The others —we just wanna push 'em to push Talbot."

Johnny: "Yeah, that's where the crunch is gonna come."

Higgins: "So what do we do that's different this time?"

Doyle: "We give your guys some protection."

Abe: "Guns?"

Johnny: "Come on, Abe."

Doyle: "Hoses."

Abe: "We gonna sprinkle water on 'em, Vince?"

Doyle: "We cut a buncha hoses into little pieces. Knock some lead in the hollow. Cover it up with friction tape. Saw a buncha two-by-fours into little walkin' sticks."

Johnny: "Yeah. Get as much real tough cardboard

as we can, stick it into the sweatbands on our hats. Everybody's gonna wear a hat."

Abe: "How are we going to stop the cops from shootin' at us?"

Doyle: "After what happened the last time, the cops aren't gonna be hot to go back out there."

Abe: "What happens if they do?"

Johnny: "Wait a minute. One way. If we split the cops up."

Abe: "You gonna ask 'em to step aside?"

Johnny: "Naw. Listen to me. Get between 'em. Drive a truck with a buncha guys in it smack into the middle of 'em."

Doyle: "Yeah. Have the guys jump out—"

Johnny: "Jump into the middle of the cops. The cops'd be afraid to shoot."

Doyle: "Cause they might hit each other."

Marr: "Boy, I gotta hand it to you guys."

Higgins: "What about those fuckin' tanks we saw out there?"

Doyle: "I'll worry about 'em."

Abe: "You'll worry about 'em?"

Doyle: "I'll take care of it."

Abe: "How? Huh, Vince? That's what I been askin' you all day?"

Johnny: "Vince and me figured that out already."

Doyle: "Dynamite."

Abe: "Dynamite?"

Johnny: "Hit the truck. No truck."

Marr: "Holy fuckin' Jesus."

Doyle: "How many of those things they got?"

Higgins: "Four."

Doyle: "Shit. You hit one, the other three are gonna run all the way to Detroit."

Abe: "But Jesus, we can't just—what about the men in that truck?"

Johnny: "What about 'em?"

Anna and Molly stood with a group of women on the floor of the huge boxlike warehouse which was Local 302's new headquarters. Behind them, men were unloading crates and cleaning up.

"What you do, Anna," Johnny said, "you go up to 'em and tell 'em what we're doin', what we want."

"Just a little contribution," Vince Doyle smiled.

"Yeah," Johnny said, "Groceries. Medical stuff. Whatever they wanna contribute."

"What if they say no, Johnny?"

"No?"

"What if they don't wanna contribute?"

"You write their names down," Doyle said, "and tell us."

"How come?" Molly asked.

"What how come?" Doyle said.

"How come we write their names down?"

Doyle grinned. "So we can send 'em a card for Christmas."

Johnny laughed. He saw Dr. Rosen at the warehouse door, and walked over to him.

"I wasn't sure you were gonna show, doc."

Dr. Rosen looked around the huge, cavernous warehouse.

"Our new hospital, huh, Johnny?"

"Not all of it, doc."

"We gonna need all of it."

Johnny laughed. "Come on, doc, I'll show you around."

He led him to a small room on the second floor. Dr. Rosen looked at it.

"What's this? The water closet? Maybe we can fit in—seven dwarfs."

"It's our hospital, doc. We aren't gonna need more room this time."

Sure, Johnny, sure." He shook his head and sighed. "Okay, Johnny. You say it's a hospital, it's a hospital."

Johnny slapped Rosen on the back. From a second-floor window, he saw Jocko, who had a piece of hose in his hand, talking to a group of union men. Johnny walked down, stood next to Doyle, and they both watched Jocko.

"What you do is," Jocko said to the men, "before the asshole can do somethin', you clobber him."

The men watched Jocko warily.

"Get him the back of the head," Jocko said, "you put him down."

"How come I should hit him if he didn't do nothin' to me?" one of the men asked.

"Cause he'll beat the shit outa you if you don't hit him first, that's how come."

"Can't we hit him in the leg?"

"The leg! You get him in the leg, you idiot, he's still gonna clobber you. You do it like this—"

Jocko moved behind one of the men and faked hitting him with the blackjack. The man turned nervously around.

"I'm just showin' you. Relax," Jocko said. "You don't put the hose over his head and bring it down—"

He faked slamming the blackjack down on the man's head.

"—He moves an inch, you miss. You swing up."

He swung upward at the man's head. "You swing up, you crack his nut."

"How's it goin'?" Johnny said to Doyle.

Doyle grinned. "Buncha nuns learnin' how to fuck."

Johnny laughed and walked away. He saw Abe speaking with a portly, bespectacled man who was pulling a child's wagon filled with wood.

"Johnny, this is Mr. Schneider," Abe said.

Johnny shook his hand.

"Mr. Schneider teaches the violin and the cello, Johnny. He brought us some wood."

"We heard that you might be needing some pieces of wood," the man said. "We wanted to help you, Mr. Kovak."

"Thank you," Johnny said.

"We don't have any money we can spare, but"—he looked at the wagon, "we had a banister."

"A banister?" Johnny said.

"My wife and I cut it up."

"You cut your banister up?"

"For the strike."

"Oh, well. Uh, thanks a lot, Mr. Schneider."

"A pleasure, Mr. Kovak."

The man beamed, shook Johnny's hand again, and walked away.

Johnny started to laugh. "He teaches the cello, Abe," he said, laughing hard. "And he cut his banister up. Jesus Christ!"

Abe got into it and laughed with him. The two of them stood there on the warehouse floor, red-faced and laughing so hard they could barely breathe.

"Get out here!" Higgins bellowed. "Will you guys get out here?"

Still laughing, they walked outside with most of the other men. A F.I.S.T. flag was being raised on the warehouse roof.

"Ain't that a sight?" Johnny said. "You ever see anything as pretty as that?"

Abe looked at him and smiled. "Never, Johnny. Never have."

Alex Papp was a rosy-cheeked, white-haired old man with a crippled left foot whose pharmacy was the largest in the Flats. He stood behind his counter in his white coat, with the red cross insignia over his heart. He looked at Anna and Molly.

"I can't give you nothin', honey," he said. "Honest. You know how it is."

"But it's for the union," Anna said. "For the federation—in case the police—"

"I know. I know. Look. You don't have to tell me.

255

Those people that were killed, they were my customers. They owed me money."

"Can't you just give us a little gauze maybe?" Anna said.

"I can't, honey. I just can't. I'd like to. I got hundreds of dollars out, people that can't pay. Nobody can pay. I know that. But I can't afford to give nothin' more."

"A couple bottles of iodine, that's all," Molly said.

"I'm sorry. Believe me, I'm sorry."

When Johnny walked into the pharmacy just before closing that night, Alex Papp greeted him happily. "Johnny, what can I do for you?"

He glanced at the four men with him: Doyle, Jocko, and two younger men with bulging suit coats.

"I'll tell you, Mr. Papp," Johnny said. "I'm here for the federation."

"I know, Johnny, I know. Those girls were here. Say, they were pretty—"

"We're askin' for contributions, Mr. Papp."

"I told them, Johnny. I can't give nothin'. Everybody wants. Nobody pays."

Johnny nodded. He paused.

"This is my friend Vince Doyle, Mr. Papp."

Doyle smiled at the pharmacist, and knocked a row of bottles on the counter to the ground.

"Here," the pharmacist said, "what are you doin'? You knocked them down. What the hell—"

He hurried over to the broken bottles.

"An accident, Mr. Papp," Vince Doyle smiled.

The pharmacist got down on the floor and nervously started cleaning up the mess.

"Accident! What the hell kind of accident was—"

"And this is my friend Jocko," Doyle said.

Jocko smashed a display case. The pharmacist looked up from the floor openmouthed. He was speechless.

Doyle smiled. "And this is Jocko's friend Al—"

"Stop it!" the pharmacist yelled.

He got up from the floor and looked at Johnny. "All right. Take what you want."

"That's real nice of you, Mr. Papp," Vince Doyle smiled.

Winthrop Talbot paced the floor of his office. St. Clair and Phillip Talbot squirmed uncomfortably in their chairs, waiting for his response.

"I don't believe it," Winthrop Talbot finally said.

"My friends assure me that their information is correct," St. Clair said.

"They can't close down the entire trucking industry of this city."

"Nevertheless, Win—"

"They can't possibly have the organiztion."

"They have help, dad," Phillip Talbot said.

"They can't possibly have the organization."

"They have some unsavory elements working with them," St. Clair said.

Winthrop Talbot turned from them and looked out his window.

"More important, dad, they have the support of the whole community down there."

"Bootleggers, petty hoodlums," St. Clair said.

"They have dockworkers, steelworkers, hundreds of volunteers. You're underestimating him, dad."

Winthrop Talbot glanced sharply at his son.

"Let me talk to him, dad."

"You want to talk to Kovak?" Winthrop Talbot smiled.

"Maybe we can put an end to this somehow."

"By giving them what they want?"

"We're going to have to live with them," Phillip Talbot said.

"With Kovak?"

"With all these unions."

"Nonsense."

"All we have to do is negotiate."

"No," Winthrop Talbot said, "we will not negotiate."

He sat down behind his desk and examined some papers.

"Let me see those June accounts you promised," he said to his son.

"You're making a mistake, dad," Phillip Talbot said quietly.

"Am I?"

"Yes. I think you are."

"These accounts are overdue," Winthrop Talbot said.

* * *

Johnny stood in his shirtsleeves in the middle of the warehouse, the sweat sopping his shirt. With him were Ed Noonan of the steelworkers, Petey Marr of the dockworkers, and Abe. They were surrounded by reporters shouting their questions.

"You got Communists helping you, Kovak?"

"You a citizen, Kovak?"

"All right, you guys gonna shut up?" Abe yelled. "If you don't shut up, I'm gonna kick your asses outa here!"

The reporters quieted down grumblingly.

"We're goin' out tomorrow morning," Johnny said quietly. "That's the announcement I got to make. We're gonna shut Consolidated down. We're settin' up lines at Endicott, Westin, and Collett trucking."

"How do you think you're gonna make a general truck strike stick, Kovak?"

"You go out tomorrow morning," Johnny said quietly. "You see how it's gonna stick."

"You got Communists working with you, Kovak?"

"I got Communists, Catholics, Protestants, Jews, micks, spicks, guineas, polacks, and every goddamn hunkie in this city."

"What if the police—"

Johnny put his arm around Noonan and Petey Marr. "We got the steelworkers with us and we got Petey Marr's dockworkers and we got all the people who believe workin' stiffs got a right to be human beings."

"What if the police try to stop you, Kovak?"

"Anybody, whatever he is, whatever he speaks,

whatever he looks like, wants to help us, come on out to the picket lines tomorrow."

"But what if the police try to stop you?"

Johnny paused. "We got a right to go on strike," he said quietly. "We don't got nothin' against the cops."

"But what if they try, Kovak?"

"They won't stop us," he said quietly. "That's all I got to say."

He turned from the reporters and started walking away.

"Are you a citizen, Kovak?"

He turned back angrily. "Yeah, I'm a citizen," he said, his voice hard. "Are you?" He glared at the man and poked him in the chest. "And it's *Mr.* Kovak to you, pal."

Petey Marr pulled him away. The reporters tried to crowd after him but Abe blocked their way.

Sweating and exhausted, Anna walked out of the five and dime, heard the horn, and walked over to the car, smiling.

"Hey, lady," Johnny grinned, "you want a surprise?"

"What you got in mind, mister?"

"You know what I got in mind," he laughed.

"No thanks, mister."

She started to walk away.

"Hey, Anna, look!"

She looked back and saw him holding a bottle of Coca-Cola high in the air.

"Straight from the icebox, Anna."

She reached for it. He jerked it back.

"First, we gotta go for a ride."

She looked at him in mock alarm.

"Nice and cold, Anna."

"Anything you want, mister." She laughed and got into the car.

They sat at sunset on a cluttered industrial beach-front on Lake Erie. Old tires littered the ground. A hollowed-out icebox was near them.

"I brought you somethin'," he said.

He handed her the imitation diamond ring he won at the penny arcade. She looked at it.

"Put it on."

She put it on and smiled.

"How does it fit?"

"Fits okay." She looked at him. "What does it mean, Johnny?"

"What do you mean?" he grinned. "It means—it means I like you."

"Do you?" she smiled.

"Maybe I'll give you a real one sometime."

She laughed. "When?"

"Jesus," he said, "I don't know, Anna. What kinda question—"

She laughed, looked at the ring.

"Johnny," she said softly, "I'm gonna be there tomorrow."

"Anna, I told you, I don't want you there. There's gonna be trouble, the cops—"

"I'm gonna be there," she said, her voice firm.

They looked at each other.

"Hold me, Johnny?"

He put his arms around her and kissed her.

Bill Rogers was a scab. He had been driving for Consolidated for more than two weeks now and as he drove down Lorain Avenue this morning on his way to the Consolidated terminal in the Flats, Bill Rogers was a happy man. Today was payday. He would get his first check.

Ahead of him, at the side of the road near a telephone booth, a freckle-faced teen-ager on a bicycle waved to him and grinned. Bill Rogers looked at the kid, tooted his horn at him, and stepped on the gas. The faster he got there, the sooner there would be money in his pocket.

The freckle-faced kid watched the truck barrel down Lorain, walked into the phone booth, and laughed. He was making five dollars a day just watching trucks and making phone calls. It must be the easiest job in the world.

He dialed the number and said, his voice excited and high, "This is Sinchik. Naw. Naw. Sinchik. Yeah, that's me. Forty-first and Lorain. A Consolidated truck just passed me." He laughed. "Yeah, the asshole's alone."

In a little room at the F.I.S.T. warehouse, Jocko said, "Okay, kid, go ride your bike."

He hung up and looked at the men crowded into the room: numbers runners, former bootleggers, small-time holdup men, all of them armed. He had personally selected all of them. They were making fifty dollars for their services this day but they were really here because Vince passed the word that he needed a favor.

"Al, Lefty, you—Lard," Jocko said, pointing to three of the men. "Forty-first and Lorain, Consolidated truck just went through there. The guy's alone."

The men started for the door. "I'm hungry," the fat man named Lard said. "I didn't eat no breakfast."

"You don't need no fuckin' breakfast," Jocko snarled. "Now get the hell outa here."

The phone rang again. Jocko picked it up and listened.

"Jesus Christ," he yelled into the receiver. "Slow down, will you, snotnose? I can't hear a word you're sayin'."

Two blocks from the F.I.S.T. warehouse, at the Consolidated terminal, a row of shotgunned guards stood behind the fence. Scab trucks were being loaded on the docks.

Across the street from the Consolidated terminal, a group of women gathered in a circle on the sidewalk. Anna and Molly handed them little bags of paprika. "Don't waste none of it," Anna said. "A little bit of paprika goes a long way." She held one of the bags up. "Open it like this and throw it in his face. And don't get none in yours." She smiled. "It stings." The women laughed.

Two trucks filled with strikers pulled up to the Consolidated gate. Men piled off it with picket signs. All of them were wearing hats with cardboard tucked into the bands. They were led by a man wearing a suit and a fedora: Ted Lettieri, who had spent four years at the Ohio Penitentiary for assault with a deadly weapon, once employed as one of Vince Doyle's rum runners. As the men herded around the Consolidated fence, a guard on the other side of the fence moved toward them with a shotgun. Ted Lettieri went to the guard, shifted his coat, and let him see the gun in his shoulder holster. Ted Lettieri grinned. "Pretty, ain't she?" he said. The guard stared at him and walked away.

Down the street from Consolidated, Mishka stood with a group of his friends from Zigi's Tavern. Jugovich, the behemoth arm wrestler, was there, as well as Zigi's cook, a pint-sized bantam rooster of a man who was dressed in his Sunday suit. Mishka held a six-quart basket of eggs and started handing them to the men.

Jugovich smiled. "We oughta eat these," he said. Mishka cracked an egg and held it under his friend's nose. Jugovich cringed from the smell.

"You ain't that hungry," Mishka said.

As Bill Rogers drove his truck down West Twenty-fifth Street, he saw a car blocking the road ahead of him. A man was lying in the street next to it; two other men stood over him, one of them very fat.

Bill Rogers stopped the truck and leaned out his window and yelled, "Whatsamatter?"

The fat man come to the truck. "Nothin'," Lard said. He smiled. "He's okay. You—you ain't." He pulled a gun from his hip and pointed it at him.

Bill Rogers was forced, at gunpoint, to drive his truck into an alley, where the truck's tires were slashed. He was ordered to take his shoes and socks off.

"Nice day for a walk," Lard said.

"Goddamn you bastards!" Bill Rogers said.

"Listen," Lard said, holding his gun up, "you wanna suck on this?"

Inside the Consolidated yard, the scab trucks had been loaded and were moving slowly toward the gate, which the strikers blocked. The strikers yelled and smashed the fence with their fists. Ted Lettieri watched them calmly, a slight smile on his face.

In an upstairs room at the F.I.S.T. warehouse, Abe was on the telephone, Johnny stood next to him.

"What's he sayin'?" Johnny said impatiently.

"They're loadin' the scabs up," Abe said.

"Okay, that's it. Let's go!"

They ran from the room down the stairs onto the main floor of the warehouse. There were a hundred men sitting there holding hats and long rubber hoses, all of them wearing hats with cardboard stuffed into them.

"All right!" Johnny yelled. "Let's go!"

The men burst out the warehouse doors into the street. Led by Johnny and Abe, holding their hats, they were a small army on a wild run through the sunlit streets of the Flats.

At the end of the street by the Consolidated terminal, a line of uniformed guards carrying shotguns formed, the four armored trucks behind them. They started moving toward the strikers blocking the gate.

At the same time, a truck roared into the street in front of the Consolidated gate and strikebreakers leaped from it carrying baseball bats. The strikers removed pieces of leaded garden hose and clubs of various sizes from their clothing. Ted Lettieri took his gun out. The strikebreakers hesitated, stunned that the strikers were armed.

"Let's get 'em!" Ted Lettieri shouted and the strikers charged the strikebreakers.

From across the street, the women ran toward the fray, the little paper bags in their hands. Anna saw one of the strikebreakers fighting with a striker. She went up to the man and hurled the paprika into his face. The man screamed in pain.

The uniformed guards walked in phalanx toward the action, the armored trucks behind them. From the sidewalk, Mishka and his friends peppered them with the rotten eggs. The guards cringed from the stink and stepped back in disarray.

Beaten and outnumbered, the strikebreakers fled from the strikers toward an alley. As they ran for it, Johnny, Abe, and their men burst from the alley toward them.

The armored trucks pulled around the phalanx of uniformed guards in front of them and headed for the strikers. As they did, a dapper little man darted from the sidewalk. He was Louis Tomasini, expert safecracker, a man Vince Doyle had especially recruited from Detroit for this day. Louis Tomasini threw a stick of dynamite at the armored truck. The truck exploded. The men inside screamed.

Abe saw the explosion and ran to the burning truck. One of the uniformed guards fired his shotgun at Louis Tomasini. Tomasini went down. Abe stood over the dapper little man, blood-covered and dying in the street.

On a tenement roof across the street, Vince Doyle watched the explosion, watched as the guard fired his shotgun. He turned to the man beside him. The man had a rifle in his hands.

"Get him," Vince Doyle said.

The man fired a shot from the roof and hit the guard who fired at Tomasini. The guard went down. The other uniformed guards looked around.

"Shoot around 'em," Vince Doyle said on the rooftop.

The rifleman pulled the trigger again. The shots hit the street around the uniformed guards, who ran toward the back of the Consolidated terminal. The armored trucks turned wildly in the street and raced away. Abe looked up at the roof.

Police wagons arrived. The policemen got off and started marching for the battling group, clubs in hand. An open truck suddenly tore from behind into the midst of the marching policemen, who desperately leaped out of the way. Tom Higgins was driving it. Strikers leaped from the back of the truck between the policemen. One of the policemen drew his gun.

"Hold your fire!" A police captain yelled. "You'll hit each other!"

Seeing that they couldn't use their guns, many of the policemen ran down the street.

Jugovich cornered a policeman against the Consolidated fence. He kept hitting the policeman, picking him up, hitting him again.

"Get up, you!" Jugovich shouted, hitting him again. "Fight!"

Still driving the truck, Higgins rammed the fence with it. The guards inside the Consolidated yard ran for the building as dozens of strikers shouldered the fence, trying to knock it down each time Higgins rammed into it. Higgins kept putting the truck into reverse and then ramming the fence.

Abe watched the armored truck burn. Near him, the body of the slain uniformed guard was trampled in the street. He could hear Higgins' truck scream as Higgins shifted gears. Abe stood there, dazed, almost in shock. A policeman swung a club at him and knocked him down. Johnny ran to him and knocked the policeman down with a piece of hose. He lifted Abe up.

"Abe? You all right?"

Abe stood glassy-eyed and didn't look at him.

"You all right?"

"We gotta stop it, Johnny!" Abe said, his voice choked. "We gotta stop it."

One of the guards inside the fence fired at Higgins' truck. The shot blew away a part of the windshield. Ted Lettieri aimed his revolver and fired. The guard went down.

Higgins' truck smashed the fence down. Dozens of

men trampled over it into the Consolidated yard. They smashed the windows of the scab trucks and started setting the trucks on fire. They headed for the Consolidated building and started throwing rocks at it. Windows broke.

On the third floor of the Consolidated terminal, Winthrop Talbot stood at a window with his son Phillip and Arthur St. Clair, watching the scene below him. His trucks were on fire. His windows were being broken. There were hundreds of men swarming over his yard.

"Let's get out of here," Phillip Talbot said.

"The police," Winthrop Talbot said. "What happened to the police?"

In the yard, one of the trucks exploded.

"For God's sake, dad," Phillip Talbot said.

He and St. Clair moved Winthrop Talbot from the window and hustled him down the stairs to a car at a rear exit.

Abe stood in the yard, dazed. The trucks were burning. Clusters of men threw rocks at the building. Others were trying to batter the door down. Higgins' truck circled the yard.

Johnny stood on top of it, yelling. "We're goin' back! Put the rocks down! We're goin' back! Everybody go back!"

Some of the men continued throwing the rocks but many turned and ran from the yard, brushing by Abe, who just stood there, staring. Johnny saw Abe from the truck. Their eyes met.

"Abe, come on!"

Abe hesitated, then leaped up on the truck next to Johnny.

"We won!" Johnny said. "We beat 'em!"

Abe looked at the burning trucks, the trampled fence, the smoke, the bloodied bodies on the ground.

"Did we, Johnny?"

Johnny didn't hear him.

"We're goin' back!" he yelled to the men in the yard, "Everybody go back! We won! We won!"

Photographers crowded around the conference room table. Winthrop Talbot got on one side of it, his son and St. Clair at his side. Johnny sat on the other; Abe, Higgins, and Vince Doyle beside him.

Flashbulbs popped as Johnny signed the paper and passed it across to Winthrop Talbot.

"Insurance, overtime, pay hike," Johnny said. "It's all there"—he paused, then grinned—"*gentlemen.*"

Winthrop Talbot took the paper and looked at it. There was funereal silence in the room.

"You gentlemen wanna *discuss* somethin' some more?" Johnny said.

St. Clair handed Winthrop Talbot a fountain pen. Talbot took the pen, hesitated, then quickly signed the paper. His expression was one of absolute defeat.

"You wanted the men to be happy," Johnny said. "That's what you said. We're happy." He grinned, paused. "Real happy, *Win.*"

Talbot looked at him and got up from the table. Johnny got up, grinned, and stuck his hand out over the table. Talbot looked at his hand and moved away from it. Johnny kept his hand out over the table and watched Winthrop Talbot walking away from him. Phillip Talbot shook his outstretched hand.

"I hope we can work together better in the future, Mr. Kovak," Phillip Talbot said.

"We're gonna work together real good, Phil, don't you worry."

Johnny smiled and winked at him.

The convention hall in Flint was a seedy old auditorium filled with rawboned, simply dressed men puffing on their stogies, F.I.S.T. banners hung from the rafters. The walls were plastered with signs which said "Reelect Rafferty" and "Go with Graham."

Johnny, Abe, and Vince Doyle were surrounded by a cluster of men.

"Where *you* from?" Johnny said to one of them.

"Flatbush."

"Where the hell's that? Place I come from's called the Flats."

"Brooklyn."

"Yeah? New York City, huh?" He grinned. "Well, how come you guys from New York City can't get what we got in Cleveland?"

"That's cause we ain't got you there with us, Johnny," a man said.

"You want me to tell you how to do it?"

"Sure, you tell us, Johnny," a man laughed.

"Okay, You look 'em in the eye, see? And then you kick 'em in the jewels. And then you wink."

The men laughed.

271

"How come you wink?" one of them asked.

"To take their minds offa how much it hurts."

As the men roared, a nervous, effeminate radio announcer moved into the middle of their group, a microphone in his hand.

"The man here in Flint who might influence this convention the most," the announcer said, "is Johnny Kovak, the new president of Cleveland's Local 302, Mr. Kovak, many of the delegates here are wondering —are you supporting Matt Rafferty or Max Graham for the presidency of the union."

"I'm no politician," Johnny grinned.

"There are rumors of bad feelings between you and Rafferty." The announcer stuck his microphone into Johnny's face.

"Horseshit," Johnny said.

The announcer pointed excitedly to his microphone. "We're on the air—"

"There's no other word for it. Horseshit."

"Thank you, Mr. Kovak," the announcer said, trying to get away.

Johnny snatched the microphone from him.

"I got a lotta respect for Matt Rafferty. He's been runnin' this union an awful long time. It's still here, right?"

He laughed.

The hotel room was airless and run-down. Vince Doyle was stretched out on the bed, a cigar in his mouth. Abe sat in a chair; Johnny sat on the floor, leaning against the wall.

"What do we need it for, Johnny?" Abe said. "Don't make any deals."

"If we could get this," Johnny said, "Illinois, Michigan, all those big states."

"All Graham has to do is make a little trade," Vince Doyle said.

"Think of what we could do for every guy in the Midwest, Abe. All the stuff we got at Consolidated."

"But you don't even know if he's gonna go for it," Abe said.

Johnny laughed.

"After what I said to that radio guy about Rafferty? Are you kiddin'?"

Max Graham opened the door. He was a middle-aged dandified man who wore a blue velvet robe. His manner was hearty and effusive; his eyes gray and cold.

"Johnny! Good of you to come."

"Max, how ya doin'." Johnny looked rumpled. His suit coat was draped over his shoulders; his tie was loose; he was sweating.

"Come in, Johnny. Come in."

Johnny looked around the lush, spacious suite.

"The dump we're in," Johnny said, "you oughta see the roaches. You ain't got no roaches in here, huh?" He grinned.

Graham went to the bar. "Bourbon, scotch, whatever you'd like."

"Give me a shot and a beer."

"I asked you to come up," Graham said, "'cause I

thought it was time we met. What you did in Cleveland, Johnny. Some victory!"

Graham handed him a glass of beer and a shot glass
of whiskey. Johnny dumped the shot in his beer glass.
Graham, drinking whiskey and soda, watched him.

"You asked me up cause you're runnin' neck and
neck with Rafferty," Johnny said.

Graham lifted his glass and smiled. "Here's to you,
Johnny."

Johnny drained his glass.

"I heard you talkin' about your friend Rafferty on
the radio," Graham said.

Johnny smiled at him. "Relax. You got my support,
Max."

"Just like that, huh?"

"You got it won, Max."

They grinned at each other.

"What do you want, Kovak?" Graham said, his voice
hard.

"The Midwest."

"The Midwest Council?" Graham laughed. "What
the hell you want that for? It's just a title."

"It is now," Johnny said. "But who says it's gotta
be? Who says we can't organize the whole thing—the
whole region—the way we did in Cleveland?"

Graham paused. He thought about it.

"Is that all you want?"

Johnny grinned. "Stay outa my way, Max, I'll stay
outa yours."

They looked at each other coldly.

Graham lifted his glass. "Here's to *us*, Johnny."

* * *

The final night of the convention, Max Graham, the new national president of the Federation of Interstate Truckers, stood on the stage of the Flint convention hall, his arms raised victoriously as the delegates cheered. He waved to Rafferty, then to Johnny, and the three of them linked their arms, raised them high, and smiled. The men roared their approval.

"I thought he was gonna jump off the goddamn stage insteada holdin' my hand," Johnny laughed the next day, as the train took them back to Cleveland. "Matt Rafferty and me, holdin' hands."

Abe and Vince Doyle laughed.

"I'll see you guys later," Abe said, "I'm gonna go take a nap."

He walked out of the dining car. Vince Doyle looked disdainfully after him.

"Ah, he's okay." Johnny said.

Doyle didn't say anything. He sipped a beer.

"The president of the Midwest Council," Doyle laughed. "You're getting up in the world, Johnny."

Johnny smiled. "Stick with me, Vince."

Doyle laughed.

"I mean it. I couldna done none of this without you."

"What about the club?" Doyle grinned. "The . . . interests . . . I got."

"I don't know," Johnny said. "Let Jocko run it for you. Keep your hand in, I don't care. Stick with me. You got a nice big job. Legit."

"A union man, Johnny? Me?"

"Listen, the sky's the limit with this thing, Vince.

Graham—Jesus, he's an asshole. Those guys at that convention, they loved me."

Doyle laughed. "Now it's me that's gonna work for you?"

"We'll do it together, Vince. We got the whole Midwest to work with. We got all that territory."

"Just look at it," Vince Doyle laughed, as the train passed a farm field. "Look at it, Johnny. All I see's a buncha cows."

'Naw, listen," Johnny said, his voice loud and excited. "I mean it. When those guys see what I can get 'em—hell, Vince—"

Doyle laughed.

The room at Local 302's warehouse, the union's new Midwestern headquarters, was only partially completed. A map of the Midwest had been taped to the wall. Johnny stood by the map. Vince Doyle, Abe, and Tom Higgins were around him.

"None of these locals," Johnny said, "pointing to the map—wherever they are—Michigan, Indiana, Kentucky—they're gettin' nothing. They ain't got the push. What we gotta do is bring 'em all together. Get every goddamn driver here in all these Midwest states to sign up. No exceptions. Everybody. We do that, the companies are gonna give us what we want."

"We'll never do it," Abe said, "a lotta guys don't wanna sign up."

"What if the companies they're workin' for sign 'em up," Johnny said. "They can't do nothing about it then."

"What do you mean?" Higgins said.

"We tell the companies they drive for—you wanna get along with us, you sign all your men up to us. That way they join automatically."

Abe thought about it. "So what if they sign the guys up and the guys don't pay their dues? That means they're not really in the union."

"Yeah, but what if the companies make sure they pay the dues?"

"What are you talkin' about?" Higgins said.

"They take the dues outa the drivers' pay. They pay us all the guys' dues in one lump each month."

"A checkoff, you mean?" Abe said. "It's not fair to the guys."

"Sure it is," Johnny said. "It's easier for 'em. They don't have to worry about comin' in to pay it."

"What if the companies won't do it?" Higgins asked.

"They'll do it," Vince Doyle said.

"That way we can really do good for the guys," Johnny said, "the locals don't negotiate with the companies no more. Like the strike that local's got goin' against the paper company in West Virginia. We'll negotiate for 'em."

"But it's *their* strike, Johnny," Abe said.

"Are you kiddin'? They're all in the Midwest Council, right? Every strike is *our* strike. We tell the locals if they can go out or not. We say they go out, then we work a deal out for 'em."

"You gonna go over all these states signin' everybody up?" Abe said.

"We'll send guys out to each state. Business agents.

277

They get a cut on each guy they sign up, each company."

"What business agents?" Abe said.

"Well, some of the guys we had helpin' us here. I don't know. They got friends in Detroit, Chicago. Right, Vince?"

"Sure. Easy."

"We'll give 'em a good cut," Johnny said. "Make it a business proposition for 'em."

"Johnny," Abe said, "you're gonna *muscle* guys to join up?"

"If we gotta muscle a few guys, it's for their own good."

"Federation of Interstate Truckers, Local 123, Parkersburg, West Virginia," said the banner on the wall of the cluttered storefront office. Johnny and Abe are talking to three men in workers' caps.

"Listen," Johnny said angrily, "I didn't ride six hours down here in the fuckin' rain to listen to a lotta guff. I say you go for the insurance and the overtime. Forget the pay raises on the contract. For your own good."

"*You say*," one of the men said, "I run this local."

"You're all in the Midwest Council, ain't you? You wanna stay in this fuckin' union, you do what I tell you."

"What are you gonna do? Throw us out, Kovak?"

"On your ass. No strike benefits. No compensation. You wanna try me?"

The men looked at each other. One of them got up angrily.

"Hey, come on," Abe said. "This way we can really do good for you guys. The companies can't screw little locals like yours no more. They gotta deal with all of us, together."

"The whole council," Johnny said. "Come on, listen to me. We're all on the same side. I know what the hell I'm doin'."

The next day in Parkersburg, they met with the company officials on the terrace of a country club.

"Insurance and overtime," Johnny said to them. "If you don't give it to us—right now—we're gonna hold out for pay raises, too."

"That sounds like blackmail to me," one of the men said.

"Call it what you like. If you want a strike like Talbot in Cleveland—"

"This ain't your local here, Kovak. What does this have to do with you?"

"I'm the president of the Midwest Council. They work for me."

"It's our company. They work for us."

"They do what the union tells 'em."

"If we agree to this contract, Kovak, how do we know you won't ask us for a pay raise next month?"

"We live up to our agreements," Abe said.

Johnny smiled. "You play ball with me, I'm gonna play ball with you."

"But what about the local here, how do we know they won't—"

"Look," Johnny said. "You worry about me. You get along with me, you got nothin' to worry about."

By winter, the warehouse had been completely rebuilt. Johnny's office was bare. There were two photographs on the wall. In one of them, he sat across a conference table from Winthrop Talbot. In the other, he and Graham and Matt Rafferty stood on stage, their arms linked. Atop a cabinet behind his desk was a tangle of wires attached to a small metal box with a red button on it: Grant's buzzer.

"How we doin'?" Johnny said.

Vince Doyle smiled. "We've got a hundred and forty-six business agents. Twelve states of the Midwest."

"Business agents," Abe said. "All those guys care about is their commissions."

"We've got almost one hundred percent company sign-ups," Doyle said.

"Anybody givin' us trouble?"

"One outfit, Johnny," Doyle said. "In Chicago. Guy named Vasko runs it. Hard-headed hunkie." He smiled.

"A hunkie, huh? It figures. How come he won't sign?"

"His guys don't wanna join, he said."

"The guy's a nobody, Johnny," Abe said. "He runs a small outfit. The hell with him."

"He'll join," Johnny said. He smiled. "They'll all join."

* * *

"Those guys are here to see you again, Frank," Smitty said.

Frank Vasko crawled out from under the truck, his face sooty, his clothes dirty. He glanced at the two men waiting outside his office.

"You want me to come with you, Frank?" Smitty said.

"Naw, you stay here. I can take care of it."

He was a big, broad-shouldered man in his early thirties and as he lumbered toward the two men, they watched him apprehensively.

Frank Vasko said nothing to them. He opened the door to his little office, walked in, and sat down behind his desk.

Then he said, his voice calm and sure, "I told you bastards already. Get it through your goddamn heads."

"Here's the contract, Frank," one of them said. "You sign it at the bottom."

Frank Vasko looked at the paper on his desk, smiled, and said, "The bottom?"

"That's right," one of them said.

He picked the paper up and ripped it into pieces.

"You sonofabitch!" one of them said. He reached for the blackjack which was in his belt. Frank Vasko knocked the blackjack from his hand and knocked the man cold. Then he ceremoniously picked the other one up, lifted him into the air, and hurled him through his plate-glass window.

Weeks later, as he decorated the Christmas tree with his wife and daughter, the doorbell rang. Frank

Vasko opened the door and a man stood there in an overcoat and hat, smiling at him.

"I'm Johnny Kovak," he said.

Frank Vasko stared at him.

Johnny smiled. "It's cold out here. Can I come in?"

Frank Vasko nodded and then turned to his wife and said, "Helen, take Aggie to mom's for a while."

His wife looked at the stranger smiling at her. She was a curvy, statuesque brunette and as Johnny smiled he said, "She don't have to go no place, Frank, on account of me."

When they were gone, Frank Vasko brought him a beer and sat down across from him and said, his voice cold and angry, "So what the hell you come here for? You can't—scare me. Those business agents you sent down, they didn't get no place."

Johnny grinned. "You gotta understand somethin', Frank. It ain't nothin' personal. You and me—shit, Frank—we probably come over here on the same boat. *Beszelsz Magyarul?*" (Do you speak Hungarian?)

"*Jobban mint Angolul,*" Frank Vasko said, his tone hard and unyielding. (Better than English.)

"Then what the hell we arguin' for?" Johnny laughed. "We come from the same country. We're on the same side."

"They don't wanna sign up, Johnny," Frank Vasko said determinedly. "They took a vote. They don't wanna pay dues. Look, Johnny. We got our own insurance. My guys, they got the best overtime of anybody in Chicago. Best rate of pay anybody in Illinois. Why the hell should they sign up?"

"Cause of the other guys workin' for other companies that don't got it so good, Frank. We gotta think about *all the guys* drivin' the road. We gotta have all the guys signed up so as we got the push."

"I don't give a shit about the other companies," Frank Vasko said. "I'm not gonna force my men to do somethin' they don't wanna do!"

"Listen, goddamnit!" Johnny said angrily. "I've seen tough guys before." He paused, lowered his voice. "We can't make no exceptions, Frank."

"I'm not gonna do it," Frank Vasko said. "Period."

Johnny smiled and got up. He got his hat and coat, and went to the door.

"Merry Christmas, Frank," he said.

Babe Milano sat in his favorite restaurant in the Loop, forking linguine, listening to Vince Doyle talk about a hunkie named Vasko and the "little help" Vince and his hunkie friend needed.

"The whole world needs a little help, Vince," Babe Milano said.

Vince Doyle and Johnny laughed. Babe's man Angel, the size of a mountain and just as talkative, was eating his food with funereal grimness.

"You're tellin' me," Babe Milano said, turning to Johnny with a grin, "that you're a hunkie and this guy Vasko's a hunkie and you can't settle this thing between you? I'll tell you somethin'. You never see no Italians goin' to no bohunks to settle no family argument."

"It ain't exactly a family argument, Babe," Vince Doyle said.

Milano smiled. "Besides that, I don't know nothin' about labor unions. All I know is that my old man sure as hell coulda used one in Wheeling. And Capone was always talkin' about 'em."

"Capone?" Vince Doyle grinned.

"Yeah. He had this big dream. He was gonna set up a whole union."

"What kinda union?" Johnny said.

"Bartenders. That way all the bartenders in the country'd push Al's booze."

They laughed. Angel didn't crack a smile.

"Al," Babe Milano said, "he shoulda paid his goddamn taxes steada havin' so many goddamn dreams. I ain't got no dreams. That's why I've got the world by the balls."

They laughed.

"You like the clam sauce?" Babe Milano asked Johnny.

"Yeah, sure. It's great."

"Garlic," Babe Milano said. "That's what does it. I have 'em cut in a whole bulb of the stuff. Cures whatever you got wrong with you. Got a cold, hangover, eat the garlic. It won't stand up for you in bed, eat the garlic. Right, Angel?"

"Right, boss," Angel said morosely.

"And have her hold her nose," Vince Doyle said. They laughed.

"Club doin' okay?" Milano asked Vince Doyle.

"Fine. Jocko's takin' care of it for me. You oughta

come down to Cleveland sometime, Babe. Haven't seen you in a while."

"We got a big operation goin' here," Babe Milano said. "Big busines, Vince. Always some shit. Last week, over in Cicero, some guy goes out into the neighborhood, tries to set up his own numbers. In Cicero! Just like that. Some *paisan*. No organization behind him. Nothin'. Goes out and does it all on his own."

"What'd you do?" Vince Doyle said.

"I talked to him," Babe Milano laughed. "Now he don't wanna set up no numbers no more."

Babe Milano was forty-two years old, a lantern-jawed, graying man with ice-cold eyes, one of the most powerful men in Chicago. The mayor sent him Christmas gifts. The Cook County district attorney, an unctuous careerist named Donald Carnes, invited him to his dinner parties. He was rich and happy, a big businessman who had a stake in four racetracks and owned two companies.

He was born in Wheeling, West Virginia, in a railroad labor camp. His father, Ippolito Milano, shifted tracks there, carried crossties, carved out roadbeds with a pick and shovel. He, his mother and father lived in a wire-enclosed company compound. There was never enough to eat and the boy, an only child, was always cold.

When he was six, his father was chosen for a work team that was to blast, shovel, and bore its way through a mountain for a new rail line. Each night his father came home covered with a light-colored dust. He had more and more trouble breathing and finally he couldn't work. His wages were cut right away, but the company permitted Ippolito Milano and his wife and son to stay in his company-owned shack. He fought for air for three months and died. The doctor said there were rocks the size of plums in his lungs.

The day after his death, the company told Luisa Milano to take her son and get out of the compound. She moved to the Italian section of Wheeling and rented a two-room apartment. The boy was seven years old when he started hawking newspapers on the streets of Wheeling. One day he walked into a saloon run by Fazio Felice, a rotund Sicilian rumored to be Wheeling's underworld kingpin, a man who always kept a derringer strapped to his boot. Fazio Felice saw the frail seven-year-old boy in his saloon and threw him out.

The next day the boy went back with his papers. Fazio Felice threw him out again. The boy went back again the next day and this time Fazio Felice screamed. "It's the kid again!" and leaped from a chair, swooped the boy into the air, and carried him toward the door. The boy dropped his papers and they scattered on the whiskey-soaked wooden floor. Fazio Felice stopped, holding the boy in midair, then sat him down on a barstool. "Kid," he said, "you ain't makin' me happy." The boy dropped from the barstool and slowly picked up his papers, straightening them into a neat pile. Then he turned and looked at Felice. "You want some papers?" he said. "Get outa here!" Fazio Felice roared.

But the next day, as the boy was hawking his papers, a big man in tight, flashy clothes walked up to him on the street and said Fazio Felice wanted to see him. The big man took the boy to the saloon and Fazio Felice lifted him to the barstool and said, "Okay, kid, what's your name?"

"Anthony," the boy said, "but mama calls me Babe."

Fazio Felice laughed. "Okay, Babe," he said. "You give me papers every day. You give me twenty in the morning and twenty in the afternoon and don't you mess up once or the deal's off."

Fazio Felice treated him like his own son from then on and by the time Babe Milano was sixteen, he was a man. He dropped out of school and, to his mother's distress, spent many nights away from home. But he brought money home for the groceries and she was was grateful for that. She didn't know that he was working for Fazio Felice, carrying messages and slips at first, then working as a bouncer and collector.

In 1921, Fazio Felice was gunned down by a man working for Guido Bertieri, his rival for the underworld gold mine along the Ohio River and, fearing for his own life, Babe Milano left Wheeling. He went to Detroit to see Giacomo Marchetti, who had been one of Fazio Felice's lifelong friends.

Prohibition had gone into effect at midnight, January 16, 1920, and Giacomo Marchetti was the biggest rumrunner in Michigan. He had set up a fleet of motor launches and schooners to import top-drawer Canadian whiskey. At first Babe worked for Marchetti as a lowly rumrunner but, reliable and intelligent, he was soon in charge of rum runs to Buffalo, Cleveland, Toledo, Milwaukee, and Chicago. He worked out the deals and percentages with gangs in each city and, where boats were impractical or too dangerous, he established truck and car fleets to transport the booze.

That's how Capone noticed him in Chicago. Babe Milano's shipments came in on time and were uncut and one day Al Capone offered Babe Milano a job. He could have protection and a chunk of the city if he was willing to take over Al Capone's bootleg supply operation. Babe Milano agreed, even though Giacomo Marchetti told him he would die if he went. Babe left him anyway, told Capone of the threat, and two months later Giacomo Marchetti was tommy-gunned to death in a restaurant parking lot in Detroit.

Capone, a man with a fine business sense, mourned Marchetti's death and realized that someone would have to take over the operation in Detroit. He picked Babe Milano to oversee Detroit from Chicago. Babe picked Shondor Elik Gerky, who had helped him make his rum runs to Buffalo and Cleveland, a soft-spoken and polite man who was a mathematical genius.

With Baba Milano plotting the overall strategy, the Capone bootlegging operations broadened. Babe Milano went back to West Virginia and down to Kentucky, organizing the moonshiners, and trucks were soon speeding out of the hills across country loaded with liquor, traveling "safe" routes created by payoffs. And in the meantime, Babe also ran his own little section of Chicago, taking care of numbers, gambling, whores, and booze. He wasn't greedy and made no effort to encroach on anyone else's territory. And after a few attempts to muscle in on his, no one tried. Periodically, he toured the cities he serviced to tighten up operations. He liked to meet the men he was dealing with: men like Vince Doyle in Cleveland. Bobby Grimaldi in Buffalo, Albert DeSapri in Pittsburgh.

On October 24, 1931, Al Capone was sentenced to prison and Babe Milano, who had watched his downfall closely, had no desire to be the new "Mayor of Crook County." He stayed in the background, avoided publicity, filed unchallengeable tax returns, and left the political maneuvering to his subordinates.

When Prohibition was repealed, he realized that the future lay in conducting legitimate business with plenty of muscle behind it. He continued his numbers and protection operations in his section of Chicago, opened a number of legitimate nightclubs, and held onto one whorehouse for old times' sake. But he was also instrumental in organizing a syndicate which purchased a string of racetracks in Ohio, West Virginia, and Kentucky. And with Shondor Gerky in Detroit, he formed the Haley Jukebox Company, a potential mother lode once the restaurant and bar owners were convinced to install their machines.

Sitting now in the restaurant in the Loop finishing his linguine, Babe Milano was pleased with himself.

It wasn't a joke. He wasn't kidding. He had the world by the balls.

"You want some spumoni?" he asked Johnny.

Johnny shook his head. "It's gonna come outa my eyes."

Milano laughed. "Angel, you want some spumoni?"

Angel's stone face cracked into a wide smile. "Yeah, that'd be great, boss."

"Goddamn guy," Babe Milano grinned. "Day he dies, his mouth's gonna be fulla spumoni."

They laughed, Babe Milano ordered the spumoni for Angel, and Vince Doyle looked at him seriously and said, "How about it, Babe?"

Milano looked at him. "Look, you want me to talk to this guy what's his name?"

"Vasko."

"Vasko. I'll talk to him, Vince." He glanced at Johnny. "For your friend here."

Doyle smiled. "We figured here in Chicago it'd be better if you took care of it."

Milano looked at Johnny. "You owe me," he said, his voice hard. Johnny looked at him and didn't say anything.

"He's gonna remember," Milano said, "huh, Vince?"

Doyle grinned. "Johnny don't forget. He's a hundred percent."

Milano looked at Johnny. "Nobody's a hundred percent," he said.

Helen Vasko hurried through the snow with Aggie, shopping bags in her hand. She fumbled with the key, then opened the door, and they rushed inside, shivering.

"Hello, Helen," one of them said.

There were three of them—big, rough-looking men wearing hats and suits.

"Who are they, mommy?" Aggie said.

Helen Vasko stepped back against the door in alarm and said, "What do you want?"

"We're just gonna talk to you a couple minutes, Helen," one of them said. He turned to Aggie. "You're gonna stay right here by the Christmas tree and tell your Uncle Jack what Santa's gonna bring you for Christmas."

"I don't have an Uncle Jack," Aggie said.

"Sure you do, honey," the man said.

"It's all right," Helen Vasko said to her daughter, "just stay right here."

The men smiled and two of them walked her into the bedroom and closed the door.

"Who are you?" she said, her voice shaking. What do you want here?"

One of them stepped closer to her. "Aw, we just wanna have a little fun, Helen."

He pushed himself against her and fondled her breasts.

"No," she said, "please."

"I bet you just love to have fun, don't you, Helen." He reached behind her, pulled her skirt up, and held her buttocks.

She started to cry. "Please."

He pulled her slip up and pushed her panties down.

The other one pushed himself against her bare buttocks and whispered, "You ever had it like this, Helen?
Two of us, at the same time?"

Her blouse was ripped open, and then her slip was
torn off. She stood there naked, sobbing, the two of
them holding her, fondling her.

One of them unzipped his fly and said, "Kneel
down, Helen."

She stood there shaking, sobbing, unable to move.

"I said kneel down."

He grabbed her shoulders roughly and forced her
to the floor, pulled her toward him by her neck and
then laughed suddenly and then he slapped her and
she slumped against the wall, naked and defenseless
and hysterical.

The man zipped his pants up and laughed. "Next
time, Helen, we ain't gonna stop."

Frank Vasko sat in the office of the Cook County
district attorney, Donald Carnes, listening, but the
words he heard didn't make any sense to him.

"I don't understand," he said.

"I've read your statement, and your wife's," the
district attorney said. "There's nothing we can do.
There's no evidence that what happened to your wife
has anything to do with your problems with the Federation of Interstate Truckers."

"No evidence?" Frank Vasko said. "But Kovak was
over my house. He came from Cleveland to see me—"

"You want me to prosecute because he paid you a

visit?" the district attorney smiled. "That's not against the law in this country."

Frank Vasko looked at him and didn't say anything.

"I'm sorry," the district attorney said, "your wife is an attractive woman. It could have been anyone that saw her on the street." He paused. "You understand, Vasko?"

"I understand," Frank Vasko said, not looking at him. The next day he called the Federation of Interstate Truckers' office and asked the business agents to come to his office.

"You sign on the bottom, like we told you," one of the business agents laughed, and Frank Vasko handed him the signed contract.

"You finally got smart," the business agent said.

"You tell Kovak—" Frank Vasko said angrily, then he stopped.

"Yeah? What should we tell him?"

"You tell him," Frank Vasko said, his voice low and broken, "You tell him Merry Christmas for me."

"Merry Christmas, Johnny," Anna said.

"Merry Christmas, Anna." He kissed her lightly.

The Christmas tree in the Kovak living room was filled with sparklers. Molly lighted one of them and as the sparks flew around the room, Abe said, "She's gonna put the house on fire."

"Let's open the presents up," Johnny said. "Anna's first." He went to the tree and picked up a present and yelled, "Ma! Come on in here!"

293

Ilona Kovak walked into the living room and said, "The duck is ready."

"You open *yours* first," Anna said.

Abe laughed. "Come on, come on, we ain't got all night. The duck's ready. You heard ma."

Anna opened the package Johnny handed her. There was a diamond ring inside. She looked at Johnny.

"This one's real," he said.

"Oh, Anna," Molly said, "let me see!"

Abe looked at the ring. "Did you rob a bank, Johnny?"

He laughed. "I got it on the layaway at Finesilver's."

Anna held the ring, teary-eyed.

"Yes or no," Johnny said.

"Listen to the big shot," Ilona Kovak smiled. "Give orders again."

Abe and Molly laughed.

"Yes or no, Anna."

"This ain't supposed to happen like this, Johnny," Anna said.

Abe laughed, "Come on, come on. The duck's ready!"

Anna looked at Johnny. "Well, sure," she said.

They laughed. Johnny put the ring on Anna's finger and kissed her.

Abe said, "Get the duck, ma, will you?"

Later that night, when they were alone in the living room by the Christmas tree, Anna said, "Johnny, do you really wanna *marry* me?"

"You think I'd spend my money for nothin'?" he laughed.

She looked at the ring and said, "Johnny, do you love me?"

"Are you kiddin'? Sure!"

"Why don't you ever say it?"

He pulled her close and kissed her.

"I say it."

Vince Doyle led Babe Milano to the table in the back of the nightclub where Johnny was waiting for them. With them was Shondor Gerky, a tall, lean man in his early thirties.

"Johnny," Vince Doyle said, "you know Babe. This is Shondor Gerky."

"Hey, how you doin'?" Johnny said, shaking Gerky's hand.

"Everybody in Detroit's talkin' about you, Johnny," Gerky said with a smile.

"Yeah? What are they sayin'?"

"They wish they had you up there, Johnny, to keep an eye on Henry Ford."

They laughed and sat down at the table.

"Hear that, Vince?" Babe Milano said, grinning, looking at Johnny. "He's a big deal, this kid."

Doyle grinned. "So when'd you get in, Babe?"

"Late in the afternoon," Milano said. He looked at Johnny. "We came down on Shon's boat. He says to me I gotta fish in Lake Erie. Shit, all you got in Lake Erie's a buncha old tires and new shit. There ain't no fish."

Gerky laughed. "You got perch in here, Babe, good bass. All you gotta do is have the patience."

"Sure you do." Milano said. "You fish much, Johnny?"

"In the Flats? For what? Roaches and rats?"

They laughed.

"He's gettin' married, Babe," Vince Doyle said.

"Congratulations," Milano said to Johnny. "Greatest thing for you, settles you down, gives you a chance to think. Steada runnin' around lookin' for it all the time."

"You married, Babe?" Johnny grinned.

"Three times," Milano deadpanned.

They roared.

Milano looked around the nightclub, which was filling with customers. A band started to play at the front of the room.

"What happened to that singer you had?" Milano asked.

"She wore herself out," Vince Doyle smiled.

"Singin'?"

"Like a bunny," Vince said.

Milano laughed.

"You're a union man, huh, Vince?" Gerky said.

"Our business agent," Johnny said.

"I never thought I'd see you a union man," Gerky grinned.

"You're doin' a lotta good things for your guys, Johnny," Milano said.

"I'm trying, Babe."

"I mean it. I wish you was around when I was workin' the mines."

"You?" Johnny grinned. "In the mines?"

"West Virginia," Milano said. "I was seventeen years old."

"He didn't like it," Gerky said.

"You're goddamn right I didn't like it," Babe Milano said.

Johnny laughed.

The car pulled up outside the warehouse which was Local 302's new headquarters and Abe jumped out and said, "I'm only gonna be a minute."

"We've got a date," Molly said.

"I gotta pick up a file, Molly."

"I'll bet you even dream about your files."

He laughed. "I do not and you know it."

"What do you dream about?" she teased.

"You know what I dream about. I'm only gonna be a minute."

He walked into the warehouse, laughing, and when he saw the light at the end of the hall, he hesitated. He didn't understand why anyone would be in the office this late. He went closer to the door and heard their voices. He started to turn away, but then he stopped in the corridor and listened to them.

"Johnny," Milano said, "they're an antilabor company, for Christ's sake. All you gotta do is go for a company that's good to its workers."

Johnny laughed. "Like yours, huh?"

297

"Hell, yes, we're good to our workers," Milano said.

"No complaints," Gerky grinned.

Milano said, "It's easy, Johnny. Your drivers don't deliver booze to any bar unless the bar's got one of our company's jukeboxes in it."

"How many jukeboxes you talkin' about?"

"Thousands of 'em," Milano said. "Here, Michigan, Illinois."

"That's a big operation," Johnny said.

There was a pause. Vince Doyle said, "Babe did us a big favor with Vasko, Johnny."

Milano smiled. "We'll help your guys, the union, whatever way we can. You know that. I've got a lotta respect for you, Johnny."

Johnny grinned. "Sure you do, Babe."

"All right then," Milano said, "is it a deal?"

"It's a deal," Johnny said slowly.

"Terrific," Milano said. "Terrific. Now. I'd like to give you a nice wedding present, Johnny."

"I don't need nothin'," Johnny said.

"Who's talkin' need, Johnny?" Milano said. "You're an important man. You got all kindsa people lookin' at you. Buy yourself a nice home. It's my gift. To you and the missus."

In the corridor, Abe turned from the door, his face a mask of disillusionment and hurt. He walked quietly down the dark hallway and out the front door of the warehouse.

In his office, Johnny turned to Babe Milano angrily and said, "I told you, I don't need nothin'."

Doyle said, "Hey, Johnny, Babe was just tryin'—"

"I know what he was tryin'."

Milano smiled. "I was just tryin' to help you, Johnny, that's all."

Their wedding was one of the largest ever held in the Flats. The mayor sent policemen to direct traffic; the newspapers sent photographers and held the Sunday edition; Max Graham sent a complete china setting as his wedding present. The ceremony was a solemn high mass, with three priests officiating. The St. Stephen's Dramatic Club Choir sang the Ave Maria. When Johnny and Anna walked out of the church with their wedding party, a huge crowd awaited them. They were bombarded with rice. Johnny's wedding party was made up of Mishka, Vince Doyle, and Tom Higgins. Abe was his best man.

At the reception afterwards in the sweltering hot church hall, there were hundreds of people, three bands, and two wedding cakes—one a Hungarian Dobos torte; the other a Lithuanian spice cake.

Anna stood in the middle of the floor in her wedding gown. A long line of men stood in front of her, waiting to kiss the bride.

Johnny watched as Mishka kissed her.

"That's enough, Mish."

Mishka ignored him and kept kissing Anna.

"Will you let her breathe?" Johnny laughed.

Petey Marr pushed Mishka away. "It's my turn."

"You wanna go get some air?" Abe said.

"I'm supposed to stand around here," Johnny said loudly, "and watch all these guys kiss my wife?"

They walked upstairs and into the sacristy, which was empty. There was a calendar on the wall with a picture of a bleeding Sacred Heart of Jesus opened to August 1938. The windows were open.

"The priest gets outa here after mass," Johnny laughed, "like some big-assed bird."

He opened a cabinet and started rummaging through it.

"What are you doin'?" Abe said.

"I'm lookin' for the wine."

"We got wine downstairs."

"You ever had any of the priest's wine? I was in the sixth grade, ma made me join up and be an altar boy. Here it is!"

He held up a bottle of opened wine and grinned.

"Every day I hadda serve, before the priest come in, I had a glass of his wine."

He found two glasses and poured wine into them.

"Best damn wine. Priests got terrific taste. They gotta drink it first thing in the morning."

He handed Abe a glass and held up his own.

"Here's to you and Molly. That frame of hers, she must be terrific." He laughed. "Huh? You can tell me. I'm a married man."

Laughing, he drank the wine from his glass. Abe watched him and put his glass down.

"What'd you do, Johnny?" Abe said quietly.

Johnny looked at him.

"Jesus, Johnny," Abe said, his voice heated but low, "what the fuck'd you do?"

"I got married," Johnny said, grinning. "If I knew you'd take it so hard, I'd—"

His grin faded. He stopped in mid-sentence.

"We had *dreams*, Johnny."

"What's the matter with you?"

"We had fuckin' dreams!"

Johnny looked at him.

"You *took*, Johnny, didn't you?"

"What are you sayin'?"

"You took!" He spit the words, his voice loud and angry.

"I took nothin' from nobody!" Johnny said angrily.

Abe paused, lowered his voice. "I heard you. I hadda pick somethin' up in the office. I heard you."

"You heard what?" Johnny said.

"You gonna buy yourself a nice home, Johnny? With your—wedding present?"

"Listen, I didn't—"

"*You* listen! You're gonna piss it all away? Everything? Every goddamn thing we built up? You and the fuckin' punks you got around you? Pushin' guys to do things they don't wanna?"

"I didn't do nothin', goddamnit."

"I don't believe you, Johnny," Abe said.

"I'm tellin' you, I didn't do nothin' except what's gonna help the guys."

"Jukeboxes!" Abe shouted. "They're gonna help 'em?" He looked away from him. "Shit, Johnny—"

"Those jukeboxes aren't gonna hurt nobody. Listen, Milano's a friend of ours."

301

"You sold out, Johnny! We had somethin' clean—"

"Clean?" Johnny said angrily. "What the hell's clean? Out there in the street? Look at what we're gettin' the guys! They got more money, they got insurance, they—we get that by bein' clean?"

They glared at each other. There was a long silence between them.

"I'm goin' to California," Abe said quietly. "I talked to Graham. They need my help with a local out there."

"When you comin' back?" Johnny said, his voice low but still angry.

"We're movin' out there. Me and Molly."

"Christ, Abe." He turned away from him, then turned back, his voice choked and imploring.

"Listen, there's highways gettin' built. Trucks all over the place. We're gonna have contracts to work out, guys to sign. We're growing big Abe. I need you."

"No, you don't, Johnny."

Abe walked out of the sacristy. Johnny looked after him.

When he walked back down to the church basement, a forced smile on his face, Anna put her arms around his neck. The band in the background was playing a czardas. It was bedlam.

"Where were you?" she said.

"I was talkin' to Abe."

She smiled. "I want you to talk to me."

He smiled slightly. "How you doin' . . . Mrs. Kovak."

She kissed him lightly.

"Talk to me more," she said.

He kissed her.

"More," she said.

In the background, Higgins bellowed, "Three cheers for Johnny Kovak, the best friend a workin' man ever had!"

The crowd cheered.

"I can't hear you, Johnny," Anna said.

He kissed her again.

II.

THE HEIGHTS

Washington, D. C. 1960. June. Four-thirty in the afternoon. A black Cadillac limousine wound its way through the early rush-hour traffic and pulled up to a skyscraping concrete and glass building near the Capitol. A long row of steps led to its front door. Beside the door was a large bronze plaque with the letters F.I.S.T. emblazoned on it.

As the limousine pulled up, a middle-aged man with horn-rimmed glasses and a freeze-dried smile rushed to it and swung open its back door.

"Welcome to Washington, Mr. Kovak."

An embarrassed black man in a chauffeur's uniform stepped out and said, "It was his idea, sir."

Johnny got out from behind the wheel of the limo, laughing. He was in his late forties. He was strong and lean, his hair graying at the sides, combed straight back. Bernie Marr, his assistant, got out on the passenger side. He was in his mid-twenties, a handsome young man wearing a button-down shirt, seersucker suit, and black cordovans.

"Welcome to Washington, Mr. Kovak," the man with the horn-rimmed glasses said.

Johnny slung his coat over his shoulder and ignored the man's outstretched hand.

"You're the official handshaker, huh?" Johnny grinned.

"I'm Peter Jacobs, Mr. Kovak, the director of public relations."

"The director, huh?"

He looked at the big ornate building and turned to Bernie Marr.

"Look at this sonofabitch, Bernie. It's bigger than the White House."

Max Graham's office was the size of a small auditorium. The carpeting was thick; the walls paneled; gold-framed photographs charting the course of Graham's career hung everywhere. A small Federation of Interstate Truckers flag was on top of his desk.

Max Graham greeted them at the door to his office. He was in his early sixties, a lean, well-kept man in a tailored suit who wore a toupee. He was very tanned.

"Great to see you, Johnny," he said effusively. "You've got to tell me how you manage to keep looking this good."

Johnny shook his hand. "You push a hundred every morning, Max, that's how. You know Bernie Marr? Petey Marr's boy? Bernie's my assistant."

Graham shook Bernie's hand. "How is your dad, Bernie? All the dockworkers I know still talk about him."

"Fine, Mr. Graham. He has a condominium in Fort Lauderdale."

Johnny glanced around Graham's office. "Sittin' in the sun, Max. Gettin' cranky as hell. Tell him about the telescope, Bernie."

Bernie Marr laughed and didn't say anything.

"He's got this big brass telescope." Johnny laughed. "Keeps an eye on the bikinis down there."

They laughed.

"Some layout you got here, Max," Johnny said.

"It's good for the image, you know what I mean, Johnny?"

Johnny walked over to the wood-paneled wall. "Public relations, huh?" He tapped the wall. "What is this stuff, mahogany or somethin'?"

"Walnut. You like it?"

"See that, Bernie," Johnny grinned. "You can reach out, knock on wood every place."

"Some days," Graham said, "I feel like doing it."

They laughed.

"We've got a masseur downstairs if you want to freshen up a bit, Johnny," Graham said.

"You've got your own guy to rub you down?" He grinned. "Isn't that somethin', Bernie?

"Sit down, sit down." Graham smiled. "How's your lovely wife?"

They sat down.

"Great, Max, great," Johnny said.

"And your boy?"

"Fine, just fine." He paused. "Gettin' bigger every day."

"I'm glad to hear it," Graham said. "We've got a suite at the Mayflower for you, you know. How long are you staying?"

Johnny laughed. "I just got here, Max, you want to know when I'm leavin'?"

Graham laughed. "I've got a big reception planned for you tonight, that's why I'm so curious."

"It's not often I get invited down to Washington for lunch," Johnny said.

"After the meeting at the Senate tomorrow," Bernie Marr said, "we're goin' back to Cleveland."

Johnny grinned. "Yeah, I'm not gonna be here long, Max. Don't worry."

Graham smiled. "Anything we can do for you Johnny. Anything at all. You know that."

Johnny looked at him and smiled slowly. "I know that, Max."

The reception that night was held at the Shoreham Hotel. Max Graham took Johnny around and introduced him to the guests. As he shook hands with them, Johnny kept his eye on a beautiful, raven-haired woman in her late twenties who was in a corner of the room. She stood straight, but the rigidity of her posture couldn't hide the softness of her curves. Her hair was swept away from her face, but kept falling into her eyes. She would brush the hair away with a smooth, fluid gesture which somehow struck him almost painfully. Their eyes met and he smiled at her. She turned haughtily away.

"Who is she, Max?" he finally asked.

"Oh, Karen. That's right, you haven't met." He

called loudly to her. The girl looked at them, obviously resenting the interruption, but she walked across the room.

"Karen," Max Graham said, "Johnny Kovak. Karen Chandler. Karen's in our research department."

"How do you do?" she said coldly.

"Just fine." He grinned.

"You don't look like your pictures."

"How's that?"

"They're very flattering."

He laughed. "You want me to send you some?"

"No, thank you," she said.

He laughed. Graham brought two men over to meet him.

Senator Donald Carnes, of Illinois, was white-haired, loud, and blustery. Senator Cole Madison, of Rhode Island, was a tall, attractive man with blond hair and blue eyes. He was in his late forties; there was an air of calm and refinement about him.

"The contracts you've gotten for your men in the Midwest," Carnes said loudly, "they've certainly earned you the respect of my constituents in the trucking industry."

"Nice of you to say so, senator." Johnny grinned.

Cole Madison smiled. "Tell me something, Mr. Kovak? How do you *always* manage to get your men such good contracts?"

Johnny laughed. "Well, you know I was barely born in this country, senator. On Ellis Island."

"We won't hold that against you," Cole Madison grinned.

"But I learned somethin' a long time ago," Johnny said, smiling. "You can get anything you want in this country—with a little bit of push."

The people around them laughed. Johnny glanced at Karen Chandler and winked at her. Cole Madison smiled wryly.

The house was in Shaker Heights, one of the most affluent suburbs in America. It was large but not lavish by the neighborhood standards. Johnny drove a late-model Lincoln into its circular driveway, got out of the car, looked around, walked up the steps, and opened the door.

"Anna?"

There was no answer.

"Anna?"

"In here."

He walked through the house into the kitchen. Anna was sitting at the table with her mother. She had retained her beauty and her figure, but there was an angularity to her movements. The years had robbed her smile of its freshness and blush, had taken from her that air of warmth and spontaneity she had had in her youth. Her hair was prematurely gray and sometimes Johnny felt as though the grayness had somehow seeped into her pores, blanched some secret vital part of her being.

"Hey," Johnny said. "Big welcome I get."

She got up from the table, smiled, and kissed him on the cheek.

"The TV star," her mother said.

"We saw you on TV," Anna said.

He laughed. "How'd I look?"

"You look better in person," Anna said.

"Older," her mother said, "like the rest of us."

He went to the refrigerator and got a can of beer, poured himself a shot of whiskey, and downed it.

"You remember we've got some people coming for a meeting tomorrow," he said.

Anna hesitated, then looked away from him. "I, uh— I promised them I'd go down to the parish, Johnny."

"Jesus, Anna, every time Babe or one of those guys come over you got somethin' to do." He paused. "Never mind. We'll grill somethin' up outside. Where's Joey?"

"He's in the yard," she said.

"Hey, Joey!" he shouted. "Joey!"

The door burst open and Joey hurled himself against Johnny. He was a large boy, twelve years old, with the thick dark hair and muscular build of his father. From birth, he had been mentally retarded.

"Hi, daddy! Hi, daddy!"

Johnny picked him up like a baby.

"Hey, how's my big guy?"

"Can we play horsey, daddy?"

"You're gettin' too old to play that," Johnny said.

"Can we play horsey?"

Anna said, "He hasn't seen you in three days, Johnny."

Johnny looked at the boy, then laughed suddenly. "All right, come on!"

He put the boy on his shoulders and ran outside

with him. The boy laughed happily. Anna and her mother watched them in silence through the window.

The following day at dusk they sat in the backyard of the house in their sports clothes, drinks in front of them. Johnny crouched over the barbecue, grilling their steaks. Babe Milano had come from Las Vegas; Shondor Gerky, who sat next to him, from Detroit.

"Now Marciano was a fighter," Babe Milano said. "These guys—you shittin' me?" Ingemar Johansson, whatever the hell his name is. The heavyweight champion of the world! A Swede?" Milano's hair was ash-white, but it was the only sign of his age. He was vibrant and muscled; he looked more like a man in his early fifties than a man who was sixty-three years old.

"How do you like your steak, Babe?" Johnny yelled from the barbecue.

"Well done."

"It's not good that way."

"I don't like it bloody."

Johnny laughed. "Pour him another drink, Tom, settle him down."

Higgins got the drink and said, "Joe Louis was some fighter, wasn't he, Babe?" He was obese. Baggy and layered from his shoulders to his knees, Higgins had trouble sitting on the lawn chair.

"Marciano took Louis out in a coupla rounds," Milano said, "what the hell you talkin' about?"

Johnny grinned. "Louis was an old man. Shit, Babe, Marciano was just another fat Guinea."

314

"That guy was a man," Milano said. "You know before every fight—he started out—a half stick of salami, then spaghetti, then steak, then half a gallon of ice cream. Then he was ready to fight."

"No wonder he was a fat guinea," Johnny said.

They laughed.

"How's my goddamn steak?" Milano said. He walked over to the barbecue. "You're burnin' it!"

"You said you wanted it well done, didn't you?" Johnny laughed.

"I didn't say I wanted it goddamn black."

Johnny laughed.

Milano lowered his voice. "Where the hell's Anna? How come she ain't here?"

"She's busy."

"What busy?"

"She's down at the parish," Johnny said. "St. Mattress of the Springs or somethin'. I don't know."

"I see you once a year, she's always down at the parish. What's the matter? She doesn't like me?"

Johnny laughed. "You ain't holy enough for her." He turned to the others. "Get your plates over here."

"I was you," Milano said, "I'd check the priest out."

Johnny laughed. "You, Babe, you'd check Jesus Christ out himself."

"You're goddamn right I would."

Johnny put the steaks on their plates.

"When the hell's that fight, Shon?" Milano said.

"Next week," Gerky said. "Yankee Stadium."

They moved to the picnic table with their steaks and sat down.

"Yankee Stadium?" Milano said. "Patterson and that Swede don't even belong in Yankee Stadium. Pass the salt, Vince, I gotta give this some taste."

"You haven't even tasted it yet," Vince Doyle said. He was heavy and balding and spoke with a thick, back-alley briskness which the years had not refined.

They laughed.

"You see the new place Graham's built in D.C.?" Johnny said to Milano. "It's somethin' you'd put up in Vegas."

"You guys paid for it, didn't you?" Milano said. He took a bite of his steak. "Look at this goddamn steak. It's coal."

They laughed.

"Each of the locals got tapped," Vince Doyle said.

"That goddamn Graham," Milano said. "He comes out last year, struttin' around. He calls me. He wants free tickets, for Christ's sake. This show and that. The cheap sonofabitch."

They laughed.

"You oughta take over, Johnny," Gerky said.

Doyle said, "That's what I've been tellin' him."

Johnny worked on his steak. "Where's the beer?" he said. "Get the beer, will you, Tom? I left it in the kitchen." He paused, then turned to Gerky. "I got time," he said.

"Who's got time?" Milano said. "Nobody's got that."

They laughed.

"Why don't you run against the guy, Johnny?" Milano said. "You'd win."

"Graham's done all right in D.C."

316

"Sure," Doyle said. "With us showin' the push in the Midwest, who's gonna screw with us at the table?"

"It's not that easy," Johnny said seriously. "If I got after him in public, Babe, it'd split the goddamn union up. The next time we're at the table to get a hike and the company reps see us weak on the inside, they ain't gonna give. It'd hurt the guys."

Higgins brought two cases of beer and started to uncap them. Milano took a bottle and looked at it.

"What the hell kinda beer is this?"

"It's Erin Brew, Babe," Higgins said. "They make it here. It's good."

"Cleveland beer? Jesus Christ." Milano looked at Johnny. "So you like what Graham's doin' in D.C., huh?"

"I don't like that goddamn palace he built, I'll tell you that. Rubdown guys, manicures—"

Milano interrupted him. "Manicures?" he said, looking at his nails. "What's wrong with a manicure?"

They all laughed at him.

Milano laughed with them. "All these years, Johnny. All these years. You're still a fuckin' hunkie."

On the wall behind the desk, above photographs of Anna and Joey, there was a large map of the Midwest with hundreds of red pins stuck into it, one pin for each local. On top of the desk was a small Federation of Interstate Truckers flag set in a silver base. Next to it, in a glass case, mounted on wood, was Gant's buzzer.

Johnny sat behind the desk, his shirt rumpled, his

tie loose and hanging low, a little black cigar in his hand. Doyle, Higgins, and Bernie Marr sat in front of him. Bernie Marr wore a blue button-down shirt, gray slacks, and a red and blue regimental tie.

"What about Senator Carnes?" Bernie Marr said.

"Give Carnes fifty thou," Johnny said. "Sixty top. But only if they bitch."

"Okay. What do you want to do about the Senate race here?"

Johnny puffed on his little cigar. "I don't know nothin' about the Democrat, what's his name? Hendricks."

"Henderson. Judge Mendelson sent you three letters asking for our support."

"Yeah, yeah. I know, Bernie. But the only time I met the guy, he shook hands like a fish. He's gonna lose."

"Five?" Vince Doyle said.

"Two. A favor to the judge."

"Two?" Doyle laughed. "Are you sure?"

"Okay. Three."

'We can't forget about the city council here, Johnny," Higgins said seriously.

Johnny laughed. His intercom buzzed.

"Send everybody at City Hall a case for Christmas. That's enough."

He pushed a button.

"There's a gentleman here to see you, Mr. Kovak," his secretary said.

The door opened. Abe Belkin stood there, grinning. His graying hair was cut short and combed over to the side. He was thin; his face lined; his eyes sunken in. He wore an off-the-rack suit which was too big on him.

Johnny got up from his desk and hugged him.

Johnny drove the Lincoln through the Flats, Abe at his side.

"Ma's gonna go nuts," Johnny said. "What the hell's it been? Five years since the last time—"

"How is she?"

"Like a rock. She won't budge. Not even with all the colored down here."

"They're not colored. They're Polish."

Johnny laughed. They passed the West Side Market.

"There's Mishka's place," Johnny said.

"He's still got his fruit stand?"

"Gets up at six o'clock every morning. Jeez, I love that old guy."

"How old is Mis now?"

"I don't know. He's gotta be—late seventies, I think."

Abe smiled.

They passed a block-long complex of new buildings, trucks all around them. Abe saw the sign: Talbot's Consolidated Trucking Company.

"God," Abe said, "that's Consolidated?"

"You wanna stop?"

"If they don't call the cops on us."

Johnny pulled up to the gate. A guard stopped the car.

"You can walk in, but you gotta leave the car here."

"I did that once," Johnny said. "I'm never gonna do it again."

Abe laughed. The guard looked at Johnny and recognized him. "Oh, Mr. Kovak. I'm sorry. Go right in, sir."

"Progress," Abe said. Johnny laughed.

The truck dock was a swirl of colors: red and amber and chrome and the flash of mirrors. Forty-thousand dollar rigs were parked next to each other; Macks, Peterbilts, Kenworths, Cummins. Lube guns shot high-pressure air. Revving engines roared. Air brakes hissed.

The truck drivers surrounded Johnny and shook his hand.

"Did you used to drive a lotta truck?" one of them asked Johnny.

"Hell, back in those days, we had rigs couldn't climb the hill outa the Flats."

The men laughed. Abe climbed in on the passenger side of one of the big trucks.

He bounced in the seat. "Air suspension seats, Johnny."

Johnny climbed in on the driver's side. "Adjusts right to your weight."

"Joe Harper sure coulda used one of these."

"Joe Harper," Johnny said. He paused, looked at the dashboard. "Look at the tach in this thing. A lotta power in here."

"Yeah," Abe said quietly. "You've got that now, don't you, Johnny?"

There was a silence between them.

"Hey," Abe said suddenly, grinning. "You want to take this thing out?"

Johnny laughed. "What the hell."

"I'll drive."

Johnny looked at him and grinned. "*I'm* driving."

Joey ran around them at the dinner table, blowing a toy horn loudly, over and over again.

"Anna, for Christ's sake," Johnny said.

"Come on, Joey, we'll play with this later." She took the horn from him. The boy started to cry.

Abe picked him up. "Come on up here to your Uncle Abe."

"I wish you woulda brought Molly," Anna said.

He rocked the boy on his knee. "I'm goin' back tomorrow, Anna."

"Did you bring me a present, Uncle Abe?" Joey said.

"Next time I come, Joey, I'll bring you one."

"I want a present, mommy."

"I'll bring you one," Abe said.

The boy started to cry again.

"Anna," Johnny said, "please."

She picked Joey up and held him.

Ilona Kovak watched Johnny and Abe. She was a frail, slight woman who still dressed in the old country manner. She wore a black dress and wore her gray hair in a bun.

"My two boys," she said slowly. "Why you don't come back from there in California, Abe? What you want there?"

Abe laughed. "You can get up in the morning, ma, you don't have to wipe the sweat off you."

"Sweat is good for you," Ilona Kovak said.

They laughed at her.

"Ma," Abe said, "you were tellin' me that ever since the time I first saw you."

"It is good," Ilona Kovak said.

"That's for sure, ma," Abe laughed.

Johnny raised his beer glass. "Well, here's to old times."

"Good times," Anna said quickly.

Abe smiled at her. "Good times, Anna."

"Is this a good time, daddy?" the boy said.

Anna said, "You know your father wants you to call him dad."

The boy smiled. "Is this a good time, dad?"

Johnny looked at him. He didn't smile. "Yeah, it's a good time, Joey."

The boy blew his horn.

Later that night, on the screened-in back porch, with empty beer bottles and a bottle of bourbon between them, Johnny said, "They were good times too, Abe."

Abe got up from the couch. He went to the screen and stared out at the darkness.

"I flew out here to talk to you, Johnny."

"Every five, six years you miss me. Is that what it is?"

"I'm serious." He paused. "You know that union flag you got on your desk? In that silver holder?"

"Yeah?"

"I got one too."

Johnny laughed. "You come all the way out here on account of that little flag?"

"Every local in the country's got one of those. You know how much they cost?"

"How much, for Christ's sake?"

"Each of those things cost fifty bucks."

"That thing cost fifty bucks? You're kidding me."

"More than a thousand locals in the country, Johnny. That's a lotta money."

"Jesus."

"How come you bought one?"

"I don't know. My secretary got it."

Abe nodded. "You got one the same reason my local got one." He paused. "'Cause we all got a letter from Graham suggesting we get a couple of 'em."

Johnny looked at him.

"You know who owns the company made those flags, Johnny?"

He shook his head.

"Graham's wife."

For a long moment, Johnny didn't say anything. Then he said, "Are you sure?"

"That's what I hear. That's right outta the guys' pockets, Johnny."

"Now wait a minute, Abe. You can't go off with your balls out on somethin' like this."

Abe smiled. "What do you want me to do, Johnny? Forget it?"

Johnny got up from the couch. "Did I say that? Jesus, Abe. Let me look into it."

"Then what?"

"If it checks, we'll do somethin' about it."

"Like what? What are we gonna do, Johnny?"

"I don't know. Somethin'. Have him give the money back to the locals. I don't know."

Abe looked at him distrustfully.

"You think I'd let anybody get away takin' from the guys?"

The next day, Johnny called Bernie Marr into his office. He told him what he had heard from Abe.

"If it's there," Johnny said, "I want it. Somebody pins you, duck. Go to Trenton. Check the guys out that have known Graham a while. You gotta spend for it, do it."

"What do you want me to take it out of?" Bernie asked.

"I'll give you ten outa the"—he grinned—"organization fund."

"How fast you want it?"

"The convention."

"Jesus, that's only—"

"You got a whole month," Johnny grinned. He looked at him seriously. "Bernie, it's important to me."

"Have I ever let you down?" Bernie Marr asked.

He watched Anna as she brushed her hair in front of the mirror in her bedroom. He walked up behind her, held her, and kissed the back of her neck. She moved away from him.

"You're *frisky* tonight," she smiled. "What'd you do today?"

324

"Frisky? What the hell kinda word—I played a little handball with Bernie."

"Did you?"

He looked at her. "What's the matter with that?"

"You never play with Joey."

"Sure I do. Joey can't play handball. He's—"

She turned on him. "He's what, Johnny? Say it."

"He's a little kid," he said. His eyes locked into hers. "What's the matter with you?"

"You never go anyplace with him," she said. "You never take him anywhere."

"I'm busy, Anna."

She smiled, measuring her words. "But not too busy to play handball with Bernie."

"Jesus Christ, Anna!" he yelled. "It's not my fault he's—" He stopped in mid-sentence.

"What isn't, Johnny?"

"Nothin'," he said sharply, turning away from her.

"No," she said, her words almost a whisper, "it's mine, isn't it?"

"I didn't say that!"

"The hell you haven't!"

She turned away from him. There was a silence between them. Then she started to cry softly. "God, Johnny."

He went to her and put his arms around her.

"This wasn't supposed to happen to us," she said.

He turned her around and smiled. "Nothin' happened," he said gently. "Talk to me, Anna. Hey, come on, talk to me."

He kissed her lightly.

"Talk to me some more." He smiled.

She smiled faintly.

"I can't hear you, Anna."

He kissed her again and, smiling, moved her toward the bed. She froze and turned away from him.

The limousine was parked at the curb outside Miami International Airport. Johnny stood on the sidewalk, looking around. Vince Doyle and Bernie Marr were behind him. Peter Jacobs, Max Graham's public relations man, tried to steer them toward the limo.

"But Max told me to pick you up, Mr. Kovak."

"Fuck the limo," Johnny said.

"We've got press waiting for you at the hotel. It's going to be embarrassing to me—"

"Fuck you too, Jacobs."

Vince and Bernie Marr laughed. Jacobs was flustered. He didn't know what to say.

Johnny grinned at him. "You know how much a cabbie makes?"

Jacobs shook his head.

"Not much."

Johnny smiled. He saw a cab and whistled loudly. Jacobs looked around in embarrassment. Doyle and Bernie Marr roared.

The cab took them to the Doral Beach Hotel and pulled behind a fleet of limousines parked in front of the lobby. A sign in front of the hotel said, "Welcome Federation of Interstate Truckers. Gain with Graham."

As Johnny got out of the cab he had his coat hooked

over a shoulder and his sleeves rolled up. Reporters surrounded him.

"Are you giving Graham's nominating speech?" a young reporter said.

Johnny pushed through the newsmen. "I'm no politician. You guys know that."

"Come on, Johnny," a crusty old reporter said. "Cut the shit."

Johnny laughed. He stopped and turned to the reporters.

"Solidarity's the word, fellows. Max hasn't asked me yet. If he does you can bet I will. In my opinion, this union's the best in the country. I don't care how Walter Reuther blows his horn about the U.A.W."

The reporters laughed.

"Now I'm glad all you guys are here to enjoy Miami Beach with us." He nodded and smiled at the crusty old reporter. "I see my friend John McCormick is here from the *News*. How are you, John? You're lookin' happier everyday."

"Cut the shit, Johnny," the old reporter grumbled.

Johnny laughed. "Now if you guys will give me some room, I'm tired. I want to have a big steak and a couple of beers. We're gonna set up a hospitality suite later on. All you guys that are from the Midwest are welcome to come."

Some of the reporters booed him.

"All right," he laughed. "I don't care where you're from, you're welcome to come."

The reporters laughed.

Johnny turned back to the crusty old reporter. "John,

I'll see you up there. We've got a special bottle of Old Crow for you,"

"Cut the shit, Johnny," the old reporter grumbled.

Johnny laughed and pushed his way through the reporters to the lobby door.

The convention hall was a gargantuan, brightly lighted place. American flags were everywhere, as were expensively printed multicolored placards that said, "Gain with Graham." A picture of Max Graham hung from the rafters. The delegates, most of them, wore expensive suits and they looked like businessmen. Johnny circulated among them, his tie loose, his coat draped over his shoulders.

"We've all got the same contract," he said to a delegate. "Max did all right."

The man spoke with a thick southern drawl. "But you've got real strength in the Midwest, Johnny. In Birmingham, Shreveport, we're still gettin' picked at by the companies, the ICC."

"Well go in and talk to Max," Johnny said. "Tell him to go down there himself and stop that shit."

The delegate shook his head. "Johnny, it ain't all that easy to talk to him."

Bernie Marr stood a few feet away with his father. Petey Marr was very tanned and almost completely bald.

"Breakfast tomorrow," Johnny said to the delegate. "Let's talk about it."

He went to Petey Marr with his arms out and hugged him.

"Look at him," Petey Marr grinned. "I used to know him when he only had one tie. Couldn't even put that one on right."

"I still can't put 'em on right," Johnny said.

The men around them laughed.

"Did you guys know," Johnny said to them, grinning, "that Petey Marr and his dockworkers—without Petey Marr and his dockworkers, we never would've won the Consolidated strike."

"Yeah, sure, Johnny," Petey Marr mumbled. "You were the one."

"You'd never know it just lookin' at him, would you?" Johnny said to the others.

"He wasn't such a smart guy then," Petey Marr said. "Scared shit what they were gonna do, weren't you?"

"Shitless," Johnny said.

The men laughed.

"A tan like a movie star," Johnny said. "Sittin' on his terrace, watchin' 'em wigglin' by on his beach. What a life you got, Petey, what a life!"

"Yeah, sure Johnny. Yeah, sure."

The men laughed again.

"We gotta go fishin' again, Petey."

"Hell, you can't fish. Why I had to teach him how to—"

The men laughed at him; so did Johnny.

"Aw, the hell with it," Petey Marr said to Bernie. "There's no winnin' with this guy. Can't a man get a drink around here? What the hell kinda setup you got here, Bernie?"

329

Bernie winked at the others. "Come on, dad."

Johnny noticed that Karen Chandler was watching him. She wore a light summer dress that accentuated her figure. Her dark hair fell below her shoulders. She smiled at him.

"Hiya, Chandler."

"I didn't think you'd remember."

"I don't look as good as my pictures."

She laughed. "You don't look too bad."

"What are you doin' down here?"

"I'm working on Graham's acceptance speech."

Johnny laughed.

"Did I say something funny?"

"I thought Max wrote his own speeches."

"I help him. It's part of my job."

He grinned. "What's the other parts of your job?"

She smiled at him.

"I'm curious," he said, leering.

"Are you?" she said coyly.

"Yeah."

She smiled. "Well, I'm not."

He laughed.

"Johnny!" a voice boomed behind him.

He turned from her and saw Max Graham coming toward him.

"Max!"

They shook hands, then grabbed each others' shoulders affectionately as some of the delegates took pictures of them.

* * *

On a terrace overlooking the hotel pool, as waiters hovered about them, Johnny and Abe sat and sipped coffee.

"When'd you get in?" Johnny said.

"About two in the morning," Abe answered.

"Christ. You better have some coffee."

"I got held up two hours at O'Hare."

"Goddamn O'Hare. Daley can't even keep his own airport goin'."

Abe drank his coffee, then said, "You sure you checked good?"

"I'm tellin' you, Abe. That's all I had Bernie doin' the last month. He checked the records inside out, upside down. I even sent him to Trenton. Nothin'. Graham's wife got nothin' to do with that flag company. The guy's just fruity about union flags. That's all."

"I guess that's that," Abe said. He paused. "You're sure, huh?"

"Abe, it's good it turned out this way. Nobody needs that kinda shit inside a union."

Vince Doyle came toward their table with a group of delegates.

"Well, I guess I'll see you later, Johnny."

"Naw, stick around," Johnny said. "Have some breakfast with us."

"Good to see you, Abe," Vince Doyle said, smiling. "Great job you're doin' out there in San Francisco."

Abe smiled. "Thanks, Vince."

As they ate breakfast, they talked about Max Graham.

"He's outa touch, Johnny," said the southern delegate. "We never see the guy. We call him, some secretary calls back."

Johnny watched the man as he ate his breakfast. "You guys eat anything except those goddamn grits?"

"It's good for the digestion, Johnny."

"So's castor oil."

"Half the time we try to reach him," another delegate said, "he's in Nassau. He sends one of those fancy PR guys around once a year tellin' us how great everything is."

The Southerner offered Johnny his grits. "It's great with this Smithfield ham, Johnny. Try some."

Johnny grimaced. "No, thanks."

"Our morale's down, Johnny," another delegate said. "I'm hearin' beefs from locals all over Texas, the Gulf Coast."

"They're makin' a good wage," Johnny said.

"Some of our young guys," the delegate said, "they're talkin' about reforms."

Johnny grinned. "Young guys are always talkin' about reformin' this and that. That's what we used to do, right Abe?"

"I'm still doin' it," Abe said.

They laughed.

"Can't we do somethin', Johnny?" the Southerner said.

"Look," he said," I hear what you guys are sayin'. But I'm not gonna run against Max. We've got a new contract comin' up. I don't want this union divided

332

up. We've gotta think of the guys. That's what it's all about, right, Abe?"

"A divided union's a weak union," Abe said, "that's for sure."

Johnny reached over and tried a forkful of the grits.

"I'll talk to Max, though," he said. "Maybe we can get him down to Birmingham insteada the Bahamas."

The delegates laughed.

"How do you like the grits?" the Southerner said.

"They're worse than they look."

They laughed.

Later in the day, Johnny and Bernie Marr, dressed in sports clothes, walked down to the pool to find Max Graham. They found him lounging in a poolside cabana in his bathing suit. Karen Chandler, clad in a bikini, was stretched out next to him, a note pad nearby.

"Mornin', Max," Johnny said.

"Johnny!" Max Graham said. "Good to see you!" He turned to his secretary. "We'll finish it up later, Karen."

Johnny winked at Karen Chandler. "Not interrupting anything, are we, Max?"

She got up angrily, note pad in hand. "I'll retype this right away, Mr. Graham." She walked out of the cabana. Johnny watched her figure.

"How about a bloody mary?" Graham said.

"Where'd you get that broad?"

"Karen? She was doing research for one of those Senate committees. Come in one day and volunteered. Bored with her life, she said. Can you believe that?

333

How about a screwdriver, Johnny? This orange juice they got down here is fabulous."

"I don't want nothin', Max."

"Bernie?"

"No, thank you, Mr. Graham."

"What about it, Johnny?" Graham said, as he made himself a drink. "Are you going to place my name in nomination? I'd consider it a real honor, Johnny. What a team we've made, the things we've accomplished for the rank and file—"

Johnny interrupted him, his voice low. "You like the ponies a lot, don't you, Max?"

"What?"

"The track. You got a—big interest in the track."

Graham looked up from his drink. "What do you mean, Johnny?"

Johnny grinned. "I don't know. I heard that—"

Graham turned away from him and continued making his drink. "Aw, somebody's always saying something. You know how it is, Johnny. Sometimes I see a race or two, sure—but—" He tasted his drink. "You sure you don't want one of these?"

Johnny shook his head and smiled. "Actually, it was Bernie who told me all about it."

"Bernie?"

Bernie reached for his briefcase. He opened it and removed a manila folder.

"You've got a horse named Danny Boy, Mr. Graham, a trainer named Guaraldi."

Max Graham put his drink down.

Bernie went on, his voice flat and ice cold. "The

trainer is on salary as business agent of Local 18 in Trenton."

"What is this?" Max Graham said.

"The only thing he does is take care of your horses."

Graham stared at them.

"How about it, Max?" Johnny said.

"What the hell do you mean how about it?" Graham's voice was rising. "I don't have to listen to—"

"Is it true or ain't it?" Johnny said.

"It's a coincidence, that's all. Sure he's on salary. There's a highway by the track in Hershey. He checks on the trucks that run up and down the road."

Johnny laughed. "Go on, Bernie."

"You've got a public relations firm in Los Angeles, Mr. Graham. Edward Harrison and Associates. Last year you paid them $145,000. Most of that money was used to buy yourself personal effects."

"Wait a minute," Max Graham said. His voice was shaky. "Sometimes he picks things up for me, sure, but—"

"Five dozen monogrammed shirts from Bullock's," Bernie Marr said, "a living room couch, a golf cart, velvet drapes, seventy pairs of socks, six pairs of shoes—"

"That's enough!" Max Graham cried.

"Enough?" Johnny grinned. "There's more."

"A twenty-foot deep freeze," Bernie Marr said, "a stereo record player, a bow tie—"

Johnny roared. "A bow tie, Max!"

"Stop it!" Graham said.

"A gravy boat," Bernie Marr said, "and salt and pepper shakers."

Graham stared at the ground and said nothing.

"It's gonna look real good for us, isn't it, Max?" Johnny said quietly. "All the PR we're gonna get. Union president steals money from his own men to buy himself a fuckin' bow tie and a—what? Salt and pepper shakers."

"What do you want?" Max Graham's voice was hoarse. His eyes studied the floor.

"What about that miniature-flag company your wife's got in Oakland, you sonofabitch?" Johnny screamed. "What'd you make offa that? A couple hundred thou?" He stood over Graham, his body rigid, his eyes burning.

"That's misappropriation of union funds, Mr. Graham," Bernie Marr said quietly. "You can go to jail."

Max Graham kept his eyes on the floor. "Just tell me what you want," he said.

As the delegates convened in the convention hall, Max Graham prepared to go on stage. He was moody and aloof, distant. He made his way to the center of the stage, slowly, and a hush settled on the hall. There were tears in his eyes.

"The past twenty years have been the best years of my life. So it is with a heavy heart I tell you that due to medical and family reasons I cannot stand again."

Some of the delegates booed. Graham silenced them.

"But tonight I want to place in nomination the man

I think most capable of leading this great union—Johnny Kovakl"

Immediately there were cheers. Within seconds the hall reverberated with a tumultuous ovation.

The applause followed Johnny out of the hall. As he walked to his suite with Vince Doyle, men crowded around him and slapped his back. Johnny grinned. Inside the suite, Bernie Marr hurried to him.

"We've got all kindsa calls about interviews, Johnny."

"I ain't got time for—"

"They want you on Huntley–Brinkley."

Doyle grinned. "Huntley–Brinkley. Jesus, Johnny."

"What do you wanna tell 'em?"

"Tell 'em okay," Johnny said. "After my acceptance speech."

He saw Abe standing in his bedroom and he went to him, taking his coat and tie off.

"They say they got air-conditioners in here," he said, "but I don't believe it."

Abe looked at him. "Congratulations," he said.

Johnny changed his shirt. "Thanks, Abe."

"You made a deal, didn't you?"

Johnny remained silent.

"And I set it up for you."

Johnny looked at him.

"He gets his pension," Abe said, "you get the union. Is that it?"

"What the fuck is wrong with you? You saw how the guys feel about Graham."

Abe turned away from him.

"Look," Johnny said, "the guy's sick. He decided to retire."

Abe turned to him and stepped close. "What about the money he took, Johnny? The money we're gonna give back to the guys."

"It's got nothin' to do with that. I told you. He's clean."

"Sure he is," Abe said. He paused. "Like you, Johnny."

Abe headed toward the door.

Johnny stopped him.

"Abe, listen to me—"

Abe pushed him away. Johnny grabbed him hard and pushed him against the wall.

"Listen to me!" he said furiously. "I'm gonna be the best president this union's ever had!"

It was a headline item on the NBC evening news. "In Miami Beach," Chet Huntley said, "the Federation of Interstate Truckers held its annual convention and elected a new president. He is John J. Kovak, a self-styled street kid from Cleveland's slums, until now the head of the union's Midwest Council."

Sitting in his Senate office with Dave Roberts, his administrative assistant, young, crew-cut, and button-down, the best the Harvard Law School had to offer, Cole Madison got up, walked to the television set, and turned the sound up.

"Well," he said, "Babe Milano must be happy today. I ought to send him a telegram congratulating him."

Cole Madison laughed. He was one of the Senate's

brightest young men, the biggest vote-getter in the history of Rhode Island, a man of limitless charm and, so it was said, limitless ambition, although Cole Madison had always been coy about his ambitions, preferring instead to dwell on his myriad accomplishments for his loyal constituents back home.

He was born with a silver spoon in his mouth, in Newport, Rhode Island, the youngest son of Clayton Madison, eccentric hunter, philanthropist, and historian, who merged his family's hundred-year-old textile operations with the mammoth Atlantic Mills Corporation, thus restructuring his family's vast fortune so that its mainstay became the business of investments.

Clayton Madison, a Yankee blue-blood, had a lifelong love of the American West. He collected old saddles and six-shooters, established a Western museum in New York City, and named his youngest son after Cole Younger, the Missouri outlaw.

He died when the boy was six months old and Cole Madison was raised by his stern and monosyllabic mother, whom he disliked from a young age. He had none of his father's love for the West, though as he grew older his mother kept telling him that he did share many of his father's "lesser qualities." He grew up in the family's compound in Newport, in love with the blazing blue sea and its crystalline air, with tennis and sailing. Even as a boy he was an excellent sailor, disdaining the broad-beamed catboats indigenous to Narragansett Bay for small, Marconi-rigged sloops and snipes.

He was always a loner, maintaining distance even

from his two older brothers, and especially from his mother. He went to St. George's School and he was profoundly bored. He tried to dodge the chapel service as much as possible and was twice almost dismissed for violations of the honor system. He found the place stodgy and dull, discovered women (easily attracted to him) at a young age (he had socially egalitarian traits, concerned only with the wealth of their bodies), and escaped to the sea as much as possible.

While he routinely accepted the comforts of wealth, he rebelled against many of its manifestations. He despised balls and Adirondack camps and girls from Radcliffe who wore short-sleeved, round-collared Mc-Mullen blouses purchased at Peck & Peck. Girls who, as Cole Madison liked to say, "had nothing between their legs and not much more elsewhere."

He went to Yale Law School, graduated with honors (further bored), and didn't know what to do with himself. Unlike his brothers, he had no wish to manage the family's finances—to "grub dollars all year," as he told his mother. A week after Pearl Harbor, against his mother's wishes, he tried to join the U.S. Army Air Corps but was told that all enlistments had been temporarily suspended due to an overload of volunteers. Undaunted, he heard about a traveling army recruiting board in Little Rock, Arkansas, and drove there nonstop, without even saying good-bye to his mother. He sold his car, filled out the forms, took his physical, appeared before the board, and was accepted as an aviation cadet in the Army Air Corps.

He loved the service and he loved flying. He was

trained at various bases on the West Coast, went through advanced single-engine training at Luke Air Force Base in Phoenix, to be a fighter pilot. He graduated in mid-September, 1942, a pilot and a second lieutenant, assigned to a squadron in the Eighth Air Force at Grafton Underwood airfield in England.

In July, 1943, he was shot down over the English Channel by German fighter attack planes. He was flying a Republic P-47 Thunderbolt, a fighter, as escort for a group of B-17 bombers returning from a bombing mission of German submarine facilities near Antwerp. A machine-gun bullet entered the lower part of his fuselage, passed upward, and struck his thigh. Instead of returning to base, he proceeded to shoot down three Messerschmidts before his plane was hit again and spiraled into the Channel. No one saw a parachute.

In September, his mother was notified that her son was missing. In October she received a notice that he was officially dead. In November, she received a letter from Cole. He said he was being held in a German POW camp. He had pulled his plane out of the spiral to the extent that he was able to bellyland in the Channel and leap out of the cockpit before it cracked up and sank. With the aid of a Mae West, he had splashed to the French shoreline and was given shelter by a French farmer. That night German soldiers had taken him captive.

In January 1944, Cole Madison escaped from captivity as he and a group of POWs were being moved to a new position camp deeper inside Germany. Traveling at night, he made his way to Allied forces. He had not only come back from the dead (in Rhode Island, a memorial service had already been said for him) but he had also escaped from the Germans. His heroics made headlines throughout the East Coast.

At war's end, he resigned his commission and went back to Newport with the Purple Heart, the Distinguished Service Cross, the Distinguished Flying Cross, and two Air Medals. He spent six months sailing, drinking, and staying in bed (never alone, and never with the same woman for more than a week).

In the next year, two events took place which would change his life. He met a Radcliffe girl unlike all Radcliffe girls. And he met Daniel Terence O'Shaughnessy, the Democratic Party boss of Providence, the weightiest politico in the state, literally and figuratively, who asked him to dinner. His mother disliked the girl and despised O'Shaughnessy and, naturally, they became two of the most important people in Cole Madison's life.

He met the Radcliffe girl at the Ida Lewis Yacht Club. She was from Pittsburgh, heiress to the Nash steel fortune, summering in Newport. Kathleen Langford Nash was five foot five, blond, brown-eyed, streamlined, gracefully elegant, and perpetually tanned. And she possessed, as Cole laughingly told her the first time they kissed, "fine tits."

She was quite proud of her tits, Cole Madison soon discovered, as well as of her all-around sexual prowess, and the morning after their first night together, he told her, "I've always said Radcliffe girls have nothing between their legs and not much elsewhere."

She smiled. "And?"

"And you can't possibly be a Radcliffe girl."

Kitty Nash (she dreaded Kathleen) was an irreverent, iconoclastic young woman with a vitriolic wit who disliked other Radcliffe girls as much as he did. She took one look at Cole Madison's sprawling family compound and said, "It really is a nice little place." She told his mother that she "adored" Newport because it was so "charmingly passé." When Cole Madison saw how much his mother disliked her, he was convinced. He asked Kitty Nash to marry him.

"Will you cheat on me?" she asked.

"Probably."

"Will you love me when you cheat on me?"

"Without doubt."

They were married in 1948 and moved into a large broken-down mansion in Providence. They began repairing the house themselves and he went to work as a corporate attorney for Jamieson, Finch, and Endicott, the biggest international law firm in the state.

A month later, Daniel Terence O'Shaughnessy called him. O'Shaughnessy was an old coot of a street politician who stayed away from Newport as much as possible. He didn't like the very rich and the very rich, who accurately considered him crude and vulgar, didn't like him. He liked what he called "little people," mill hands and factory workers and the men of the shipyards. He drank beer with them and kept track of thousands of birthdays and anniversaries, and every election they turned to Daniel Terence O'Shaughnessy for his "advice."

Why did you want to see me? Cole Madison asked Daniel Terence O'Shaughnessy, a bear of a man, over dinner.

"I want you to run for Congress," Daniel Terence O'Shaughnessy said.

"Why me?"

"You came back from the dead and you escaped from the Germans. You can become a legend.

"Do you think I can be a good congressman?" Cole Madison asked.

"Now what in hell does that mean?" Daniel Terence O'Shaughnessy laughed.

"Let me put it this way," Cole Madison said. "Do you think I'd do well in Washington?"

"Absolutely."

"Why?"

"Two reasons," the big man smiled. "You obviously know how to survive. We know that from the war. And in the course of my research, I discovered that you showed a rather cavalier attitude toward the honor system at St. George's. That, my boy, is a winning combination."

Cole Madison laughed. Bored with the law firm, he agreed to make the race. With Daniel Terence O'Shaughnessy beside him, he campaigned hard. He kissed thousands of drooling babies, attended innumerable clambakes, and shook hands until his right hand was swollen. He was a fine campaigner: his boyish charm and his blond good looks attracted the women; his masculinity drew the men. He down-played his background, made fun of it even some-times, referring to St. George's as "that boring high school my mother made me go to." He spoke up everywhere for "Little People"—the poor, the elderly, the "men and women trying their damnedest to make a living in this country." They listened to his fiery, idealistic words, delivered in a staccato, hard-edged style, and when the speech ended (it was basically the same speech everywhere), they asked him what the German POW camp had really been like.

On election night, with only one precinct out, he was trailing by 102 votes. The precinct remaining was where Daniel Terence O'Shaughnessy had lived for thirty-eight years. Cole Madison went to Congress by forty-three votes. It was said that some dead men in the precinct voted four times that day. But Cole Mad-ison ignored the scuttlebutt, made a fervent and high-toned acceptance speech, and moved to Washington with Kitty. He was relected in 1950 and 1952 by wide margins and in 1954 he was elected to the Senate in a landslide.

Daniel Terence O'Shaughnessy taught him well. He went back to Rhode Island often, campaigned hard for other candidates, had an excellent legislative rec-ord in Washington, and kept making idealistic speeches for the Little People. He was liked by his fellow senators as well. He had natural charisma, a wide following, but he went out of his way to play the game by the old rules. He deferred to seniority

345

and to Senate protocol. He enjoyed sitting around the Senate cloakroom with the powerful Southerners and shooting the bull over bourbon and branch water.

In 1956, at the age of sixty-nine, Daniel Terence O'Shaughnessy suffered a massive heart attack.

"You're the best I've seen, Cole," he said two days before he died. "You can be the President of the United States. Even without me."

Cole Madison held Daniel Terence O'Shaughnessy's hand and said, "It would've been a landslide with you, Danny."

O'Shaughnessy smiled painfully. "Bide your time. Use the Senate. Find a big issue. Ride it into the White House."

In 1958, Cole Madison was relected to the Senate with the biggest vote in Rhode Island's history. That same year, he became chairman of the Senate Rackets Committee. He had found his big issue.

He barnstormed the country, always in fund-raising efforts for other candidates, talking about the power of organized crime. He was a snow-white figure with blond hair battling the forces of corruption. It was the perfect issue. No one could really disagree with him. He became more and more electric on the stand, crusading, gathering bold headlines all across America.

There were those jaded Washington gossips who said Cole Madison had gone to Congress thanks to Nazis and dead men and was now about to ascend to the White House atop a black cloud of his own creation. But Cole Madison denied Presidential aspirations (always with a smile), took good care of the Little People in Rhode Island, and reminded Americans everywhere that there were gangsters in their cities dedicated to the corruption of their children.

Meanwhile, he lived happily in a Virginia mansion with Kitty and his two young daughters, going back to Rhode Island to sail as much as possible (although he was finding it increasingly difficult to do that because of the photographers who followed him everywhere). Sometimes Kitty was along on these trips; sometimes she was not. He had not lied to her: he had been unfaithful often, but he loved no one else. It was an arrangement which Kitty Madison, an intelligent woman, accepted handily.

The picture on the television set in Cole Madison's office flickered now as the delegates to the Federation of Interstate Truckers convention in Miami Beach applauded their new president.

Johnny Kovak stood in front of them and said, "I'm gonna get you the biggest pay hike in the history of this union! It's gonna be the best pay of any union in the world! You work hard! You deserve the best! I'm gonna see that you get it! I promise you that!"

The delegates roared.

Cole Madison shut the set off.

"What do you think, Dave?" He smiled. "Should I send Milano the telegram?"

"Maybe we should look into Kovak as well," Dave Roberts said.

"Let's just keep working on Milano now. And see what turns up." Cole Madison laughed.

"What is it?" Roberts asked.

"Kovak. There's something about him," Cole Madison said. "You know what, Dave? I almost think I'd like him."

They stood on the back porch of their home in Shaker Heights, arguing. Johnny was impatient. Anna was adamant.

"But that's where I'm gonna work," Johnny said. "You've gotta come with me."

"This is where I belong, Johnny. Not with all those people, those parties you've got to go to all the time."

"You used to like parties."

"That was—different."

"How was it so goddamned different? Tell me that." A door slammed.

"Joey's home," she said.

"Just tell me that, Anna. How was it?"

"It was different," she said softly. "That's all."

The boy ran to them, holding something in his hand. "Dad!" he said excitedly. "Look what I made you in school today."

Johnny took his son's offering. It was a ceramic ashtray.

"It's beautiful, Joey. Hey, Anna, look at this."

"Don't you like it, dad?" the boy said.

He laughed. "I love it. What do you mean?"

"Aren't you gonna try it out?" Joey smiled.

"Well, sure." He fumbled in his pockets. "I don't have any cigars."

Anna said, "They're on top of the TV, Joey."

The boy ran into the house. Anna held the ash-tray and looked at it. "It's pretty, isn't it?"

"There's all kinds of schools like that in D.C. Come on, Anna, I even checked."

She kept her eyes on the ashtray. "You could come back here all the time, couldn't you? Couldn't you, Johnny? And I could go up there sometimes and—"

He turned away from her. "Anna." His voice was choked. "Anna. Is that how you want it?"

"It's better this way," she said.

He put his hand on her cheek. "Anna, please."

"You'll see," she said softly.

Joey ran toward them from the house. "I got your cigars, daddy! I got 'em."

His new Washington office looked remarkably old. The wood paneling had been ripped off the walls. His desk, piled high with account ledgers, was the old and battered desk he had used in Cleveland. On top of it were Gant's buzzer and Joey's ceramic ash-tray.

"They juggled the money all over the place," Vince Doyle said. "They'd take it out of one fund and stick it into another."

Johnny sat behind his desk, looking at a ledger. "Did you see what Graham spent on entertainment last year?"

"I know, Johnny," Bernie Marr said. "We're not even sure where the pension-fund investments were made."

"Goddamnit!" Johnny said. "Get those accountants

we were talkin' about. I want 'em to go over all this stuff with a magnifying glass."

They nodded and started out of the office.

"And let's get rid of that public relations asshole!"

"There are four of 'em, Johnny," Bernie said.

"Christ! Can all of 'em."

Vince Doyle grinned. "Anything else?"

"Yeah. Keep an eye on Higgins. Bernie, you do it. Anything that's outa the ordinary in Cleveland, I want to handle. Every couple weeks, kick Tom in the ass."

Doyle laughed. "Don't you think we're in good hands back there, Johnny?"

"Very funny, Vince, but I ain't in the mood."

Doyle laughed and the two of them walked out of the office. Johnny kept going over the ledgers. Karen Chandler walked in with an envelope.

"All you people ever did around here," he growled, "was throw parties."

She smiled. "All we people?"

"The entertainment money last year," he said angrily. "It's a lot more 'n a lotta locals bring *in*."

"Well," she said, "maybe you want me to cancel your reception tonight."

He looked at her and grinned. "You're a real wise guy, Chandler, aren't you?"

She smiled and put the envelope on his desk.

"It's the acceptance speech I wrote for Mr. Graham at the convention."

"What the hell do I want with it?"

"I thought you'd enjoy reading it." She paused and

350

smiled sweetly. "Considering the way it turned out."

He laughed. "Get the hell outa here, Chandler. I've got work to do."

"Yes, Mr. Kovak." She turned and walked out of his office.

That night at the reception, Johnny wore a $300 tailored suit. He stood in the middle of the gathering with a bottle of beer in his hand.

"You have no idea, senator," he said to a silver-haired, elderly man, "the things you can see from a rig. Honeymooners. He's drivin'. She's startin' the honeymoon right there on the road."

The senator laughed.

"The rig gives you a real overview of life," Johnny said.

"I didn't realize you had driving experience," the senator said.

"I drove enough. It taught me about life."

The senator smiled. "But what can you learn about life in a truck?"

"Never to hit the brake when steppin' on the gas can get you out of a tight squeeze," Johnny said. "Never to step on the gas when hittin' the brake can keep you out of a ditch."

The senator laughed.

"And another thing, senator. You've got a big wheel in a truck and you've got a big load. Either you've got the muscle to move the wheel fast, or the load's going to come down on top of your head."

The senator looked at him, assessing him. "Yes, that's a valuable lesson," he said.

Karen Chandler interrupted them. Cole Madison was with her.

"Mr. Kovak, do you know Senator Madison, the chairman of the Senate Rackets Committee?"

"Sure," Johnny said. He shook hands. "Glad you came by, senator. What's the Senate Racket Committee up to nowadays?"

"Oh," Cole Madison smiled. "Investigating 'push' of various kinds."

Johnny grinned. "Push is something I bet every politician knows a lot about."

"Even politicians in the labor movement, Mr. Kovak?"

Johnny laughed. "I'm no politician, senator. I'm just a street kid from the slums."

"Yes, of course you are," Cole Madison smiled. "Well, I have to be leaving. Congratulations, incidentally."

"Thank you."

"And give my regards to Babe Milano."

Johnny grinned. "You know Babe?"

"Only by reputation." Cole Madison smiled.

"I'll do that."

"Leaving so early, senator?" It was Karen Chandler.

"I've got an early game of tennis." He turned to Johnny. "Do you play, Mr. Kovak?"

"Handball. I could never afford a racket."

Madison laughed. "A tennis racket, you mean?"

Johnny grinned. "Yeah."

"Too bad," Cole Madison said. "I would have enjoyed playing you."

He said good-bye to Karen Chandler and walked out the door. Johnny watched him as he left.

Her apartment was in Georgetown. It was small but tastefully furnished: prints, ferns, Persian rugs, fresh flowers. Johnny sat on a couch, his legs stretched across a coffee table, his tie loose. She stood at a portable bar.

"What would you like?" Karen Chandler said.

"Give me a beer. You got any bourbon?"

"I think I can find some." She poured him the bourbon. "Don't you ever drink anything else?"

"Ain't it classy enough for you?"

She handed him the shot and the beer.

"Do you really like this stuff or is it just part of your street-kid routine?"

He grinned. "What are you drinking?"

"Benedictine and brandy."

"That's cat piss."

"Thank you." She lifted her glass. "Cat piss to you, too."

Johnny laughed. She sat down on a couch across from him.

"You're the expert on shitheads in this town, Chandler. What's Madison like?"

"For openers, he's not one of the shitheads in this town."

"What else?"

"Rich. Good-looking."

He smiled. "Give me the goods."

"Let's see. Ambitious. Many people think he's going to be President some day. Some say he's ruthless, some say he's idealistic. He's married. His wife is the heir to a—soap fortune, I think, or was it steel?"

"Does he fuck around on the fortune?"

"Who doesn't . . . fuck around . . . in Washington?"

He grinned. "What do you hear?"

She looked at him. "Why?"

"I wanna know, that's why."

"He has a—certain reputation. He's a very magnetic man."

He laughed. "You sound like you—"

"I never had the pleasure."

"I didn't mean—"

She smiled. "Of course you did."

"You like that kinda guy?"

"I like to see what's inside them."

"What's Madison got inside him?"

"I'm not sure. You'll have to find out yourself." She sipped her drink. "Why are you so interested in Cole Madison?"

"I get interested in any guy that's interested in me."

"Who says he's interested in you?"

"He says."

"I didn't hear him say that."

He grinned. "I did."

"Well," she said. "It's getting late."

"You want me to go?"

She smiled. "Why would I want you to stay?"

"What if I wanna stay?"

"Sorry, that's not part of my job."

"I didn't think it was," he said.

She smiled. "Do you . . . fuck around . . . on your wife?"

He grinned. "I'm a—what'd you call it? I'm a magnetic guy."

She smiled. She looked at him. "I bet you're a terrible lay."

"What the hell thing is that to say?"

She laughed. "Did I embarrass you? I'm sorry."

"I'll see you around, Chandler."

He got up and put his coat on. He went to the door.

"I didn't say I wanted you to go," she said.

She got up and went to him. She kissed him on the lips once, gently.

"Did I?"

Afterward, as they lay in the bed in silence, she smoked a cigarette. Johnny sipped from a glass of bourbon.

"How come you got bored with your life?" he said.

"Who told you that?"

"I'm askin' the questions."

"Does it matter?"

"Yeah."

"Why?"

"I like to know what I'm gettin' myself into."

"You mean who, not what," she said.

"You've got a dirty mouth, Chandler."

She smiled. "Don't you like my mouth?"

"Come on, I asked you—"

"Yes, sir, Mr. Kovak."

"Christ."

She smiled. "I was disillusioned," she said. "I'd lost my *innocence*." She laughed sarcastically.

"Who was he?"

"A whole series of things."

He grinned. "Gangbang."

"So to speak."

"Where'd the chip on your shoulder come from?"

She smiled. "You don't like my shoulder, either? What else don't you like?"

"Forget it."

She laughed. "I grew up in Richmond. My father was an executive. He was never home. My mother wanted me to be a nun."

He laughed. "A nun? You?"

She smiled. "I know. I discovered that myself and went to college. I believed a lot of garbage."

"Like what?"

"I read too much."

"It screws up your eyes."

"You're right. I believed in change. In making things better."

"What happened?"

"I got out of school and came up to work on the Hill."

He grinned. "To make things better?"

"Yes."

"Beautiful."

"Yes."

"So?"

"So I got bored with my life and came to work for Graham."

"You still bored?"

She looked at him. "I don't know. Have you got any other questions?"

He grinned. "You still think I'm a terrible lay?"

"I need more proof."

He laughed. "Smart mouth."

She got out of the bed. "I thought you said it was dirty."

"Where you goin', smart mouth?"

"To take a shower." She turned to him, naked. "Do you want to take one?"

"I already took one today."

"Not with me."

He looked at her.

"What's the matter, Kovak?" She smiled. "Haven't you ever taken a shower with a lady?"

Much of his first month as the national president of F.I.S.T. was spent at truck stops all over Pennsylvania and Maryland. In Breezewood, Pennsylvania, at a place called the Mid-America Truck Terminal, a place which offered complete laundry and diesel service, he sat in a room on a folding chair, surrounded by truckers, many of them wearing baseball caps and T-shirts. There were two wall-sized posters in the room: one of a naked girl standing in front of a Mack truck; the other of a truck in a rainstorm, the arms of Christ protecting it.

"At the warehouse, see," one of the truckers said to him, "they put all the weight on the back of the trailer. It oughta go as much up front as—"

"Hey," Johnny grinned. "I don't need no lessons from you guys loadin' a truck."

The trucker gave him a buck-toothed smile. "So they put it on the rear cause they're gonna get nailed at the weight station for having too much damn weight on one axle."

"Which would cost the company dough," Johnny said.

"With the weight in the rear, Johnny, the rig—"

"I know. It jitters all over the road."

"It's causin' a lotta accidents, Johnny."

"Too many," another trucker said.

"That shit's gonna stop," Johnny said, "I'll tell you that."

"Another thing that gets me—" the trucker said.

Johnny interrupted him and turned to Bernie Marr. "Round me up a bowl of chili, will you, Bernie? And let's get all these jugs filled up again."

Bernie collected the drivers' Thermos bottles.

"The fuckin' dispatchers, Johnny," the trucker said.

"What about 'em?"

"To get a load, I gotta tip the sonofabitch. Every damn trip he wants more."

"No more tips," Johnny said. "I promise you."

Outside, in the vast parking lot, they showed him their rigs.

"Johnny," one of them said, "let me show you where I'm supposed to sleep in mine."

He took him to a big Peterbilt and opened the passenger door.

Johnny grinned. "I ain't gettin' in the business side of no rig."

They laughed. Johnny climbed into the cab on the driver's side with the trucker. The trucker showed him a sleeping compartment with a thin mattress on top of a board.

"Now how in hell's a man supposed to sleep in here, Johnny?"

"What company you with?" Johnny said.

"Knowles."

"Bernie," Johnny yelled, "write that down. Fuck Knowles."

The men laughed and as he and Bernie headed back to their battered old Plymouth, they slapped him on the back and shook his hand again. He waved to them.

"My old man used to say," he said to Bernie, "if a trucker will shake your hand, you got it knocked."

"Did he really say that?" Bernie said.

"Whattaya mean?" He looked at Bernie and laughed.

Karen Chandler sat in his office, taking notes. Johnny was in his shirtsleeves. He looked tired and drawn.

"I want a breakdown of all their profits," he said. "Get those hotshot accountants on it."

"By region?"

"Every single company that their Trucking Association represents."

"Annually?"

"Month to month. Broken down separate. Exact dollars and cents."

"Right."

"Then have the accountants total the whole sonofabitch up and estimate a figure the companies'll lose if we got out."

"Anything else?"

"Yeah. I want you to dig out all the contracts Graham got."

"All of them?"

"Every single goddamn year."

"What do you want that for?"

"So I can show the contract we're gonna get is better on every single point, that's why."

"Is that it?"

"That's it for now," he said.

She got up and looked at him, then started out. But she hesitated.

"You're sweating," she said.

"Huh?"

She smiled. "You're sweating."

"I always sweat when I'm workin'."

"You need a shower."

"A shower?"

"I've got a shower at my place."

He laughed. "Get the hell outa here Chandler, will you?"

The regional vice-presidents of the Federation of Interstate Truckers were gathered around the conference table—aging, paunchy men who wore tailored suits and smoked Cuban cigars. Johnny stalked about the room, talking to them. They listened impassively.

"I want you to talk to your men! I want you to get yourself seen! I want you to go down to the truck stops!"

One of them smiled. Johnny glared at him.

"What's so funny, Cavelli?"

"You want me to climb into the rig, too, Johnny? Make a run?"

There were a few laughs.

"No. Cavelli, I wouldn't ask you to do that," Johnny said. "The shape you're in, you'd get a heart attack."

The men laughed.

"I wanna know what the guys in the different regions are bitchin' about!" Johnny said. He turned to one of the men.

"When's the last time you've been inside a warehouse, McQuinn?"

"I've been busy with the routine, Johnny."

Johnny turned on him. "Bullshit! Nine holes every morning and gettin' your nails done in the afternoon, that's what you've been busy! We've got a contract comin' up! It's gonna be the best national contract this union's ever had! Any union's had! Two weeks from now, I want all of you back here to tell me what you found out!"

"Johnny," Cavelli said quietly, "I've got a regional meeting in two weeks."

"Yeah? Where?"

Cavelli hesitated. "In—Acapulco."

The men laughed.

Johnny stood there, grinning at them. "This is a whole new crap game, gents. I've got the roll. There ain't no more fuckin' Acapulco."

It was just past seven o'clock and the morning was chilly. Johnny walked through the street of the nation's capital, fresh and alert. He carried the final edition of the *Washington Post* and a bundle of manila folders, and as he watched the last streetlights blink off he thought back to the night he made his acceptance speech.

He could hear the applause roaring through the convention hall, pumping through his veins. He could hear his own shouted words. "I'm gonna get you the biggest pay hike in the history of this union! It's gonna be the best pay hike of any union in the world! You work hard! You deserve the best! I'm gonna see that you get it! I promise you that!"

On this morning, the beginning of negotiations for a new contract between the Federation of Interstate Truckers and the National Trucking Association, it was time to make good on that promise.

The first session was scheduled to begin at nine o'clock in a conference room at the Mayflower Hotel. There was time to spare, but Johnny walked briskly. He wanted to get there early. He wanted to study the facilities, particularly the suite of rooms which the Trucking Association had reserved for use between bargaining sessions. He wanted to give himself every possible advantage because he knew that the man on the other side of the table, the man he had to deal with, Phillip Talbot, had every reason to dislike him personally and professionally.

Since his father's death in 1943, Phillip Talbot had built Consolidated into the nation's largest trucking firm. That accomplished, Phil Talbot turned his attention to the interests of the trucking industry at large. In 1955 he was elected president of the National Trucking Association and since that time had done everything in his power to deregulate the trucking industry and undermine union advances. He was, Johnny knew, a man not to underestimate. Phil Talbot negotiated the last national contract with Max Graham and Max came home with a half-empty bag.

Through the years, Johnny and Phil Talbot maintained a formally cordial relationship. Though they went their separate ways following their confrontation in the thirties, their paths crossed frequently. And though Phil Talbot always treated Johnny with seeming courtesy and respect, he knew in his guts how Phil Talbot really felt.

Johnny strode into the lobby of the Mayflower Hotel. As he made his way to the elevators, a tall man with silver hair turned from the bell captain's desk. He was striking and dignified. He wore a dark cashmere sport coat, soft black leather shoes. He carried a large black leather attaché case with gold fittings.

"Hello, Johnny," Phillip Talbot said.

"Hiya, Phil."

They shook hands, smiled at each other, and got into the elevator. The doors closed and the elevator started to rise.

Phil Talbot looked at Johnny, an amused expression on his face, his gray eyes twinkling. He smiled slightly.

"It's good to see you, Johnny," he said.

Johnny nodded, grinning. They were silent for some moments.

"Well," Phil Talbot said, "I guess we can say this is a big day."

"Could be." Johnny smiled.

"Little early, aren't you?"

"No earlier than you, Phil."

The elevator came to a stop. The doors opened and they walked out. Johnny laughed.

"Come on. I want to show you the place we got when we're not gonna be talkin'." He waved an arm and started down the hallway. Phil Talbot smiled and followed him.

They entered a suite of rooms.

"Just like yours, huh?" Johnny grinned.

"Nothing this lavish," Phillip Talbot smiled. "Ours is much more modest."

Johnny laughed. He walked to a desk and picked up the telephone. He looked at Phil Talbot and winked. "Listen," he said into the phone, "I want you to send up a couple pots of coffee, some doughnuts and rolls, maybe a couple orange juice. Okay?"

Phil held up a finger. "I've had breakfast, but thank you. I really must go."

"Hey, come on," Johnny said. "Long time. Let's talk."

"No. Thank you."

Johnny shrugged. He turned to the phone. "Skip it, I'll call you back."

Phil Talbot smiled, waved, and walked out of the room.

"See you later, Phil." Johnny grinned.

As he walked down the corridor to his own suite, Phillip Talbot was not pleased with the beginning of this day. He had wanted to arrive ahead of time to have a chance to think, not to get into a shadow-boxing match with Kovak.

During that long ago battle in Cleveland, Phillip Talbot had felt a grudging admiration for the man who had stormed into his father's office and humiliated him. But in later years, as he came to understand Winthrop Talbot better, as well as the forces driving Kovak, he came to see Johnny Kovak as the enemy—not only of his family, but of the free-enterprise system as well. He had come to understand that his father was right. Money and business, in its many and varied forms, was America's most sacred institution.

When Winthrop Talbot died at the age of seventy-two of a heart attack, still working ten-hour days on the top floor of the Talbot Building, Phillip Talbot was forty-one years old. By that time he knew as much about the trucking industry as any man on earth. Within eight years he succeeded in making Consolidated the industry leader in both size and profits. He had more than twenty-five thousand employees on his payroll; he owned more than twenty-eight thousand trucks, tractors, trailers, and shipping containers. He had routes in forty-five of the fifty states, with interlines in the remaining five states; and he had moved into Canada and the Yukon Territory.

Through all of this, Phillip Talbot had managed to go over, around, or through the increasingly complex maze of federal and state regulations which applied to interstate truck traffic. He also made peace with the unions, especially with the Federation of Interstate Truckers, if only because it was expedient. He was a consummate politician. His timing was precise and he knew exactly when to retreat and when to advance.

But now, as he opened the door to the National Trucking Association's suite, Phillip Talbot realized that he was afraid. Kovak played by a different set of rules. Kovak refused to embrace those niceties which made difficult situations tolerable. Kovak made deals, Phillip Talbot knew, but only if the people he was dealing with were already on his side of the fence. But if you employed truck drivers, "his" men, Kovak recognized no common ground. You saw it his way, Phillip Talbot knew from painful experience, or you got sledgehammered.

He paced the room restlessly, thinking about these things, when suddenly he realized how hungry he was. He had lied to Kovak; he didn't want to have breakfast with him. He never ate breakfast, but this morning it must have been his nerves. He went to the phone and dialed room service, but before he could place his order there was a knock at the door.

"Just a moment," Phil Talbot said. He put the phone down and answered the door. A waiter stood there with a cart loaded down with rolls, toast, eggs benedict, and coffee.

"You must have the wrong room," Phillip Talbot said. "I didn't order this."

"Compliments of Mr. Kovak, sir," the waiter said. He handed Phillip Talbot a card.

"Nobody oughta negotiate on an empty stomach," the card said.

Phillip Talbot sat at one end of the long boardroom table; Johnny at the other. Flanking them were two of Talbot's aides and Vince Doyle and Bernie Marr. A stenographer sat in the corner.

"Let the record show," Phillip Talbot said, "that discussions between the Federation of Interstate Truckers and the National Trucking Association relative to a three-year contract began at—"

"I don't want to do it like this, Phil," Johnny said.

Talbot looked at him.

"Let's just kick things around. We don't need the stenographer in here. Everything's off the record." He grinned. "Man to man."

Talbot smiled. "Thank you, Miss Osborne. We'll call you later."

The stenographer got up and walked out of the room. As soon as she closed the door, Johnny stood up.

"I'm not gonna blue-sky you guys," he said. "I know

the profits you had last year. I tell my guys to go out, they're gonna go out. Phil, you know that. I'm not Max Graham. This is the first national contract I'm workin' out. I've got somethin' to prove to the guys. You don't fight me this time, we're gonna get along better next contract around. I give you my word."

"We'll do our best, Johnny," Talbot said. "The price of living increase is five and a half percent. You want an eight percent hike. We'll go seven."

"Eight, Phil, the number's eight."

Talbot got up and walked around the room. "We'll go seven only with a flat guarantee you'll stop any wildcats within forty-eight hours. Plus—the meal allowance hike isn't fifty cents, it's a quarter. The living allowance isn't a dollar, it's seventy-five cents."

"No rear loadings," Johnny said.

"No rear loadings."

"You can any dispatcher that—"

"We'll do our best to watch the dispatchers," Talbot said.

"Fuck that! I'll do my best to stop the wildcats."

Talbot smiled. "All right, Johnny. As a good-faith gesture, we'll lay it down flat. We don't have to, but we will. Any dispatchers whom your locals can prove took a bribe will be dismissed." He paused. "How about it, do we have a contract?"

Johnny grinned. "Not so fast, Phil, not so fast. We've got time. You trying to rush me into something?"

That night, Johnny discussed Phil Talbot's offer with Vince Doyle and Bernie Marr.

"Take it," Doyle said, "we can't get a better deal."

Johnny shook his head.

"You don't like it," Bernie Marr said.

"I want eight."

"They're not gonna go eight," Vince Doyle said.

"The goddamn hell they won't!" Johnny said. "Talbot's gonna screw with me? His old man tried that."

As negotiations resumed the following morning, there was a noticeable chill to the proceedings. Both sides seemed braced for battle.

Johnny put it bluntly.

"Eight it is," he said.

"No deal, Johnny," Phillip Talbot said.

"You got any idea," Johnny said, smiling, "what you guys are gonna lose?"

"I'm sorry, Johnny."

Johnny stared at Talbot. "It's your balls, Phil."

Johnny announced the outcome himself. He stood on a stage at a union hall in Baltimore, his arms outstretched. Hundreds of men were before him, stomping their feet, cheering, and applauding.

"You asked for eight," he shouted to them, "I got you eight! I got you the biggest hike this union's ever had!"

A copy of the new issue of *Time* magazine was on the committee table in front of Cole Madison. The headline said "Blue Collar Push" and the cover was a color photo of Johnny stepping from the cab of a truck.

Cole Madison looked at the seven other senators

around the table. One of them was Donald Carnes of Illinois.

"I asked for this closed executive session, gentlemen," Cole Madison said, "because I believe the Rackets Committee should expand its investigation in another area. Our investigation of the activities of Mr. Anthony Milano has shown Mr. Milano's friendship with the Federation of Interstate Truckers and its new president, John J. Kovak. We have also uncovered traces of a link between the Midwest Council and organized crime. I make this suggestion with some regret. I have long had a profound respect—as I am sure have all of you—for the labor movement and its accomplishments. But I find frightening the possibility that the head of one of this country's largest unions, a hero to the workers of America"—he held the magazine up—"may have ties to the bosses of organized crime."

In the corridor afterward, Carnes stopped Madison. Carnes looked agitated.

"Is something troubling you, Don?" Cole Madison grinned.

"Well, bluntly," Carnes whispered, "are you sure all this is good idea?"

"All what?"

"Well, getting into this Kovak business."

Madison smiled. "It seems to me we have a responsibility to get into it, don't you think, Don?"

Carnes smiled. "Maybe, Cole, maybe. But you have such a bright political future. You don't want to bite off more than you can chew."

"Are you telling me," Cole Madison grinned, "that Johnny Kovak is too big a bite for the Senate of the United States?"

Carnes laughed. "Frankly, Cole, no. It's not the future of the United States Senate that I'm concerned about."

"Oh?" Cole Madison said. He slapped Carnes on the back. "I appreciate the advice, Don."

Babe Milano sat in the Rutherford B. Hayes suite of the Statler-Cleveland Hotel, a club sandwich in front of him. He took a bite of it and grimaced. He put the sandwich down.

"You come to Cleveland on a Sunday, Johnny," Milano said, "forget it. Only thing open is the goddamn hotel coffee shop."

"You should've called me."

"I didn't want to call you. We can talk better here. So how about it, Johnny?"

"It's not smart, Babe."

"It's a free country, Johnny. Who says we can't make a deal between friends?"

Johnny shook his head. "Madison's got some guy lookin' for me with a subpoena in D.C."

"I've got dozens of subpoenas," Milano grinned. "They can't prove nothin'."

"We're gonna land you a million bucks with those rackets guys sniffin' around? It's not smart, Babe."

"It's business, Johnny. You make loans outa the pension fund to all kindsa people. You're gonna give

us the same rate as anybody else. There's nothin'
wrong with that."

Johnny walked away from him. With his back to
him, he said, "What do you know about Madison?"

Milano laughed. "He's a flash in the pan. He'll get a
couple write-ups, fold the committee, go on to somethin' else."

"Carnes says he's running a crusade."

"There's no such thing as a crusade. Carnes got a
guilty conscience."

Johnny smiled.

"What do you say, Johnny?"

"All right, Babe," he said, his voice low, his back
still to Milano, "you work out the numbers with
Vince."

He turned on Milano suddenly, his voice harsh. "You
put up good fuckin' security, you hear? You make
your payments on time! It's comin' outa the guys'
pockets."

Milano smiled. "What are you worried about,
Johnny? Our Dun & Bradstreet, it's the best."

Dave Roberts handed Higgins the subpoena and
smiled. Higgins stared at it. Johnny walked into the
office.

"What's goin' on, Tom?"

"This man's from the Senate Committee, Johnny,"
Higgins said. "He's got a—"

"My name's Roberts. I'm an investigator for—"

Johnny looked at him. "I know what the hell you
are."

Higgins got up from the desk hurriedly and handed Johnny the subpoena. Johnny sat down and looked it over.

"It's a subpoena," Roberts said. "It requires you to—"

"You tell me what it is you want," Johnny said.

"A list of Local 302's financial assets from 1952 to—"

"We don't have 'em."

"A list of banks where those assets are deposited."

"We don't have 'em."

"Names and salaries of Midwest Council business agents."

"We don't have 'em."

"Records of Local 302's property investments."

"We don't have 'em."

"Records of Local 302's political contributions."

Johnny smiled. "Sorry. We ain't got those, either."

"What do you mean you don't have them?" Roberts was angry.

"We had a burglary last week. Somebody cleaned out the files. Right, Tom?"

"That's right, Johnny."

"A burglary," Roberts said.

"That's right," Johnny said. "There's robberies all over the place."

Roberts smiled. "And of course you made out a police report."

Johnny looked at Higgins. "Tom?"

"Absolutely, Johnny."

Johnny grinned at Roberts. "They got any suspects yet?" he said to Higgins.

"Not yet, Johnny."

"Give 'em a call today," Johnny said. "Make sure they're workin' on it."

Johnny grinned, picked up the subpoena, and ripped it into pieces. He handed the pieces to Roberts.

"You tell Madison," he said, his voice calm, "he's fuckin' with the wrong guy. He wants to play a game, it ain't gonna be tennis."

Ilona Kovak stood over the cake for her sixty-fourth birthday in the living room of her house in the Flats, surrounded by her family and her old-country friends. She looked at the cake and the smiling faces around her and, obviously touched, said, "Cake no good. Make you fat."

Johnny laughed. "Stop crabbin', ma, cut it up."

"Make a wish, mom," Anna said, "blow the candles out."

"Old age," Ilona Kovak smiled. "No more wishing."

They laughed and Ilona Kovak looked at her grandson, his big eyes on the single candle at the center of the layered chocolate cake, and said, "Joey, you blow out the candle with granma." The boy looked at her and smiled. He drew in a big breath and, together, they blew the candle out.

Johnny led the applause and as Ilona Kovak cut the cake up, he looked at Zigi Zagon, his beer belly sagging, who was huddled in a corner with Mishka. Mishka had become very thin and feeble.

Johnny went to them. He put his arm around Mishka. "How's business, Zigi?" he said.

"Going to hell like everything else," Zigi Zagon said. "More bother than it's worth."

Johnny laughed. "Yeah? How many times over are you a millionaire?"

"It ain't funny, Johnny," Zigi Zagon said. "Everybody movin' outa the Flats or into the grave. Damn niggers movin' in."

Johnny looked at Mishka and said, "Well, Mishka is still here."

"Him," Zigi Zagon said, "stay in his house like an old man. He don't drink."

"I drink my own," Mishka said.

"His own. Poison even the niggers." Zigi Zagon laughed.

"You taste it, Johnny?" Mishka said, and Johnny said sure, and laughed.

In front of them, Joey handed his grandmother a multicolored throw rug. She took it, and kissed the boy, and said, "It's beautiful, honey."

"Granma's birthday!" the boy said.

"Yes, honey, it's granma's birthday," Ilona Kovak said.

"He made it himself, mom," Anna smiled, "from cigarette packs."

Ilona Kovak held the boy, and kissed him again, and said, "Best birthday present granma ever got."

Johnny watched them, smiling.

"You no want to taste it?" Mishka said.

Johnny laughed and Mishka led them into the kitchen and poured the wine into three glasses.

"It's better than the Ex-Lax," Zigi Zagon said.

Mishka said, "I brought it special for your mom."

Zigi Zagon grinned and said, "He want to poison your mom, Johnny."

"Where do you make it?" Johnny laughed.

"I got a shack in the backyard," Mishka said.

"In his shack," Zigi Zagon said, "the old fool, dancing on his grapes."

Johnny tasted it and grimaced.

"Good, Johnny?" Mishka said.

"Terrific."

"Better than what Zigi sells?"

Johnny grinned. "Much better, Mishka."

"More?"

"Sure."

Johnny drank the wine and Zigi Zagon laughed.

"See?" Mishka said to him.

Behind them, Joey came into the kitchen, crying, the throw rug in his hands. It was in pieces.

"It broke, daddy," he cried.

Johnny picked the boy up in his arms and held him.

"It broke," the boy said, tears running down his face.

"It's okay," Johnny said. "Here, daddy'll help you fix it.

He got down on the floor, his arms around the crying boy, and he tried to put the cigarette wrappers together again.

Rain beat against the station wagon's windshield as it pulled up to the lobby of Cleveland's Hopkins International Airport. Anna was driving. Johnny sat next to her and Joey was in the back seat. The radio was on and an announcer was reading the news.

"You comin' back Saturday?" Anna said.

"I don't know, Anna. I got all kindsa stuff."

In the back seat, Joey said, "I don't want you to go, daddy. Can't you stay?"

"Did you hear that?" Johnny said. He turned the radio up.

"The San Francisco local of the Federation of Interstate Truckers has threatened a wildcat strike for tomorrow morning. Abe Belkin, the president of the local, said his men will walk out—"

Joey said, "I want daddy to stay, mommy!" Anna shushed him.

"—because of a dispute with Bay Area trucking officials over the dismissal of three men yesterday from Trans-Bay Freight Lines. The walkout could cripple the trucking industry from Seattle to Los Angeles. After this message, sports."

An upbeat jingle came on the radio.

Lost in his thoughts, Johnny stared into the rain.

Joey said, "I love you, daddy! I love you!"

He turned back to the boy, distant and preoccupied. "I love you too, Joey."

When he got off the plane at Washington National Airport, reporters crowded around him.

"Your contract with the National Trucking Association prohibits wildcats, are you—"

Johnny grinned. "We're gonna honor our contracts, fellas."

"Have you been in touch with Mr. Belkin in San Francisco?"

"This union always honors its agreements."

"But have you—"

He smiled. "That's all, fellas. Give me a break. We'll have something for you as soon as we can. Thanks for comin' out."

In the limo with Vince Doyle and Bernie Marr, Johnny said, "Tell Talbot I'm workin' on it. There ain't gonna be no wildcat."

"I talked to Abe before we picked you up," Doyle said.

Johnny smiled. "What'd he say?"

"He doesn't give a shit what the contract says, he's goin' out tomorrow."

Johnny grinned, then shook his head. He turned to Bernie Marr. "Get me out to San Francisco first plane tomorrow."

"Do you want me to come?"

"Keep the lid on," Johnny said, "I don't want no press."

"Johnny," Vince Doyle said, "what's the use of you runnin' out there?"

He turned to Doyle angrily. "This thing could tie up the whole West Coast. What if the whole region goes out, for Christ's sake? It could bust the contract wide open."

"He's not gonna change his mind," Doyle said. "He don't listen to reason."

There was a pause. Johnny didn't say anything. Then he turned to Bernie Marr.

"Bernie, I want to know everything there is on Madison."

"Madison?" Doyle said. "Abe's gonna fuck up the agreement we got, what are you worrying about Madison for?"

"Listen, I can handle Abe, Vince."

"Nobody can handle him."

Johnny ignored it. He looked at Bernie Marr. "I want that stuff when I get back."

"That's only a couple days, Johnny, that's not much time."

"Fuck that!" Johnny said, his voice loud. "I don't want to hear that. *Get it.*"

At Karen Chandler's apartment that night, Johnny sat in the living room in his robe, smoking one of his little cigars. He had a drink in his hand. Karen came out of the bathroom with a towel around her. She looked at him.

"What's wrong, Johnny?"

"Nothin'."

He got up and went to the window, his back to her. She watched him.

"Johnny," she said after a while, "there are no strings."

"Everybody's got strings."

"Not me, Johnny."

He looked at her, then turned back to the window.

"It's Abe. He's gonna screw up the whole thing. The contract. Everything we got."

"But he's a friend of yours, Johnny."

"He's got these cockamamie ideas."

"What ideas?"

He paused and looked at her. "He ain't—realistic. He's like you. Before you lost your cherry." He smiled. "Ain't that what happened?"

"Maybe," she said, "maybe you're right." She grinned. "Isn't he ever going to lose his?"

Johnny laughed. "Abe? Not him."

The house in San Francisco was on Vallejo Street. He got out of the cab and walked up the steps. He rang the bell. Molly opened the door.

He grinned. "Hello, Molly."

"Johnny," she said, "what a—"

He looked at her. She was wearing slacks and a blouse. The blouse was unbuttoned and he could almost see her breasts.

"Look at you, Molly," he laughed. "You're still a sight."

At the dinner table that night, Abe's children, Benjy, twelve, and Betsy, ten, sat with them.

"What did you do then, Uncle Johnny?" Benjy said.

"Your dad and me, we sat down and we said—'We're takin' no more of this. We're gonna talk to the men.'"

Abe Belkin laughed. "We prayed Gant wouldn't find out, that's what we did."

"We waited for the tomatoes," Johnny said, "and we said, 'We're not puttin 'em inside. We're gonna let 'em freeze.'"

"Didn't they get mad?" Betsy asked.

The boy made a face. "Aw, Betsy," he said.

"Yeah," Johnny grinned, "sure they got mad."

Molly walked into the dining room from the kitchen. "All right, to bed you two."

"Did you win, Uncle Johnny?" Benjy said.

He glanced at Abe. "Sure we won."

Abe laughed. "Everybody lost their jobs."

"No!" the boy said. "They didn't!"

Johnny smiled. "Later on. Later on we won."

Molly brought the children to him and he kissed them good-night.

When they were gone, Abe said, "Whatever happened to Gant?"

"He had a stroke. Croaked right on that goddamn platform of his."

Abe laughed.

"We bought that warehouse, you know," Johnny said.

Abe laughed. "You bought Fleckner Foods?"

"They went bust, the place was up for sale."

Abe laughed. "What do you use it for?"

"Nothin'," Johnny said, now laughing himself, "but it's *ours*."

Abe roared.

"Are you kiddin'?" Johnny laughed. "I woulda spent a million bucks to own that place."

They looked at each other and roared. Their laughter faded, then died, and they looked at each other uncomfortably.

Later that night, as they sat on Abe's patio, they again looked at each other, and again they were uncomfortable.

"I can't let you do it," Johnny said.

"It's my strike, Johnny."

"We've got a contract with 'em. No wildcats. You're gonna screw up everything we got."

"They fire three of my guys for no reason and you want me to—"

"Take it into mediation, Abe. That's all. That's what the contract says."

"Screw around for six months waitin' for a decision?"

"Give 'em their benefits until then," Johnny said.

"Benefits? It's the principle of the thing."

"Goddamn your principles!" he said angrily. "You want me to take out hundreds of thousands of guys cause three clowns on the West Coast got canned."

There was a pause.

"Is that what they are, Johnny?" Abe said it quietly.

"You get 'em back to work tomorrow," Johnny said. His voice was cold.

"This is my local, Johnny. We're stayin' out."

"You do what I tell you! It's my union."

There were more than five hundred people in the grand ballroom of the Sheraton-Cleveland, many of them from Shaker Heights and Hunting Valley and Pepper Pike and Gates Mills; women who belonged to the Junior League and men who sipped their noonday martinis inside the cathedral walls of the Union Club. The women wore evening gowns specially ordered for the occasion; the men were black-tied, their manner as stiff as their collars. It was a testimonial dinner, a civic occasion in a city of few civic occasions, and so Mayor Norris was there, a beaming ward boss of the old school chosen by the suburban, old-money Union Clubbers to run "their" city for them. And the governor had sent his top aide, Martin Kalb, who hated Johnny Kovak, hated the way he had to get down on his knees every four years to get the union's support, but who sat next to Johnny and Anna at the speaker's table, and who was now saying in his most earnest manner how much the governor regretted that he couldn't come himself. The owners of the Cleveland Indians and Cleveland Browns were there as well, as were four congressmen, eight judges, and an entire table of churchmen.

Phillip Talbot stood up after the plates were cleared and stepped up to the microphone. He squinted into the cigar smoke drifting in gray-blue clouds toward the top of the red velvet curtains at the sides of the room. He smiled and told a few clumsy jokes cribbed from the pages of the *After-Dinner Speaker's Manual*, and then he talked about Johnny Kovak's accomplishments and career, and after five minutes of that he paused and looked over at Johnny and he grinned.

"Those of us who knew Johnny Kovak," Phillip Talbot said, "and I must say he and I met under somewhat strained circumstances—"

The audience laughed.

"—know that Johnny Kovak is a man of his word. That's only one reason why the city of Cleveland is proud of him, why we're here tonight in his honor. But I'm especially happy to introduce to you a man who has often been witness to Johnny Kovak's personal generosity, the archbishop of the Diocese of Cleveland, the Very Reverend Edward C. Mooney."

Archbishop Mooney was a Cleveland institution, a man with the fragility of old bone china. He spoke in hushed, dramatic tones which underlined the import of each of his words. He said he had known Johnny Kovak for many years and had always found him a strong, generous, and compassionate man, a Catholic in the finest sense of that word.

"Whenever the need arose," the bishop said, "when Catholic Charities looked like it wasn't going to meet its goal, when the diocese organized our Sheltered Workshop for the Retarded, Johnny Kovak and the Federation of Interstate Truckers were always there to lend us a hand. So it is my great honor tonight, as a small token of this city's feeling for one of its favorite sons, to present Johnny Kovak with this check—for eighty-five thousand dollars—to be used for whatever charitable porpose he desires."

The audience applauded. Johnny got up and shook hands with the bishop. He took the check.

"Thank you, Bishop Mooney. Thank you very much. I really don't know what to say."

The audience laughed.

"It's a helluva long way from here down to the Flats."

The audience laughed.

"I know what I'm going to do with this check, though." He paused. "You know, when I was growin' up in the Flats, I wondered if the day'd ever come when anybody—no matter how poor—would get the

best help a doctor could give. This check is gonna
be the start of that kind of a hospital. The Joe Kovak
Memorial Hospital. In the memory of my old man."

The audience applauded. Johnny smiled.

As the wildcat strike against Trans-Bay Freight in
San Francisco went into its third day, Abe Belkin got
an official notice from F.I.S.T. headquarters in Washington. It was short and to the point: the strike was unauthorized and had to be called off immediately. Abe
smiled to himself when he saw the signature at the
bottom of the page: Vincent Doyle, general vice-
president.

Later the same day, other California union officials
who had earlier sworn support to the wildcat expressed second thoughts. Al Howard down in San
Jose called Abe and said he had come to the conclu-
sion that the wildcat was ill advised. Trumbull Max-
well came down from Sacramento to see Abe. He told
him he was in a no-win position; every local west of
the Mississippi had been notified to withdraw support
of the strike. And over in Oakland, Tom Babcock, who
controlled an East Bay empire even larger than Abe's
San Francisco territory, said in no uncertain terms
that there would be trouble unless Abe fell into line.

Abe called a meeting of the striking drivers. He read
the message from F.I.S.T. headquarters and told the
men of the follow-up calls. Then he asked the drivers
for their decision. They voted unanimously to continue the strike.

At daybreak the next morning, Abe made his way to

the Trans-Bay Freight Lines truck terminal on the Embarcadero, the main street along San Francisco's waterfront. The morning was the color of plumber's putty. The air was chilly and damp. A mist clung to the ground and as the Embarcadero yawned with morning's first stir, men with upturned collars, their hands thrust deep into their coat pockets, moved toward the glowing yellow lights and brewing coffee of the waterfront cafés.

Toward the sea, the steel prows of ocean cargo ships and giant concrete pier fronts all but obliterated the view of the bay, leaving a jumble of boom derricks, boat davits, and ship stacks on the horizon. On the far side of the Embarcadero, away from the docks, were brick warehouses painted with black and white graffiti, rusting railroad tracks from an earlier day, and the truck terminals, among them Trans-Bay. And looming over it all, like a giant silver rainbow curving up and into the fog, was the Bay Bridge, the eight-and-a-half-mile structural connection to Oakland. It was an area near the part of town called Tar Flat, close to where the western end of the bridge had been anchored to the earth.

At seven o'clock, Walt Simmons, Abe's right-hand man and vice-president of the San Francisco local, was already on the line, organizing pickets along the chain-link fence and gate bordering the truck depot. Walt was a small man, about five foot six, but he had strength and tenacity of purpose that far outweighed his physical size. The son of a farmer, he had served both Abe and the local with unswerving loyalty for four years, frequently at the expense of his family. Walt Simmons considered the Federation of Interstate Truckers the most important thing in his life. "If it weren't for the federation," he always said, "I'd still be driving a hay wagon in Livermore."

"How many you get?" Walt Simmons grinned as Abe walked up to the picket line.

"What?"

"Calls. How many death calls?"

Abe smiled. "Four."

"I got you beat," Walt Simmons laughed. "I got five."

Walt looked at the row of silent Trans-Bay trucks nudged into the terminal dock behind the fence. "Way I see it," he said, "they're gonna try and bust out from the inside."

"No way," Abe said, "they're gonna bull their way in."

An hour went by without incident, then another and another. The Embarcadero's morning rush slid into a midday hum, and along the picket line the forty or so drivers abandoned their militant spacing. Many of them sat down with their signs.

Walt Simmons was the first to spot them. They came down Rincon Hill, straight for Pier 24, then made a right turn onto the Embarcadero. They bore down on the pickets slowly, a row of 2½-ton panel trucks, unmarked except for the Ford nameplates on their engine hoods. They slowed as they reached the picket line, passed at a crawl, then turned and made a second pass.

On the far side of a side street across from the pickets, the truck pulled into a weed-strewn vacant lot
next to a gas station, a telephone booth nearby. They
lined up as if offering themselves for review, then cut
their motors. The cab of each truck contained a driver
and a man riding shotgun, and for long minutes the
new arrivals and the pickets studied each other.

A powerfully built man with black hair and a pock-
marked face finally got out of the lead truck and
slammed the door. He wore heavy twill pants and
boots, with a gray flannel shirt tucked beneath a
broad leather belt. He carried a clipboard in one
hand, some rumpled papers clamped beneath the
silver clasp. The man crossed the street alone. He
walked directly to the main knot of pickets.

"Abe Belkin?" he said.

Abe looked at him coldly. "That's me."

The man nodded. Then he looked at his clipboard
and began to read, as if from a writ. "You got an
unauthorized strike here. We been instructed, national
office, Federation of Interstate Truckers, not to honor
this here picket line."

"Who instructed you?"

The man glanced down at his clipboard. "Vincent
Doyle, general vice-president."

Abe looked at him. "Every man on this line is a
member of the federation."

"We got our orders," the man said.

"Okay. You've got your orders," Abe said. "Now
take a look at this truck terminal." His voice was hard.
"There's one way in and there's one way out, right

through this gate. You want to come in, you want to ignore this picket line, okay. But you're gonna have to run us down."

"Suit yourself," the man said. He turned and walked back across the street to the vacant lot. The other drivers, now out of their trucks, gathered around him. The man talked to them, then walked to the telephone booth. He dropped some coins in the slot and dialed.

Across the street, Walt Simmons said, "Looks like the shit's in the soup."

The big man in the gray flannel shirt stayed in the phone booth more than fifteen minutes. Then he hung up and walked briskly to his truck. "That's it, let's go," he said. The engines roared and the trucks exploded with life.

The lead truck driven by the pock-marked man headed straight for the gate. It was followed by a second truck. The other two trucks swung out, one toward the pickets on the left, the other toward the pickets on the right.

Ten feet from the pickets guarding the gate, the lead truck stopped. But off to the sides, the flanking trucks bore down on the two ends of the picket line, and when they reached the ends, the rear doors of the trucks flew open. Ten men jumped from each. Their fists were clenched and they swung clubs and blackjacks.

With collective instinct, the pickets broke and headed for the flanks.

"No!" Abe screamed. "Get back to the gate!"

Walt Simmons heard his warning and pushed and

dragged four or five men with him as he threw himself in front of the gate.

At that moment, the lead truck shot forward. There was no warning. The man with the pock-marked face simply slammed the accelerator to the floor. He didn't brake until he was halfway through the gate.

Walt Simmons screamed, his left leg under the truck's rear tire. The truck ground into reverse and the right tire rolled over Simmons again. There was a sudden hush, then someone shouted, "Let's get the fuck outa here."

With grinding, wrenching noises, the trucks backed away from the pickets.

Abe bent over Walt Simmons, covering him with his jacket, holding his face.

"Walt," he said, "Walt."

Simmons was white and cold. He coughed once and was silent. Abe cradled him in his arms. Tears rivered his face.

Johnny sat in his office with Vince Doyle, watching the television set.

The television reporter said, "Union organizer Walt Simmons was dead on arrival at San Francisco General Hospital. Two federation organizers from a San Jose local were charged with the killing. Abe Belkin, the president of San Francisco Local 43, said his local was ending the wildcat walkout."

On screen, Abe said, "We're goin' back to work because I don't want anymore of my men gettin' killed.

You've got more punks and hoodlums in this union than you've got decent rank and file."

The television reporter said, "In Washington, Senator Cole Madison, of Rhode Island, the chairman of the Senate Rackets Committee, said he will hold public hearings to probe alleged underworld ties to the union."

On screen, Madison said, "I just don't think we can stand by and see people killed because they don't follow Mr. Kovak's orders."

"Will you call Kovak to testify?" the reporter asked Madison.

Madison smiled wryly. "I don't see why not."

Johnny shut the set off. He turned furiously to Doyle.

"I said push 'em, Vince! I didn't say kill nobody!"

"Nobody wanted to kill anybody, Johnny. It was an accident."

"An accident?" he shouted. "A fuckin' accident? You think Madison's gonna buy that? You think Abe's gonna buy that? What the fuck you want me to say to those fuckin' reporter out there? I'm sorry? We didn't wanna kill nobody? We just wanted to squeeze 'em?"

He walked behind his desk.

"Goddamnit, Vince!" he said. "Goddamnit!"

An hour later, when he walked down the steps of the F.I.S.T. building and the reporters besieged him, he was calm and composed.

"What's your reaction to Senator Madison's announcement, Mr. Kovak?"

"Madison's got no evidence," Johnny said. "This union's clean. I think it's a real insult to the working man in this country."

"Why do you think Senator Madison is holding these hearings?"

Johnny grinned. "Maybe the eight percent hike I got the men's got somethin' to do with it."

Some of the reporters laughed.

"Listen, this is nothin' new and you fellas in the writing game know it. The average guy in this country is always gettin' screwed by the big-money boys. They used to use shotguns and baseball bats on us. Now it's politicians."

"What about Abe Belkin's statement?"

"I'm glad he ended that wildcat," Johnny said. "Our contract says no wildcats. And as you know, we live up to our agreements."

"But what about the hoodlums he says are in your union?"

"I'm sorry, but I didn't hear him say that."

"But he says there are hoodlums—"

"Look, fellas. I don't know what he said, but I do know that he was speakin' rash, probably on account of what happened. I've got a lotta respect for Abe Belkin. He's a great union man. We're all sorry that guy Simmons was killed in that fight. Even if he was in an unauthorized strike, I'm gonna make sure that his family gets all the benefits. And let me tell you somethin' else. This union's gonna make sure all the facts come out about what happened. I've instructed my assistants to begin our own investigation."

* * *

In his office the next day, Cole Madison sat with Dave Roberts and Charles White, an ebullient young speech writer only a year out of Yale.

"Senator," Charlie White said, "I'm only thinking about all this in terms of a presidential campaign."

Cole Madison poured coffee for them from a silver container.

"If I decide to run," he said.

Charlie White grinned. "Well, of course. But I think we should—"

"You guys are so damned eager for me to run," Cole Madison said.

He laced his coffee with a shot of cognac.

"Well, consider the possibility," Charlie White said.

Cole Madison laughed. "The possibility, Charlie?"

"Well, yes sir," Charlie White said.

"All right, Charlie," Cole Madison said. "I hear you starting to itch. Let's hear it."

"I certainly don't want to see us trapped in an anti-labor posture," Charlie White said, "and judging from what Kovak said yesterday, he's going to try to—"

"He was *good*." Cole Madison grinned. "Wasn't he?"

"When you look at those big industrial states," Charlie White said, his voice trailing off.

Cole Madison lounged back in his chair. "I think we can get most of the labor vote," he said.

"Going after Kovak?" Charlie White said.

Madison grinned. "Look, Kovak's got tremendous popular support, I know. But let's say we can knock some of the halo off him. Let's say we can prove some of the things we suspect. I think a lot of the other union heads would abandon him."

"I don't understand, senator," Charlie White said. "Why?"

"Because I don't think they want to be investigated themselves. Some of these other unions aren't snow white, either. I think they'd condemn Kovak to curry favor with us."

Dave Roberts laughed. "If that's true, I wouldn't be surprised if you got their endorsements."

"I wouldn't, either." Cole Madison smiled. "*If* I decide to run."

"Jesus, senator," Charlie White said, "that's a brilliant piece of strategy."

"No, it's not," Madison said. "It's a lot of political crap, that's what it is. Kovak scares me. Talking about his 'push.' That's why I want him. This guy lives it. It's in his eyes. With his power unchecked, his friends —what if he applies that push against the government?"

"The government?" Charlie White said, "but certainly you don't think—"

"Wake up, Charlie," Cole Madison said. "Johnny Kovak could shut this country down."

John Howard Harper, the Federation of Interstate Truckers' new legal counsel, was one of the most highly priced corporate attorneys in America. A civilized and genteel man in his mid-sixties, he sat in Johnny's office and puffed his hand-made Savinelli.

Bernie Marr had just presented the circumstances of Walt Simmons' death.

"Perhaps we should make some gesture of cooperation," Harper said.

Johnny looked at him angrily. "Fuck Madison. We ain't cooperatin'. Listen, counsel, this is no Boy Scout troop we've got. Madison thinks he's such a big deal. Let him try to serve his subpoenas."

"Well, if you want my advice," Harper said, "you should at least revoke the memberships of the men charged with Simmons' death."

"I'm revokin' nothin'," Johnny said. "They got carried away, that's all. They were members in good standin'. We're gonna pay their court costs, we're gonna see they get their salary."

"While they're in jail?" Harper said in disbelief.

"Hell, yes."

"It's a mistake, Mr. Kovak. I advise you against it."

Johnny smiled. "Thanks. That's why I'm payin' you for, counselor, to give me advice."

Harper returned the smile. "It is indeed, Mr. Kovak." He paused. "How about this man Belkin in San Francisco? Will he cooperate with Senator Madison?"

Johnny laughed. "Abe? Listen, I know Abe. We had a fight, that's all. He's pissed off. He's been pissed off before."

"I don't know, Johnny," Vince Doyle said. "I'm not so sure."

"He's got his head in the clouds, Vince. He don't know what makes the world go round. That's just Abe."

"All right," Harper said, "let's assume that's true. But how will we handle Madison?"

"I'll handle him," Johnny said flatly.

"But how will you do that, Mr. Kovak?"

Johnny laughed. "Bernie," he said, "what'd we get on Madison?"

"Zero, Johnny," Bernie Marr said, "the guy's clean."

"Clean?" Johnny said bitterly. "Nobody's clean. What the hell's wrong with you, Bernie?"

Cole Madison, meanwhile, was finding it difficult to line up witnesses willing to testify in front of his committee. He visited Max Graham at his home in New Jersey and when he asked him to testify, Graham laughed at him.

"I've been with the federation all my life," Graham said. "I've got my pension. What do you want me to do. Lose everything?"

"We could subpoena you," Cole Madison said.

Graham smiled. "Go ahead. It wouldn't do you any good and you know it. I wouldn't give you a thing."

"Off the record, Mr. Graham."

"Come on, senator," Max Graham said, "there is no off the record. Johnny Kovak got the membership the biggest pay raise in our history." He paused and laughed bitterly. "He's a living legend, senator."

When he visited Abe Belkin in San Francisco, Cole Madison got no further. He barely got through the front door. Abe looked at him suspiciously and didn't mince words.

"You're wasting your time, senator," he said. "I'm not gonna testify against Johnny."

"But why? If you don't like what he's doing—"

"Because we've got a *union*. I don't know if you really understand what that means, senator. Johnny and I built it up. You're asking me to tear it down."

"What if it's larger than that, Mr. Belkin? What if Kovak's power becomes a threat?"

Abe smiled. "To what?"

"To the country."

"What if, what if," Abe grinned. "I'm not gonna fight with Johnny in front of a Senate committee. I'll settle it inside the union."

Madison laughed. "You're an idealist, Mr. Belkin."

"Maybe," Abe said. "What are you, senator?"

In the limousine back to the airport, Madison said, "If only I could get Belkin to testify; he's the key."

"You'll never convince him," Dave Roberts said.

"Can you imagine what he must know? I've got to get to know Kovak better. Maybe then I can somehow reach Belkin."

"What are you going to do, senator," Dave Roberts laughed, "invite him to dinner?"

Madison looked at him. "Dave, you're a genius."

"No. Please. I was joking."

"Why not, for God's sake?" A formal dinner with Kovak in the middle of it? I'm going to enjoy it. He'll be completely off balance."

"You don't even know that he'll accept the invitation."

Madison laughed. "He'll accept. Don't you worry about that, Dave. He'll accept."

A uniformed doorman watched pop-eyed as a cab, its front fender bent and rusted, pulled behind the long row of parked limousines in front of Cole Madison's Virginia mansion.

The doorman moved to open the cab's back door but before he could manage it the cabbie himself bounded out and pushed him out of the way. The cabbie, a sweaty, fat little man with a smile all the way down to his kneecaps, opened the door and said, "Here you go, Mr. Kovak, sir."

Johnny climbed out of the back with Karen Chandler. She looked stunning in an evening gown that matched her hair. Johnny wore a dinner jacket which was slightly wrinkled. He shook hands with the cabbie, then he and Karen walked up the steps to the mansion. Cole Madison, with Kitty at his side, greeted them.

"You remember Karen Chandler?" Johnny said.

Madison smiled. "Of course."

Johnny grinned and looked at Kitty Madison. "Mrs. Madison, I heard you were an attractive woman. I heard wrong. You're gorgeous."

Kitty Madison laughed. "Thank you. You didn't tell me about Mr. Kovak's charm, Cole."

"I always liked blondes," Johnny grinned.

"Yes," Cole Madison said, "your wife is blond, isn't she?"

"Yeah, yeah. Anna's blond. We're all gettin' a little older though. She's back in Cleveland."

Madison smiled. "How unfortunate."

"Please excuse me," Kitty Madison said.

"As long as you promise I'll see you later on," Johnny smiled.

"Oh," she laughed, "you'll see me, Mr. Kovak."

She greeted some other guests and Cole said to Johnny, "Well, how is everything at the federation?"

"Subpoenas all over the place," Johnny said, "it's a snowstorm."

"Is that right?"

"Some guys come around with 'em yesterday to a local in Detroit. They almost got hit by a car."

Madison laughed. "Miss Chandler, didn't you work for the Ways and Means Committee at one time?"

"For several years."

"Yes," Madison smiled, "I thought I heard your name . . . making the rounds."

"Like yours, senator?" Karen Chandler smiled.

Madison laughed and stopped an elderly couple nearby.

"I'd like you to meet Ambassador and Mrs. Lawrenson," he said. "Johnny and Karen Kovak." Madison stepped away with a smile. Johnny laughed. The ambassador and his wife, gray-haired patricians, stared at them. Nobody knew what to say.

"Well, ambassador," Johnny said finally, "what country you workin' as ambassador to?"

"I'm the ambassador to the Vatican, Mr. Kovak."

"Jesus!" Johnny said excitedly, "I'm happy to meet

you." He thumped the old man on the back and grinned. "You mean you actually know the fuckin' Pope?"

At dinner, Johnny and Karen were seated next to the ambassador and his wife. The old woman turned to Karen.

"Do you help your husband to recruit his men?" she asked.

"Well," Karen Chandler said, "sometimes I help him, but actually he—"

"She ain't my wife," Johnny said.

"I beg your pardon?" the old woman said.

"She ain't my wife."

The old woman looked at him openmouthed.

"Hell," Johnny grinned, "that's okay. Don't worry about it."

When the wine was poured, he tasted it and, raising his voice, said to Cole Madison, who was sitting at the other side of the table, "This is good wine, senator."

Madison smiled. "Thank you."

"You ever stomped any grapes?"

The others at the table stopped eating and stared dumbfounded at him.

"I never have." Madison grinned.

"It's terrific. My old man used to make some wine in the basement. I'd go down there with him; we'd get our shoes off, stomp the grapes."

"Really," Madison smiled.

"Used to make great wine. Tastes better, you know, if you stomp it yourself."

Madison laughed.

"This is good wine, though," Johnny said. "My favorite wine's Hungarian wine. Best wine in the world."

"I've never had Hungarian wine," Madison said.

"You oughta try it."

"What do you recommend?"

"Egri Bikaver."

"Egri Bikaver?"

"You got that pretty good," Johnny said.

"What does it mean?"

"Bull's blood."

"*Bull's blood?*" Madison laughed.

"They just call it that."

"I'll try it," Madison said.

"You really oughta."

The other guests started eating. Johnny watched them, then picked up his lamb chop and started to chew it loudly. The others at the table gradually noticed and stopped eating—except Karen, who started to laugh.

Johnny looked up and grinned.

"This chop, Cole," he said. "Jesus. It's a hundred percent." He winked at Madison and started chewing on his bone again.

Alone with Madison in his den after dinner, Johnny walked around the spacious, comfortable room and examined the cut-glass ashtrays and Chinese vases.

"So this is how the stinkin' rich live," Johnny smiled. Madison returned the smile.

"Quite a performance you put on out there," Madison said.

Johnny grinned. "What do you mean?"

He walked around the room looking at the photographs on the walls. Madison saw him looking at a picture of him in lieutenant's uniform.

"You were never in the service, were you? High blood pressure wasn't it?"

Johnny grinned and looked at him. "I'll make you a deal."

Madison smiled. "What kind of deal?"

"We cut the shit and get down to what we're here for."

Madison laughed. "No deals," he said.

"Everybody makes deals," Johnny said.

Madison opened a humidor. "Cigar?"

Johnny took the cigar and smelled it. "What is it?"

"Davidoff. Havana."

Johnny smiled. "I smoke Pirogis sometimes."

"Are they Italian?"

"Scranton, Pa. Union made."

Madison laughed. They sat down and Madison lit his cigar for him, then lit his own. They puffed on their cigars, watching each other through the smoke, smiling.

"What is it that we're here for?" Cole Madison said.

"We're here to talk politics," Johnny said.

"Oh? What aspect of it?"

Johnny grinned. "Vote-getting."

Madison puffed on his cigar. "Difficult business, vote-getting."

There was a pause.

"You know something?" Johnny said, his voice low, "there's other ways of gettin' votes."

"I could say I don't know what you're talking about."

"Yeah, but you didn't ask me over here to tell me that."

Madison laughed, then looked at him seriously. "I've got an old rule. Power corrupts. Absolute power corrupts absolutely."

Johnny grinned. "So?"

Madison said, "Your power is pretty absolute."

Johnny laughed and puffed on his cigar. "I've got an older one than that. Fight fists with fists."

"Is that a threat?" Madison smiled.

Johnny grinned. He slowly took an envelope from his pocket and threw it on the coffee table between them. Madison looked at it. The name "Dorothy Rohr" was neatly printed across it.

Johnny laughed. "Open it, senator."

Madison smiled and opened the envelope. He withdrew three photographs of a young blond woman and placed them on the table. He stared at the pictures. His smile faded.

"Get off it, *senator*," Johnny said viciously. "You can't win."

Madison looked at him. He collected the pictures and put them back in the envelope. He threw the envelope across the table.

"No deal, Johnny."

"Just think," Johnny smiled. "You could've been President."

Three days later, in a small banquet room at the Washington Hilton, the young blond woman, Dorothy Rohr, stood before a battery of microphones and television cameras. She was in her mid-twenties and she wore no makeup. Her hair was cut short. She held a dimple-cheeked little girl, and next to her stood her attorney, a moon-faced man in a shiny black suit.

"Have you heard from Senator Madison since the baby was born?" a reporter asked.

"Gentlemen, please," the attorney said. "Please. I'm sure you all appreciate that this is a moment of great emotional anguish for Miss Rohr."

The reporters laughed.

"I will only say that she has had no contact with Senator Madison since she left his employ," the attorney said.

"Intimate or otherwise?" a reporter asked.

"Both."

The reporters laughed again.

"Has he paid her any money since—"

"He paid her a thousand dollars as a 'going-away present,' " the attorney said, "when Miss Rohr left his employ. I have a Thermofax of the check here."

He held up the Thermofax for the photographers.

"Why is she suing him after all this time?"

"Gentlemen," the attorney said, "she just wants this

lovely little girl"—he pointed to the little girl—"to have a father. That's not asking too much, gentlemen, is it?"

The reporters laughed. The little girl started to cry.

The newspapers were spread out on Cole Madison's desk. Their front pages were all monopolized by pictures of Dorothy Rohr and stories of his paternity suit. Madison glanced at the stories, shook his head, and grinned. Dave Roberts and Charlie White watched him.

"Maybe we should postpone the hearings," Dave Roberts said, "until this business fades off the front page."

"Not a chance," Madison said. "Not a chance."

"What about the press, senator?" Charlie White said.

"Charlie," Madison said, "I want you to write me the most fervent categorical denial you're capable of. I want it to sizzle with moral outrage. I'm shocked by the bald nature of the lie. So on and so forth."

"It's character assassination, senator," Charlie White said.

Madison grinned. "Don't overdo it, Charlie."

He looked at the newspapers again and scrutinized a picture of Dorothy Rohr.

"She looks downright virginal here. I wonder what she cost Kovak. Dave, see if you can find out."

Roberts nodded, Charles White looked at the paper. "Halfway virginal, maybe," he said.

"What?" Madison smiled. "She certainly didn't get halfway pregnant, did she?"

* * *

The Senate caucus room was a stately chamber with vaulted ceiling, red carpets, arching windows, marble pillars, and glistening chandeliers. Cole Madison sat at the center of an elevated table, Dave Roberts behind him. Senator Carnes sat at the table's end, and smiled for the photographers. The room was filled with spectators and reporters.

Cole Madison banged his gavel and said, "We will call our first witness, Mr. Frank C. Vasko."

Frank Vasko was a broken and haggard man who looked older than his years. He sat at the witness table alone, his shoulders slumped, his head down. His speech was halting; his manner tentative.

Responding to Cole Madison's questions, he talked about the small trucking firm he had once headed in Chicago. He told how Johnny Kovak visited him and told him to sign his men up into the union. His voice breaking, he described how four men broke into his house one day and took his wife into the bedroom, tore her clothes, and threatened to rape her.

Cole Madison paused. The room hushed.

"Mr. Vasko," he said, "had they tried to convince you to sign your men up before Mr. Kovak paid you the visit?"

"Yes, sir."

"How?"

"Their business agents came to the office. I got phone calls."

"What did Mr. Kovak say when he visited you?"

"He said if I didn't sign up, then some of the other companies wouldn't."

"Anything else?"

"It was a long time ago, senator." Vasko paused. "But before he left, I'll never forget, he said, 'Merry Christmas, Frank.'"

"But you didn't sign up?" Madison said.

"No, sir."

"Why not, Mr. Vasko?"

"Senator, my men voted not to join the union. I wasn't gonna make 'em do somethin' they didn't wanna do."

"But you signed up nevertheless after what happened to your wife?"

"Yes, sir."

Madison paused. "Mr. Vasko, what—uh, what were the, uh, personal consequences of what happened to your wife?"

Vasko hesitated. "Well, she was afraid, senator."

"Can you be more specific, Mr. Vasko?"

"To go out on the street. To shop. To go to church. She said they were following her. She kept the house dark at night, rolled the shades down during the day. They were watching her, she said."

"Did you go to the police?"

Vasko looked at Senator Carnes and hesitated. Carnes watched him poker-faced.

"Yes, sir," Vasko said. "District attorney, Cook County, state of Illinois." He kept his eyes on Carnes.

Madison saw him looking at Carnes. "What did the district attorney say?"

"He said there was no connection between the union

407

and the men who—who did what they done to my wife."

"I see," Madison said. He conferred with Dave Roberts a moment, then continued. "And what was the district attorney's name?"

Vasko looked at Madison a long moment before answering. "I forget, senator." He lowered his eyes to the table.

"Do you, Mr. Vasko?"

"It was a long time ago, senator," Vasko said, his voice low.

Madison paused. "Yes," he said finally, his eyes on Vasko's, "it was." He changed his tone. "You sold your trucking company?"

"With our hospital bills and everything—"

Madison interrupted him. "I only have one more question. I know this will be painful to you. Believe me, Mr. Vasko, I wish to cause you no more pain."

Vasko smiled. "I know that, senator."

"Was your wife institutionalized after what happened to her?"

"Yes, sir."

"For how long?"

"Two years."

There was a buzz among the spectators in the hearing room. Some of the reporters hurried out of the room toward the telephones.

"What are you doing now, Mr. Vasko?" Madison said.

"I run a body shop in Cottonwood, Arizona."

"Why did you move there?"

"It's a small place, senator," Frank Vasko said. He smiled. "A pretty place. A lotta trees. Big sky. I knew nobody was gonna bother us there."

That afternoon, Babe Milano sat at the witness table, smiling, oozing confidence.

Asked if he would tell the truth, the whole truth, and nothing but the truth, he said, "Absolutely!" It got a big laugh.

"State your name, please," Cole Madison said.

"Senator," Babe Milano said, "you've been investigating me for I don't know how long. You've sent me a million subpoenas." He paused. "Senator, you don't even know my name?"

The spectators laughed. "For the record," Cole Madison said.

"Anthony Giuseppe Milano. Two Ps in Giuseppe, senator."

"And your occupation?"

"I'm a businessman."

"And your age?"

"Sixty-three, senator. But Jesus, I feel younger than that."

The spectators laughed.

"And your address?"

"The Palms Hotel, Las Vegas. Penthouse suite. It's got a helluva view, senator."

The spectators laughed again. Cole Madison smiled, then looked at him seriously.

"Mr. Milano," Cole Madison said, "you're a friend of John J. Kovak's, aren't you?"

"I know him, sure."

"How long have you had this friendship?"

"I don't know. A long time, senator."

"Five years? Ten? Twenty?"

"Closer to twenty, I'd say."

Madison smiled. "Now Mr. Milano, you have quite a lengthy arrest record, isn't that right?"

Milano grinned. "Well, I got into some scrapes, if that's what you mean, senator. A long time ago. I'm not gonna deny it."

"Can you give us a list of your arrests?"

"I can't recall, senator. I know I beat a guy up pretty good once in a fight. He was welshin' on a bet. I'm glad I did it too, senator, the no good son-of-a—"

The spectators laughed.

Madison looked at a piece of paper Roberts handed him. "Extortion, bribery, suspicion of murder, suspicion of conspiracy to commit murder. Isn't it a fact, Mr. Milano, that you are one of the leading figures of organized crime in this country?"

Milano smiled. "I'm a businessman is all, senator. I'm trying to make a living like everybody else. Besides of which, there's no such thing as that."

"No such thing as what?"

"Organized crime. The reporters just make it up for the headlines. They gotta sell their papers. They gotta sell the ads for the TV. I don't blame 'em, senator. They're just businessmen like you and me. They're just trying to make a living like you and me. I don't mind, senator."

"You don't?"

"Hell, no, senator," Milano grinned. "They don't make much."

The spectators laughed.

"I see they've been writing a lot about you, too, lately, senator."

The spectators laughed again. Madison grinned.

"I don't believe that stuff about you, either," Babe Milano said.

Madison smiled. "Thank you very much, Mr. Milano. I appreciate that."

"Any time senator."

"But tell me, Mr. Milano, isn't it a fact that for the past thirty years you've personally known most of the dangerous criminals in this country?"

"I don't understand, senator," Babe Milano said.

"Do you know Albert Grimaldi?"

"Sure."

Madison smiled. "Do you see him often, Mr. Milano?"

"Not no more, senator." Milano paused. "He's under the ground."

The spectators laughed.

"Did he die of natural causes?" Cole Madison asked.

"I wouldn't say that, no," Milano said.

"Why not, Mr. Milano?" Madison was straightfaced.

"Because he died in the gas chamber in Pennsylvania."

The spectators laughed again. "I see," Madison said. His eyes twinkled. "How about Robert Battaglia, Mr. Milano, do you know him?"

"Bobby's under the daisies, too," Milano said.

The spectators laughed again.

"And how did he get such an intimate view of the daisies, as you put it?" Cole Madison asked.

"He sat down in an electric chair, senator," Babe Milano said.

The hearing room exploded in laughter.

"Was he also a friend of yours?" Cole Madison asked.

"I knew Bobby, sure."

"Now Mr. Milano," Cole Madison said, "since these men were executed for their crimes, don't you think it's fair to say they're dangerous criminals?"

"They're not dangerous no more, senator."

The spectators roared.

"You're right there," Madison grinned.

"I think I know what you're gettin' at, senator."

"I'm glad."

"But it's not fair. I know thousands of people in this country. I know senators and governors and congressmen. I can't help it if some of the people I know sometimes get into trouble with the law."

The spectators laughed.

"Do you introduce your friends to each other, Mr. Milano?"

"Well, sometimes, sure."

Milano's lawyers consulted with him.

"Have you ever introduced any of these men," Cole Madison said, "these criminals that are friends of yours, to your friend John J. Kovak?"

"To Johnny?" Milano said, surprised.

His lawyers talked to him again.

"Please answer the question, Mr. Milano."

"I don't know," Babe Milano said, "I'm trying to think. I've got a lotta friends."

"You aren't answering the question," Madison said.

"To the best of my recollection," Milano said. "I cannot recall."

"I see," Madison said. He paused. "Can you recall, Mr. Milano, that you own the major interest in the Aquacade Entertainment Corporation of Las Vegas?"

"Sure I can recall," Milano smiled. "It's all in my income-tax forms you've got, senator."

The spectators laughed.

"Thank you. And didn't the Aquacade Entertainment Corporation recently negotiate a one million two hundred thousand dollar loan from the pension fund of the Federation of Interstate Truckers?"

Milano consulted his lawyers.

"That's no secret," he said. "We're building a new casino that looks just like Miami Beach. Swimming pool on the main floor. Water skis. Cabanas. And you can gamble right there."

The spectators laughed.

"Did you talk to your friend Mr. Kovak about lending you that money?" Cole Madison said.

"I talked to the trustees of the pension fund. They approved it. We've got security down, our payments are on time—"

"But didn't you talk to your friend Mr. Kovak about giving the loan to you?" Madison's voice was strident, and accusing.

"Nobody likes to negotiate with him, senator," Babe

Milano said. "Jesus Christ, I'd rather talk to the trustees any day."

The spectators laughed.

"Did you or did you not talk to Mr. Kovak about it?"

"I'll tell you the God's truth, senator," Babe Milano said.

"That will be refreshing."

The spectators laughed.

"I can't recall."

The spectators roared. Milano smiled. Madison looked exasperated.

Cole Madison leaned back in his Senate office that night, a bottle of Chivas Regal in front of him. His feet were on the desk. He looked worn out and dispirited.

"What do you think, Dave?"

"Well," Dave Roberts said, "it could be worse."

Madison laughed. "How?"

"Vasko was effective," Roberts said. "He got a lot of TV play."

Madison looked at him. "That's really great, Dave. I'm overwhelmed with how great that is."

"I almost hate to bring this up, senator," Roberts said after a pause, "but what happens if Doyle and Kovak both take the Fifth?"

Charlie White laughed. "We're up shit creek."

Madison glanced at him sharply.

"As they say, senator," Charlie White said.

Madison glared at him, then turned to Dave Roberts. "Kovak won't take the Fifth. He's going to make Milano look like the amateur hour."

"What about Doyle?" Roberts said.

Madison took his feet off the desk. "I hope he does," he said. "Goddamnit, Dave, I hope he does. Once he takes the Fifth, he has to keep taking it." He paused and smiled ruefully. "No matter what I ask him."

At a union hall in Brooklyn, Johnny stood in front of three hundred loudly cheering men. His shirtsleeves were rolled up. He was without a tie. Sweat streamed down his face.

"The man that's tryin' to railroad us with this great crusade," Johnny shouted, "the man paintin' us all kindsa dirt, he can't even keep his own life in decent order!"

The men cheered.

"We know why they're drivin' their railroad against us! We know the eight percent hike in our paychecks is what's up their craw! Well, I'm tellin' you, it ain't gonna work! The next time out, we're goin' up to ten!"

The men cheered.

"And then to twelve!"

The men cheered.

"And then to fourteen!"

The men cheered wildly.

Johnny paused and watched them.

"This country's truckers ain't gonna get railroaded by no committee!" he cried. "The hell with them! We're the ones that put the railroads outa business!"

* * *

Vince Doyle was a model of rectitude as he walked into the hearing room. He wore a gray suit, a white shirt, a navy-blue tie, and the horn-rimmed glasses which he usually only wore when reading. He was somber and deadpan and as he sat at the witness table, he looked almost professorial. He was flanked by two young attorneys, John Howard Harper's assistants, who sat protectively beside him whispering advice even before Cole Madison began asking questions. Vince Doyle swore to tell the truth and Cole Madison smiled, as if on cue.

"State your name, please," Cole Madison said.

Vince Doyle looked at him and in a flat monotone recited, "I respectfully decline to answer because I honestly believe my answer might incriminate me."

Cole Madison grinned. "Did you say *honestly*, sir?"

Some of the spectators laughed.

"Sir," Cole Madison smiled, "do you honestly believe that if you told us what your name is, your name, what people call you, that it would incriminate you?"

Doyle talked to his lawyers.

"It might," he said.

"I must say," Cole Madison said, "that I have never met anyone whose name is such a cross to him."

The spectators laughed.

"I am going to assume, sir," Cole Madison said, "that your name is Vincent Doyle, that you are a national vice-president of the Federation of Interstate Truckers, that you were born in Cleveland, Ohio, and

416

that you have been a lifelong friend of Mr. John J. Kovak."

"I respectfully decline to answer—"

"I haven't asked any questions," Cole Madison said. "All I made were assumptions."

The spectators laughed.

"Isn't it a fact, Mr. Doyle," Cole Madison said, "that previous to your association with the Federation of Interstate Truckers, you were a business partner of Mr. Anthony Milano?"

"I respectfully decline to answer—"

"In an interstate bootlegging operation?"

"I respectfully decline to answer," Vince Doyle monotoned, "on the grounds that my answer might incriminate me."

"And wasn't the third partner of that bootlegging operation Mr. Shondor Gerky of Detroit?"

"I respectfully decline to answer."

"Didn't you introduce Mr. Milano and Mr. Gerky to Mr. John J. Kovak?"

"I respectfully decline to answer."

"And didn't Mr. Milano and Mr. Gerky have a controlling interest in the Haley Jukebox Company, headquartered in Pontiac, Michigan?"

"I respectfully decline to answer."

"And didn't the Midwest Council of the Federation of Interstate Truckers, under the aegis of Mr. Kovak, force businesses to patronize the Haley Jukebox Company—because of your friendship with Mr. Milano and Mr. Gerky?"

417

"I respectfully decline to answer."

"I keep hearing the word 'respectfully,'" Cole Madison said. He smiled. "You seem to have a great deal of respect, Mr. Doyle, for this whole process."

The spectators laughed.

"I respectfully decline to answer," Vince Doyle said.

"Yes, I know," Cole Madison said. "I somehow assumed you might say that."

The spectators laughed again.

"Now. Reaching more recent times, Mr. Doyle, isn't it a fact that you helped your friend Mr. Milano secure a one million two hundred thousand dollar loan from your union's pension fund?"

"I respectfully decline to answer."

"Let me understand," Cole Madison said. He paused. "Do you feel that if you gave a truthful answer to this committee about helping gangsters with union money —with funds of your members—that your answer would tend to incriminate you?"

"It might," Vince Doyle said.

"You honestly feel that way?"

Doyle consulted his lawyers.

"I do."

"That's a marvelous self-admission, Mr. Doyle," Cole Madison said. "I applaud your candor."

The spectators roared.

"Isn't it a fact, Mr. Doyle," he continued, "that without their consent, your membership's funds are being used to further the interests of organized crime in this country?"

"I respectfully decline to answer the—"

"That you and Mr. Kovak are indirectly subsidizing drug traffic, prostitution, illegal gambling in this country?"

"I object to this line of questioning," one of Doyle's attorneys said.

"Answer the question, Mr. Doyle!" Madison snapped.

"I respectfully decline to answer," Vince Doyle said, "because I honestly believe my answer might tend to incriminate me."

Madison smiled. "*Tend*, Mr. Doyle, is that what you said?"

"Tend."

"Let the record show," Cole Madison said, "that Mr. Doyle has made a wise choice of four-letter words."

The spectators laughed.

"Mr. Doyle," Cole Madison said slowly, "is there any question I can possibly ask you the answer to which will not incriminate you?"

Doyle consulted his lawyers.

"Are you a man, Mr. Doyle," Cole Madison smiled, "or are you a worm?"

"I refuse to answer the question—"

The spectators roared.

Cole Madison banged his gavel. "Thank you, Mr. Doyle. I think you've finally answered one of my questions."

The spectators roared. Cole Madison smiled. Vince Doyle glared at him.

* * *

The plan was simple. They would paralyze the nation's capital. They would cause the greatest traffic jam in the history of Washington, D.C.

As Vince Doyle testified, more than two hundred trucks—tankers, flatbeds, vans, panels, tractors—would converge on the city. The majority of them were simply to circle through the city in a show of solidarity, greeting each other with blasts of their air horns.

But other trucks were to suffer "accidents" or "breakdowns" in strategic locations. The locations included the Capitol Building, Washington Circle, the Pentagon, the Baltimore–Washington Parkway, and three of the six major bridges leading across the Potomac. In all cases the mishaps were to occur in the outbound lanes so that traffic leaving the city would be brought to a standstill while incoming traffic would be unimpeded. The White House was a special case. Here there were to be two disruptions, one in the front and one in the rear. Of the two, the one in the front was considered the more important, for the breakdown at 1600 Pennsylvania Avenue was tailor-made for the television cameras.

This special job, putting the "push" on the Oval Office, was delegated to a man named Wally Brubaker, a burly ex-marine and F.I.S.T. organizer from Hagerstown, Maryland. A feisty man of forty-three with a hair-trigger temper, Brubaker came from a family of hard-core union men. His father was a steelworker, his brothers with the meat packers and railroad men. In addition, Brubaker harbored a smoldering hatred of the federal government stemming from his discharge from the Marine Corps for a minor infraction of regulations. At the time of the infraction, Brubaker had fourteen years of service, and it was his contention that the government had given him the boot to deprive him of his retirement pay.

So now, on this day, as Wally Brubaker prepared to visit Washington, he had no compunctions about "hitting" the White House. He was, he felt, many years overdue. He climbed into the cab of a Diamond T tractor in Hagerstown at 12:30 P.M. Behind him was a battered and rusted drop-bed trailer loaded with a dirt-encrusted yellow bulldozer. The bulldozer, which had been out of service for more than two years, was tightly chained in place. As he eased his rig onto Interstate 70, Wally Brubaker looked like a down-on-his-luck contractor heading for some distant and dubious excavation site. His trip to the White House would take him two and a half hours.

Elsewhere, other drivers were already on the road or preparing to leave. Jake Grabsky, heading north on Interstate 95 out of Richmond, Virginia, was piloting a gleaming silver and red eight-axle tanker rig consisting of a full trailer tank, a semitrailer tank, and a Mack diesel tractor with a turbo-charged engine. Grabsky, whose eventual destination was the Pentagon, was heading for the intersection of 95 and Route 1, where he hoped to nail down a considerable number of the more than nine thousand vehicles in the Pentagon parking lots.

Eli Jennings, at the wheel of a rig loaded with soft drinks destined for District of Columbia beverage stores, was also on Interstate 95, but moving south out of Camden, New Jersey. His assignment was to knock out the Francis Scott Key Memorial Bridge.

Ramsey Johnson, a giant of a black man, was moving south on Interstate 83 from Harrisburg, Pennsylvania. Johnson was known inside the Federation of Interstate Truckers as a strong-arm, a man who could be relied on to get results. On this day, Ramsey Johnson was hauling a Dorsey flatbed trailer loaded with steel rods, the kind used to reinforce concrete. Johnson had drawn the Capitol Building, and the tie lines on his load had been specially designed to break away at his command from the cab. The dump was to be made at East Capitol Street and First Street, directly in front of the Capitol, with the Supreme Court Building and the Library of Congress on either side.

And there were others: Charlie Drake, out of Altoona, Pennsylvania, with a load of electronics components meant to jam the Arlington Memorial Bridge; Dick Newman from Baltimore, hauling a load of refrigerated produce, headed for the Mason Memorial Bridge; Rudolph Alonsky, of Wilmington, Delaware, headed for a breakdown near Anacostia Park on the Baltimore–Washington Parkway; and Teddy Heater, dispatched from Philadelphia to create a hindrance around Washington Circle with a load of furniture.

To them were added platoons of support personnel, men who wore blue or green work clothes over their gray sweatshirts, each of them behind the wheel of a monster headed for the nation's capital, each of them ready to throw a special monkey wrench.

They began to arrive in force about 1:30 P.M. But instead of heading into the city, they circled the District on the Capitol Beltway, stalling for time, waiting for the appointment. By 2 P.M., there were more than one hundred and fifty trucks lazily circling the capital, some going clockwise, others counter-clockwise, in the manner of a mammoth motorized picket line. They kept their horns silent and as they passed one another in counterrotational sweeps, they looked not unlike an armada of whales coming in for the kill.

Meanwhile, business in Washington was going on as usual. At the Mayflower Hotel, both the Rotary Club and the Lions Club were lingering over coffee after their weekly meetings. At the White House, the seemingly endless line of visiting tourists, who would number more than nine thousand that day, continued their patient rounds. The changing of the guard at the Tomb of the Unknown Soldier took place as usual; and at the Pentagon more than a few generals were recovering from lunch with a visit to the Meditation Room. Hot air hung over the city; the doldrums of summer; a lassitude that put dogs on their sides and pigeons to rest.

Exactly at 2:15 P.M., the rigs driven by Brubaker, Grabsky, Jennings, Johnson, Drake, Newman, Alonsky, and Heater swung off the Capitol Beltway and moved into the city. These trucks, the advance guard and main-body muscle by virtue of their missions, were to slip into the city before the authorities realized they were being invaded. These trucks alone could tie up Washington traffic and make the dramatic point; each

423

additional truck which succeeded in entering the city would only further the dramatization of the goal.

Brubaker made his way toward the White House by way of Connecticut Avenue. Only once, just outside of Georgetown, did he run into trouble. A mounted policeman pulled his horse next to the cab and asked Brubaker if he had a permit to transport a bulldozer through town. Brubaker looked at the officer and said, "Look, buddy, if you want to hold up the project at the White House that's okay with me. All I know is they told me to deliver this equipment." The policeman brushed him on with a wave of his hand. The other drivers encountered no opposition at all.

At 2:30 P.M., the main body of trucks swept off the Capitol Beltway. At each of the nearly twenty off-ramps and exits and feeder roads leading to the city a convoy of trucks suddenly materialized. Most of the exits were able to handle the strain. But at both the Baltimore–Washington Parkway exit and the Henry Shirley Memorial Highway exit there were delays. More than thirty-five trucks hit each of them at once.

Yet one by one the drivers threaded their way into Washington. Those approaching from the southwest immediately saw that Jennings, Drake, and Newman had successfully sabotaged the bridges over the Potomac. Outgoing movement on the Key, Arlington, and Mason bridges was either stopped completely or reduced to a creep.

On the Key Bridge, Jennings moved his rig diagonally across all lanes of traffic and cut his motor. He was the victim of a "jammed transmission." He got out of the cab and inspected his motor with a wrench and a screwdriver. His transmission was then, in fact, jammed.

Drake simply stopped in the middle of the Arlington Bridge and turned on his flashers. He probed around underneath his motor and a large pool of slippery fluid formed around his truck.

On the Mason Bridge, Newman stopped his truck and deliberately severed his main brake lines.

At other key points it was the same. Grabsky stopped his rig at Interstate 95 and Route 1, popped his flashers, and got out to investigate. By the time he had circled the truck in search of the trouble, every tire on his rig was deflating. Within minutes, the two silver and red tankers sat on puddles of rubber. That took care of the Pentagon.

Alonsky ripped his ignition wires apart, then swore he didn't know what was wrong as the Baltimore–Washington Parkway became a slow-moving nightmare.

Outside the Capitol Building, Ramsey Johnson arrived with his load of steel rods and pulled the cord that released the entire cargo into the street. More than nine hundred rods tumbled to the pavement like a giant stack of twisted toothpicks. The black man got out of his cab and sat down on the curb, shaking his head and shrugging his shoulders to all questions.

Brubaker, meanwhile, had made his way to the White House. Approaching from the east along Pennsylvania Avenue, he drove his bulldozer past the front of the executive mansion, then onto Jackson. At

Jackson, he nosed the Diamond T catty-corner across the intersection, aiming it straight for Blair House, the President's traditional guest quarters.

When he had the rig straddled diagonally across the intersection, the bulldozer approximately dead center, he cut the motor and got out to investigate. He was immediately surrounded by a contingent of White House guards, Secret Service agents, and police.

"I'm tellin' you," Brubaker shouted to them, "there's something wrong with my rig. I felt it up front. It jerked me right through the intersection."

A tall middle-aged man built along the lines of a concrete power station stepped up to him. He wore a dark suit and his hair was clipped short. His face was noticeably devoid of laugh lines.

"You're going to move this thing," he said quietly.

"Fuck you," Brubaker said. "I know what I'm talkin' about." He jerked a thumb toward the bulldozer. "There's somethin' screwed up back there."

The tall man remained expressionless. Then he touched a finger to Brubaker's shirt and said, "Move it. No questions. No trouble."

"Listen, you sonofabitch," Brubaker said, "I—"

"Move it."

"Move it?" Brubaker yelled. "You want me to move it? All right, I'm gonna move it."

He leaped into the cab of the Diamond T and gunned the Cummins diesel engine. It screamed and roared. The stacks shot open and clouds of black smoke blew into the air. Brubaker sat there for some seconds, vibrating in his seat, scowling at the tall man in the dark suit, and then he popped the clutch. There was a thunderous crash, the wrenching sound of metal. The Diamond T leaped forward but the trailer and bulldozer stayed in the same spot and dropped to the pavement with a multiton thud.

Brubaker pumped his brakes and stopped the tractor not more than ten feet from the fallen trailer. He jumped from the cockpit and stalked toward the man in the dark suit.

"Goddamnit, you sonofabitch," Brubaker yelled, "I told you there was something wrong. Now what the fuck am I supposed to do? Huh? Smart guy?"

"The first thing you can do," the man in the suit said calmly, "is move the tractor. Out of the way." He pointed to a bus zone. "Over there."

"The fuck I will," Brubaker said. "You move it."

He flipped the man the key and walked away, leaving the astonished group of policemen and the dirty yellow bulldozer, nosed deep in the pavement, behind him.

At the same time, behind the White House, Gilbert Orlander, a member of F.I.S.T. Local 44 in Alexandria, Virginia, hauled a forty-foot aluminum trailer down Madison Place and jackknifed it in front of a White House driveway. He got out and walked to the guard shack at the White House gate.

"Steering column broke," Orlander said simply. When the Secret Service tried to move the truck, they discovered that the steering wheel spun free as a Yo-Yo.

By 3:45 P.M., the paralysis of Washington was complete. Traffic on virtually every major artery had been reduced to a crawl. As the success of the operation became clear, truck drivers who had joined the assault as a lark were inspired to other, unplanned actions. Some stopped their rigs anywhere and erected barricades around them with red rubber traffic cones or fiery highway flares. And on the north side of the city, on Sixteenth Street near Rock Creek Park, persons unknown stole a District of Columbia highway maintenance truck, a small flatbed which was equipped with a Wald Town and Country Push-Button Striping Machine, a piece of machinery used for painting traffic lanes on the city's streets. By mid-afternoon, squiggly newly painted lines were in the streets all over Georgetown.

At 4 P.M., the first of hundreds of thousands of government and civilian workers began leaving their offices. The Pentagon alone disgorged some 25,000 people. Summer tourists visiting the Smithsonian Institution, the National Archives Building, the Washington Monument, or any of a hundred other historic attractions, now began searching for their cars or taxis to take them to hotels or out of the city.

They found they couldn't even get their cars out of parking lots, let alone through city streets. Public transportation was at a complete standstill. Throughout the nation's capital, the fastest means of travel was by foot. The air was filled with the menacing sonorous rumble of air horns, now backed by the piercing, shrill wail of a hundred police sirens.

* * *

Their limousine was stalled in traffic. Hundreds of car horns created a deafening cacophonous roar.

Cole Madison turned the radio up. "Motorists are advised to avoid the Key Bridge," a radio newsman said, "where a tractor-trailer has broken down with a jammed transmission."

"A jammed transmission," Cole Madison laughed. "Did you hear that, Dave? That's pretty good."

"This is incredible," Dave Roberts said.

Cole Madison smiled ruefully. "It's 'push,' that's all. Why shouldn't he push us?"

They listened to the radio.

"More than two hundred drivers, mostly from New Jersey and Pennsylvania, are taking part in today's action. Among those caught in the squeeze was the President of the United States, whose driver was forced to take an alternate route after a jackknifed truck carrying a bulldozer blocked a White House driveway."

"Sure," Cole Madison smiled. "Why not bulldoze the President? Anyone else who gets in his way."

"At his home in Shaker Heights, Ohio, Federation of Interstate Truckers president Johnny Kovak denied that his union's leadership had any knowledge of today's action. Kovak said he would speak to his membership to avoid a similar 'mass breakdown' when he appears in front of the Senate Rackets Committee next week."

"We must remember to thank him for that, Dave." Cole Madison smiled.

His words were nearly drowned out by the roar of hundreds of car horns.

"I'll tell you something, Dave," Cole Madison said, his voice crackling and firm, "all the trucks and all the horn honking in the world won't keep me from putting Kovak on that stand."

The St. Stephen's courtyard was decorated with red, white, and green bunting. Bunches of grapes had been strung together and were hanging from a thin rope which circled the dance floor. A gypsy band played the czardas. Sausages were being grilled on open fires. The courtyard was crowded.

Johnny sat at a long table next to his mother and Anna. At the other end of the table, Zigi Zagon was having a loud and animated discussion with Mishka and a group of older Hungarian men. Johnny sipped a beer, puffed on a little black cigar, and watched the dancers.

"How come you don't bring Joey?" his mother said.

"My mom's there," Anna answered. "Johnny didn't want to—"

"You shouldn't be ashamed, Johnny," Ilona Kovak said.

He turned to her angrily. "I'm not ashamed, ma. Anna's mother just happened to be there. Okay?"

She looked at him accusingly. "Joey likes the music."

He looked away from her without response and watched Zigi Zagon gesture floridly at Mishka. He grinned. "Law and order, Zigi," Johnny said, "that's all you talk about."

"Mrs. Toth," Zigi said, "she makes the strudel. You know her, Johnny? Yesterday she come to the early mass. A guy jumps out at her with a knife. He takes her money, knocks her down."

"What about the cops?" Johnny said.

"The cops come, write everything down, go away."

Johnny smiled. "I'll talk to the mayor, Zigi, get some more cops down here."

"It's terrible, Johnny," Zigi Zagon said, "all the riff-raff down here."

Johnny grinned. "I said I'd take care of it, Zigi. I'll talk to the mayor. Relax."

"Okay, Johnny," Zigi Zagon smiled. He turned to the other men. "What we do without Johnny, huh?"

They laughed.

Mishka said, "I saw Abe on the television, Johnny."

Johnny forced a smile. "I saw him too, Mish."

"You two—you get in a fight?"

"A little disagreement, Mish, that's all."

Mishka looked at him. Johnny avoided his eyes and turned to Anna. "You wanna dance?"

"That Vasko on the television, Johnny," Mishka said.

Johnny helped Anna up. He looked at the old man and grinned. "You just watch the set all day? Is that what you do, Mishka?"

Mishka said, "He's a Hungarian boy too, no?"

"Yeah."

They looked at each other. Mishka nodded and said nothing.

"Come on, Anna," Johnny said. He led her to the dance floor. They danced the czardas. The other dancers moved quickly away when they saw them. The people in the courtyard gathered around and clapped. Johnny grinned and showed off for them. Anna smiled at him. Then, suddenly, tears came to her eyes. Johnny stopped dancing and the music stopped harshly.

They stood at sunset on the bridge overlooking the Flats. Johnny chewed on his dead cigar. Anna, huddled together, hugged herself.

"What happened to you back there?" Johnny said.

"I don't know. Tired, I guess."

"You feelin' better?"

"Sure."

They looked down into the Flats.

"Jesus, look at that, will you, Anna? You can hardly recognize the place."

"It don't look so different," she said.

He laughed. "Are you kiddin'? Colored all over the place. Parkin' lots. Look at this bridge. Remember when there were only two lanes. Cars droppin' down all the time."

Lost in her thoughts, she stared down at the smoky industrial valley.

"Don't you miss it sometimes, Johnny?"

He didn't answer her.

"I do," she said quietly.

"How the hell can you miss it?" he said. "We're living in Shaker Heights. We've got a big house, trees, the yard—"

"I don't know," she said, her voice cold. "I just miss it sometimes, that's all."

"You sound like ma. She's gonna live down there till the day she dies."

"It's hers, Johnny. Her priest is there, her bakery, her butcher—"

He laughed. "Jesus Christ, Anna. There's bakeries all over the place. Priests. You can order the sausage, get it delivered."

She stared at the Flats. There was a silence between them.

"I always liked it best when the sun was going down like this," she said without looking at him. "The bridge was right in the middle of the sun. It was beautiful."

"I never thought it was," he said. "Come on, Anna, let's go."

He led her toward the car and with his other hand flipped the dead cigar over the side of the bridge into the Flats.

She didn't really know what had caused it. Doing the czardas with Johnny outside the same church hall where they had danced the czardas the day of their marriage. She had spun back to that day on that old hardwood floor and the memory had stabbed at her core.

She had dreamed so many dreams then. They would live happily ever after. They would raise children who would live happily ever after them. There would be no pain. No remorse. No disillusionment. God would be good to them because God was good.

But now, minutes after midnight, trying to fall asleep in her bedroom, her husband a few doors away in his own room, Anna was no longer certain of the goodness of God. She was a strict and practicing Catholic: the Infant of Prague stood crowned and velvet-robed on her dresser; a simple wooden crucifix hung from the wall above her bed. Her faith had provided her increasing solace and strength, but her life had taught her that God wasn't good. Only just.

Just? What was the justice of their lives? One miscarriage; another child stillborn; and then Joey. Why Joey? Why afflict her loving and towheaded little boy with the curse of a lifetime? Why doom him to pasting together cigarette wrappers and crude ceramic ashtrays?

She thought then of the ruined, empty look on Frank Vasko's face which she had seen this week on television. Johnny had wished him Merry Christmas. And then the men had gone into his home while Frank Vasko was away and taken his wife into the bedroom and . . .

We weren't even married then, Anna thought. If I had known. If I had only known.

Yes, God was just. How Johnny had dreamed of having a son. When they lost their first child, his first words had been, "Was it a boy?" When the nurse said no, he had nodded slightly, said nothing else. And when the second was stillborn and he was told that— yes, it had been a boy, he had railed at her in that nightmarish, brightly lighted hospital room.

"I told you to stay off your feet, Anna! I told you to take it easy! Don't you want any children? Is that it?"

He couldn't seem to comprehend what had happened. That it had been a fault of no one's. That the child, only hours before his birth, had had a bowel movement in the womb and had choked and strangled on his own waste. Johnny listened wide-eyed and unblinking to the doctor's explanation but Anna could see that it wasn't sinking in. It was an absurdity of fate. Johnny had no comprehension of absurdities of fate. Johnny believed in creating his own fate.

Then, when she got pregnant again, it was as if he was going to will this child to life. He painted and decorated the baby's room himself, something they had feared doing since the loss of the first child. He had three different doctors coming to the house. He talked about the baby all the time; almost, she thought at times, like he was daring fate.

It would be a boy. A boy named Joey. A boy who would grow into a big, strong man like his grandfather. A handsome boy who would play quarterback for Notre Dame. He came home with a football one day, months before the child's birth, and put it on top of the dresser in the baby's room.

She had laughed. "What's that for?"

"Joey's gonna need it."

She had started to cry, then, afraid once again, the hospital memories flooding her. He had held her. "It's gonna be all right, Anna. I'm tellin' you. He's gonna *need* it."

A quarterback for Notre Dame, Anna thought bitterly in the darkness of her bedroom. She remembered the incredible joy they had both felt at Joey's birth. Yes, it was a boy. Yes, he was healthy. Yes, he would be named Joseph Kovak. Yes, he would need that football on top of the dresser.

"You see?" Johnny had laughed, holding her, hugging her and the child. "What did I tell you? What did I tell you?"

Three days after his birth they discovered that Joseph Kovak was mentally retarded. Brain damage, the doctor said.

Johnny had stood there in the hospital room, staring at him. "Goddamn you!" he said. "What the hell was I payin' you for?" He pushed the doctor to the wall. The baby started to cry. "Johnny, please," Anna had said. He released the doctor and turned on her, his face twisted, his eyes huge. "You!" he said. That was all. A single word. "You!" and something was dead between them.

And then he had bolted from the room, almost knocking the doctor down, and Anna hadn't seen him for the rest of her hospital stay. He came for her the morning of her release and took the two of them home. He was solicitous and kind. He cooed to the baby and played with him. But the football on top of the dresser was gone.

A man like Johnny with a mentally retarded son. A powerful and attractive man, a man loved by thousands of people. With a son who would be forever pitied. Forever the butt of a thousand vicious jokes. Forever victim. Forever loser.

She saw Frank Vasko's face again in the darkness of her room and heard the words she had tried to block out, the words which had been a wild scream inside her head for days: "She kept the house dark at night, rolled the shades down during the day. They were watching her, she said." Yes, Anna thought. God was just. Johnny had created her son's fate.

After Joey's birth they had grown further and further from each other. He always seemed to have too much work to do and she always tried to busy herself as much as possible. They were superficially affectionate with each other but making love became more and more difficult for her. She didn't believe in birth control, of course, and he didn't believe in taking chances. And she felt, everytime he touched her, that he was blaming her for Joey. She heard the single word over and over again: "You!"

They were self-conscious with each other physically, almost afraid. He brought his paperwork home at night, finishing it in the bedroom, working very late. Finally, because, he said, he didn't want to keep her up late, he suggested they sleep in separate bedrooms. She felt heartbroken and relieved and said, "Whatever you want, Johnny."

He traveled often and was gone much of the time, organizing other locals, always giving speeches, and she was left to the boy, the house, her mother, and a few friends. She noticed that as she grew older, she liked the house in Shaker Heights less, drawn increasingly to her roots, to her Lithuanian friends, to the Flats. She felt the big house in Shaker Heights wasn't meant for her; it was comfortable and attractive and she didn't feel she belonged there.

She tried to talk to Johnny about the house once

and he had laughed and said, "Stop talkin' like a hunkie, Anna."

"I am a hunkie," she had said.

"No, you're not," he had kidded, "you're Lithuanian."

"You know what I mean, Johnny."

"Come on, get off it," he had said. "Next thing you know, Anna, you're gonna wanna go back to the old country. Like ma. She's always talkin' about goin' back before she dies."

He didn't understand. He had people waiting for him at the office. New members to sign up. New locals to organize. Interviews to do. Appointments to keep. Schedules to meet. Problems to solve. Never enough time. Never enough time to understand.

She didn't like his friends, either. Vince Doyle. Gerky, from Detroit. Milano from Las Vegas. Even Tom Higgins; Tom had somehow changed. They were friendly to her and treated her with great respect and the coldness of their eyes sent chills down her spine. So, after a while, she stopped going with him to many places—claiming headaches, claiming that Joey needed her at home, that the little boy would not understand the presence of strangers putting him to sleep. And though he had objected to it at first, he soon accepted it.

As they spent more time apart, she grew stronger in her faith. She got involved in the Sacred Heart Society and the diocesan program for the mentally retarded. She made novenas and observed First Fridays and tried to fill the awful gap in her life with God.

438

She knew what she was doing, knew that her marriage was hollow now at its center, knew that she said prayers the way some people drank whiskey, but it didn't matter. He had his union and she had her retarded son and her just God.

Her just God. She thought of Frank Vasko again, of the fear in his eyes, the things he had said. Of Babe Milano and Gerky and Doyle and the coldness she saw in them and she started to cry. She had never understood why Abe had left Johnny, had never been able to get a straight answer all these years, only that they had had an argument, but now it made sense to to her. Abe had seen that coldness, too; and maybe he had seen it where she had never seen it: in Johnny.

She cried harder in the darkness now, remembering that day in the Flats against Consolidated when she had gone out with the other women to help Johnny and his men. When, at the end of that day, Johnny had won and there were bodies in the streets. Bodies of guards and strikebreakers she hadn't thought about until now.

Was that where it had all gone wrong?

Since she had helped him, was she guilty, too? Had she, too, created her own fate?

Did she deserve the sentence handed out to her by her just God?

To be married to a man she could never leave but whom she would never really love again?

In the bedroom down the hall, Joey started to cry. Anna got up from the bed, brushed her tears away, and hurried to him. She held and shushed him, told him that it was only a nightmare. He'd see. In the morning everything would be fine once again.

Late at night, Cole Madison paced the living room floor of Abe Belkin's home in San Francisco.

"I can't do it without you," he said. "Without you he's won."

Abe smiled. "You've lost. Isn't that what you're worried about?"

"The hell with me!" Madison said furiously. "We're talking about this country! When he sent those trucks into Washington Friday—what was he saying? 'I'm Johnny Kovak. You push me and I can shut this country down.'"

Abe didn't say anything. He sat on the couch and avoided Madison's eyes.

"Do you want the Babe Milanos of this country to have that kind of weight?" Cole Madison said.

"I know Milano is a friend of his," Abe said, "but I don't know—".

"Don't be naive!" Madison said loudly. "How long do you think he can control Milano and his friends? When are they going to start telling him what to do. Where will it end? Pushing the President? Shutting the highways down? Forcing the Justice Department to look the other way while the underworld gets rich?"

Abe smiled. "You don't really believe that yourself."

"The hell I don't!" Madison snapped. "*He can do it!*" He paused. "If he shuts the highways down, what the hell would we do? Call the National Guard out all over the country? Bring paratroopers in? Fight a war on the turnpikes and interstates?"

"He's the only brother I ever had," Abe said. His voice was choked. "Don't you understand that?"

"For God's sake," Cole Madison said. "Is that what you've fought all your life for?"

Abe looked at him, then looked away. He put his head in his hands.

Waking up alone on a sun-drenched Sunday morning in her Georgetown apartment, Karen Chandler fought her depression. She made herself a cup of instant coffee—to go with my instant depression, she thought—scalded her lip, said "Oh shit" very demurely, then got the paper and went back to bed.

There he was on the front page. There was no escaping him. Two sidebars inside. You would think, reading the *Washington Post,* that Johnny's appearance in front of the Rackets Committee tomorrow would be some sort of globally resounding event. A mini-summit meeting or something. Reporters, Karen Chandler thought bitterly, what a breed. Summer doldrums in the nation's capital and not much for the pack rats to feed on. So Johnny would be their meat.

She hadn't seen much of him in the past week. He came over late at night once but was moody and distant. She woke around dawn, reached over and touched him, and found he was wide awake. He pushed her hand away with a brusqueness he had never shown in bed before.

Karen Chandler put the newspaper down, rested her head on the pillow, and closed her eyes. Damn it. She wondered what he was doing in Cleveland. With his son. With his wife. His wife. A friendly Sunday morning thought guaranteed to rid you of your depression, right, Karen?

His wife. She had told herself, in the beginning, that his wife didn't make any difference. Wives never made any difference. Rule number one in Washington. She slept with him because she liked him. Liked his go-to-hell stance. Liked whatever it was that drove him. And, later, liked what she saw in bed. Not just the sex. The gentleness. Who would believe it? Her proletarian hero. Mr. Blue Collar Push. He was the gentlest lover she had ever had. The most unselfish lover she had ever had. So forget his wife, Karen. His wife didn't matter. Right?

Then why was she so depressed whenever he went back to Cleveland? Why was she just lying around her apartment on this bright, gorgeous day with her eyes pressed shut against the world? Damn it. She opened her eyes suddenly, looked up at the ceiling, and closed them again quickly. Ceilings were no relief.

It was all getting so very complicated. She had listened to that man Vasko's testimony and thought—did Johnny do that? Did Johnny really ruin that poor man's whole life? Johnny, who was always talking about helping his "little guys." Johnny, who told her, late at night, about the "little guys" he had seen beaten and left for dead on the streets of Cleveland. Wasn't Vasko the classic "little guy?" Hadn't he been figuratively beaten bloody, a part of his life left for dead in Chicago?

And Milano. Everybody knew what Milano was. The things Milano represented horrified her. She had made a decision just after she got out of college that, never mind its byzantine complexities and imponderable shades of gray, the world was a place of good and evil and she would devote her work to the good. And now she was not only working for, but sleeping with, a man who, she was convinced, believed in the goodness of what he was doing. But was it possible that this man was a friend to a . . . a Babe Milano?

No, she told herself quickly, getting out of bed, going to her window, watching the sun play off her living-room rug. No, it wasn't. She knew Johnny. Men who believed in the goodness of what they were doing didn't pal around with gangland chiefs. And Vasko— well, that was simple. Johnny had had nothing to do with it. Somebody else in the union must have made that decision. Somebody lower down. It couldn't have been Johnny.

She looked at the clock. It was almost time for her brunch with Paula. Paula Eaton was her best friend, but she didn't even feel like seeing Paula today. Not that she felt like staying cooped up in her apartment either. Maybe Johnny would get back from Cleveland early tonight, she thought. Maybe he'd come over to see her. The thought suddenly brightened her. Then, just as suddenly, the fact that it had brightened her caused her to become further depressed.

An hour later, she sat in the back room of Billy

Martin's Carriage House picking at her eggs benedict, watching Paula devour her plateful of Sunday morning veal parmigiana. She had never understood how anyone could eat veal parmigiana for breakfast— brunch was, after all, nothing but a breakfast—and as Paula twirled another forkful of spaghetti, she found herself staring at the fork disappearing into Paula's heavily lipsticked mouth, hardly hearing what Paula was saying.

It was just another one of Paula's Sunday brunch stories, anyway. Along with her unending complaints about her weight, Paula insisted on relating to her the always predictable details of her previous night's amours.

"Can you imagine, Kar," Paula was saying, the forkful of pasta twirling and disappearing again, "I haven't seen him in a year. He gets here from Denver, takes me out to dinner, I was hoping for the Jockey Club but no, he has to take me to this absolute dump, and then, we're hardly finished with the crepes, which aren't very good anyway, when, right away, it's up to his hotel room and it's tug-of-war time with my skirt."

"And you resisted," Karen laughed. "Naturally."

"What?" her friend laughed, actually halting a forkful flight in midair. "Resisted? Of course not. Why in the world would I resist? I'm simply objecting to his lack of style."

"Denver," Karen said. "What did you expect? Who is he anyway?"

"He's a schmuck," Paula said. "Obviously. I met him last year. Besides that, I wouldn't be so haughty about Denver. At least he's not from Cleveland."

They laughed together and Paula held her pudgy hand up for the waiter, then held two fingers up and said to Karen, "You will, naturally, resist another martini?"

It was an old joke between them. Karen rarely had a second martini and to have a second one at breakfast was almost a sin. But it was a sin which she nevertheless committed, although guiltily, whenever she had brunch with Paula.

"Naturally I'll resist," she smiled, "and naturally I'll drink it."

Paula laughed.

They had worked on the Ways and Means Committee together, had shuttled around the Hill working in the offices of too many congressmen, and had become first friends and then roommates, an arrangement which ended one morning when Karen woke up and realized she simply could not put up with Paula's consummate untidiness, with underwear all over the floor and pieces of week-old chicken on the kitchen counter. They had had a petty and ugly little scene, had moved into separate apartments, and had realized, after a few months that they missed their friendship. So now they got together, almost ritualistically, for Sunday brunch, and never visited each others' apartments.

The martinis arrived and Paula held hers up and

smiled an impish, almost catty smile, and said, "Here's to Cleveland. They call it the best location in the nation, don't they?"

Karen laughed. "You finally found out," she said. "I was wondering when you'd ask me about him."

"Found out?" Paula said archly, draining half her drink. "I'm surprised you didn't put billboards up on Wisconsin Avenue. After that dinner party, you may as well have."

"Yes," Karen said. "I suppose you're right. She sipped her martini and said nothing else.

"Well," Paula said after a moment, "is that all you're going to tell me?"

Karen laughed. "What else should I tell you?"

"*Everything.*"

Karen raised her eyebrows in jest. "Everything? Paula, you really are a voyeur."

"Oh, stop it," Paula said impatiently. "Tell me."

"Well," Karen said confidentially, lowering her voice to a whisper, "he's Hungarian."

"Will you please stop it?" Paula said. "I read that in *Time* magazine. Tell me."

Karen rubbed the side of her glass and, her face suddenly serious, finally said, "I don't know what to tell you."

"I was right," Paula said. "Trouble indeed. You, Kar, at a loss for words?"

They laughed.

Karen looked at her friend, smiled coyly, and said, "Yes, he is very good in bed, if that's what you want to know."

"Aha, I've got you now," Paul said. "The surest sign is a red herring."

"A red herring?"

"Well," Paula said, "if you are willing to tell me *that*, almost immediately, there must be many things you'd rather not tell me."

"Such as," Karen said evenly.

"Such as," Paula said, "considering the way you're slugging down your martini, you're probably in love with him."

Karen laughed loudly and self-consciously as her friend smirked at her knowingly. Then she looked down at the table, noting, once again, the bread crumbs around Paula's plate, and said, "You're silly."

"Okay, I'm silly," Paula said, "but I thought we agreed. Never, ever, fall in love with anyone who has anything to do with this hellish town. I thought we decided that a long time ago."

"I told you, I'm not in love with him," Karen said, an edge to her voice. She waited, then smiled. "Besides, he's not like the people in this town."

"Kar, really," Paul said. "You'd better have another martini. It will send the blood rushing to your brain. You can think clearly." She laughed, held two fingers up for the waiter again, and Karen noticed, surprised, that she had already drained her second glass. And she still didn't feel a thing.

"He's not," she insisted. "He's not like anybody up on the Hill. He really believes in what he's doing."

"Bull," Paula said. "Of course he is. He's just better at it."

"You don't even know him."

"He must be *awfully* good in bed," Paula said.

The color rushed to Karen's cheeks. "That," she said, "is below the belt."

"Yes, I know," Paula laughed. "That's what I was saying."

When Karen didn't laugh at that, Paula looked away from her friend's eyes and said, "Honestly, Kar. Look, we've been around this town. We know about politicians. If your friend decided to, he could probably run quite a race for the White House. I think he's the perfect demagogue."

"How can you say that?" Karen said angrily. "He doesn't even care about these things. He just cares about helping his men."

"Yes, yes, I know," Paula said dismissingly. "You don't have to tell me. You sound like you're writing one of his speeches. That is what you do for him, isn't it?"

"No," Karen said icily, "as a matter of fact I don't do that for him."

"Pity," Paula said, "he could utilize another of your talents."

The waiter brought them their third martinis and Karen Chandler took a long sip from hers, put it down, then looked at her friend, "Paula," she said finally, "what is all this?"

"I don't know," Paula said. "I'm sorry." She sipped her drink and said, her voice rushed and plaintive, "I'm afraid for you, Kar, that's all. Do you really know what you're doing?"

"Yes," Karen said softly, "I think so."

"But do you really know him, Kar? What about all this Rackets Committee business? All these—*connections*—he has."

"Talk about demagoguery," Karen said. "There's Cole Madison at his best."

"Are you sure?" Paula said.

Karen thought about it a moment. "I'm never sure of anything," she smiled. "I have learned that lesson." She paused. "See? I haven't lost all my senses. But Johnny isn't a . . . a gangster. I knew that. Underneath that Halloween mask he wears, all that street-kid stuff, he's an intelligent, sensitive man."

"There you go again, Kar," Paula said.

"And he does believe in the things he says. I've seen the things he's gotten for the rank and file."

"A real populist hero, right?" Paula smiled.

"As much of one as we're likely to see, probably," Karen said.

Paula laughed and drained her third martini. "God, Kar," she said, "you lied to me."

"I don't believe in lying, you know that."

"Okay, then you dissembled."

"When did I dissemble?"

"When you said you weren't in love with him."

"But I'm not," Karen said.

Paula laughed again. "Just keep your eyes open," she said. "Promise me that. Your slobby ex-roommate loves you."

"Oh, Paula," Karen said, reaching over and holding her friend's hand, "I'll be all right. Don't worry."

Realizing, as she said it, that she was, in fact, dissembling. That she was, in fact, very worried. That she wasn't sure she would be all right at all.

When Johnny walked into the Senate Caucus Room with John Howard Harper and Bernie Marr, many of the spectators cheered. A few people had signs that said, "Stop the Railroad!" and "Senate Scab Committee." A trucker went up to Johnny and said, "They ain't gonna push us." Johnny grinned. "Goddamn right they ain't."

He walked to the witness table and sat down. Harper and Bernie Marr sat behind him in the first row. Johnny looked at Cole Madison and smiled. He took his coat off and draped it over an empty chair next to him.

"May we have quiet, please?" Cole Madison said. He banged his gavel. "I'm sure we all want to hear every single word Mr. Kovak has to say."

The spectators fell silent. Johnny grinned.

Cole Madison smiled. "First, I'd like to thank Mr. Kovak, since it seems this city is free this morning of the many truck breakdowns which took place the day Mr. Doyle testified." He paused and looked at Johnny. "It's nice of you to permit the nation's capital to go about its business today, Mr. Kovak."

Johnny grinned. "Anything I can ever do to help you with law and order, senator, I'm always happy to do."

Madison smiled. "Thank you."

450

"Sure. Anytime you need help, senator, call me."

The spectators laughed.

"For the record," Cole Madison said, "can you state your full name, please?"

"John Joseph Kovak. But I've never gone by all that formality stuff, senator. Johnny sounds okay."

The spectators laughed.

"And where were you born, Mr. Kovak?"

"On Ellis Island, right off the boat."

"Then you're a citizen of this country?"

"I got the birth certificate put up and framed on my wall."

"Your occupation?"

"I'm the national president, Federation of Interstate Truckers."

Some of the truckers in the audience cheered. Johnny smiled.

"Thank you," Cole Madison said. "That takes care of the formalities."

"You mean we can cut the crap," Johnny said, "and get down to what we're here for."

The spectators roared.

Madison looked at him and smiled. "Yes, Mr. Kovak, we can." He paused until the room was silent.

"Mr. Kovak, how many members do you have in your union?"

"We've got more than seven hundred thousand guys."

"And what exactly is the scope of your authority as president?"

"We represent the guys that drive your cabs, haul your furniture, pick up your garbage, and deliver anything else."

Madison smiled. "Is that all?"

"Everything that's on the road is mine."

"Yours, Mr. Kovak?"

"I get raises for all of 'em."

"Doesn't it frighten you," Cole Madison said, "to think of all this power—in the hands of one man?"

"No."

"Why not, Mr. Kovak?"

"I don't scare that easy, senator."

The spectators laughed.

"And the reason is that it's in *my* hands."

The spectators laughed.

"It might be bad if it got in the wrong hands," Johnny smiled.

"But your hands are the right hands?"

"My hands are the ones that got the guys the eight percent hike."

The spectators laughed.

"I *see*," Cole Madison said. He smiled and paused, looking at his notes. "Now isn't it a fact, Mr. Kovak, that in your hands the federation has gained a reputation for strong-arm tactics?"

"All the guys in the union have strong arms, senator."

The spectators laughed.

"Please answer the question," Cole Madison said.

"I don't know what you mean, senator," Johnny said. "I'm just a street kid from the slums. Nobody's gonna put me down on my knees, I got a reputation for that. Nobody's gonna put my union on its knees, we got a reputation for that."

The truckers in the audience cheered.

"But isn't it a fact, Mr. Kovak," Madison said, "that many of your members, especially many of your business agents, have criminal records?"

"Yeah, that's a fact, senator." Johnny smiled.

"You admit that?" Cole Madison said.

"Sure. Any union man that went out on strike in the thirties, forties—he's got a criminal record. The policemen in those days didn't have nothin' to do except put us in jail. You wanna find a good union man, senator, all you gotta do is make sure he's got an arrest record."

The spectators laughed.

"Isn't it a fact," Cole Madison said, "that you've paid the legal fees and continued to pay the salaries of those business agents arrested for criminal offenses?"

"Absolutely, senator. If he's a union man in good standing, we'll pay those things. Every man is presumed innocent until he's proven guilty. It's part of our Declaration of Independence, senator. You don't want me to start giving you civics lessons, do you, senator?"

The spectators laughed.

"No, I really don't want you to do that, Mr. Kovak," Cole Madison smiled.

The spectators laughed again.

"Why do you keep criminals—convicted criminals—in your union?" Madison said.

"I don't know what you're talkin' about, senator. I threw the Communists out."

"I'm talking about former bootleggers, armed robbers, extortionists, musclemen—"

"Guys that lift weights?" Johnny said.

The spectators roared.

"Answer the question, Mr. Kovak," Cole Madison said.

"As long as they've done a good job for this union, senator, that's all I care about."

"Has Vincent Doyle done a good job for your union?" Cole Madison said.

"Topnotch," Johnny said. "The best."

"He's an official of your union?"

"General vice-president."

"Mr. Kovak, do you believe a union official should be suspended from office if he refuses to answer questions on the grounds of self-incrimination?"

"If he takes the Fifth?"

"That's right."

"It's part of the Declaration of Independence and the Bill of Rights. The whole package, right, senator? A guy's got a right to refuse to answer somethin' if he don't want to and I ain't gonna can him for it."

"Why not, Mr. Kovak?"

"Why not? What kinda question is that, senator? You want me to screw around with George Washington and Thomas Jefferson and all those guys that thought up that stuff?"

The spectators laughed.

"Mr. Kovak," Cole Madison said, "do you know Anthony Milano?"

"Yes, I do."

"You're friends?"

"I know him."

"And your union recently gave one of Mr. Milano's concerns, Aquacade Entertainment Corporation of Las Vegas, a loan of one million two hundred thousand dollars from your pension fund?"

"That's right."

"Did Mr. Milano ask you to give him the loan as a favor to him?"

"He talked to the trustees, senator."

Cole Madison smiled. "Did he, now?"

"Yes, he did, senator."

"You're one of the pension fund trustees, aren't you, Mr. Kovak?"

"That's right."

"And you voted to give him the loan?"

"Along with the other eleven trustees."

Madison smiled. "How long have you known Mr. Milano?"

"A long time."

Madison grinned. "Have you and Mr. Milano ever been involved in previous business transactions?"

Johnny hesitated. "I don't remember one."

"Let me try to refresh your memory," Cole Madison said. "What about the Haley Jukebox Company of Pontiac, Michigan?"

"I don't know nothin' about that firm," Johnny said slowly.

"Isn't it a fact, Mr. Kovak, that when you headed the Midwest Council of your union, you forced businessmen to buy Haley jukeboxes?"

Johnny grinned. "How could I force any businessman to do that?"

Madison smiled and looked at him. "By telling bar owners that unless they used Haley jukeboxes, your drivers wouldn't deliver liquor to them."

There was a buzz among the spectators. Johnny looked slightly uneasy.

"No," he said, "that's not true."

"Isn't it a fact," Cole Madison said, "that the Haley Jukebox Company was at the time owned by Mr. Anthony Milano—"

"I don't know nothin' about—"

"And Mr. Shondor Elik Gerky?" Madison said.

"I don't know nothin' about who owned some company I don't know nothin' about," Johnny said forcefully.

Madison grinned. "And isn't it true that to convince you to help his firm—Mr. Milano paid you a bribe?"

There was a lot of noise among the spectators. Johnny looked startled.

"That's a lie," he said.

Madison paused. "A bribe in the form of a wedding present?"

Some of the reporters ran from the room. Johnny looked preoccupied. Madison banged his gavel for silence.

"It's a lie you dreamed up for your headlines," Johnny said.

456

"You're under oath here," Madison said sharply.

"I don't give a damn what I'm under. I never took nothin' in my life."

Madison grinned at him. John Howard Harper got up from the front row, sat down next to Johnny, and whispered to him. Johnny did not acknowledge his presence. He stared at Madison and waited.

Madison looked up from his notes. "Have you ever killed anyone, Mr. Kovak?" he said.

There was pandemonium in the hearing room.

"You know goddamn well," Johnny said, "if you asked me that outside this room, I'd sue you for everything you got."

"Is your answer no?"

"That's right."

"What's right?"

"That's right," Johnny said angrily. "I never killed nobody."

"You're sure?" Madison said.

Johnny said nothing. He glared at Cole Madison.

There was a long pause. Madison looked at his notes.

"Isn't it a fact," Madison said loudly, his voice crisp, "that you once killed a man with your own hands?"

Johnny looked stunned. Several reporters ran from the room. Madison banged his gavel for silence.

"Isn't it a fact," he said, "that in the strike against Talbot's Consolidated Trucking, you beat a man's head against the floor of a boxcar and left him in a pool of blood?"

457

Johnny stared at Madison. Harper talked excitedly to Johnny. There was bedlam in the room.

"Answer the question, Mr. Kovak!" Madison said.

Johnny kept staring at him.

"Answer the question!"

"I'm not gonna sit here," he shouted, "and be called all kindsa names and be accused of all kindsa things without—"

"Answer the question!"

"—a shred of evidence. I tried to give you the truth. That's not what you want—"

"You're not answering the question!" Madison said. "You wanna see your name in the paper tomorrow next to a buncha crazy charges!"

"We can hold you in contempt," Madison said.

Johnny got up from the table. "The hell with you! Do anything you want! On my lawyer's advice, I'm not gonna answer nothin' more."

He turned and walked out of the hearing room as Madison pounded the gavel for order and the photographers tried to take his picture. Bernie Marr and Harper helped him through the crowd. Johnny looked dazed.

Madison watched him. "This meeting is adjourned," he said. "We will reconvene next Tuesday, July the seventh."

He hurried through the long, echoing Senate corridors, Bernie Marr and Harper on either side of him, and as he walked out the front door of the big marble building, he stopped suddenly on the top step and stood there. The big trucks were down in the street, dozens of them, and as their drivers saw Johnny, they blasted their air horns and waved to him.

"You want me, you got me!" Johnny yelled, his voice hoarse, his fist high in the air. The men hit their air horns again and he walked down the long stairway to the limo.

"Is it true?" Harper said the moment the door was closed.

Johnny didn't even look at him. The limo wound its way through traffic. Harper fidgeted and cleared his throat.

"Look," Harper said finally. "I won't ask you if it's true. But what can he prove? He sounded sure. He was setting you up. He has to have a witness. Who can the witness be? What will he say? Did someone see you—"

Johnny stared straight ahead and smiled. "Who knows, counselor?"

"You don't seem to understand," Harper said. "This can destroy you. I'm simply looking out for your interest. Who saw you—"

"Why don't you shut your mouth, counselor?" Johnny said quietly.

Harper slumped back against the seat. No one said anything. The limo raced through traffic.

"Soon as we get back," Johnny said to Bernie, "I wanna see Vince."

There was a bottle of bourbon on the desk in Johnny's office. He walked around the room, smok-

459

ing a little cigar. He looked exhausted. Vince Doyle stalked him as he walked.

"I don't care how many years ago it was," Vince Doyle said angrily. "The guy died. Madison's gonna have Abe sayin' he tried to stop you. You kept poundin' the guy's head. Jesus Christ, Johnny. It's a murder rap. Think what it's gonna do to the union—"

"What the hell you want me to do?" Johnny said. "How's I supposed to know he'd—" He paused. His voice was low, broken. "We grew up in the same house, Vince."

"I told you. I told you the day'd come that sonofabitch would knife you."

"All right, Vince, you told me."

There was a momentary silence.

"There's only one thing to do," Vince Doyle said.

Johnny looked at him, then looked away in disgust.

Doyle said, "I'll talk to Milano."

Johnny turned on him furiously. "No! We'll deny it. We'll hammer it through."

"Deny it?" Doyle laughed sarcastically. "What about that stuff about the wedding present? The only way he could know about that, he heard us. He's gonna pin you for takin' a bribe."

"I didn't take nothin'!" Johnny said angrily. "You were there. I didn't take it!"

"How's it gonna look?"

"I don't care. I'm not gonn—"

"He's gonna ruin you, Johnny!" Vince Doyle said angrily. "He ruins you, he ruins the union! Think about the men, Johnny! You gotta do it for them!"

"No!" Johnny said furiously. His voice was choked. "Goddamnit, no!"

In the State Office Building, Cole Madison sat behind his desk, Dave Roberts in front of him.

"I want Belkin here," Madison said angrily. "He can stay at my place."

"He says he's not going to hide anywhere," Roberts said.

"We're asking him to be smart," Madison said, "not to hide."

"He says he's the head of his local and he's not going to hide like a criminal."

"Goddamn his idealism," Madison said. "He still doesn't really believe me."

"I talked him into agreeing to two men from the bureau."

"Make sure they're with him twenty-four hours a day," Madison said.

"They'll fly out with him Monday night."

Madison shook his head. "Belkin should be here. I don't like it."

"Senator," Dave Roberts said, "do you really think Kovak would—"

"Dave," Cole Madison said wearily. "Please. Don't you realize the stakes?"

The bottle of bourbon on his desk was empty. He sat slumped in the darkness of his office, staring out his window into the rain. His eyes were red-rimmed, his complexion pale. He lit another little cigar, threw the match into the wastebasket, and looked at the clock. It was almost midnight. Nine o'clock in California.

"It smells horrible in here," Karen Chandler said. She stood at the door tentatively, afraid to intrude.

"Then stay the hell out," he said.

She walked across the room to his desk and stopped. She looked at him. "How are you?"

He didn't look at her. He said nothing.

"He's won, Johnny, hasn't he?"

"He's won nothin'," Johnny said. His voice was a growl.

"He wouldn't have said those things if—"

"He can't prove shit," he said, louder now. "He's just pushin'."

She paused. "But why, Johnny?" she said. "Did you really . . ." The words trailed away. She stood there, her eyes on the floor.

"Listen," he said, "you weren't down there in the goddamn Flats. You don't know." He got up from the desk and stood in front of his window, watching the rain, his back to her. "It was a war," he said, "we were fightin' a war."

"But people like Milano," she said.

He turned on her. "How the hell do you think we got the push? You think the companies just *gave* everything to us?"

She didn't say anything. The rain beat against the windows.

"What are you going to do?" she said softly.

"I'm gonna fight," he said, turning from her again. "That's all I really know how to do." He paused and laughed softly to himself. "Jesus, this town," he said, "it ain't a whole lot different than the Flats."

"Is there anything I can do?"

"Yeah," he said, his back still to her, "you can leave me alone."

She looked at him and stood there a moment, then turned wordlessly and walked out of the office. He stood at the window, staring at the rain. He could see the White House a block away. "Jesus Christ, Abe," he said to himself, He looked at the clock. Twelve-twenty. Nine-twenty in California.

He lit the stub of his cigar, sat down, and reached for the telephone. He hunched over it, dialed, ran his fingers through his hair. He waited. He waited. Three rings. Six rings. The rings stopped. He heard her voice. "Hello?"

"Molly," he said, his voice controlled. "Listen, this is Johnny. Johnny Kovak." He paused. "Don't bullshit me, Molly," he said, his voice rising. "I gotta talk to him. I'm tellin' you, just put him on." He waited. He heard Abe's voice.

"Listen, Abe," he said. He paused, listening. "I don't wanna hear that," Johnny said. "We can work it out." He paused. "Abe," he said, "this is crazy." His voice was shaky. "I can fly out there tomorrow and—"

He paused. "What the fuck you mean there's nothin' to say?" he cried. His voice was choked. "Abe, for Christ's sake. You don't know what you're doin'. You're cuttin' my guts out, you're—"

The phone went dead in his hands. The dial tone blared at him. He put the phone down calmly and leaned back in the chair, the cigar in his mouth. He got up suddenly and, in blind fury, hurled the phone against the wall, then the whiskey bottle, then the ceramic ashtray which Joey made him. He hesitated a moment, his breathing checked, then picked up the glass case and smashed it against the wall. It exploded in a hundred pieces. He went to the wall and got down on the floor and picked Gant's buzzer up and he stood there in the darkness, the tears running down his face.

Saturday afternoon in San Francisco and Abe Belkin was upset. He had spent the morning reading the *San Francisco Chronicle's* account of Johnny's testimony in front of the Senate Committee. Then he had lunch with Molly and the kids. Now the kids were playing with their balloons in the back room and Molly sat working a crossword puzzle. Abe paced about, annoyed.

The object of his irritation sat not more than eight feet away on his living room sofa: special agent Thomas Brown of the FBI. He wore a dark suit and a conservative tie and he had a remarkable ability to look alert and indifferent at the same time.

Outside the house on Vallejo Street, an agent named DaSilva sat in a dark-colored Plymouth sedan. He and Brown worked in teams, three shifts a day, guarding the house. A ridiculous precaution, Abe thought. But he had agreed to it—only because it seemed to reassure Molly.

Abe looked at the FBI man sitting there on his sofa

and stopped pacing. "All right," he said to no one in particular, "I'm goin' out for the groceries. Same way I do every Saturday." He looked at Molly challengingly. "You comin' with me or not?"

"Abe," she said, "let them go for it."

Agent Brown, faultlessly courteous, said, "I'd be happy to go for it, Mr. Belkin. We've got instructions from Washington to—"

"You know what you can do with your instructions?" Abe Belkin said, seething. He controlled himself. "Now look. I got two things I do Saturday. I watch the ball game. And I get the groceries."

Brown looked at Molly and, getting no support, shrugged.

"Abe," Molly said, "the kids."

"They'll stay here," Abe said. He pointed to the FBI man. "He's here. It'll give him something to do."

The children ran into the living room. "Can we come too?" Betsy said. Benjy held a large orange balloon. He put the stem in his mouth and blew; his eyes grew huge.

"No," Abe said, "you stay here."

Benjy released the balloon. It looped around the room in a crazy series of twists and swirls.

"Tell you what," Abe continued, "I'll get some ice cream. What kind of ice cream you want?"

"Chocolate!" Benjy yelled.

Betsy screamed, "Strawberry!"

"Chocolate!"

"Strawberry!"

"Okay, all right," Abe said. He dropped to his knee

and hugged them. "I'll get chocolate *and* strawberry. How's that?" He stood up and looked at Molly. "You got the list?"

She nodded and as they walked toward the door, Brown said, "DaSilva will follow you, Mr. Belkin. Wherever you usually go, don't go there. Go to a different store. And drive around first."

"Yeah, yeah, I know," Abe said. "What if I wanna go to the can, is he gonna follow me there?" He walked out, grumbling. Brown whispered into a walkie-talkie to his partner on the street.

As Abe pulled slowly away from his home, the dark-colored Plymouth eased in behind him. They made their way past a row of large stucco homes, their roofs tiled with red and green terra cotta, their doors embroidered with iron. When they reached Divisadero Street, they turned toward the bay and dropped down a hill.

Abe turned right on Lombard, drove past a stretch of motels, restaurants, dry cleaners, and small bank branches, then made a left on Laguna. He worked his way around the children playing in Funston Park, turned left on Bay Street. At Cervantes Boulevard, he angled off to the right and drove on to Marina Boulevard. Making a sharp right, he passed Marine Park, alive with romping dogs, couples with their arms entwined, and kites dancing in the air.

Then he pulled into the first supermarket he saw. It was a large Safeway, with an asphalt parking lot the size of a football field, and as he nosed his car into a parking space the dark-colored Plymouth glided to a stop behind him. Agent DaSilva nodded. Abe shook his head.

Inside the store, Molly loaded the grocery cart as if preparing for a family reunion. As Abe pushed the chrome cart along the gray tile floor, watching the short list become a mountain of boxes and cans, he asked Molly what the hell she was doing.

"You like to go out and shop every Saturday?" she said, peeved. "Well, when we get done, we're going to be set for a while."

Trying to look unobtrusive, DaSilva trailed behind them with a grocery cart of his own. Now and then he put something in it: a package of Kool-Aid, some biscuits, several cans of vegetables. At the beverage cooler he added a six-pack of beer.

Abe watched him and grinned. DaSilva was a man of medium height, sandy-haired, and groomed to a clean-cut shine. Like Brown, he wore a dark suit and conservative tie; and like Brown he had a Smith and Wesson Model 19 Combat Magnum strapped to his right hip. It was a large weapon, chambered for .357 Magnum cartridges.

The store was crowded. At the check-out counters, Abe and Molly found eight long lines. An even longer line threaded back from the counter identified by a blinking sign that said, "Express Lane, ten items or less." Abe and Molly pushed their cart into lane four. DaSilva quietly got into lane five, even though he only had seven items in his cart.

They waited. Five minutes went by. A man in a white apron who was the store manager walked up to

DaSilva and told him he was eligible for the express lane. DaSilva thanked him for the advice and said he liked his lane better. The manager shook his head and walked away.

Abe smiled and watched the agent. He was intrigued by the way DaSilva slowly slid his eyes about, studying, appraising, noting each customer, accomplishing it all without drawing attention to himself. He wondered exactly what DaSilva was looking for and he tried to follow his eyes. He saw Toledo scales on the check-out counters, displays of razor blades, candy and gum, and stacks of Reader's Digest. Tracking DaSilva's eyes, looking up, he made a note: there were 18 rows of fluorescent lights, sixteen tubes in each row, 288 tubes in all.

"Damn," he said suddenly.

Molly looked at him.

"The ice cream."

Molly turned and started back toward the aisles. Abe reached out for her. "I'll get it," he said.

He made his way past a row of Huffmann meat coolers, down an aisle stocked with canned soft drinks, macaroni, and dried soups, and passed under an archway of paper flowers. At the freezer compartment containing the ice cream, the refrigeration unit made a clanking noise, and on top of the cooler, stacked in neat rows, were cans of Hershey's chocolate-flavored syrup, boxes of sugar cones, and containers of fudge topping.

Abe took a gallon of chocolate ice cream and a gallon of strawberry from the compartment. He retraced his steps, moving back through the archway of paper flowers, down the aisle with the soft drinks and macaroni. When he reached the check-out counters, he stopped cold.

Two men dressed in work clothes and ski masks over their heads held shotguns trained on the check-out stands. A third man, also wearing a ski mask, was making his way from one cash register to the next, dumping the money trays into a cloth sack.

Abe moved slowly to Molly's side.

"Nobody moves!" one of the gunmen yelled. "Nobody gets hurt!" He waved the barrel of the shotgun in front of him like a wand.

Abe glanced at DaSilva questioningly. Almost imperceptibly, DaSilva shook his head.

At one of the two entrances to the store, a security guard in a tan uniform—around the corner and out of sight when the gunmen entered—was creeping into view. He had his gun drawn. He seemed terrified.

Something in the customers' eyes at the check-out counters caused one of the holdup men to whirl. The security guard fired. A split second later there was a shotgun blast. The guard screamed and slapped his hands to his face. He staggered backward. Tiny crimson holes appeared on the front of his tan shirt.

"Run!" DaSilva screamed to Molly and Abe. He drew his weapon suddenly and pulled the trigger, sending a bullet whizzing by the head of one of the holdup men. Then the shotgun exploded again and DaSilva doubled over as a cloud of steel pellets tore into his stomach.

The gunmen ran for Abe and Molly. They aimed their shotguns. Blasts ripped the air. Abe went down first, then Molly, both blown off their feet by shots fired at their heads.

The gunmen pumped their weapons and fired wildly in the general direction of the customers. The customers bolted, panicked, and dove into the aisles screaming.

One of the gunmen moved over Abe and Molly. He pointed his shotgun down at them. He fired four times, each shot for the back of their heads.

The gunmen backed out the store. They got into a late-model Chevrolet, started the motor, then pulled slowly out of the parking lot and into the flow of Saturday afternoon traffic. The ski masks came off and one of them said to the driver, "Real careful, now. No speeding."

"I'm not speeding, Arnie," the driver said petulantly.

The Chevrolet swung onto Van Ness Avenue, made a right turn on Turk Street, then zigzagged to a small garage on Bartlett Street, not too far off Market. One of the double sliding doors was up and the Chevrolet pulled in next to another car. The garage was dark.

"Come on, hit the light," one of the gunmen said.

"Will you let me get outa the car first, Arnie?" someone said.

The instant the light blinked on two men stepped from behind the second car. They held large handguns with silencers. They fired twelve shots in all. Four for each man. No misses.

* * *

Cole Madison and Dave Roberts hurried down the corridor of San Francisco's Letterman Hospital, an FBI supervisor and detectives alongside them.

"Two of them were DOA, senator," the FBI man said. "I don't know how this one is still alive."

"Have you got a name?" Cole Madison said.

"Arnie Jurek. He's thirty-four, born in Saginaw, Michigan."

"What about his record?"

"We haven't got anything on him the last four years, senator."

"Before that?"

"He was an enforcer for Shondor Gerky in Detroit."

Madison smiled. "Gerky," he said.

"Witnesses?" Roberts said.

"Nobody saw. Nobody heard. It's that kind of neighborhood."

"Perfect," Cole Madison said. "Hit Belkin. Hit the hit men."

The FBI man stopped by a door guarded by three policemen. "In here, senator."

They walked into the room. Madison nodded at the doctor and walked to the bed. The man was red-haired, his face bluish and swollen.

"Jurek," Madison said, leaning close to him, "can you hear me?"

The man didn't respond.

"You're going to die, Jurek," Madison said. "You haven't got a chance."

"Senator," the doctor said.

471

"Who hired you?" Madison said. "Was it Milano? Did Gerky hire you? You were supposed to hit Belkin, weren't you?"

There was silence in the room.

"It's too late, senator," the doctor said quietly. "He's dead."

At the press conference in the crowded Senate Caucus Room, Cole Madison stood next to the Attorney General of the United States.

"I regret to announce, therefore," Cole Madison said, "that the Senate Rackets Committee is concluding its hearings. I believe the Attorney General has an announcement of vital significance."

The Attorney General, a reed-thin, elderly man, stepped to the microphone. He spoke quietly.

"I will only make this brief statement, ladies and gentlemen, and will answer no questions." He read from a prepared text. "At seven o'clock this morning, the Justice Department—acting in concert with the Federal Bureau of Investigation, the Internal Revenue Service, and several other government agencies—launched a wide-ranging investigation of *all* the activities of the Federation of Interstate Truckers. This investigation will be conducted jointly with Senator Madison and the members of the staff of the Senate Rackets Committee. As you know, a separate task force of fifty-six FBI agents was yesterday assigned to probe the execution-style slaying of Mr. and Mrs. Abraham Belkin and special agent Theodore DaSilva."

The Attorney General stepped away from the microphone.

"Senator Madison," a reporter shouted, "was Belkin's testimony going to be damaging to Kovak?"

Madison paused. "Yes."

"What was he going to say?"

"Mr. Belkin was going to confirm some things we had probed earlier."

"Can you be more specific, senator?" a reporter shouted.

The Attorney General whispered something to Madison.

"No, I can't," Cole Madison said. "Mr. Belkin is dead. No one can speak for him."

Johnny stood in front of the television cameras and reporters in his office. He wore a black suit and a black tie. He looked worn out.

"Abe Belkin's death in San Francisco," he said, "shows how law and order is breakin' down in this country. Everyplace you go, you hear about robbings, beatings, people gettin' killed over a few bucks in the cash register. The police look like they can't do nothin' to stop it. That's why, to help stop crime, the Federation of Interstate Truckers has decided on organizin' policemen into the union. Most policemen get such a terrible wage that they gotta hold down a job on the side. They're overworked and they're underpaid. We're gonna get 'em a decent wage. They won't have to hold other jobs. They won't have to be overworked. So that way they can put everything they've got into stoppin' crimes like the senseless supermarket holdup that caused the deaths of my good friends Abe and Molly Belkin in San Francisco."

He knocked on the door to her apartment. Karen Chandler opened it and looked at him.

"Not even a hello?"

"I'm not feeling well," she said.

"You didn't come to work." He smiled.

"I didn't feel like working."

He walked inside. Suitcases were spread around the floor.

"What are you doin'?" he said.

"I'm taking a trip."

He grinned. "A trip? Where?"

"I'm going to Europe."

She walked to one of the suitcases and packed it. He watched her.

"What the hell is this?"

She laughed. "I saw your little speech, Johnny."

"What the hell's so funny?"

"It was funny," she said, "didn't you think it was funny?"

He went to her and grabbed her roughly. "Listen, goddamnit."

"You were right," she said. "You're a magnetic man. I like magnetic men. I believed in you."

He held her.

"And I found out what you've got inside," she said, "didn't I, Johnny?"

He said nothing.

"Shit, Johnny," she said, "that's what."

He slapped her.

"You're shit."

He slapped her again. She started to cry.

"What are you going to do now, Johnny, kill me?"

They stood facing each other in the cabin of the yacht, which was making its way peacefully down the Potomac.

"You know the kind of heat we're gettin'?" Babe Milano said angrily. "I'm not just talkin' about me. All my friends."

"I didn't ask you to hit any FBI guy," Johnny said.

"It's not the FBI guy," Milano said. "It's you and Madison. We've got the attorney general on us, Johnny. The whole goddamn government."

"I can handle 'em."

Milano laughed.

"What the hell you want me to do, Babe?"

"I don't know," Milano said. He turned from him, and softened his tone. "I was talkin' to some of my friends. Maybe you oughta let Vince run it a while, Johnny. Take a leave of absence or somethin'."

Johnny grinned. "Resign? Is that what you're sayin', Babe?"

"I didn't say nothin' about that," Milano said.

"You don't tell *me* how to run my union," Johnny said angrily.

"I didn't say that, Johnny."

"Nobody tells me that!"

"All right, Johnny," Milano smiled. "All right. I'm just tryin' to help you."

They looked at each other. There was a long pause. Milano walked away from him.

"Listen, Johnny," Milano said, "we helped you out" —he hesitated—"we need a little help from you."

"What kinda help?"

"We're buildin' a new resort in Florida. We're gonna need another loan."

"You haven't paid off on the one to Aquacade," Johnny said.

Milano smiled and looked at him. "Sometimes, you're doin' business, Johnny, things don't work out."

"That money ain't mine," Johnny said, "it's outa the guys' pensions."

Milano paused. "You take a loss," he said softly.

"I can't do that."

"You can't, huh?" Milano said. He turned on him furiously. "That guy was gonna put you outa business. Is that what I told you? I can't do that?"

"That money pays their pensions, Babe, when they retire—"

"Fuck their pensions!" Milano shouted. "I saved your ass! Look where it got us. Look at the heat." He paused. "I don't give a goddamn what happens when they retire!"

Three weeks after Abe's death, Ilona Kovak died of a heart attack. She was buried alongside her husband in the little cemetery on the hillside in the Flats.

On the way down the hill toward the limo, Johnny

saw Mishka and hugged him. "Mish," he said, "we're gonna miss her, Mish."

"Yeah, we will, Johnny," the old man said coldly. He walked away.

Johnny walked down to the limo with Anna and Joey and glanced back. The old man was walking slowly across the hillside, flowers in his hand.

"Wait in the car," Johnny said to Anna.

He walked back up the hill. Mishka had stopped in front of a large marble stone that said, "One for All and All for One—In Memory of the Victims of the Funeral Day Massacre. Cleveland, 1935." Mishka put the flowers on a grave. Johnny looked at it. The tombstone said, "Michael P. Monahan, 1880–1935, He Was a Union Man."

Mishka walked over to him. They stood there, staring at the gravestones.

"She was a fine woman, your ma," Mishka said.

Johnny didn't say anything.

"After Abe died, her heart. It get tired."

Johnny didn't reply.

Mishka looked at him. "Is it true, Johnny? What they say?" He paused. "It was you—get Abe?"

"It's a lie, Mish. Madison's lie."

"The senator's lie?"

"Yeah."

They looked at each other, then Johnny looked away. There was a pause.

"I don't believe you, Johnny," Mishka said quietly. He looked at Monahan's grave. "Him," he said, "all of them. They die for nothing, Johnny."

He walked down the hillside. Johnny stood there.

In the limo on the way home from the cemetery, Johnny sat at one end of the back seat, staring out his window. Anna sat at the other end, her face a mask. Joey sat between them.

Joey said, "Why did we throw the flowers into the grave, mommy? Why did we throw the flowers?"

Johnny looked at him.

"Daddy's crying," the boy said. "Daddy, don't cry."

Johnny turned away from him.

"Why is daddy crying, mommy?" the boy said.

Anna put her arm around the boy. She drew him close to her, and stared straight ahead.

Dave Roberts stood beside Dorothy Rohr in the Senate Caucus Room. They were surrounded by reporters. Dorothy Rohr was crying.

"I didn't want to hurt nobody," she said, "I just needed the money."

"Who paid you the ten thousand dollars?" a reporter asked.

"Miss Rohr has identified the man," Roberts said, "as Paul Bernard Marr, a high-ranking union official, an aide to Johnny Kovak."

"What did Marr tell you?" a reporter said.

"If I said it was Senator Madison's baby," the girl said, "they'd pay me ten thousand dollars."

"Why did you come forward now?" a reporter asked.

"Miss Rohr had a guilty conscience," Dave Roberts said.

The reporters laughed.

* * *

Two men followed Johnny out of the Mayflower Hotel in Washington and as he got into the limousine, he glanced back at them.

"Everywhere I goddamn go," Johnny said as the limousine pulled away from the curb. "Bugs all over the place. Guys watchin' us."

"I talked to Carnes," Vince Doyle said. "He says Madison's got more than three hundred guys workin' on it."

"They're subpoenaing everything in Cleveland," Bernie Marr said. "Higgins said he's got FBI camping on the front door."

Johnny said nothing. The limousine moved through traffic.

"Babe called me yesterday," Vince Doyle said. "He says they've got more FBI at the crap tables than they've got marks."

Johnny smiled thinly. "Goddamn Madison," he said. "He wants us to *know* they're there."

Cole Madison stood behind the desk in his Senate office and grinned.

"Is this a social visit, Johnny?"

Johnny sat in the chair, his legs crossed. He smiled. "What'd you pay the girl?"

"Which girl?" Madison grinned.

Johnny laughed. "Rohr."

Madison paused and looked at him. "You paid her ten. We paid her thirty. She's getting rich."

"You and your attorney general friend," Johnny said. "Get your guys offa me!"

Madison smiled. "Can't you take the pressure, Johnny?"

"You're pushin' me!"

"You're through, Johnny. We've got more 'push' than you do. More men. More money. Sooner or later, we'll find somebody. Somebody will sell you out."

"Nobody's gonna sell me out!"

Madison laughed. "There's always somebody to sell anybody out." He paused. "We'll get you for something. Maybe not Belkin, but we'll find something. You're going to jail, Johnny."

Johnny looked at him in disbelief. "You know something?" he said. "You're crazy."

Madison smiled. "You don't believe that yourself."

Vegas was Babe Milano's town and the 1,300 delegates to the Federation of Interstate Truckers' annual convention got a big welcome. Blazing marquees in front of the big byzantine hotels on the Strip said "Welcome F.I.S.T.," "Welcome Johnny Kovakl," and "Las Vegas Loves Truckers."

Inside the Las Vegas convention center, banners hung from the rafters saying "F.I.S.T. Is a Fist" and "We Will Not Be Railroaded."

As Johnny's limousine pulled up to the convention center it was momentarily blocked by ten young men carrying placards that said, "Get the Gangsters Out of the Labor Movement" and "Who Killed Abe Belkin?"

"Who the hell are they?" Johnny asked Bernie Marr inside the limo.

"College kids from Berkeley. Do-gooders."

"Get 'em out," he snapped. "I don't wanna see 'em on TV."

An hour later, the picketers were arrested by Las Vegas police and charged with disturbing the peace. They were told that they didn't have the necessary permit for a "public march." When they were released the next day, they went to the mayor's office seeking their permit. They were refused. Their presence, they were told, could create an "incident" with the convention delegates. "We don't want you to get hurt," an aide to the mayor told them. "We are acting in your interest."

On the convention's final night, Johnny addressed the membership. He gave a fiery, bare-knuckled speech which got front-page coverage from the *New York Times* the next day. "Our biggest objective in the next year," he said, "is to sign up every policeman in America into this union. It's the least we can do for as good a union man as my friend Abe Belkin." The delegates cheered.

"Cole Madison can go to hell!" Johnny shouted. "The Justice Department can go to hell! Nobody's gonna destroy this union!"

They were alone in Milano's lavish penthouse suite overlooking the Strip.

"It's Madison, Babe," Johnny said. "He's causin' the whole thing. Without him, they're gonna back off." He paused. "There's no other way."

"You gotta be out of your mind, Johnny," Babe Milano said. "You don't hit somebody like him."

"He wants to send me to jail, don't you understand that?" Johnny said angrily.

"He's a United States senator!"

"The guy's crazy. I'm tellin' you. There's no other way."

"Johnny," Milano said, "he's got the Justice Department, the Treasury, the FBI, I don't know what goddamn else." He paused. "You're fightin' the whole government."

Johnny looked at him. "We're in this together, Babe," he said quietly. "He gets me, he'll get you too."

There was a long silence.

"It's too big for us," Milano said.

"Not for me it ain't."

Milano looked at him. There was another pause.

"I can't give you an answer, Johnny. I've gotta talk to my friends."

"There's no time for talkin', Babe—"

"Johnny!" Milano yelled. "I gotta talk to 'em."

"How long?"

"I don't know. I'll let you know." Milano turned away from him. He changed his tone. "How's Anna?"

Johnny nodded.

"The boy?"

Johnny nodded.

"What do you think about the Browns this year?" Milano said.

Johnny didn't say anything.

"You know that Jimmy Brown, he ran up eighteen hundred and sixty-three yards last year."

Johnny didn't say anything.

Milano grinned. "Eighteen hundred and sixty-three yards! What a guy! Supernigger! That's what they call him."

Johnny reached for his coat. "I'll see you, Babe."

"Look, Johnny," Babe Milano said. "We'll work somethin' out. I'll talk to my friends. Everything's gonna be all right."

Milano smiled. Johnny looked at him and grinned.

"I gotta go to New York in a couple of weeks," Milano said. "I'll stop by and see you, let you know. Okay?"

Johnny smiled. "Okay."

"Hey, Johnny," Milano smiled, "what are friends for?"

Johnny laughed.

Babe Milano had breakfast in his suite the next day with Vince Doyle and Bernie Marr.

"So that's it," Milano said. "I've gotta say it looks like the only thing we can do."

"There's gotta be another way," Bernie Marr said.

Doyle turned to him angrily. "What other way? There's so much heat nobody can make a move."

Milano smiled. "I've gotta have this place checked out every day, make sure it ain't bugged."

"Jesus," Bernie Marr said. "There's just gotta be another way."

"What other way?" Milano said. "What choice've we got?"

"But think about the reaction," Bernie said. "You just don't do somethin' like this."

"It'll be in the papers a year," Milano says. "On TV a couple months. After that, who's gonna care?"

"But, he's—he's a powerful man," Bernie said. "A lotta people admire him."

There was a pause.

"It'll stop the heat," Milano said.

Bernie shook his head.

"You've got a good future, Bernie," Vince Doyle said. "Relax."

The sign outside said "Jocko's Lanes" and when Johnny walked into the deserted cavernous place on Cleveland's West Side two weeks after the Las Vegas convention, Jocko greeted him effusively. He was paunchy and bald and his gold teeth still flashed.

"Babe here yet?" Johnny said.

"Babe's in town?"

"I'm supposed to meet him here."

"Hey, that's great, Johnny," Jocko beamed. "Babe's comin' here? That's great. Siddown."

They sat down and Jocko poured him the beer and after two or three of them he started to reminisce. "Those were the good old days, Johnny, weren't they? We were young then, Johnny. Maybe that's why." He laughed. Johnny looked at his watch.

"That singer Vince had, Johnny," Jocko said, "remember her? You banged that broad, didn't you? Ah, I know you did. You banged all those broads."

Johnny looked at his watch again. "I gotta make a call," he said.

"She musta been good," Jocko said. "The ass on her. Jesus."

He went to the phone and called Anna. No, she told him, he had received no calls. Johnny went back to Jocko and said good-bye to him. He walked out of the bowling alley, puzzled and nervous.

He was getting into his car in the parking lot when the other car pulled up to him. Bernie Marr swung the passenger door open and grinned.

"What are you doin' here?" Johnny said.

"Get in."

Johnny got into the car. "What the hell's goin' on?" he said.

"Milano didn't wanna meet you here. Too many people."

"Why the hell didn't he call?"

"I don't know," Bernie Marr grinned. "He changed his mind the last minute. Asked me to pick someplace out and come get you."

"What about my car?"

"Leave it here," Bernie smiled. "I'll bring you back. Chauffeur service."

Johnny grinned. "Chauffeur service, huh? Where we goin'?"

Bernie began driving.

"That old warehouse we got," Bernie said. "Down in the Flats."

Johnny grinned. "Fleckner Foods?"

"I figured nobody's gonna be there."

Johnny grinned. "I used to work down there."

"Yeah?" Bernie said. "What'd you do?"

"Loaded stuff," Johnny said. "Fruit. Vegetables." He paused. His voice softened. "Tomatoes."

"That sounds like fun," Bernie said.

Johnny nodded and said nothing. He stared out the window as Bernie drove through the city.

"Whose car you got?" Johnny said after a while.

Bernie laughed. "It's a rental. My fuckin' radiator's shot."

"Again?" Johnny said. "You oughta trade that thing in."

"Yeah," Bernie Marr smiled. "One of these days I will."

The Fleckner Foods warehouse had been unused for years. It was ramshackle and tottering; its windows had been boarded up.

Bernie got out of the car and opened a garage door. The whole block was deserted. Babe Milano hadn't arrived.

Bernie got back into the car and drove it into the dimly lighted warehouse. Johnny sat in the front seat and looked the warehouse over. That place by the wall there, he remembered, that was where they used to sit waiting for the damn deliveries.

"Look at this place," he said to Bernie.

"I'm gonna go out front," Bernie said, "maybe they missed the place."

Johnny kept staring at the warehouse. "There used to be this platform there," he said. "The guy had a buzzer."

Bernie got out of the car and walked outside. He pulled the garage door down. It was so dark now that Johnny could barely see. He got out of the car and walked around. He walked to the spot where Gant had had his platform. He stood there.

He could hear the buzzer now, tearing at his nerves. Gant was up there, pushing at it. Dombrowsky was down on the floor, scurrying after the peaches. Dorsett was up on the platform, the guard clubbing at his head. Dorsett fell and hit the cement. Then Dorsett was saying, "You can't beat 'em, kid, you'll see." Then Dombrowsky was saying, "Ain't everything that's fair." Then Abe, "You can do it, Johnny. You can get even with 'em." Then he was saying to Abe, "We'll do it together, you're my brother, ain't you?"

The buzzer got louder and louder. And then he was up on the platform, tearing it out. Taking it home. Putting it down on the kitchen table that night, thinking of the old man. Keeping it in that glass case all these years. On top of his desk. So everyone could see it. And then, that night, talking to Abe, smashing it against the wall. The buzzer in bits and pieces. Shattered. Everything shattered.

But he had beaten them, hadn't he? Hadn't he? It had all been for the men. They were the best-paid men in the whole country. They were his men. He had done it.

But then why had everything shattered?

Why wouldn't the goddamn buzzer stop eating at his insides?

The garage door opened, jarring him. Two of Babe Milano's men walked in. He liked Angel, Babe's top guy. He didn't know the other one.

"Where's Babe?" he asked Angel.

"He's outside, Johnny," Angel said.

"Jesus Christ," he said, "why the hell didn't he come in?"

He stepped in front of them angrily and headed for the door.

Angel aimed the Magnum and shot him point-blank in the back.

He went down, then rose and staggered toward the garage door. There was a shaft of light there. The buzzer kept going off in his head.

Angel fired again. Johnny sank to his knees, swayed. Someone slammed the door shut outside. The shaft of light darkened. He couldn't hear the buzzer any more. He pitched forward on the warehouse floor.

Angel stood over him and fired the Magnum again.

"Get the bag," Angel said.

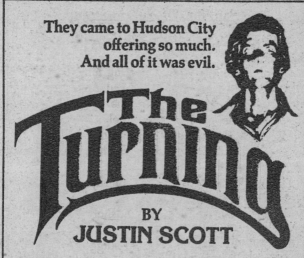

"WE ONLY HAVE ONE TEXAS"

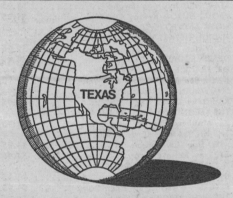

TEXAS

People ask if there is really an energy crisis. Look at it this way. World oil consumption is 60 million barrels per day and is growing 5 percent each year. This means the world must find three million barrels of new oil production each day. Three million barrels per day is the amount of oil produced in Texas as its peak was 5 years ago. The problem is that it is not going to be easy to find a Texas-sized new oil supply every year, year after year. In just a few years, it may be impossible to balance demand and supply of oil unless we start conserving oil today. So next time someone asks: "is there really an energy crisis?" Tell them: "yes, we only have one Texas."

ENERGY CONSERVATION -
IT'S YOUR CHANCE TO SAVE, AMERICA

Department of Energy, Washington, D.C.